Praise for Ferrett Stein

Automatic Reload

"I came for the shoot-'em-up action, but the relationships in this book have more punch than the most well-tuned gun."
—Alex Wells, author of *Hunger Makes the Wolf*

"A wicked techno-thriller full of gut-punching action, sharp twists, and surprisingly tender moments."
—Spencer Ellsworth, author of The Starfire trilogy

The Sol Majestic

"A feast of a book!"
—*New York Times* bestselling author Seanan McGuire

"Strange, rich, thoughtful, and just plain fun."
—Cherie Priest, Hugo and Nebula Award–nominated author

"There are moving tales and clever tales. This one happens to be both." —Ken Liu, Hugo, Nebula, Locus, and World Fantasy Award–winning author

"Dizzying, beautiful world-building—damn, this book is good."
—Mur Lafferty, Hugo Award finalist

"We arrive at the Sol Majestic for a meal and are served a new outlook on life. Triumphant." —*The Washington Post*

"With lush details and vividly rendered characters, crafting a memorable love letter to the nourishment of body and soul."
—*Publishers Weekly* (starred review)

"A charming coming-of-age tale with an appealing cast of unforgettable characters." —*Library Journal* (starred review)

Also by Ferrett Steinmetz

The Sol Majestic

AUTOMATIC RELOAD

Ferrett
Steinmetz

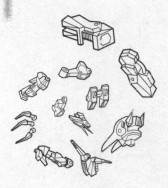

A Tom Doherty Associates Book

New York

TOR

AUTOMATIC RELOAD

Copyright © 2020 by Ferrett Steinmetz

A Tor Book
Published by Tom Doherty Associates
120 Broadway
New York, NY 10271

www.tor-forge.com

Tor® is a registered trademark of Macmillan Publishing Group, LLC.

The Library of Congress Cataloging-in-Publication Data is available upon request.

ISBN 978-1-250-16821-4 (trade paperback)
ISBN 978-1-250-16820-7 (ebook)

Our books may be purchased in bulk for promotional, educational, or business use. Please contact your local bookseller or the Macmillan Corporate and Premium Sales Department at 1–800-221-7945, extension 5442, or by email at MacmillanSpecialMarkets@macmillan.com.

First Edition: 2020

Printed in the United States of America

0 9 8 7 6 5 4 3 2 1

The most unbelievable aspect of this book is that we will still have an open internet by 2050.

The freedom of the internet is currently being dismantled by huge corporations and venal politicians. That is why this book is devoted to the Electronic Frontier Foundation, which fights the good fight. Thanks, folks.

www.eff.org

ACT

1

Reluctantly
Crouched
at the
Starting Line

I can't help but ask: one day, many years later, when you find your previous awareness, cognition, and choices are all wrong—will you keep going along the wrong path, or reject yourself?

—Gu Li, the last world-class Go player beaten by Google's artificial intelligence, realizing that humans had finally been obsoleted in a game originally thought to be unplayable by computers.
January 2017, *The Wall Street Journal*

I'm not a fan of human arms. That quarter-second delay between visual confirmation and trigger finger movement is, quite literally, a killer in a combat situation. Compare your sluggish meatware to the baseline friend-or-foe targeting routines on my Zentrine-Gauss upper-limb armed prosthetics—they have their own sensors, and can put three rounds into an emerging hostile in under .04 seconds. Even if you have your gun aimed at me when I walk into your line of fire, I'll outdraw you, with computer-targeted accuracy, with .21 seconds to spare. You'll be dead before either of us realizes what happened.

So to survive, you must realize this: the human body is the least reliable component of your combat equipment. The more you can minimize its influence, the better.

Which leaves good maintenance as the only thing that will protect you.

Yet the sole advantage your organic appendages have over my sweet darlings Scylla and Charybdis—yes, I nickname my limbs—is that your meat-arms are self-lubricating and self-repairing. Your daily maintenance consists of pull-ups and a salad.

Me? I spend hours fieldstripping my arms and legs, clearing out debris that could jam the delicate machinery. I recalibrate my artificial musculature. I optimize the computerized routines that govern Scylla and Charybdis—their baseline friend-or-foe identification routines take .04 seconds to acquire a noncombatant target, but I've shaved my capture-to-fire time down to .0125 seconds, *and* my onboard computers can differentiate between happy children and gun-toting criminals with dwarfism.

It's the little details that matter.

Yet even if you do proper maintenance, you must do your pre-combat prep then *stow your ego away.* Too many body-hackers tether their self-worth to their in-combat contribution—if they don't fire a few bullets manually, they figure they're not real soldiers. These assholes get themselves killed, relying on their high-latency nervous system.

If you do it right, the fighting's all but done before you arrive at your drop zone. You tune your reaction packages for the killing ground, you ensure your armed prosthetics are combat-ready, and you let the computers do the work.

Case in point: two men just died while I dictated this sentence.

The kidnappers I'm engaged with now—whoops, there goes a third one—are not, it must be said, particularly bright. The smartest kidnappers in Nigeria stopped when they realized the global fuel shortages were forcing oil companies to cut out unwanted expenses like, say, ransoms paid to kidnappers who targeted petroleum workers. The middling kidnappers gave it up when Aishat Njeze, current managing director of the state-owned Nigerian National Petroleum Corporation, started cracking down on kidnappers with bloody hi-tech reprisals.

These dumb motherfuckers kidnapped Aishat Njeze's daughter.

That poor kid's eleven years old, the worst age to be kidnapped—old enough to understand what's going on, young enough for the trauma to kick her right in the formative stages. If I don't get her out soon, little Onyeka's in for years of desensitization therapy.

Ferrett Steinmetz

So here I am, a one-man rescue squad sweeping through rusted sheds in the Niger Delta's ankle-deep silt. Which is a shame, because I love Nigeria—Lagos is a friendly city, almost as nice as my hometown of St. Louis, Missouri, and there are even some really scenic views to be had from the Niger River. But dirt-poor brutes don't take a kidnapped kid to places the Nigerian tourist board would approve of. I'm watching the numbers tick up on my readouts as Scylla and Charybdis auto-target and kill five kidnappers in under forty-five seconds.

(I should say "disable," not "kill"; my sensors have not verified these men's deaths, only confirmed these former opponents are sufficiently maimed to be combat-irrelevant. Too many body-hackers get off on tracking their exact body counts—but me? As a drone pilot, I not only had to call in air strikes but had to circle the kill zone for hours afterwards, watching dismembered bodies rot in case their terrorist friends showed up to bury the corpses. I am *done* with watching corpses. So my IFF routines mark anyone unable to fight back as "disabled"—even though, knowing how high I've dialed in the mortality factors for Scylla and Charybdis, they're probably dead.)

We're now a minute into the kill box. I started the assault just as dawn glimmered over the Niger's muck-slick waters; the kidnappers are realizing someone big has come for them. My sensors track movement behind the soft wood and tin walls, assign high probabilities to which folks are going for their guns and which ones are diving for cover.

Less ethical hackers have their IFF routines set to fire through cover. But I won't take any chances harming innocents in their houses. If these bozos emerge to snap off a shot at me, they'll find a bullet smashing through their brain long before their slow, slow nervous system pulls the trigger.

As my ground routines scan for little Onyeka's biosignatures, I have time to compile a partial list of items I personally would have gotten around to before kidnapping a politician's daughter:

- a drone net to warn me of incoming hostiles, as opposed to the two guys chugging banana beer outside the perimeter
- automated turrets keyed to exclude white-listed biosignatures, ready to fire on any hostile
- networked subvocal implants among my commanders on a tight-beam, encrypted frequency, instead of crappy text-message codes that got cracked by the Nigerian National Petroleum Corporation
- mines, or at the *very* least buried grenades, to stop me from sauntering through their compound (Would it *kill* them to at least try digging a good old-fashioned punji stake pit?)
- a bucket of fine sand. (I'm not saying it's a *great* plan, but it's at least *possible* some errant dust might work its way past my environmental seals to clog a vital servo and throw off my targeting systems.)

But I suppose if these guys had the money for non-sand-buckety tech, they wouldn't have gone for the Hail Mary pass of kidnapping Aishat Njeze's daughter. Nigeria as a whole is thriving in the new world economy, but this is the starving part.

I don't like people living in poverty. These thugs are skeletal, scabbed, overwhelmed. I feel sorry for them—

—until I remember there's a crying girl sobbing into duct tape, wearing the most adorable bow tie and blue vest jacket, held hostage somewhere in these shoddy huts. I'd seen the footage of her kidnappers pulling up in a rusty van to yank her off the street on her way to school.

She'd had two human guards—antiquated meat-technology. Njeze's daughter Onyeka had watched these assholes murder her protectors; that's not something any kid should have to experience. Each passing minute scrapes deeper scars into her psyche.

Scylla kicks off another three rounds. An eighth person gets sorted into the "disabled" column. And as Scylla and Charybdis clear the path, I fine-tune their scanners, adjusting for the unexpectedly damp morning fog, homing in on poor Onyeka—

A ragged kid in a tattered Cleveland Cavaliers T-shirt emerges, hands up. My IFF routines switch to manual intervention, identifying the object in his hand as a harmless Apple cell phone, asking if I wish to disable.

Kid's lucky I've configured my software to accept surrenders.

"Speak your piece."

The kid trembles. He's emaciated, his dark skin prickling with fear-sweat. He turns the phone towards me to show it's on speakerphone—

But the button is green underneath his thumb, as opposed to the red "disconnect" icon.

It's an inverted speakerphone. A dead-man's call.

"If you do not leave," he says in a quavering adolescent voice, "we will shoot the girl in the head. If this call disconnects"—he mimes dropping it—"we will shoot the girl in the head. Your only hope to keep her alive is to leave."

I smile.

That's the first smart thing they've done.

"That's some mighty fine improvisation," I tell him. "Which moves us on to the negotiation stage of events."

When I have Scylla and Charybdis trained on someone, my Missouri drawl comes creeping out. Can't keep the cowboy out of the boy, I guess—or maybe I swagger when I'm uncertain.

Yet from the way he flinches, I'd wager that Kidnapper Intern here has seen a few Westerns too. Though I don't look much like a cowboy to him—Scylla and Charybdis are massive spidery prosthetics bristling with weaponry, so overdesigned for combat that they bear little resemblance to human limbs. My legs are hulking contraptions like walking bulldozers, my slim meat-torso covered in thick armored plating, my head hidden behind a bulletproof HUD.

"No negotiation," he says. The blood-pressure readouts I've got aimed at his throat inform me it's 87 percent likely he's telling the truth. Still, I'm activating my linguistic analyst modules, chopping up the thirty-seven words he's spoken in an attempt to narrow down his accent. "You killed too many. Go."

Forty-two words in, and my linguistic analysts tell me his vowels have a distinctly Ibibian tang. Not that I know what the hell that means, but that's why I loaded up my knowledge banks with a full accent database before heading to hot ground. (I could stream the data off-site for refined language analysis, but the three-second delay might prove deadly.)

"Oh, you wanna negotiate with me," I say. "If I go home empty-handed, the Nigerian National Petroleum Corporation will decide *nobody* can get the girl out safely."

He squints, uncertain what I mean. Under different circumstances, I'd fill in the gaps. As it is, I nod helpfully, as if I'm guiding him to the inevitable conclusion.

"They will pay us." He glances up at the cell phone, hoping his bosses will give him answers. "Or the girl will die."

He's using a Dr. Seuss vocabulary. That's good. "I'm not so sure I agree a hundred percent with your police work there, Lou."

He glares. "My name is not Lou!"

"It's a reference, kid. *Fargo.* It's an old movie. I love old movies. You love old movies?"

He grips the phone like he wants to chuck it at my head. He'd probably prefer I shot him; that would at least make him look good in front of his buddies. Now he can't decide whether negotiating with me is what his bosses would want, or whether he'll get murdered for talking too much to the enemy.

"You have thirty seconds to leave," he tells me.

"That's generous. I'd have done ten."

"Or she dies."

"I got that already."

Ferrett Steinmetz

"Thirty. Twenty-nine. Twenty-eight . . ."

Each syllable loads more precious data into my analyst programs. I triangulate Scylla's tasers, set the disabling targets on Charybdis, multitasking hard enough to blunt my incipient panic. "Kid, I just took out your friends without blinking. I'm the friendly option. If I walk away, my bosses won't give you cash—that'd tell every other cut-rate kidnapper it's still payday in Nigeria.

"No, sir." I pull a cigar out of my leg-mounted humidor and light it—which is less dangerous than you'd think, as Scylla and Charybdis's front-facing armaments are shoulder-mounted. "This is about money. Right now, you kidnappers have been an unwanted expense on NNPC's balance sheet. Then they figured out that hiring *my* metallic ass cost less than the future payouts they'd be obligated to shell out if they continued to play nice with you kidnappers. And if *I* don't work out, well . . .

"The Nigerian National Petroleum Corporation doesn't want to owe anyone else. But they're gonna have to call in the Yak."

The kid stops counting.

The Yak is the acronym for the International Access Consortium—the IAC—who are the modern world's deep-process gods. If you think Scylla and Charybdis can pull off some terrifying stunts, envision black-budget AI networks staffed by the nastiest ex-CIA, ex-MSS, and ex-GRU agents—each of whom can break into any network you've ever touched, read every email you've ever written, compile a list of every place you've visited, then use that to compile a profile that knows you more intimately than you know yourself. They've driven strong men to suicide.

I say they're gods because they are the closest thing to infallible I've ever witnessed. I've only seen them unleash their data-fueled mayhem three times, and the longest it took from "contract acceptance" to "delivery of the corpse, as agreed" was five hours.

They are digital gods, and I pray they never notice me.

Yet as the kid's dark skin flushes darker, understanding just what deep feces he's in, I realize that *I* have a future if I walk away—whereas this kid's bosses will shoot him in the head twenty minutes from now if he hesitates. This kid is an unwise equation, the sum of every bad decision he's made compounded by wretched starting circumstances. Though he clearly regrets his decision, his outs have narrowed to "hope he gets lucky sticking with the side he's already picked."

"Nuh-nine," he continues. "Eight. S-seven . . . ?"

"Isaac!" a distorted voice cries from the phone. "Stop talking! He's checking your voice against the worldwide video feeds to identify you!"

His cheeks flush with embarrassment. I *am* running a default social-media trace, in fact, but what good would it do reading this asshole's Facebook posts while these assholes put bullets in Onyeka's chest?

Still, the veins in Isaac's neck bulge as he realizes I was never negotiating in good faith. He opens his mouth to yell words that look like "kill the girl"—

Takedowns are a lot like being in car crashes.

I've spent the last minute programming *how* Isaac is going down, but the actual mechanics are like being fired down a highway. I've set my legs to accelerate at speeds that won't quite concuss me. Still, I'm launched from zero to twenty miles per hour in under a half second. My head snaps back, putting strain on my reinforced spine. Charybdis injects headache-suppressant drugs as my tightfoam neck braces stiffen.

And when my vision unblurs, the haptic feedback from Scylla indicates I am holding a convulsing 125-pound male by his right wrist. He makes muffled choking noises, the taser wires in his throat silencing him before he could complete his sentence. No surprise: if my aiming routines couldn't target anatomical vulnerabilities to a 2-millimeter variance, hell, I might as well use meatarms to shoot.

I check his phone even though the "objective accomplished"

Ferrett Steinmetz

light on my readout is glowing green. Sure enough, his fingers are mashed against the phone by a thick artificial muscle loop wrapped around his hand—a fibrous mesh handcuff that had been charged with electricity when Charybdis fired it from a secret compartment, but shrank like a cramped muscle fiber once removed from the charge station.

Contemplate the algorithms needed to calculate what residual charge the goopcuff should have. Ponder the heavy-duty physics calculations required to determine what trajectory the goopcuff should be fired at. Envision the skill required to know what anatomical area Charybdis should target to guarantee the primary objective that "Isaac cannot drop his phone."

Now imagine the weeks spent cloistered in my firing range, a mad programmer-combat monk, endlessly firing a glorified rubber band against a spare arm set to "maximum flail" mode, and realize that *practice pays off.*

And while I'm staring with dumb triumph at Isaac, goggle-eyed for the .75 seconds it takes to visually verify this successful field trial to my sludgy brain's satisfaction, Scylla and Charybdis are carrying out the next phase of their programmed mission, bless their CPUs. They grab the phone, verify it's still connected, and slam in the connection jack.

Readouts blossom across the HUD as my crypto routines analyze the kid's phone. He's patched his phone to the latest OS—a pleasantly diligent act of security in a slipshod operation—but guess who keeps a list of zero-day vulnerabilities for occasions such as this?

Preparation, my friends. Preparation staves off ruination.

An intake of breath from the speakerphone. His bosses are about to demand that Isaac check in. When he doesn't speak up, it's lights-out for Onyeka.

Cold sweat trickles down my neck. Here goes the big trick—creative improvisations like this are where missions get saved or go FUBAR.

"I don't care if he sees my Facebook posts!" I say, my linguistic routines mimicking Isaac's Ibibian accent. "What if he's right about them bringing in the Yak?"

I cringe—if Isaac doesn't have a Facebook account, and they know that, this mission's over. Plus, I know the façade isn't perfect; he didn't speak enough for my linguistic modules to get a firm handle on his speech patterns.

Then again, they're not expecting me to have pulled the ol' switcheroo on him. If he's speaking funny, maybe that's stress talking. And each second they spend talking to fake-Isaac is a second I'm rootkitting his phone, injecting spyware programs, following his bosses back down this open call to compromise their phone and activate their GPS.

Maybe someone in this village is watching me from a slit in their hut, taking live video they're selling to the kidnappers, sat so far back in shadow that my sensors can't pick them up. Then again, I *did* just disable eight armed guards in under three minutes. Most sane people dive for cover when they hear shots fired.

Yet anyone who sees me cradling Isaac's shivering body could call his bosses to inform them their agent's been compromised.

Every passing second shoves Onyeka deeper into danger.

"When I committed, you committed!" his boss shouts, each word transmitted helping my spyware to close in on his location. *"You do not back out now, Isaac! Get that body-hacker to leave!"*

A dot blooms across my HUD map; the boss has been back-traced to a location six hundred meters northwest. The fucking NNPC got their data wrong; they handed me the location the kidnappers' mooks were sleeping in, not where Onyeka was.

Then again, if combat was a predictable exercise they'd have sent in drones. They pay me the big bucks to improvise.

"The Yak is more than our lives," I-as-Isaac say. "They go after families. They kill everyone."

And I drop Isaac before my legs propel me through the shanty city, my artificial musculature cornering at top speeds like a

Ferrett Steinmetz

computer-enhanced quarterback, splicing in satellite maps taken an hour ago with current visual data. Merchants are poking their heads out to see if it's safe yet.

As I take off, my routines ask me if I want to terminate Isaac. Which would be simpler. He's a scummy kidnapper who'll probably get involved in some other crime if I let him go—one shot from my rear-facing armaments, and he's gone.

But the kid stood up to me. Knowing he'd die.

I respect Isaac's bravery, knowing how messed up that is, and let him live.

My chest tightens again as I head into the streets. I remind myself that I programmed my IFF routines personally. Scylla won't shoot a kid who darts out in front of me; Charybdis won't cap some grandmother who's opening a window.

I've prepared for this. I won't hurt anyone who doesn't deserve it. Not anymore.

And I'm rounding the corner to the target zone as his boss shouts through the compromised phone: *"Wait. When the fuck do you care about families?"*

Oops. If I'd checked his Facebook, I'd have known he was an orphan. "The IAC is a different danger," I say, knowing I only have to stall until I can get to the green dot on the map.

"After everything we've been through?" the boss yells. *"After— wait. What's our passphrase?"*

Fuck.

The only consolation is that I am now at the green dot.

Except I'm standing in an empty hut, my metal feet planted on the location where Isaac's phone thinks Onyeka is being kept, and no one is here.

"Say that passphrase, Isaac, and I will shoot you in the head," I say in my own voice over the phone—a response that makes zero sense, but I'm not aiming for coherent conversation. I'm trying to confuse the bosses into hesitating, which buys me time to figure out what to do next.

My heart's pounding. I don't let it distract me.

The trace tells me the call is coming from here, but all I see is an empty house. It has a cooler with a few banana beers soaking in half-melted ice, three cots, and zero occupants.

Are my traces borked?

Have I just doomed Onyeka?

"Report in! Report in!" the bosses say.

I remember that computers never give you the data you wanted. They only give you the data you asked for.

I asked for the latitude and longitude of Onyeka's kidnappers.

I ask for height, and sure enough, the signal is 2.3 meters below ground level.

These folks have a bunker.

My respect for their operations ticks up slightly.

I move the table with a stealth that only computer-assisted servos can manage, find the padlocked trapdoor beneath. It's a heavy metal door, at least three hundred kilos.

"What is your passphrase?" the bosses cry. Thank God they're a little panicky.

The padlock's easy—I drop into stealth mode, enmeshing the padlock in a laser-targeted sensor-web so Scylla and Charybdis won't make any boss-alerting clanks as they move it. The lockpick flips out of Scylla's index finger—it's not flashy, but the lockpick's the most reliable piece of my arsenal—and pops it open.

The trapdoor, however . . .

If I'd known I'd have to move heavy objects quickly, I would have outfitted myself with a different artificial-musculature configuration that would catapult this massive door off.

But I don't have that loadout. I can lift it myself, but it'll take 0.7 seconds.

Ferrett Steinmetz

If they're as dedicated as I think they are, they might kill Onyeka before I drop inside.

My biological-response packages inject me as they sense my stress rising, warding off PTSD shock. I can't have anyone else innocent die on my watch.

I had military orders back then. Someone else would have thumbed the "fire" button if I hadn't. And mistakes happen during combat, even with all the preparations we took; sometimes that satellite-enhanced blur you thought was a stray dog—nothing worth aborting a high-priority terrorist-killing mission over—turns out to be a six-year-old kid running in to see his daddy, who wasn't even a terrorist, just a waiter unlucky enough to serve terrorists.

The whole reason I went solo is so I'd never have to make those choices again. No kids, no waiters—just the combatants, and only the combatants.

The phone clicks off—or tries to. They want to disconnect, except the spyware I've implanted won't let them drop the call.

I heave open the trapdoor, rust flakes falling into the fluorescent-lit chamber below. Scylla takes out someone in midheave, some poor bodyguard unlucky enough to sit below the newly opened line of fire.

I drop down two meters; my artificial legs cushion the fall, but I'm still seven hundred pounds of metal crashing into the floor. Even though my shoulders, hips, and spinal cord have been reinforced to handle the weight of my prosthetics, I'll need an MRI to check the remaining bone for microfractures.

There's Onyeka. She's still dressed in her bright blue school outfit and knee-high socks; her mother won't let her wear makeup yet, but she snuck on purple eye shadow on the way to school. Her hair is cornrowed, her soft brown eyes wide and terrified.

A thin man has a long, curved knife pressed against her throat. He's hauled her into the corner, squeezing as much of his body as he can behind her soft body—creating enough cover that my auto-targeting routines ask for manual approval before they take the shot. He keeps his elbows tucked in close to his ribs so he doesn't expose any limbs, his knife hand hidden behind her collarbone. Shooting the knife might drive it back hard enough to slice Onyeka's jugular.

He trembles, clutching her like a fearful child grabbing his teddy bear.

Blood trickles down her throat. He's cut her to show how serious he is.

"It's over," I whisper. "Put the knife away."

Which isn't quite true. Because I wasn't expecting a knife. I have flechette loads that'd jam a normal human's trigger—but using the tasers on this guy might cut Onyeka's neck open, and there's not enough of him out in the open to chance the goopcuffs.

"I'm down to fatal options," I tell him. "Let's negotiate and walk away from here alive, shall we?"

"It's not my choice." My truth-sensors inform me he believes that. "You leave or she dies."

Onyeka had been trying to be brave, so brave, but hearing her death spoken in her ear breaks her. She slumps, letting out a wordless gasp that saws deep into my heart.

"I don't want to hurt you," I say, my mouth dry. And it's true. Scylla and Charybdis have automated death, made ruinous injuries as clinical as spreadsheets. I've incapacitated eight men today and I couldn't tell you what they looked like.

I can look a man in the eyes and kill him.

But I'm really tired of doing that.

He giggles, pressing his knife deeper into Onyeka's neck. "They tested me, five. Now they're testing you, four," he titters, almost offering an excuse. "The culling destroys us all, three. The refining, two. It never stops, one."

His muscles tense, sawing the blade across her neck.

Scylla and Charybdis fire before he completes the stroke.

And I'm scooping up little Onyeka in my arms as she cries hysterically, convinced she's bleeding out—but I cradle her close,

Ferrett Steinmetz

squirting microadhesives and blood-clotting crystals into the cut before I pinch the wound shut. It's serious, but good stitches will turn the cut into an ugly scar.

"Is she safe?" Onyeka's mother pulls rank to override the comm channel. "Is my daughter safe?"

I look down. She'd have bled out from a slit throat if I hadn't given her immediate medical attention. She may have hearing damage from the gunfire. Her heart's thumping so hard I can feel it through my prosthetics.

I fish out a handkerchief to wipe her kidnapper's blood off her face.

"Is she safe?"

I inject Onyeka with anti-PTSD drugs to blunt her trauma. She'll be fine. But for one brief moment, she was certain she was dead, and that certainty will wake her at night when she shivers back to consciousness and realizes how fragile her whole existence is.

"I have retrieved the target with minor injuries." I send the signal for Onyeka's newer, beefier bodyguards to come to the extraction point. And I've carried out my contract, and the money will be deposited into my bank account, and I can afford the maintenance costs on Scylla and Charybdis for another month. The NNPC will recommend me for other jobs.

Yet I look down at Onyeka trying to shove me away as I maintain the pressure on her wound. We both want out of this bunker. Instead, I sit down heavily on a kidnapper's bed and wait for my own anti-PTSD drugs to kick in.

I failed my mission.

Someone got hurt.

"Take off your arms," the customs agent says. "Legs too. Place all potential weapons on the table."

"And what, exactly," I reply with glacial politeness, "do you think I'll take the fourth limb off with once the first three are on the table?"

I'm not in a good mood to begin with after watching the child psychiatrists take Onyeka away, even though that was hours ago. And New York customs agents are always ready to pick a fight with a living weapon, so I keep telling myself: *Don't get confrontational. They're just bureaucrats. You need to get your butt home to analyze the mission; don't give these jerks an excuse to pull your permits.*

I should add that even my biggest loadouts don't have extensive weaponry—for the flight back to Missouri, I've switched to Butch and Sundance, with a single (unloaded) gun in each forearm. Yet those guns use unmodified .38 rounds—they'll fuck up your day, but they're not punching through tank armor.

Scylla and Charybdis have .45-caliber accuracy, not the brutal stopping power of .50-caliber antiaircraft rounds. If I strapped bazookas to my shoulders, I'd have cop cars sniping me the minute I headed down to Starbucks to get a coffee. Which is why all my embedded armory are modified versions of handguns you could purchase legally at any reputable gun shop.

(Note: handguns, not rifles. Computer-targeted rifles can outshoot any human sniper, so only cops are authorized to use them. Wiring my capture-to-fire routines up to a .308 rifle would let me machine-gun incoming threats from a mile away—which is why even the most gun-happy states will throw your ass in jail for possession of auto-targeted long-range weapons, and why the infantry has a hell of a time attracting recruits for modern warfare.)

Before I cross state lines, I have my onboard lawyer-modules scan each county's local gun laws to tell me which locales I can safely enter, then send text messages to the local law enforcement to tell them when I'll arrive so they don't open fire on the killing machine. And I have to do it whenever I plan a trip, because legislators keep passing new laws to restrict the usage of mechanically grafted auto-targeting weaponry.

Except down South, where they *loooove* flashy weaponry. Even though most folks can't afford the $125,000 non-insurance-covered surgery to neurally decode your stump's nerve endings and make your baseline $45,000 myoelectric prosthetic-armament platform do your bidding.

People think body-hackers are rich. But we're like those couples who drop too much on their dream McMansion and wind up house-poor—I have a lot invested in limbs and limb-enhancement, and not much else. Certainly not enough that I can afford lawyers to haul my ass out of jail regularly.

Needless to say, I stick to open-carry states, stopping in gun-hostile states like New York only for as long as it takes to get my ass on another plane. And the American customs agents would prefer it if I'd get shot in Nigeria.

The hard-ass customs agent slaps his palms on the examination table. His co-worker rolls his eyes. Agent Hard-Ass here has seen the same old cop movies that I have; he apparently thinks intimidation works against a walking armory. "Don't give me lip, tin man, or I'll have the feds haul you away."

"On what charge?" I give a whatcha-gonna-do shrug that exposes the clip feeds on the underside of my forearms—which are, as per federal regulation, opened for examination at all times and have bright-orange hard-plastic plugs inserted into them to make it visually apparent there's nothing fireable in the chamber. "All my prosthetic armaments are peace-tied, to the letter of the law, and you will note I am glowing a reassuring purple."

Peace-tied is a federally mandated software configuration that legal prosthetic armaments must have; once I activate it to demonstrate my willful surrender, neon bands on the deactivated limb glow purple and any weapons are unable to fire until fifteen minutes after the peace-tie codes are deactivated.

(Supposedly. I once spent three days figuring out how to subvert the peace-tie lock software, then realized I'd create much harsher laws if I fired in a public space with peace-tied weaponry. Considering the peace-tie is for the cyborgs' benefit, giving them a legal, irrefutably visible way to demonstrate their harmlessness to a police force who'd prefer to snipe any body-hacker on sight, why should I fuck it up for everyone else?)

Yet *not only* am I peace-tied, I have allowed the government access to record my credit-card purchases and social-network posts; there are deep-data analyst AIs that comb my records for evidence of psychiatric malfunction, alerting the authorities in case me purchasing the wrong deodorant signals an incipient danger to innocents.

The customs agents have access to these stability reports. I know my latest report is sterling, or I would have been greeted by EMP grenades instead of two toothless paper pushers.

"You aren't cooperating," Hard-Ass splutters. "Put your prosthetics on the table."

"Each of these limbs are anchored at fifteen nuBone hardpoints," I explain, "and requires a special attachment station to remove without permanent damage to my body. In addition, a safe removal process takes at least half an hour, as the multiple nerve-to-CPU interfaces need to be carefully disconnected—"

Hard-Ass crosses his arms. *"Take your time."*

"—which is why the Amputee Protection Act of 2043 states amputees are not required to remove Class IV prosthetics for government searches unless there is reasonable suspicion of criminal activity."

My left leg whirs, printing out the Act's highlighted passages; I tear it off and present it to him.

Bureaucrats do not like being beaten at their own game, which is why I try not to encourage showdowns; they can stuff you full of niggling regulations until you crap paperwork. Yet this souped-up rent-a-cop is hell-bent on making a case out of today's hapless body-hacker, so I have no choice but to grab the big-form firepower.

Sure enough, I can see Hard-Ass figuring out other ways to fuck me over—because a bureaucrat can always enforce some obscure clause that'll make your day worse. So I try the side exit.

"Look," I say to his buddy, as cheerfully as I can manage. "Truth

Ferrett Steinmetz

is, you don't want me here. You can hold me for a day or two before you let me back into the USA, but that'll dump more paperwork on your desk. I'm just a citizen with a few more circuits; all I wanna do is get home to Missouri and have a beer. You like a beer at the end of a long day?"

His buddy—clearly the more experienced agent—gives a little nod and steps forward. "I like a beer," he allows. "I also like knowing I'm letting the right people into this country I love."

I envy him. I used to have that unalloyed American adoration.

"I'm not gonna hurt my country." I tap my right arm. "I gave up too much for her."

He squints. "You lost your right arm in combat?"

"I wish. We'd already dropped the payload through our drones. *This* happened at the party afterwards. ISIS had spent months figuring out where our remote HQ was located, then planned an operation to take us out during a post-sortie celebration. I'd guzzled six Budweisers when the shell hit."

The old guard guy gives a little disapproving wince—I should have given him the military-friendly version. The one where we discover an ISIS council meeting through remote drone reconnaissance, then drop missiles on them from the stratosphere before they fired cowardly missiles at us when we weren't looking. Guy like him's never been in the military, but wants our brass polish to rub off on him through high tales of adventure. There's plenty of warriors out there—good men, mostly—who want to tell those tales to justify their lives.

Hell, I used to *be* that guy. Like every drone pilot, I grew up guzzling military recruitment games. We honed our remote reflexes with realistic weaponry profiles housed in G.I. Joe story lines.

But these days? I take my fighting straight. I've seen too much combat—and I know how much work I put in to ensure no bystanders get hurt. The government makes an effort to protect civilians, sure, but . . . it wasn't enough for me.

The agent wants to drink deep on my heroic patriotism. Yet that devotion goes down sour once I ponder the casualties it takes to keep America afloat.

"So you lost your right arm." His gaze flicks down to Sundance, my left leg, my right leg. "What about the rest?"

I flex them proudly. "I only lost the first limb. The rest? I upgraded."

Hard-Ass's face goes green. He stares down at his palm, imagining lopping off his fingers to replace them with machinery.

I gaze coolly back at him—because yeah. I remember looking down at my functioning meat-legs and finding them inferior to my right arm's hotswappable functionality. I remember dragging a bowie knife across my shaved thighs, leaving a thin trail of blood, trying to envision what my body would feel like once I amputated the limbs I was born with.

Both customs agents scratch their legs uncomfortably, bathed in the lambent purple glow of my peace-tied limbs.

"Get a move on," they say, and just like that I'm on my way back to Missouri.

Welcome to America.

Now, St. Louis is a fine town—big enough to enjoy the benefits of living in the big city, without that "packed in like cockroaches" feeling you get from New York or Chicago—but the reason I'm so darned eager to skip past customs has nothing to do with my hometown love.

It's because the perfect mission waits in my workshop.

To you, dear reader, me making the right on-field calls to save Onyeka Njeze's life (if not her well-being) was the exciting part. But knowing one wrong decision could cost a young girl her life is exhausting, panic-inducing, demoralizing—the furthest thing from "exciting" there is.

"Exciting" would be entering a mission with all decisions made in advance, and exiting without a single thing happening outside mission parameters.

Ferrett Steinmetz

So as I booked the first flight out of Lagos, I was pondering ways to safeguard people in future missions—I'd mentioned Isaac's Facebook account when I didn't have to, so I'll prepare scripts to handle future situations where I'll need to masquerade as someone. I didn't have my GPS traces default-configured to provide altitude; a few lines of code will correct that. I'd relied on tasers and goopcuffs for close-combat hostage situations; I've been relying too much on firearms, neglecting my hand-to-hand combat routines.

On the flight back home, I listed every error I made that endangered an innocent. Those mistakes were scars; I could never remove them, but their pain goaded me to improvement. I vowed to replay my mission logs until I discovered the ideal approach that would have preserved both Onyeka's life and her innocence.

If I ever carry out a mission where no one is injured but the enemy, that unblemished combat will be born in Yoyodyne Labs, my private workshop in the Olivette suburbs.

I snag a cab back home, thumbing extra cash to St. Louis's networked driver-AIs so I can legally run a few red lights. My mind races with weaponry loadouts that might have disarmed her assailant without traumatizing Onyeka, and the only place to test them is in the lab, so . . .

Yoyodyne Labs—bonus points if you get the reference—is an unassuming loft stashed in a secure apartment complex where the successful bohemian artists live. My neighbors below are a pleasant gay poly triad who run a home data-analysis lab. If they find my habit of showing up with different limbs at every condo meeting unsettling, well, they're well versed in gossiping discreetly.

My biometrics unlock the door to my private space. As I walk in, eye-easy lights glow on to illuminate the spacious loft before me—revealing the neat racks of local servers with their blinking lights, the medical whitebays where I swap and fine-tune my limbs, the acoustic-foam-swaddled firing range at the far end, the cubbies of spare parts tagged with RFID chips so I can track down any of my personal inventory instantly.

My limbs are programmed to keep me standing in perfect posture, yet I feel an urge to straighten with pride. Yoyodyne Labs looks like a showroom waiting for a big brass inspection—each repair station has every tool I'd need within arm's reach.

I'm the only one who works here. That makes me the big brass. I like how this place has been customized to fit me; I like how it's been customized to *impress* me.

Haptic sensors register something snuffling at my ankles.

I lean down to pet Opposite Cat.

Opposite Cat purrs—well, its internal vacuum systems clicking on is purr-*like* as its carbon-whiskered geometric face plucks the dirt from my lower extremities. Its angled limbs are shaped from Stormtrooper-white plastic, its quickstrap artificial musculature designed to leap with greater agility than any feline.

The few friends I have told me I should get a pet. But a pet would seed my clean room with loose hair that would infect my muscle-knitting factories. So I built a pet that would not add mess, but subtract it—a tiny bot patrolling my workspace to remove dirt.

Hence: an Opposite Cat.

My friends now tell me I should get a life.

Speaking of my friends, my message lights are blinking—I forgot to put my accounts into stealth mode, and so my social networks have pinged people to inform them I'm back. My local social crew is an uneasy network of novice body-hackers who want to hang with me to feel tough, do-gooder veterans asking me to donate free security to their anti-war protests, lovers who fetishize the attachments more than the man, and a handful of people I actually trust.

I put them all on hold with a single message: **brb saving the world**.

Everybody knows that means "Two weeks minimum until I poke my head out again."

So I settle into my changing station with a grunt as my servos start the elaborate dance of decoupling Butch and Sundance to

Ferrett Steinmetz

swap them out with Scotty and Geordie, my maintenance arma- tures. As I download the massive dump of mission data to my local servers for MapReduce and reprocessing—no way I was streaming *that* precious combat data over a porous internet—I instruct my massive-screen movie theater to queue up *To Kill a Mockingbird* for what it informs me is the forty-seventh time.

And as my stations ready me for repairs, I remember what my Air Force therapist told me about my love of old movies:

You watch old movies to experience a time when men mattered, she'd told me. *You like* High Noon *because there were no automated gun turrets who could outshoot any human. You like* There Will Be Blood *because back then, a clever man didn't have to outrace satel- lite data to find oil deposits. You like* The Terminator *because back then, people thought they could escape a tracker machine.*

So why do I like old movies? I'd asked her. *New movies still pre- tend like we humans are better at things.*

Because old movies had to do it without CGI, she'd replied. *You want to live in a time when computers didn't exist.*

I told her she was wrong, of course. As a drone pilot, my job was to meld myself with computers, to fuse complex AI with human judgment to create moral and ethical outcomes that would protect the United States. How could I hate computers?

I told her I liked old movies because back then, the good guys won.

Do Fargo *or* There Will Be Blood *have happy endings?* she asked.

And then Scotty and Geordie are attached, these great spidery rotating tool armatures that snap in and out of position, and I put Scylla and Charybdis on the stand as I fieldstrip them, inspecting every artificial muscle strand and gearbox and timing pulley.

I fall into a meditative trance, as I always do, hunting for poten- tial failure points. I'm quoting movies under my breath as I disas- semble my prosthetics, because I need to hear human voices when I'm elbow-deep in tech. I listen to Gregory Peck telling Jem, *There's a lot of ugly things in this world, son. I wish I could keep them all away from you. That's never possible,* and he helps me remember why I'm trying to make a difference.

Sure enough, an anchor-point popped on Charybdis when I hauled up the trapdoor; my rerouting modules kept her operating at 93.6 percent efficiency, but that'll require replacing the drive schemata.

I check warranties. Nobody in the old cyberpunk movies mentions warranties, but the fact that the anchor-point is still service-friendly just saved me $1,600.

Gregory Peck's magnificent speeches end as the film switches to *Singin' in the Rain,* all frothy musical numbers, and the camaraderie between Gene Kelly and Donald O'Connor is so intense I feel like *I'm* friends with them, except I don't have to interact with them—which is good when I'm head-down in the schemata.

Sure enough, the alignment is off again in Scylla's lateral gun-actuators—she's been pulling left for months—so *that* needs to be retooled, and the rust flakes kicked up from the trapdoor got sucked in when the anchor-point popped and must be edged out before they cause short circuits. Some of the microbatteries have reached their end of use-life and must be swapped out before their effective power potential drops below combat standards.

Your profile shows you never watched movies, let alone old ones, before your honorable discharge, my therapist had said. *You played video games. Why did you stop?*

The theater auto-switches to *The Terminator.* Which is a movie about a killer death robot, and most people think it's an action adventure, but to me it's a comedy. Because I always imagine how trivial it'd be to destroy a real-life Terminator—these great military kill-machines running on magical nuclear batteries that never required coolant. Their drivetrains were covered in gooey meat; those delicate finger-armatures would clog long before they pulled a trigger.

I laugh. I'm the only one who gets my jokes.

Hell, I'm the only who hears them.

Ferrett Steinmetz

With each repair, the tally goes up: each deep-well battery another $600 sourced in bulk from the manufacturer, each gun realignment requiring delicate microfibers that are $3,359 on sale from CircuitCo. Each expense a tempting shortcut until you realize someone's life—often my own—depends on it.

The NNPC has dropped $250,000 into my account, pre-tax—and by the time I've refurbished Scylla, Charybdis, Butch, Sundance, and my legs, the post-mission maintenance has already chewed up $43,589. I think I've been awake for days. It doesn't matter; I have stims for that, and when I tire I do endless sit-ups, upgrading the slim core of organic muscle I still have available.

I have to be perfect, or other people will get hurt.

And then I'm rushing to the firing range, setting a printed-meat pseudo-dummy coursing with gelblood beneath an automated human arm simulacra wielding a knife. Good nonlethal weapons always cost ten times as much as a bullet to the brain. Still, the expensive sample prototypes of yank-tasers and splatter guards and dazzlers tell me which tools might have saved Onyeka from her kidnapper.

(I binge-watch *Arsenic and Old Lace* over and over again as I fight the pseudo-dummy, because it's a dark comedy where Cary Grant discovers his favorite aunts are serial killers, and I need black humor to cope when I'm endlessly reenacting Onyeka's throat-slashing.)

And I'm battling replicas of the best martial artists, tweaking my hand-to-hand routines to ensure I can take down world-class knife fighters, which reminds me I'm running out of memory for reaction packages *again* and so I spend $1,400 to upgrade to another googolplex of combat-shielded RAM.

(The martial arts makes me pull up *Seven Samurai*—good warriors dying fast by the sword, and their battle-born closeness makes me feel less like I'm swinging at combat dummies and more like I'm testing my skills against a stalwart comrade.)

And I'm tweaking my gun-targeting routines, because I've had nightmares about Scylla and Charybdis accidentally firing on some poor old man walking out into the marketplace, and I can't stop thinking how easy a false positive would have been in that crowded rush, and so I compensate for this new environment while pondering how many probability percentages I can shave off before someone splatters my skull due to a false negative.

(And as I panic thinking about the innocents I've hurt, I put on *Léon: The Professional* to see an assassin who's done much worse things redeem himself by rescuing a small girl.)

And then the combat sims ping me to inform me I can replay the missions now, with predicted behavior scraped from the incapacitated kidnappers' social media, and I'm glad to hear the extra time I could have spent scouting the area would have gotten me caught. I'm listening to my subvocalized, real-time mission recording, my constant narration allowing me to replay my line of thought as I made my worst decisions—a combat habit I've carried into my civilian life.

You use movies like addicts use methadone, my therapist had told me, just before I stopped seeing her. *They've become your replacement for human interaction.*

My in-in-box flashes red—my real in-box. My second- and third-tier buddies get filtered out until I have the energy to deal with them. What's left are the people I call my actual friends, and paying employers.

It's Trish, who best exemplifies a mixture of the two—she gets me jobs because she likes me. She's a veteran who somehow makes friends with people she's shot at, and she does her best to steer me towards riskier, high-yield employment activities. Sometimes I'm tempted. I've burned through $115,000 in eight days' worth of frantic deconstruction, reconstruction, and knife-wielder's *destruc-*tion, and if you're starting to see why I can't afford to pass up a good job, well, now you understand why most body-hackers get into the security business.

We have to talk, Trish says. That sounds uncomfortably relationshippy to me. It shouldn't be—we're not compatible.

Ferrett Steinmetz

I'm making the world a better place, I shoot back. **Catch you when I'm done?**

3:2, Trish says.

That's . . . not a real number.

She senses my hesitation, then types it again to confirm: **3:2.** What she's typing is a code we share to obscure the money a potential job might bring in.

The code for the Nigerian job, for example, would have been "25:96." As in "$250,000 for an estimated ninety-six hours of work, including travel time and prep." Considering I spent seventy-two hours sifting through the NNPC's data to prep the right mission approach, that was a conservative estimate.

"3:2" means "$3 million for two hours of work."

If it was anybody *but* Trish telling me this, I'd assume it was either a rip-off or a suicide mission. Yet if Trish is pinging me during maintenance time, she thinks this is a genuine offer.

I'm listening, I type.

Be at the Express Mart in ten hours and I'll shoot you coordinates from there, she says. **Look passing. I will. But come hot.**

Which is her code for "wear Thelma and Louise, my arms that can pass for human in a crowd if I wear long sleeves and no one looks close." The fact that she's sending me coordinates once I've arrived at a downtown location means she doesn't want anyone intercepting this communication to know where we'll be; an hour's drive from the Express Mart could put me anywhere in St. Louis.

If Trish is going to the effort of passing, well, she's serious. I don't think I've ever seen her shaved.

Yet that final phrase—"come hot"—means to arrive armed, just in case. Which I don't like. Thelma and Louise have no internal loadouts, which makes them legal anywhere—but if their sensors spot trouble, I have the second-plus delay of them unholstering a gun from my waist and drawing across a much greater range of motion.

But $3 million?

That'd buy me months' worth of maintenance time. Maybe a whole year.

I tell the lab to prep my nice arms.

I don't like Thelma and Louise much.

There's always this awkward moment between loadouts, a time between when the docking stations have removed my old arms and have yet to attach my new ones. When those incoming arms are Scylla and Charybdis, or Butch and Sundance, or even the antiquated weaponries of Jekyll and Hyde or Bonnie and Clyde, I feel like my limbs have been stripped away to reforge myself into a more efficient weapon.

But with Thelma and Louise, well—their specs barely register above human standards. I could, theoretically, be outwrestled by a beefy bouncer.

I feel my sockets exposed as Thelma and Louise revolve into place—my left socket smoothly surgical where they scooped out the shoulder joint to allow direct attachment to a reinforced collarbone and ribs, my right socket a puckered crater from where the rocket launcher shattered my arm into pink mist.

I am not a human being in those moments. I am a Ken-doll-with-the-limbs-plucked-off showroom mannequin—a useless torso, squirming in midair. I know my docking stations have triple redundancies so they won't fail, and even if they did my legs can be hacked to attach spare arms in a pinch, but . . .

Only with Thelma and Louise do I feel so nakedly helpless.

When Thelma and Louise are anchored to my nuBone hardpoints, I am reduced. With Scylla or Butch or Bonnie, the sole design consideration is brute efficiency. They can have bulky compartments to hold batteries, have multiple joints terminating in variable grippers.

I look at today's hands. Thelma and Louise's primary design considerations are to blend in—if it would cause a bulge or a joint

Ferrett Steinmetz

that couldn't pass for baseline human, it has to go. Alas, despite the fact that my prosthetics need their own sensors and storage, circuits are far bulkier than nerves, leaving the manufacturer with the unfortunate design consideration of having to pack more functionality into a cramped space.

So the artificial muscles have to be thin enough to be strapped over batteries molded to look like biceps. The sensors jammed into the remaining crevices must be small and underpowered. I'm capped at a percentage multiplier of human speeds because the muscles have to mimic human movement convincingly.

Thelma and Louise feel like I'm trying to imitate a body I've already amputated.

Opposite Cat hops down from her charger to vacuum my neck. I wriggle. I never taught her that trick—she's just learned to vacuum me when I'm stressed out. I could dig around in her neural networks to root out her motivations, but then I'd find some pragmatic rationale like my body temperature rises when I'm upset and I shed more skin flakes.

I prefer to think she harbors some affection for me. So I "pet" her, thumbing the reset button on her neck to send her back to her charge dock.

Slightly more relaxed, I buckle a pair of .45s to my hips; Thelma and Louise can draw and target independently. That's something, at least. And my showroom legs have a few tricks, though my sensors will be almost useless underneath the blue jeans. This button-down shirt's too light, lacking my body armor's reassuring weight.

I don't bother putting on clothes in the lab unless I know I have visitors, which I never do. In combat, I'm naked beneath my protective layers of body armor.

Putting on clothes feels like attending a masquerade.

I take my motorbike—a Harley so elderly it's grandfathered in under St. Louis's otherwise-strict auto-drive rules. It's so old it doesn't have onboard computers to log where I travel, which can be handy on the occasions I want to disable my GPSes so my location traces won't be subpoenable in a court case. (They could piece my route together from the images the auto-drive cars snap as they navigate the roads, of course. Or by scanning social-media accounts to find people posting photos of the old-timey guy on the gas-powered bike. There's no way to go completely dark these days; the best you can do is make it difficult to track you.)

I roar my Harley into gear and head out to the first staged rendezvous at the Express Mart, feeling underpowered and underequipped for a $3-million mission.

The meetup locale is Shaky Joe's, a biker bar on St. Louis's edge. I walk in as the opening band bursts into an uncomfortable flourish of crunchy guitar chords; they're working a little too hard for the room. Tonight's crowd has come here to have a beer, blow off some steam, maybe find a cheerful fuck.

I close my eyes, breathe in. There's too many people here. I should pop a tranquilizer, but I need to be sharp in case something happens.

The crowd looks cheerfully scraggly, as I'd expect them to in this day and age. They're mostly ex-truckers who still haven't figured out what to do twenty years after the self-driving trucks rolled out and devastated America's economy. That little technological achievement rendered 6 percent of America's workforce redundant, though the trucker culture remains; some have become spare-parts mechanics, others have taken to doing small jobs for anyone who'll pay 'em beer money in the underground economy. A too-significant number have curled up inside any bar that'll let them drink themselves to death on their government stipend.

Yet though America's remaining blue-collar work is drying up, destroyed by increasing automation, there'll always be a residue of folks who bellow out old Kid Rock songs—even though Kid Rock was in a wheelchair when they were teenagers.

These bandana-wearing motherfuckers are America's new Amish, and they'd stomp my ass hard if they noticed my prosthetic arma-

Ferrett Steinmetz

ments. They'd take my technology as a challenge, another souped-up replacement for human skill, and some drunk asshole would see whether he could take me down before my defenses came online.

And what would happen then? Would I have to kill someone if they all rushed me?

I stare out at the crowd, calculating threat responses, unable to make eye contact because I keep envisioning myself hurting them.

"Hey, sailor." A pretty redheaded white girl curls her arms around my bicep. I freeze, not encouraging her; Thelma's batteries generate heat akin to body warmth, and I've got a millimeter-thick pseudoflesh layer that'll pass on casual touch, but if this girl squeezes she'll discover unyielding titanium beneath her fingers.

I can't hurt her. I *can't.*

"Buy a girl a drink?" she asks.

"Sorry." I scan the crowd for Trish. "I've got a date."

"Damn right ya do, dipshit. It's me."

I look down at the girl's face for the first time. Fresh razor burn peeks out from beneath a layer of discreet foundation makeup. But Trish's lips have been painted a deep kissable burgundy, her sharp cheeks softened with rouge; and instead of her usual off-the-shoulder cocktail dress to show off her stubbled legs, she's wearing the obligatory hip-hugger blue jeans and leather vest that the other local girls are wearing.

Her ample cleavage? Also shaven clean.

She's unsettlingly feminine, going bare-armed to show off the tribal military tattoos laced around her pale biceps—yet she manages to make the gun tucked into her leather boots seem stylish.

"You, uh . . ." I stammer. "That's a . . ."

She snorts a laugh, gets up on tiptoes to kiss me on the cheek. "I *told* you I was gonna pass, silly." Then she flicks her long red fingernails across her denuded cheeks if to say, *I know, crazy right?*

Trish normally sports a thin fuzzy beard and mustache in addition to her long auburn hair. Some of the other body-hackers have tried gossiping with me about her "real" gender—but Trish asked me to call her "she." That makes her a she as far as I'm concerned. I mean, I cut off my legs to replace them with hardware, what right do I have to judge anyone else's body?

Still, it's a little weird seeing her pretending to be something she's not. There's a scattering of other bearded female-reading guests here, and some very masculine men with child-bearing hips—as long as you're willing to pound Budweisers and root for the Cardinals, nobody cares much what you look like.

But Trish has completely altered her appearance. If *I* didn't recognize her, no one will.

She keeps her head down as she leads me to a wooden booth whittled away by carved graffiti. Her not working the crowd gives me the heebie-jeebies. I imagine saying hello to a stranger without Trish serving as social lubricant, then realize maybe I rely on Trish too heavily to curate my social life.

She slides into the booth like a dancer.

"You . . . you look good." Which she does, but I'm not thrilled; seeing Trish like this has the squirmy, distant charm of realizing your little sister could be thought of as "cute."

"I spruce up nice." She buffs her fingernails on her collar. "So what date are we on? Fourth or fifth?"

"We're . . ." I frown. "We're not dating."

"We are tonight." She looks around at the crowd; a handful pay vague attention to us. "I'm happy to be here, you're grumpy; everyone's assuming I've gotten bored with you, so I've dragged you out somewhere dangerous to see if you'll lighten up. Once we start negotiating, they'll assume we're arguing because you're no fun."

It's a nice bone thrown in my direction: she knows I'm nervous the crowd might figure out what I am, so she's framing how they view this meeting in romantic-comedy terms. (Because oh God does Trish *love* terrible rom-coms.)

I respond in my best Harrison Ford deadpan, "I'm fun."

She shakes her head. "You have the *potential* to be fun. But do you know how I know you're falling short of that goal?"

Ferrett Steinmetz

"How?"

She reaches across the table to cup my gloved hand. "When a girl tells you to buy her a drink, son, you buy her a drink."

That "son" is comforting. It's Trish's quiet way of reinforcing how she's flirting with me to project the illusion that we're a couple. Which is good; she's a lesbian, I'm half machinery, we're not meant to work out.

"I was waiting for you to introduce me to the bartender," I demur.

She wriggles uncomfortably. "Yeah, I don't . . . I don't know her."

"You don't know the *bartender* here?"

Her eyes narrow as she scowls. "Of course not. That's why I *chose* this place. But even glammed up as I am, someone might still recognize me—so seriously, sweetie, buy me a drink? No—buy me multiple drinks."

"Okay, okay," I mutter. "I didn't know there *was* a place you didn't know the bartender."

Trish knows everyone. You can't go out to dinner with her without a waiter waving hello. And during drinks she'll stumble across an old buddy she hasn't seen in years, then compress the last decade's worth of history into a brief conversation so expertly this distant acquaintance will walk away believing Trish is their best friend.

Yet somehow, despite the fact that she's spent half the night introducing you to other people, you always feel like Trish came out just to see you.

As I push my way through the crowd to the bar, I note the bartender's presence—at the hip bars downtown, the bartender would be a pleasant old-timey statement, their sign they could afford to pay someone for what amounted to performance art. At Shaky Joe's, the bartender's an old Mexican woman who I suspect has been working the counter since long before the drinkbots put bartenders out of business, and will work here until she's dead. These truckers would turn any drinkbot into a piñata.

The bartender's presence is both reassuring and troublesome: a bog-standard drinkbot would never overpour Wild Turkey as flagrantly, but on the other hand a bot has zero chance of noticing my electronic hands.

By the time I get back to Trish the younger guys are eyeing her, wondering if they should take a shot. I sit down, glaring at them; they fold.

"So . . . three million?" I ask, sliding the drink over.

"They're looking for a very specific skill set."

"I don't have skills worth three million for two hours," I tell her. "That's Yak-level money."

She sips her drink, avoiding eye contact. "Funny you mention that . . ."

I'm halfway to my feet before she grabs me hard enough that my limbs ask me whether to flip into violence mode. I realize she's chosen the bar not only because the band's noisy enough to drown out casual eavesdropping, but also because I won't dare make a scene leaving.

"It's not a *direct* contract with the International Access Consortium," she whispers, speaking quickly—and I'd *still* stomp away if it wasn't for that sliver of hurt in her blue eyes asking, *Do you think I'd hurt you?* "I wouldn't set you up with the Yak. I wouldn't set my worst enemy up with the Yak. There's some lines even *I* wouldn't cross."

"So who—"

"*Sit down,*" she hisses. The crowd's staring because Trish's hair is practically standing on end.

The Yak does that to people.

I lower myself back down. She hands out apologetic smiles to the crowd.

"Fifth date, and we won't make our sixth," she whispers, her fingers trembling. "Are you gonna drink that drink? I'm gonna drink mine."

"I don't drink alcohol," I inform her. "I get enough brain damage in the course of combat. And I'll get more damaged getting involved with the Yak. So what the hell are *you* doing getting in-

Ferrett Steinmetz

volved with the IAC? You're better off flying under their radar, because if they notice you, well . . ."

Rumor was the Yak paid world-class prices . . . the first time. After that, they dug up deep blackmail to get past employees involved in increasingly sordid missions, because the Yak viewed its independent operatives as an ablative meat-shield. You only got involved with the Yak if you were balls-in-the-garbage-disposal desperate.

"*I'm* not on their radar," she says. "But Ancillary Force is."

I'm not good with politics. But Trish is, and we are about to enter into a complex web of alliances where she thinks she can come out on top.

And $3 million, well . . . that's enough to stash in a bank and collect interest. It wouldn't be enough to retire on—not yet. But it *would* be enough that the cash from my future jobs could go towards saving for a future, instead of endlessly dribbling down into the maintenance sinkhole.

Three million dollars could be enough to, at some point, stop shooting people for a living.

"Let me explain," she says.

I gulp the Wild Turkey.

"You know Ancillary Force, right?"

"That's Donnie's outfit, isn't it? He—"

I splutter, realizing my fingers are massaging my temples. Just mentioning Donnie's name has made me tense enough to kickstart Thelma and Louise into auto-soothe mode.

Trish looks into her empty glass disconsolately, wanting more. "So you know Donnie."

I sigh. "He *loves* me."

Remember when I talked about the novice body-hackers who hang with me to feel badass? The ones who my email filters filter out when I'm in a bad mood?

Donnie's the king of those.

If Donnie had his way, we'd be best buddies—and the problem is, Donnie's just useful enough that I don't feel comfortable telling him we *aren't*. He's almost as good at optimizing systems as I am—maybe better—so if I get stuck, Donnie's someone who I can conference in when I need to squeeze extra performance out of compressed sight-models. (Which is fancy talk for "Not shooting people you didn't mean to shoot.")

And Donnie, well, he's rich. I try not to sell out to people overmuch, as it makes me feel like a used-car salesman, but Donnie has all the new toys—I have to save for months before buying a replacement for Scylla or Charybdis, reading every review. But Donnie doesn't think twice about ordering in a $500,000 Dyson-Grantha armatured leg prosthetic to see if it operates as smoothly as the ads claim. He tinkers on any piece of equipment that catches his fancy, taking it apart, improving his craft; if I need to test some prosthetics, no matter how obscure, Donnie can loan them to me.

(In fact, on some loan requests I suspect Donnie's secretly bought equipment he didn't own to avoid admitting that he didn't have it.)

Trish cranes in, trying to get a look at my face under my head-massaging hands. "So . . . do *you* think Donnie runs a good organization?"

I start to order Thelma and Louise away, but the more I think about Donnie the more I realize they're all that's staving off a headache. "That depends."

"On?"

"Which side of the paycheck you're on."

Because that's the other problem with Donnie: he wants to be the biggest badass in town. I optimize for bystander safety; Donnie optimizes for maximum effect, ensuring every shot's a splattery skull-breaker, gearing himself with the largest weapons it's legally permissible to own.

Donnie's been bugging me to go out on a mission for years, his eyes widening as he burbles at me: *Think about how cool it would be! For us! The biggest badasses in the USA! Working together!*

But I've seen how he tunes his IFF routines. He believes any potential danger should be shot. If they're not dangerous, he asks, then why are they in a firefight?

Except he's working local missions—with America's unemployment rate nudging 43 percent thanks to automation, there's plenty of riots that need quelling. Hell, in this bar alone there's fifty ex-truckers who'd love to take a wrench to the auto-drive eighteen-wheelers. And the riots get worse if automated drones quell them, so having a human face on your walking armory has some benefits.

Unless they're of the opinion that anyone who fucks with them deserves a groin-shot kill.

Donnie's casualty rate is higher than I could live with. Even if he's on a no-kill mission, the man thinks it's a giggle to put out someone's eye with a rubber bullet. I've gotten queasy just rubbing titanium shoulders with him, let alone teaming up.

Trish nods. "Yeah. Well, Donnie's got the history the Yak wants—he's never failed a mission."

"Because if he gets backed into a corner, he blows his way out with excess firepower?"

"And lawyers up afterwards." Trish slumps. "Donnie keeps asking me for assignments. I don't give him much. You hear me?"

I do. This industry's too small to piss people off. Trish isn't thrilled about dealing with him either, but she has to give him little leads or Donnie will know she's not a fan. It takes a lot for Donnie to understand you're not on his side, as he blithely assumes everyone adores him, but . . . neither Trish nor I have wanted to see what happens when you get on Donnie's bad side.

"So you're giving me a mission with the Yak *and* Donnie," I say. "Why the hell would I want this?"

"Three million?"

"Three million's bought you the time to explain."

"All right." She ticks off her reasons on her fingers. "First off, it's three million *if everything goes right*. This is Donnie's first mission for the Yak, and as far as he knows it's a cakewalk—just babysit a package as it's transferred off the docks in New York into a secure location. It's three million if it goes clean, without any casualties—if there's any conflict that makes the news, that reward drops to a million. Still extraordinary pay for two hours. If they can't deliver the package, you get nothing."

"So Donnie's eager to ensure his first mission for the IAC goes well, and is willing to overpay to impress his new masters. Is there *that* much money in future IAC contracts?"

"It's not so much the money as that Donnie thinks the IAC will let him cut loose. He wants those black-book contracts where he can really do some damage."

My eyes roll so hard it hurts. "Of course."

"But the Powers What Be At The IAC want to see whether he's capable of keeping a mission low-key."

"So they saw his legal record."

"They're the IAC. They saw *everything*. But his legal record is why you're perfect for this mission. Only you can get Donnie and his trigger-happy mercs to calm down. Hell, he's so eager to work with you, he'll install whatever reaction packages you want. You can keep his men restrained to safe parameters."

"Have you told him you're scouting me for the job?"

"Oh hell no," she says. "I'm surprised he didn't contact you directly."

I have a firm suspicion that once I scan through my mail filters, I'll find several blocked texts from Donnie begging me to come along on this mission.

She squints. "*Did* he contact you directly? This won't fuck my finder's fee, will it?"

"*If* I take this mission, I'll tell him you had the pull to yank me out of maintenance mode. But shepherding Donnie still puts me in the Yak's gunsights."

"It doesn't. You'll be an independent contractor, hired for a single mission. They haven't asked Donnie for a roster list, they didn't ask Donnie for security clearances for his men—"

Ferrett Steinmetz

"Because they've broken into his files?"

"Yes. That's why we're having this discussion off the record. He's bringing in a secret ringer in case the shit hits the fan. Donnie doesn't want the Yak to know he's pulling extra muscle onto this mission. This whole contract takes place off-line—he pays me with a bag of cash he set aside years before he came to the Yak's attention, I launder it to find ways to get it to you, and none of this appears in any transactional record."

"Except for me physically showing my face at the site."

"Your face will be hidden behind your HUD-shield. Babysit the package well, and nobody at the Yak will even know you were there. Officially, Donnie's crew will be the only agents on the ground. Except . . ."

Trish swoops her empty drink around in the air, then sets it down on the table as if she's not sure how to put this.

"You're not sure they're telling the truth," I say.

"Nope. This might not be a babysitting job, but a total party kill. The Yak doesn't have loyalty to long-term employees, let alone first-time contractors."

"So you're thinking the Yak knows something big's coming for their package, and are throwing Donnie's men in the way?"

She grimaces. "Could be cheap distraction. Maybe the Yak's counting on Ancillary Force to be the expendable defense line before their real muscle swoops in to do cleanup."

"Awww. And you thought of me."

"I wouldn't assign this mission to someone who couldn't handle it," she shoots back. "Donnie isn't vetting me either—for all his techno fetishery, he doesn't give a shit about human resources. I could toss some wannabe into the soup and hope for an easy finder's fee."

She pauses, holds me with her eyes.

"But you. You've pulled off impossible missions. You just saved that little girl in Nigeria."

"I didn't save Onyeka. That kid will spend the rest of her life—"

"Stop right there. *Those words are enough.* 'That kid will spend the rest of her life.' Objective *complete*."

I squeeze my drink so hard the glass cracks. I look down, baffled, realizing I need to recalibrate Thelma.

"You're too hard on yourself, Mat. You got through when the NNPC gave you bollixed information. You pushed on when you realized—correctly—that the NNPC's next move would be a scorched-earth mission. You spend so much time working to fix the things that went wrong, you never consider the things that went *right*."

"The things that go right happen *because* I consider all the things that went wrong—"

"Don't," she says, cutting me off. "Just don't. For the record, my finder's fee is fifty thousand dollars—that'll pay off my mortgage. But I *will* walk away if I can't put the right man on this job. I've done the research. That right man is you."

"Trish, three million dollars isn't worth getting on the Yak's radar."

"The money's not why I called you."

"Then why?"

"Because Donnie will do this mission with or without you. Even if it *is* a milk run, those docks are crowded with union workers—you think Donnie's default IFF settings will protect bystanders from being blinded by rubber bullets?"

The injected hiss of mild sedatives; Thelma decides my blood pressure's rising too much. "That's low play, Trish, I can't be responsible for—"

"If a firefight breaks out during the transfer and you're not there," she says, leaning forward, "what do *you* think will happen?"

I imagine armor-piercing bullets smashing through hard hats, panicked workers cut down, blood-dripping headlines with DOCK FIREFIGHT KILLS HUNDREDS. Donnie's career would be over, even his lawyers couldn't save him then, but . . .

I think of the kids those union laborers are raising.

Ferrett Steinmetz

I think of a thousand sad Onyekas standing at funerals.

"Saving innocents will be what lets you sleep at night," Trish says, nodding. "That three million's your consolation prize."

Thelma and Louise massage my temples again as I realize yeah, I'm on this case.

I'm going dark for this mission, but there's no sense making it easy for the Yak to know where I am. I'm assuming they'll break into my files.

So I hack my own system, installing a virus designed to simulate me.

Yoyodyne Laboratories is now infected by a silent macro that runs endless random simulations against the last mission logs, searching for the perfect outcome. (I call it "Ferris Bueller" and have it set to save its experiments, in case Ferris stumbles upon a casualty-free approach.) Ferris periodically switches approaches—ordering replacements from vendors I'd been meaning to buy, initiating test shots at the firing range, flushing the toilet, surfing porn.

I look at the full list of what I do when I'm in maintenance mode. It's both accurate and a little humiliating, seeing my sad behaviors laid out.

But if the Yak breaks in to check if I'm the mystery member of Donnie's squad, they won't notice Ferris working silently beneath the hood—they'll see the stream of data and conclude I'm at work.

I hope.

All the while Opposite Cat tickles my ear, following me around, vacuuming anything from me she can get at—which, given she's been designed to be able to leap to get at anything in the room, is pretty much all of me.

I savor one last cigar to leave Opposite Cat a bowl of ashes so she won't get bored while I'm away. That's not weird, is it?

Once I've strapped on Scylla and Charybdis, I sneak out the back door in the dark of night, run the 1.5 miles to the *highly* illicit hackmobile I have set up. I call him "Herbie the Love Bug," and he will log a fake identity to each city's networked driver-AIs it drives through, his "windows" illegal television screens that broadcast an illusory interior with a nice, happy white dad and his kids taking a cheerful vacation.

I do, however, bring an empty milk jug with me. Such a low-tech solution to being unable to stop for bathroom breaks.

I settle in for a twelve-hour drive. Trish said it was a two-hour job including travel, but she thought I'd be taking Donnie's private jet. I'd rather go the slow ninety-miles-per-hour auto-drive route to ensure the Yak has as little ability to trace my trail as possible.

And finally, Herbie the hackmobile pulls into the distribution center I'm supposed to meet Donnie's men at. This distribution center, in turn, is roughly twenty minutes away from the docks where we'll pick up the package after we've coordinated strategies.

Just seeing the rendezvous site makes me glad I've taken the job.

Because I'm arriving at the midday shift-change, and there's streams of auto-driven cars pulling up to the guard stations, beaming their credentials, then dropping off blue-collar workers at the safe zone well beyond the concrete barriers and electrified fences.

A couple of low-level body-hackers—friendly human faces who've only replaced an arm, wearing brown button-down security-guard shirts instead of body armor—amble alongside the protestors waving signs outside, smiling, making sure nothing boils over into yet another riot.

Still, whenever an auto-driven truck pulls into the guard stations, the protestors swarm in, milling close so the trucks have to inch forward, their three-dimensional hazard-processing sensors working overtime. The protestors don't quite lie down in front of the trucks—that'd get them hauled away—but they definitely slow down the unloading process.

Protesters and workers alike would be slaughtered if Donnie's kind of fight broke out here.

Ferrett Steinmetz

Yet as we pull into the distribution center, I ponder that this is one of the last jobs humanity will get to do before computers turn the lights out on us. I remember being young enough to hear the astonished yelps as general practitioners got replaced with medical-AIs, as law clerks got replaced with smart legal neurals, as architects got replaced by cunning design programs.

Oh, you still need human bodies for the tiebreakers, of course; we'll always want human judges. (Except for computer-mediated arbitration, which is picking up in popularity.) We'll always want surgeons monitoring our heart surgeries, even if one surgeon can now oversee an entire surgical ward.

But the distribution center? That's where shipping containers full of merchandise get broken out to be shipped to local warehouses. You *could* theoretically build a robot flexible and smart enough to unload refrigerators *and* corn *and* glass panes *and* the millions of other things America buys.

Yet you've seen how expensive it is, maintaining my arms. Why bother with robots when you can pay some poor schmuck minimum wage, and let workers' comp pick up the difference if the meat-hardware breaks down?

As I roll down the window so the guards can verify my access, I wonder if Donnie came up with the idea to meet up here or if the IAC did. Either way, it's a smart move. Nobody will question a few extra body-hackers at a place that needs so much security, and there's a truck pulling in every three minutes. If the IAC is looking to transfer its cargo cleanly, then this is a good place for them to covertly insert an extra layer of defense before heading out to pick up their package from the docks.

Then again, I've had twelve hours to ponder what cargo needs six heavily armed cyborgs to guard it.

We're supposed to meet out in the truck yard, down by the railway where the trains come in. Another good choice: the distribution-center owners don't want people knowing how many auto-driven trucks are parked here, lest protesters choose an optimal time to sneak in for sabotage, so the entire area is blocked off with camouflage netting. Including the huge wire net overhead, designed to stop protest drones from firing Molotov cocktails into the repair holding zones.

I get out of Herbie the hackmobile, ports hot, IFF tuned tight. Someone would have to actively draw a gun on me for Scylla and Charybdis to authorize fire. But this is a poor zone for automated combat; it's shadowy, dappled with scant sunlight from what the netting filters through. I have to squeeze through the bug-splattered hoods from where computer-driven trucks have parked door-to-door to maximize space. It's also a hot summer day. Between the hot trucks cooling down and the ambient air temperature, there's lots of ways to have embarrassing false positives—or deadly false negatives.

Yet I hear Donnie's goons—sorry, the fine employees of Ancillary Force—shouting excitedly from a few trucks over.

I triple-check that I'm broadcasting my location on the prearranged encrypted frequency: the problem is that body-hackers are, by definition, threats. There've been some ugly situations where two body-hackers surprised each other and their software initiated fatal firefights before either had realized what happened. So making Ancillary Force aware of my approach is *high* on my agenda of Not Getting My Ass Shot.

As I approach, four Ancillary body-hackers—none of them Donnie—are crouched in the empty spot where our truck will eventually arrive.

Each has gleaming limbs, stenciled with Ancillary Force's logo—a gold-and-diamond reticle hovering over a silhouetted criminal. I don't need my ID systems to catalogue their armament prosthetics: I can recognize their model and make by silhouette, so I mentally catalogue their offensive capability. They all pack top-quality merchandise, though a couple bear the telltale marks of a refurbish.

They're huddled in a semicircle around one of the parked rail cars, whispering to one another.

Their mounted guns are twitching, aiming at something.

Ferrett Steinmetz

That's not good.

I stride forward. Donnie's brought serious chrome with him—of the four, I can spot only one organic limb left between them. A few dedicated enthusiasts will trade off one limb for the combat advantage, the serious will give literally an arm and a leg to become a killing machine, but Donnie's hired maniacs were willing to toss 40 percent of their body mass into the dumpster in exchange for pure firepower—

I'm slammed up against a truck's hood hard enough that my neck stabilizers don't quite kick in. My HUD comes ablaze with readouts in bold letters my adrenaline-shocked mind can read:

Shot fired no threats detected.

I *think* I heard the shot, a silenced round, but my preprogrammed reaction routines have acted to protect my slow human body. Even though my sensors haven't yet figured out what's dangerous enough to warrant Ancillary Force entering into a firefight, it's flung me against cover while it maneuvers me towards the combat zone to get better information.

Attempting to sync.

My legs propel me in a four-foot standing jump to leap backwards onto the truck's drive axle, the truck creaking under my weight. My strategic simulators thrash as they reach out over the encrypted LAN to gather data from combatants closer to the threat, hungry for tactical information, but we haven't established protocols yet so there's no—

I have no idea why my routines are climbing up for cover, but my GUI feeds me what information it knows. One of Donnie's men, a woman actually, is limned in bright yellow, indicating she fired the shot, the projected line of fire showing she shot low, beneath the train. Some threat was emerging from there.

Yet while my IFF routines are in overdrive, hunting for new dangers, I wonder:

What the hell would crawl from underneath a train that would be worth shooting?

I hear coarse laughter—the kind that knocks me right back to fourth grade when bullies used to pick on me because my mom couldn't afford new clothes. "Look attim leap!" the girl who fired laughs. "Our new recruit's a scaredy-cat—another kitty!"

Oh, they did not.

Oh, they fucking *did not*.

I manually dampen the combat alert—because my tactical simulators are designed to assume that if someone fires, there must be a threat in the area. My sensors can feed me information, but it's up to me to provide the context.

I push my way past the now-doubled-over-with-laughter hackers to see what these assholes shot.

Sure enough, there's an anguished orange tabby with a gunshot between its legs. My sensors tell me it's dying from shock.

I command Charybdis to give it a mercy kill, then whirl around to face them as my left arm puts the poor cat out of its misery.

"What the fuck are you doing, shooting strays?" I bellow.

Their laughter dies. The woman who shot steps forward, setting her smoked helmet transparent to show me the sneer on her ragged white face. She'd been pretty once, but her nose is shoved to one side from an old bar brawl, her cheeks festooned with zits from clogged pores, her body odor so offensive she's clearly nurtured her stench as a mark of pride. The kind of hacker who concentrates on the tech and makes a point of ignoring the flesh, then.

Her gunports clack noisily; my HUD alerts me with:

Terminal threat detected.

Indicating she's cut off the encryption network so I'll have no idea when she starts shooting.

Ferrett Steinmetz

"Why?" she asks, licking chapped lips. "You a stray?"

I take her in; her four limbs are Endolite-Ruger, a beautifully matched set—and her body armor has a nice bright Endolite-Ruger logo printed across the front. She's a walking advertisement, having opted to stay on technology's cutting edge by signing her body away to her sponsor.

And what she's advertising is mayhem. Her arms are top-of-the-line Ordnance 6000s with inset weaponry, her legs gleaming new Panzertron Mark IVs. We're both struggling to talk as our reaction packages instruct our legs to put us in optimal positions for the potentially impending firefight, jerking us to and fro as our guns twitch.

"Kiva," one of the other cat killers says nervously, his legs carrying him backwards to get him out of the line of fire. "Power down. That's—"

"I know who he is," Kiva snaps, low and deadly; dangers of having a reputation, I guess. She's clearly been itching to put her tech up against mine.

"Funny," I drawl, taking my time to stare her up and down. "I've never heard of you. But I'd bet you twenty bucks you've got a nice Endolite-Ruger tattoo under that armor."

Kiva's face flushes as her mooks groan—they've clearly wanted to say that to her, but didn't dare. What I just implied, probably correctly, is that she's so in hock to Endolite-Ruger that she's had to contractually emblazon their logo on her skin.

I don't need my HUD's audio analysis to inform me that that series of clicks is her limbs loading armor-piercing bullets into the chamber.

"I'm proud to wear my Endolite-Ruger Ordnance 6000s," she says, a bit too theatrically; she's doubtlessly got a permanent recorder on to ensure she never says a bad word against her sponsors. "I told these fellas my upgraded Osprey 3.1 operating systems can shoot sharp enough to spay a stray cat. Which I *did*. Wanna try for two, junkyard?"

And again, though my HUD tells me where her four guns are aimed, I had already guessed.

I pop my faceplate, then withdraw yet another cigar from my pocket and light it with the butane torch in Scylla's index finger. This is a peaceful cigar. Gives me time to cool the waters.

Also, anyone who can light up a cigar with four guns aimed at his dick is someone worth listening to.

"Funny thing about those Ordnance 6000s," I say, after exhaling a blue cloud in Kiva's direction. "It's a mighty *theatrical* set of armaments. You know they brought in acoustic engineers to specially curve the chambers on your inset guns? Just to amplify that badass little *click-clack* when they're loading so everyone within range can hear you?"

She frowns. "Yeah. So?"

I step closer, puffing on my Macanudo. "Funny thing about that; it *also* amplifies the sounds of its *other* internal mechanisms loud enough for other systems to pick up. A properly prepared person could, say, profile the noise of your four guns to know when they're locking in to shoot."

The bead of sweat rolling down her nose is delectable.

"So?" she says. "Even if you did know when I was about to fire, the Ordnance's default reaction time from 'capture target' to 'firing' is point zero three seconds!"

If you're forever shilling for your employer, you'd better know your equipment's stats by heart.

"That's the *default* reaction time, darling," I say, smiling. "If you jailbreak your Osprey software to install some leaner routines, maybe swap those proprietary armatures for a nicely greased Khaw-Schrodinger Multikinetic loadout, you could shave that CTF down to a slim point zero two four seconds.

"But I've got my guns aimed at yours, and *my* CTF is point zero one three."

It's nice hearing the mooks gasp. There are so few people who can appreciate the depths of my fine-tuning. And Kiva, well, she didn't look great in the first place, but she goes positively pale.

"So here's what happens," I tell her. My faceplate snaps back down and our leg armatures do an intricate dance around each other—her looking for more distance, me not letting her get away. "If you authorize that fire, my microphones will pick up that you've given the green light to kill me. And my countermeasures will blow the *shit* out of your Ordnance 6000s before your hammers fall on ammo."

Then I might rip your arms off for good measure, I think. I mean, I did just upgrade these hand-to-hand combat routines.

"Fuck you!" she says. *"There's no way you've got the specs to my arms memorized!"*

And again, the "uhhhhh" from the mooks who know my reputation is like hearing angels sing.

"You don't tell me who to shoot!" she cries. She looks around, betrayed, ready to take it out on someone else—but we're dancing, me driving her backwards, our guns twitching.

"I'm telling you to stand down. *Now*. Because on this mission, *I* am your second-in-command. If you don't reauthorize me on your IFF, *I'll* shoot first to disable your weapons and then upload the video of how useless your Ordnance 6000s were against these— what did you call them? Junkyard arms?"

"You don't even have a matched set!"

I shrug. "Scylla and Charybdis look pretty balanced to me. But what do *you* think? Will your corporate sponsors keep you on board once I've made you famous for demonstrating the manifest weaknesses in their design?"

Her larynx twitches as she subvocalizes something. I frown; it's unlikely she has any surprises up her Endolite-Ruger sleeves, as her corporate masters would *not* approve of nonfactory settings . . . but who knows whether they've given her beta weaponry?

Still. She doesn't know what I have either. And I'm famed for my experimentation.

"Calling the Endolite-Ruger help desk?" I ask.

Three terminal threats detected.

She smirks. "Not quite."
I hear the clanks as the three mooks take positions from behind.

The irritating thing about computerized combat is that your tactical systems never point you in the direction *you* want to be looking—they're positioning you for a maximal balance of effective firepower, cover, and retreat. You're always facing the wrong direction for your meat-eyes to take in what's happening. And while I could pump camera-views into my feed, in practice I find multiple screen-in-screens more distracting.

My combat overlay tells me I'm in deep. I have some surprise weaponry stashed in my legs, and Scylla and Charybdis have some tricks I didn't reveal. My defense scans tell me I could outfire them one-on-one.

But four combat-tactical machines? I don't have enough weaponry to go around. My tactical sims give me a 29 percent chance of victory if this goes to gunpowder.

That seems mighty generous.

Yet I'm okay with that. The only people getting fucked up today will be voluntary participants.

It's a good fight.

We're all dancing, this crazy jujitsu maneuvering done at insect-fast speeds—me feinting, them cutting me off, my legs doing football-style bluffs to get my back against the train for cover, the four darting into position around me to capitalize on their advantage.

Yet though it's smarter to watch them as dots on a map, I want to see them with my own eyes—it's a weakness, I know some body-hackers can give themselves over to the overlay, but me?

This is no video game. I like to see who I'm shooting.

Ferrett Steinmetz

We should be trash-talking—but we've got our heads down, programming in improvements, upgrading our tactics. And though I could probably do that and talk at the same time . . .

I'm terrified.

Fighting other body-hackers isn't like fighting baseline humans. With baseline humans, you see them raise the gun, you see them pull the trigger—it's comprehensible.

Whereas when—if—someone opens fire, the response will take place at processor speeds. If you count "Mississippi one, Mississippi two," the fatal shots will be fired before you've finished your first "M."

Every blink takes forever when you're not sure if your eyes will open again.

Except they're scared too. That's why they haven't fired. Their tacticals are probably telling them they have a 71 percent chance of victory—but that 29 percent is a considerable disincentive to commit.

"Come on!" Kiva snarls. "Eighty-three percent chance we win! Go for it!"

"That's a seventeen percent chance you all die," I say, puffing on my cigar, grateful for my customized HUD-helmet that allows me to smoke petite coronas while I fight. "And my odds say I'll take at least two of you down with me."

"Fuck you, junkyard." My bioreadouts show her rising heartbeat—she'll accept the terms and conditions within the next minute, and then we all live—or not—with the consequences.

"Now *that's* what I like to see!" a cheery voice calls out "Everyone armed and ready for the *shit*!"

Donnie walks in, his face lit up like a kid watching fireworks.

Belay that; he's fucking *applauding* as he strolls into the middle of a firefight. A slow, appreciative clap. And—

Is he smoking a cigar?

My cigar brand?

As he walks into five intersecting lines of fire with his faceplate open?

Then again, Donnie can afford to be relaxed. He's got bulky ceramic-coated Symbiotech-Walther legs, flared out like chaps but bristling with gunports—a high-end military spec that's outlawed for public carry, but I guess Donnie has the lawyers to fight that one.

And his arms are things of beauty: massive Gressinger-Sauer Omnipotents, fresh off the line, barely resembling human arms except for the extendogrips on the ends—gracefully curved swathes of tanklike machinery alternating with classic, tried-and-tested guns.

Of course he's had the entire thing detailed too. His million-dollar-per-limb rig is spray-painted a royal purple and gold—what does he care about camouflage?—with the Ancillary Force target-on-a-criminal logo in actual gold plating.

He's beautiful death. He could slaughter us all and I don't think we'd scratch his paint.

"*Kiiiiva*." He cocks his head, spreading his arms wide open as if going for a hug—and despite the fact those hydraulic-assisted limbs look more like a garbage compactor, Kiva gives a schoolgirl's giggle and glances away, blushing behind her faceplate. "Who's afraid of nothing? *That's* my girl. Ready to *explode!*"

Donnie's meat-body has a Californian surfer's good looks— his sandy hair and toothpaste-whitened smile melts panties. He pays megabucks for transparent body armor so he can show off his tanned six-pack. And if the bulge in his pants isn't artificial, well . . . I'm not a man who envies much, but it's hard not to notice the anaconda he swings.

He chucks Kiva under her chin, his brass knuckles cruising to stop a micrometer away from her faceplate. Even I have to admire how well he's tuned his Omnipotents' motion controls—they probably gave him beta access because, well, Donnie's tweaks tend to wind up as factory defaults.

He snorts with glee, turning around to face his other men. "And you! I *love* your enthusiasm! You *knew* how dangerous this SOB was, yet you piled in! You put the 'T' in 'teamwork'!

"But." He shakes his head. "You fellas gotta tweak your tacticals.

Ferrett Steinmetz

Your simulators gave you an eighty-three percent chance of success? Against *this* man? Why—"

A car smashes into me.

I don't understand what's happened—the emergency airbags have smashed into my ears like boxing gloves, my legs have stiffened to brace against the impact, my arms are shrieking that a 120-pound weight just smashed into me at eighty miles per hour.

"—this man has countermeasures for *everything*," Donnie finishes.

And as I stare at the corrugated metal spikes inches away from my nose, I realize:

Donnie punched me. At superhuman speeds.

If I hadn't upgraded my hand-to-hand combat routines, he would have punched my head off.

"That's why I love you, man," he whispers, pulling me in a little too close before kissing the top of my helmet. "Today's mission is gonna kick. Ass. You and me. Together at last." He waves to his crew. "Let's *roll*."

The plan is that we ride in two automated trucks to the pickup point at the docks; though trucks don't have drivers anymore, most long-distance vehicles have seats they'll rent to folks who need cheap cross-country transport. And of course the Yak's kitted out the trucks with the same illegal video-windows that I used, which will make it appear to casual inspection that the trucks are empty.

Me? I'm trying to get my head back in gear while the six of us clank towards the trucks. My body shivers from adrenaline shock from Donnie's punch. And my mind, well, it's yelling at me for being so damned stupid for tussling with people I had to work with.

What the hell was I thinking, provoking a face-off with Kiva?

I have conversation-boosting diplomatic assistants I could have pulled up to ease the waters. I wasn't acting like a problem-solver—I was acting like a damn sheriff in a western.

How could I have been so stupid, boxing myself into a situation with a 29 percent chance of survival?

Then I look at Kiva, who's side-eyeing me as she pointedly dry-fires her guns at the other stray cats, and I think:

I'd rather die than kiss a cat killer's ass.

"If everything goes to plan," Donnie says, oblivious to the bad blood between us, "the dock drops off two shipping containers—one has the package, the other's a decoy—we accompany them both to a lab at an unknown point in New Jersey, then head out to a well-deserved steak dinner."

Kiva snorts. "What happens if something goes wrong?"

Donnie pats me on the shoulder, his rubber-padded palm thumping onto my armor. "We let the man with the plan guide us to a smooth victory."

I'm still running tests to see which actuators need realignment after absorbing Donnie's punch, so it takes me a moment to realize Donnie's left the mission up to me.

Donnie floats me the dreamy look of a teenager expecting to see his favorite band take the stage. Kiva and her mooks are exchanging uneasy glances—I'm pretty sure they didn't know I'd be arriving until this morning, let alone running the show.

I splutter out a protest before realizing, yes, in fact I spent several hours on the drive here preparing reaction packages.

"All right, folks," I say, broadcasting my mission parameters out. "Everyone install these IFF routines—they're designed to protect civilians, so no cranking up the threat profiles. I'll notice."

"It's in his contract that if Ancillary Force disobeys his suggestions, he's not responsible for any resulting mayhem," Donnie says; I thank God Trish thought to negotiate that. "That means if you 'forget' to install his mission-mandated routines, I pay him three million no matter *how* the shit goes down." He stabs his cigar in their direction. "And I *will* deduct the difference from your salary."

They flinch. I know damn well they don't have a hundred thousand to spare, but Donnie talks about a million-dollar garnished paycheck like he's docking them next week's lunch money.

"Now," I say. "I've calculated seven different potential combat situations on this trip that would require different tactical reactions, and created a starter reaction package to handle each of them—you'll have to customize them to match your own loadouts. We've got a few minutes before the trucks roll out, so let's run some simulations to coordinate our firepower—"

As Donnie's mooks gather around me, asking for assistance in dealing with the inevitable protocol conflicts, their belligerence melts away into hopeful uncertainty. They ask the right questions—which is to say they've got the basics covered, but don't try to hide their ignorances with bullshit once we delve into advanced configurations.

Which is . . . pleasantly surprising. Our artificial limbs are the intersection of neural-decoding technology and AI-backed pattern recognition and myoelectric artificial muscles and laser-based targeting webs and customized device drivers backed with complex operating systems. Anyone who claims they know it all is lying. People think I'm some miracle worker, but most of my work involves hunting through poorly written documentation until I figure out what the hell has gone wrong.

Scotty never talks about how he checked stack overflow before he fixed the *Enterprise*, but he totally did.

And in fact, they seem *enthused* as I go over the seven potential combat situations in detail—as if they've thirsted for improvements. One of the mooks, a Caucasian three-limber named Marcy, agrees that combat situation number four (highway chase) is likely, but have we considered potential police intervention? A young black kid who calls himself Defcon, his skin striped with badly done Semper Fi tattoos, frets about what happens if we enter combat situation number seven (ambush at the delivery station) and the IAC friendlies are wearing the same uniforms as the IAC hostiles. "How would we prevent shooting the guys who sign our paychecks?" he asks.

"Jesus fuck." Kiva sighs, rolling her eyes. "How likely do you think that is?"

Marcy and Defcon and Saladin turn on her, staging a mild rebellion—Saladin slaps his brushed steel Össur Magnums, showing off his rotational targeting .22 rifles. "My default packages can put four bullets through an eyeball before I've noticed what happened," he scoffs. "Do *you* want to explain to the IAC why you killed their man on the ground?"

"No," she says sullenly. "But . . ."

"If I'm in a highway chase and a cop pulls up behind us, my Fillauer-Mossbergs will engage before I notice them. Which means their patrol car's defensive systems will go toe-to-toe with mine, and then yours, and then *all* of ours because threat-lights are gonna go up across the board without a proper filter."

"Classic system-based escalation," Defcon mutters.

Marcy steps closer to Kiva, almost bumping chests. "You think the IAC will thank you when their secret package gets called in as evidence on cop murders?"

"All right, all right," she snaps. The biomonitors show her upper prosthetics filtering out angry twitches sent by a nervous system that wants to start swinging punches.

As experienced vets, we ignore it. Being linked into a multisystem combat bio-network means I'm also uncomfortably aware of Saladin's precombat erection.

Make no mistake: Donnie's men are dripping ooo-rah, doing their best to nudge my IFF routines towards settings more conducive to dead bystanders. Our network med-readouts show me their increased adrenaline levels as they dream of explosions. They'll complain if things *don't* go in the shit. But . . .

They're each committed to ensuring that when the bullets fly,

Ferrett Steinmetz

our limbs are engineered to do the smartest possible thing to save our package and then save us, in that order.

They just don't give a shit about anyone else.

Thank God that yes, Marcy's concerns aside, I *had* ensured our IFF routines were geared to use nonfatal reactions on policemen.

And by the time we squeeze ourselves into the trucks—Donnie and me in the truck designated to hold the IAC package, everyone else in the decoy, splitting our firepower as evenly as possible in case one truck gets obliterated—there's a lively debate on overcoming the truck's camera's blind spots.

Donnie squirms in the seats, which aren't designed to accommodate his oversized limbs. I keep glancing over the long list of his loadout inventories, which could take on black-ops helicopters without blinking. That weight gives him the profile of a squat, 1,500-pound man, his reinforced spine creaking under the support.

Yet he's sat back the entire time, smiling as he tosses in light interjections that are more like suggestions, scooted over uncomfortably close.

"This is great!" He bounces as he hooks into the truck's sensors. "Can't wait to see how those reaction packages work when the shit goes down. We've never tried a mission that minimizes casualties before!"

He offers me a cigar from a humidor in his right thigh.

And as I light up, I realize: other men would have been threatened by handing over total command. But Donnie's either so confident in his abilities or so enamored of my work—or both—that it literally doesn't occur to him to be jealous.

"So," I say, choosing my words carefully. "What would you have done if Trish had sent someone else? Or nobody? What would the plan have been then?"

At first, I think Donnie is shrugging. But then I hear the whirrs as a total system check ripples across his arms, every one of his military-grade weaponries shifting as they verify full range of motion. His legs go next, flexing as they check their cornering speeds, my flash-protection dimming as his micron-accurate laserweb maps the cabin's interior.

He sends me the complete readout:

All systems functional.

"Violence doesn't need a plan."
He thumbs the truck's start button.
We pull out into the line of trucks ready to hit the highway.

It's a fifteen-minute ride to the docks, and I'm scanning the freighter trucks surrounding us as we cruise in computer-assisted formation past the decayed highway exit signs; nobody needs signs these days, not with constant GPS feeds to tell you where you are, but it'd cost money to take them down. They've become high-profile graffiti war zones instead, with artists getting into firefights over who gets to paint their elaborate murals over exit 13A.

We're quiet for different reasons. I'm scanning for any signs of combat situation number one (vehicle hijacking before delivery), fretting that only three of us—Donnie, me, and Kiva—have biological-response packages installed. (Which makes sad sense; getting a doctor to give you a license for auto-prescriptions is a helluva bureaucratic hoop.) If our enemy hits us on the way to the drop zone, then they know we're in the cabins; the best time to do the swap would be when we're surrounded by automated trucks and no witnesses.

The most effective and surreptitious takedown, barring unknown technology—and anyone big enough to tangle with the IAC would have *really* unknown technology, but let's not consider that—would be drugs designed to knock us unconscious.

Without blood-stabilization packages to maintain their body chemistry within established parameters, Saladin, Defcon, and Marcy could go down in under thirty seconds.

Ferrett Steinmetz

Not that their limbs would. I've ensured if any of us are rendered unconscious, our prosthetics will switch into automatic threat-detection and defense mode. But the idea of three killing machines running loose without human judgment makes me grind my teeth.

Whereas Donnie drums his leg with his small-scale gripping hands, eager for the action. The bioreadouts show me how Kiva's humming, how Saladin's squeezing his cock, how Defcon keeps checking his ammo inventory.

When the bullets fly, none of them want to miss a moment.

Not that this precombat eagerness is unusual—I was in the military, for God's sake—but the Drone Corps tended to be much more sedate. We weren't in personal danger, and we had to train our cameras on the corpses for hours afterwards to monitor the zone. Sometimes we got to watch the mothers bring their kids to see the splatter we made of their daddies.

There's not a lot of people in the trucks headed towards the docks. But on the freeway's far side, the side headed *away* from the docks, there are poor young couples starting their low-budget, cross-country vacation. While I know I've programmed our IFF routines to avoid firing on civilians, any firefight here will pile up the casualties.

Which is why I breathe a sigh of relief when we pull into the docks.

The Newark-Elizabeth Port never sleeps: trucks and cars wind their way into the great corrugated steel maze of shipping containers the ships bring. Most of the work's automated nowadays, with cranes lifting containers off the boats and a complex priority-algorithm determining where the various intermodal freight-storage facilities will reside until someone can pick them up.

(Not that I knew that before I started the trip here. I do a lot of research en route.)

Yet as we ease into the automated traffic flow, I note the hundreds of people: hard-hatted maintenance workers ensuring the complex machinery never breaks down, union men to clean up the inevitable spills, inventory clerks who do surprise inspections to reduce theft, and even tattered travelers clustering in a predetermined safe zone, ready to pay to hitchhike to Iowa because it's the cheapest way to see their families.

"Switch packages," I say. "Remove number one, install combat situation number two: dock shoot-out. My install is complete."

The HUD shows me Donnie swapping out his vehicle-hijacking response package for the dock–shoot-out response package, which is a complex one: it wires into Donnie's (expensive) live-time satellite feeds that map out the docks every seventy seconds, then creates a customized threat-inventory of anything that moves.

It takes him six seconds to finish the installation, importing terabytes of carefully programmed parameters designed to take every reasonable consideration into account. Then Saladin starts, as is proper procedure; the nightmare scenario would be a firefight breaking out while the six of us are reconfiguring our mission parameters. Saladin goes green, then Marcy, then—

"What the fuck?" Kiva yells. "What the *shit* does 'Malformed YAML in module Osprey colon colon TRPI colon colon oAuth' mean?"

Defcon sighs. "Jesus, Kiva, you fucked up your import settings *again*?"

"*I* didn't fuck them up! *You* wrote the XSLT transformation scripts!"

"Hold on, hold on," I say, my skin going cold. "You're relying on *someone else's* transformation scripts to provide reaction packages for your armory? You—"

But I realize the broadcast isn't going out to anyone, because Donnie's cut off my audio connection, the first superuser action I've seen him take.

"I've got it, Keeves," he says, quietly logging into her system with what I realize with sick horror is root access.

Nobody but the body attached to the prosthetics should have root access. *Ever.*

Ferrett Steinmetz

"They set her up at the factory," Donnie explains, troubleshooting the Osprey OS merge conflicts with an ease I envy. "She's their showroom model, remember."

"Donnie." My mouth is dry. "She doesn't know how to import bog-standard response packages. That's prosthetic armaments one-oh-one."

"Awww, Kiva doesn't like to sweat the technical details," Donnie mutters, clucking his tongue as he looks up obscure settings in the Osprey Threat Response Protocol Import documents. "That glorious little bitch just likes to kill. And Endolite-Ruger likes having her in a high-profile outfit where they can get footage of their platforms in flashy urban combat. They pay me a nice stipend to keep her on board—it's a win-win-win situation."

I blink. "I didn't know you cared about budgeting."

His manipulation-limbs shoot me galvanized fingerguns. "Keeps Mom happy." He winks at me, a little *Let's keep this between us, okay?* "All right, Kiva, you're good to go. Now Defcon, you finish and let's rock this town."

His confidence is like an undertow; I can't fight it, not effectively. Though I do note with interest that he's at least vaguely concerned with keeping his mother, the CTO of an advanced AI investment firm, appeased.

We pull in. The massive cranes dwarf the trucks, engulfing us in darkness as impossibly large clamps haul shipping containers overhead.

"Our secret signal is confirmed." Donnie points his cigar at an approaching shipping container—a corrugated green steel box the size of an RV, lurching towards us. My research reminds me whatever's in that is housed in a smart container—there's dumb containers, boxes that keep nonperishable goods dry, and then varying levels of smart containers that have sensors and environment control. That can be as simple as keeping an even airflow so the bananas don't go bad, all the way up to complex air-lock environments with hygrometers and temperature and humidity controls.

Whatever the IAC is putting under our control has thick electrical cables.

We go quiet as the container gets placed on the truck's suspension, automated routines ensuring that the electricity flow isn't interrupted in the transfer so the container's end-state readouts remain within the contractually mandated parameters.

There's a metallic clack as the clamps are released and the truck rolls out to let the next shipment be placed on Kiva's decoy truck.

"Anyone else feel a little disappointed?" Donnie asks.

I hate to admit it, but . . . I *am* disappointed.

This is the mysterious secret package we've committed our lives to protecting? It should be limned with a glowing purple, or have an oily black substance leaking out the bottom.

Instead, it looks like every other furniture shipment on the road. And though I've planned for a thousand different assaults, today's endgame may be a quiet ride down to a temporary IAC facility, and never ever knowing what was in the container.

I'll get $3 million. But I'd spend the rest of my life curious about what the IAC was up to.

"Don't." Donnie rests a hand on my shoulder. "Just . . . don't."

I start to protest that I wasn't thinking anything, but . . . yeah. I *was* thinking about sniffing at the readouts, seeing what I could scope out.

"Let 'em do what they want." He flexes his shoulder shotguns. "And they'll let us do what *we* want."

I forgot: he's hoping to not void his contract so he can get assigned to the thrill-'n'-kill missions the IAC is famed for, whereas I'm hoping to vanish before the IAC knows I'm here. Though that's gotten trickier now that Donnie's put me in charge of this mission; if they get future work, there's a good chance they'll mention what they learned from me today. They might even recommend me as an expert.

Fuck.

We pull out of the docks without incident, though I'm fuming;

Ferrett Steinmetz

why didn't I turn the assignment down? Why didn't I let Donnie take the lead?

Saving innocents will be what lets you sleep at night, Trish said. Which is great, except we won't *have* any innocents. We're halfway to the drop-off point and my presence hasn't made a damn bit of difference because this is in fact a milk run to ensure Donnie can stay on his leash when the IAC needs it, and I just tipped my hand to a goddamned blackmail organization because I *had* to supervise these wet-eared hackers.

There's a muffled *whump* from the front of the truck, followed by a rhythmic flapping noise. I don't need my HUD to tell me the front tire blew. Donnie chuckles.

"Combat situation number three." Donnie draws the words out, low like a wolf whistle, as the truck pulls over. "Yeah, buddy."

"Wait," Kiva says, confused. "What's number three again?"

"Vehicle disablement followed by ambush," I say, realizing I should be careful what I wish for.

The driver-AI adjusts for the blown tire, pulling over to wait for one of New Jersey's roaming mechanicbots to arrive.

I'm glad I've programmed in this contingency, because by default our truck would stop immediately, leaving us in an exposed position. Instead, it pulls over so far onto the shoulder that it bumps up against the sad-looking trees choking on fumes from the freeway. Kiva's truck, the decoy truck, pulls in next to us, providing cover if anyone attacks from the road.

I climb out of the cockpit, watching the incoming trucks even though I know my sensors are doing a much better job tracking them. If any heavy forces ambush us, it'll most likely be from a vehicle turned into a combat carrier.

This rush-hour fight could get bloody.

I need to stay focused.

I want to shout orders just to make myself feel better, but the

HUD shows me everyone's headed for their preassigned stations. Donnie positions his immense firepower by the roadside, where hopefully he can deflect any incoming suicide bombings. Saladin has hopped out to scan the woods for incoming hostiles. Marcy, Defcon, and Kiva are flanking the shipping container, each aligning their 120-degree protection zone so there's no uncovered spaces.

Me? As the ex–drone pilot, I'm tasked with linking into Donnie's satellite feeds, my analyst modules scanning the last live-time reading for threats while I examine the blown tire.

This isn't FUBAR yet, I think, kneeling down to look at the torn rubber-and-steel weave. *Six body-hackers milling around isn't a hundred percent guaranteed to attract police attention.* Even if they are, the cops are distant—people still think cops and freeways go together like cops and donuts, but that was back when humans drove the roads. Now that city AIs control traffic, crime and accidents on freeways are rare. These days the cops cluster in residential neighborhoods, monitoring the citizenry.

I check the last sat-feed, which shows nothing unusual overhead—some flocks of birds flapping over the woods, the usual crisscross of bulletproofed delivery drones, but no inbound choppers. If anyone's in the woods, they're real hidden—but the woods make "real hidden" easy to achieve.

I long for a remote drone to scope out living creatures in the woods, but those are the first things to go whenever serious combat breaks out; any body-hacker worth his salt has anti-drone countermeasures. Besides, if you don't register your drone's flight path in advance with the FAA then they shoot it down before slapping you with a massive fine. Donnie's right to rely on the eye in the sky; it's slower, but nothing blocks it.

"Shouldn't they have attacked by now?" Donnie asks, already sounding bored.

"Maybe it's a legit blown tire," Kiva says.

"I wish." The scan shows me the whiff of cordite still attached to a flap of tire tread. Someone scattered flattened smart caltrops in the road, each primed to detonate when it sensed our vehicle's signature. "They knew we were coming."

"Who's 'they'?" Marcy asks, her bioreadouts spiking. *"Who the fuck's coming for us?"*

"Fuck that," Kiva says, then asks the first smart question she's asked all day: *"Why aren't they here yet?"*

Which is what worries me: what's so big they need to move it into position? We've had more than enough time for Kiva, Marcy, and Defcon to assume a 360-degree defense.

Which means either they fucked up the timing—unlikely—or whatever they'll hit us with doesn't care that we're in the way.

I scan the satellite update again, and nothing significant's moved—the drones are on their authorized flight plans, I hear the squawk of birds cresting the—

Scylla fires, a single shot, my sound-filters dampening the noise.

One of the birds swooping over the treetops six hundred yards away explodes.

"Dammit!" I yell, spooked. Fucking long-range false positives. You have to assume anything tossed in your direction is a threat—but occasionally a bird will dive for an insect in a way that, if it doesn't change trajectory, could impact with you. And at the speed with which both birds *and* incoming projectiles move, you can't take the chance of shooting a splattery Molotov cocktail when it's two yards away. "Don't tense up, it's just—"

Then two other armaments go off—Saladin detonates another bird into intestinal fireworks, then Donnie launches a microfusillade of bullets into the squawking flock whizzing over the treetops. Seven birds go up like a string of firecrackers, cawing in protest as they swirl in erratic loops around their fallen—

"Dammit, Donnie!" I yell, my HUD noting the rapid descent of a drone I'd been monitoring as a potential threat. "You shot down a delivery drone!"

Donnie squints, double-checking his combat logs. "I didn't," he protests. "My targeting routines were configured to exclude delivery drones."

But by then Defcon and Marcy's guns are taking potshots at the bird-swarm roaring over the trees, and my auto-zoom on the fallen drone shows it's intact but on *fire*, blue electricity sparking out of its engines as a dying bird thrashes in its propellers—

—and the refreshed satellite image shows the bird-swarms converging onto our position, flying in from all sides—

—and my analyst modules are auto-zooming bird images at me, showing the glint of metallic talons embedded in fast-moving organic bodies, noting how this bird isn't native to the New Jersey area, cataloguing it as some unknown bird of prey except birds of prey don't fly in flocks—

"Incoming!" I scream, adjusting my IFF routines to handle a barrage of fast-moving aerial threats as our armaments blast birds from the sky.

"All right! Genetically altered aerial combat hawks!" Donnie fires so many rounds, the light strobes around us.

I'm too busy tweaking our IFFs to react appropriately to this threat—my image-AIs are combing through blurry combat photos to capture what "a hawk" looks like so they can refine their capture routines, and I'm blinking at good hawk-images and shaking away bad ones to improve the target profile ASAP.

That drone falling? That was *luck*. If a bird hadn't panicked when Donnie fired, smashing into a stray drone and demonstrating how they can do—*something*—to machinery, we wouldn't have deemed them threats until they'd swarmed us.

The *only* reason we're keeping hundreds of birds at bay is that we fired at twenty yards instead of five.

I think of that old guy at customs, wanting grand tales about warfare's majesty. Well, here's the truth of war: sometimes, you survive for reasons that had dick-all to do with skill.

Still, we've kept the flocks at a healthy distance even though the birds are doing their best to dive-bomb us, or maybe they're trying to bomb the package—it's hard to tell what they're aiming for because we're shooting them out of the sky before they get within twenty yards. The flock's feathered arc is driven back as they impact our kill zone.

Detonated birds are splattering on the ground around us. They *sizzle* when they hit.

"What do these things do if they hit us?" Marcy asks.

I shoot her an image of the downed drone, sparking with electricity. "Don't find out."

Damn if Donnie's not right; who the hell genetically engineers hawks? Not only is gene modification an inexact science—any body's a complex meld of factors, so you're way more likely to cause an avian cancer than you are to create a supereagle—but animals are *slow*.

"*Yeah!*" Kiva shouts, laughing manically as she goes into auto-fire, mowing the birds down as they approach. "Take that! And that! And *that*!"

"*Slow down, goddammit!*" I scream. "Donnie! Switch to high-impact explosives!"

"Look at 'em!" He laughs, switching to tracers to demonstrate how many bullets he's putting into the air, a great neon fan-dance display that rains blood down upon the grass. "They go up like piñatas! Ha! You little fuckers!"

"Switch to grenades and make them go up like fireworks!" I yell.

Defcon interrupts, a high-priority signal: "Sir, the shrapnel from any explosives overhead could harm the package—"

"Couple massive bursts never hurt anyone," Donnie says. "Let's put on a show for the crowd!"

The surrounding traffic has triangulated the gunfire's source, and they've either sped up to get away from it or slowed down to *stay* away from it. Which is good; we're firing into the air, but our collective fire-to-disable ratio hovers in the low 60 percents. Every miss sends a stray bullet arcing out that risks killing someone half a mile away.

Yet those misses are our enemy's genius: humans are slow, but these birds are *fast*. Not quite as fast as our capture-target-and-fire times, but we didn't program our weaponry to know what a bird's idealized kill zones are—so our guns are firing at wings, at talons, at blurs.

Even if I didn't care about shooting innocent vacationers huddling in the trucks, logistics will throttle us. Seconds into the fight, and our shared ammunition supplies have dropped by 42.6 percent. We're not equipped to fight swarms, which is doubtless what our enemy counted on; if we don't adjust strategy, we'll be down to using harsh language.

God forbid this is their opening salvo.

Donnie lobs a couple of terrifying fireballs into the air; they go up in a *whoomph*, taking out massive numbers of birds and shattering windows up and down I-78. But more hawks are charging in, and I don't have time to check the satellite feeds to see how many are left because I've assembled a bird–kill zone profile that's boosted my fire-to-disable ratio to 96.2 percent.

I'd prefer to run some test cases, but occasionally you just gotta live-deploy to production—so I save the profile as HITCHCOCK.KZP and push it out to the network.

That'll keep our defense zone clean until the second wave arrives. I don't know how many birds they've got—maybe the plan is to run us out of bullets before sending in the heavy hitters, but this will slow our ammo expenditure as Kiva, Marcy, and Defcon defend the package.

I check the newsnets; sure enough, the cops are inbound, the trucks having called them the moment their audial processors noted gunfire. ETA is ten minutes, and I'm not sure whether I'm looking forward to their arrival or dreading it.

"Donnie, Saladin, cut fire and move in," I say, squeegeeing bird blood off my helmet. "We'll let them defend the package while we plan our exit—"

Ferrett Steinmetz

"What the *shit*?"

The volume dims as guns stop shooting. The birds swarm in towards Kiva as she stares down at her arms, making frantic punching motions as she tries to get her gunports active again—

She was supposed to add the HITCHCOCK.KZP enemy profile to her response package as a hot-patch.

Except instead of *adding* a new enemy to her existing threat profile, she told her system to *replace* the active profile with HITCHCOCK.KZP—which caused a combat cessation as her systems imported the data from scratch.

I curse as she curses: "Reboot, you piece of shit, *reboot*! You—"

A taloned blur rockets towards her, pulling up in the last second to extend its claws.

Spiked metallic nails punch through her body armor

A crackle of blue electricity flares through her as the bird falls down dead.

Her neck snaps back, her prosthetics jerking into auto-target mode as her protective seizure-filters kick in. But more raptors dive-bomb her, soaring in to jab their claws through her helmet, unleashing torrents of currents into her before dying.

Her flesh sizzles.

Crazily, I think: *Man, her corporate sponsors are gonna be angry her last words were spent trashing their product.*

"You fucking—" Donnie moves to take her position, so angry he actually screams instead of subvocalizing over the encrypted channel. "You fucking *cyborg birds*!"

I don't know what *I'd* call them, but I do know that poor Saladin—who obediently cut fire—got hit by one, and his medical readouts show his heart stuttering with defibrillation before his connection shorts out.

Then he's obscured by a ball of smoking feathers.

"Close up, people!" I yell, thankful Donnie's already moving into position to seal up Kiva's fire zone—

—except Donnie's screaming, "Jesus fucking shit, how dare you make me look bad, how the fuck will I explain *two* casualties to my contact?" at the birds, unleashing such a fusillade that his ammunition drops 10 percent in a single second. He's plowing right into their center mass as they regroup to lead him away from the truck, maimed birds tumbling from the air like a gory hurricane, sacrificing themselves—

—which is terrifying, they have a *strategy*—

—sacrificing themselves so a squadron of bio-falcons can swoop low past Kiva's body and punch their curved claws into the side of our truck, unloading voltage into the frame.

The faked video-windows that provide an illusory interior fuzz and go black.

Something inside the containers clicks off.

"Marcy, Defcon!" I yell. "Get over here, I'm wiring you into the shipping container!"

"*What?*"

"These fucking birds overloaded the container's deep-well batteries—which means whatever's inside the package powered down! I've gotta get your power supplies feeding this thing until we can fend off these psycho falcons and hook the container over to the other truck!"

I'm thankful they move over, even though they're confused. "You can't just hook us in—we don't have plugs—"

"I have converters." I pop my leg-compartments open and start the wiring process.

I don't tell them this will drain their power to emergency combat levels; their legs will shut down, and they'll be reduced to armed turrets. I could take the hit and power this myself—but after watching Kiva and Donnie in action, I would not trust this crew to wipe my nose.

Donnie's running up and down the freeway shoulder like a six-year-old chasing seagulls at the beach, albeit with far more screaming of "*Take that, motherfuckers!*" and aerial explosions. Yet he's chewed his way through a significant portion of the flock, which means I can handle defending the package on my own.

Ferrett Steinmetz

I'm *praying* the IAC was smart enough to install a backup generator to maintain whatever's in there—though the scorched claw marks on the shipping container's sides indicate the electrohawks may have shorted *that* out as well.

Did we let the enemy destroy the IAC's secret package?

No. No. It's only been fifty seconds since the truck went dead, fifty long seconds because I have to do the connection with clumsy manual control since I have to jury-rig the adapter to handle both Marcy *and* Defcon, and the current's back on.

I freeze, knowing whatever systems are inside have been returned to functionality—but have you ever seen what happens to a sophisticated software kernel when you crash it without warning?

Scylla and Charybdis's active fire has slowed to a shot every two seconds, most of the birds dead, the remaining ones dispersed. They flap away like drunkards from a bar. I feel a weird sympathy: given how much electricity they pumped out, I doubt they were engineered to live long.

Quietly, I think: *Self, take either side of this bet for a thousand dollars: Have the birds accomplished their mission, and whatever's inside that container is toast? Or have they succeeded in softening us up, and now our enemy's sending in the big guns to retrieve the package?*

I check the satellite feeds again. But my attention's plastered to my audio pickups, which detect the subtle hum of equipment clicking back on again, servers warming up—

And the anguished screams of someone waking up inside the container.

"*Mama?*" the woman inside the IAC's container yells, her voice rising with each syllable. "*Vala? Can you hear me? What's happening?*"

Her trust is heartbreaking. I can't think of anyone I'd call out to if I woke up kidnapped, but she sounds like a woman who phones her mother after every date.

I didn't need to know who she was.

"Where are y—"

My sensors pick up her choked gurgle. Then the real screams start:

"What did they do to my body?"

My heart rate spikes in sympathy with her so quickly that my biological-response packages administer antianxiety medication. Something's been done to her that, judging from the way she can't stop screaming, is not something I ever want to see.

She's got family. I don't want to think about that either.

Donnie grips my shoulder hard enough that my haptic feedback registers it as pain.

"Get in there." Donnie shoves me towards the container. "Get in there and *shut that bitch up.*"

I shoot him a glare more intense than a laser. "Don't you have some birds to chase?"

He shakes his head as if he can't believe I'm not keeping up with him. *"I* have a mission to salvage. The cops will arrive in seven minutes and forty-five seconds, and *I* need to be out here to have my lawyers explain this firefight was a legal defense of a private transport vehicle. Saladin and Kiva are charcoal briquettes, Defcon and Marcy can't move, which leaves *you* to go inside and put the kibosh on Miss Yappers."

It finally dawns on me: he's speaking verbally. He's shut down the mission's audio recorders—this is off the record.

"No," I say, realizing what he's asking. "I am *not* breaking into an IAC secret container. Stealing secrets from the Yak is a guaranteed route to assassination."

Donnie's so furious he fires twenty rounds into the air for emphasis. "Come *on,* man! If their equipment was online, Scream Queen there wouldn't say a word. The gates are down! Which makes it perfect for you—the famed cyber-espionage expert—to sneak in and knock her out. Clearly, this is a prisoner transfer, so if we deliver the prisoner—"

Ferrett Steinmetz

"—prisoners are made by *governments*, Donnie, this is a *kidnap-ping—*"

"Yes! Yes! It's a *three-million-dollar kidnapping*! Which you are being paid to *anesthetize* any moral quandaries you might have had! Spend a million on therapy—you've still got two million left over to get every upgrade you ever wanted! Go to fucking *Disney World!*"

"That's not the way it works—"

"The way it works is this." He turns his wrist towards me to display a red cop-countdown clock. "I have six minutes and forty-five seconds before the cops show up. My lawyerbots inform me that *if* the cops hear a woman screaming in the back of our truck, there will be no amount of law in the world I can throw at them to stop the NJPD from breaking into the Yak's private vehicle. At which point our contract's null and void and *I* will never get to fight anything near as cool as these weirdo electrobirds again."

I look over at Kiva's and Saladin's smoking bodies—charred torsos hanging between blackened artificial limbs. "You thought this was *fun?*"

His laugh would be infectious if it weren't so psychotic. "This was the *shit*! You know you'll be telling this story to your buddies—haven't you been subvocalizing this narrative the whole time? You're always muttering to yourself."

"I don't—wait, do I?" I know I constantly subvocalize, half syllables my language modules clean up into full text—but do I *mutter*? I thought I—

"We both record for posterity, bro. And you, you monstrous electronic cat burglar you." Donnie sweeps one arm across the shipping container as though it's a grand set of mountains to be explored. "*You* will break into the IAC's lab and cover up anything that happened so *I* can keep getting sweet contracts like this."

"I'm good at what I do because I research, Donnie. We know *nothing* about that container's interior. An improv break-in against the best security in the world has almost *zero* chance of—"

"Yeah, yeah, yeah. You know, I thought this mission would be a lot more fun with you on board."

I make a strangled noise. "Missions aren't *fun*. They're the *opposite* of fun. You—"

"Did you notice how I made sure nobody used your name or your call sign today?"

He looks up as though he's reading skywriting, his words so light that it's impossible not to sense him tap-dancing around the threat.

"Or maybe you noticed how I covered up your hardware addresses and masked your voice?" he continues, hopping from foot to foot in a frightened mocking dance. "Trish told me, 'Ooo, he doesn't want the IAC chiefs to know he's there!' and fuck if I didn't do my best to conceal your presence—even though we both know these Yak missions are the only way to get your hands on their advanced equipment."

I *should* have known that. Trish surely knew, but I stay out of hacker gossip, so . . . I didn't.

But yeah. If I put myself in the IAC's pocket, I'll get access to cutting-edge technology that even the US military doesn't get to play with unless the IAC bosses approve the sale. I look around at the dismembered birds, which are deliquescing into goo—the IAC's enemies have made secret advances in genetic technology.

What gifts does the IAC have for its loyal squadrons?

Assuming I can let the kidnappings slide.

Donnie breathes a sigh of relief, taking my disgruntled concern for tech-lust. "So," he says with the calmness of a man who believes the matter's settled. "You sneak in there. You shut her up. You seal the case and hope nobody notices. We have five minutes and forty-five seconds to quiet the evidence before the cops arrive."

"She's not evidence, she's a person. And if I botch the break-in? Three million is *not* enough to risk pissing off the IAC."

"Or I tell my IAC contacts that you were the reason this mission failed."

So there it is.

"Play along, man." He hunkers down to whisper. "Everyone here

Ferrett Steinmetz

has a good reason to keep this quiet. But if we don't *all* have a good reason, well, I'll tell them the reason for our mission failure was a last-minute hire who, I don't know, was a saboteur. Wonder what the IAC's deep analysts would find if they rooted through your background?"

He sees the disgust on my face, takes a hurt step back—I remember that *he* still thinks we're *friends*. He shakes his head, trying to figure out how to apologize for this, but Donnie's not a man who apologizes for much.

"Look. I wanna give you three million dollars and a spotless win-record. Just . . . make everything work. When it's done, I will buy you the best box of cigars in existence and you and I will run rampant through the Yak's secret prosthetic technology. Okay?" He pats my shoulder. "Gotta talk to my lawyerbots."

He could have a private communiqué without moving an inch, but instead he walks over to the other side of the trucks, making exaggerated cell-phone gestures.

Leaving me alone to listen to the poor woman, still panicking inside the truck.

"*—how am I moving what is* happening *no it's* okay *break it down one step at time don't hyperventilate* I can't control my lungs I don't control my breath *no okay you've got to do what you've got to do Silvia remember what Mama told you you've got to do what you've got to do so* please God help *and God provides so what you've got to do is get* out *of here so get it* together *Silvia get it* together . . ."

I didn't need to know her name was Silvia. Silvia's moved onto a running monologue of incoherent prayers.

She's talking to herself because that's better than being alone.

Whereas I'm headed towards the shipping container's doors, unable to tell my audio-filters to mask her voice.

Whoever sent in the electrobirds knew we were coming, so I'm pretty sure they disabled the IAC's defenses. It's in their interests not to leave evidence in the IAC's hands—so maybe I *can* walk in and not have them know I was there.

Donnie's right: we probably *can* slip in.

The trick is, Silvia—the package—can't know I was there either. Covertly cracking open the seal on the container's back doors so it can be repaired without detection is a cinch. I set Charybdis to disable anyone inside, squeezing my eyes shut as I poke her in through the door.

"*Hello?*" I hear, just as Charybdis informs me there's a human-like figure—but she's trapped, spread-eagle, behind a transparent barrier, so my tasers can't reach her. "Please, my name is Silvia Maldonado, they kidnapped me, you have to get me out."

She's struggling to keep her dignity now that she knows someone else can hear her.

Don't reply, I think, keeping my head down, letting my HUD guide me around the stacks of equipment to the lock on her bulletproof cage. *Don't engage with her. The IAC will fucking kill you. Just take the three million dollars and run, you can buy the best psychiatrists.*

"Please," she whispers. "Tell me what they did to me. I can't see my body."

I look up.

I shouldn't, but I look up.

I gasp.

It'd be bad enough if she'd just been manacled, naked, to the table—and she's racked up like a car on a hydraulic lift, roughly at chest height. She's a medical marionette, her arms flowering with bruises from the multiple IV sites hanging from the ceiling. Her head's clamped back, her arms and legs shackled so every inch of her is available for viewing, the cage wide enough for doctors to hold conferences over her restrained body.

It isn't sexy; it's gynecological. And if that medical violation were the only thing, well, I've seen worse in war, but . . .

Her head's been transplanted onto something inhuman.

You can see the ragged "V" where her dark-brown skin has been fused with clumps of dragonfly-green twitching fiber molded into a vague torso shape. The spasming pseudoflesh has been shaped

Ferrett Steinmetz

into a hyperattractive Barbie hourglass, complete with nippleless breasts and an undulating vagina—almost sculpted smooth, except tiny hairlike tendrils on it ripple individually, sensing my entrance, forming hypnotic spirals as they focus in on me.

Yet the female shape is clearly designed to distract—put sexy clothes on that, and men would be too busy staring at her curves to notice how her head's a little too big for a proper fit, how her arms hang too low.

Because her arms are human . . . at least until you look past the elbow, at which point her skin mutates into prickling green flesh. Same with the way her legs look normal up until just above the knee, at which point her skin transforms into bristling emerald—

"What do you see?" she asks.

The hairs on her belly twitch like flies washing themselves.

I slam back against the far wall, confused, before remembering: my legs are programmed to retreat from unknown threats.

And she *is* unknown. I've programmed my sensors with an extensive database of every animal: this is not on the books.

Whatever the IAC bioengineers are doing, they've got black-ops tech that's centuries ahead of modern science. They've genetically engineered an organism from scratch, an organism that runs on no biology principles my onboard data banks are familiar with, then fused a human brain to it.

If they can do that, what *can't* they do?

The shipping container constricts around me. If the IAC knows I saw this—her—they'll come for me. And they won't hire Donnie: they'll bring their experienced operatives to take me down.

My legs sense the threat, retreating . . .

"Don't leave!" she shrieks, slamming against her restraints with such inhuman speed that I'm glad there's an inch-thick layer of bulletproof glass between us. "You have to get me out of here! I can't do this myself! If you leave me, they'll do *worse!*"

My legs cruise to a stop. Because they know, just as I know, that I can't leave a terrified woman behind.

I concentrate on her face. Silvia is—was?—in her midthirties, her long black hair coiffed as though she was sent through a beauty salon before being packed away for transport. Her features are pretty, but whittled gaunt by years of stress. If she wasn't strapped to the table, I could envision her behind some desk as a harried middle manager, trapped in a job she's been meaning to quit.

Her wide brown eyes are squinched up as she loses her shit.

"This was supposed to be *therapy* Mama and Vala said it would *help* and now whatever I am sends fucking *body-hackers* running for cover and I'm a *freak* I'm a goddamned—"

"Ma'am, *calm down.*" I shouldn't initiate contact, but—

"Don't you think I'm *trying?*" she sobs. "That's what this was supposed to *solve*! If I could calm down just because somebody *told* me to, my family wouldn't have booked me into experimental therapy to *solve* me, Jesus, if you ever had a panic attack you'd know you *can't* just calm down, it's not that *simple*, I can't—"

"You're right," I say, shamed.

She stops, shocked. "What?"

"I've had panic attacks. You're right. I shouldn't have said that."

She blinks away tears, struggling to focus on me. I must look threateningly alien; four bulky blood-spattered limbs, my gunports still smoking, my combat helmet darkened to an impenetrable onyx. "*You* have panic attacks?"

"They wouldn't diagnose me with PTSD," I whisper. "They said you couldn't get it from watching people die through a computer monitor. But . . . you can. And . . . yeah. I should know better. I can't just yell at you to get it together." There's an awkward silence where I feel I have to offer her something, so I add: "I fix it by doing maintenance. Rerunning mission logs. It calms me down."

"I've been doing the breathing exercises they taught me," she says. "But my breathing's different. I don't think I have a heartbeat." She chuckles. "I don't . . . I don't know what you're seeing, but I suspect my biofeedback class will be at a loss when I get back."

Ferrett Steinmetz

"Yeah."

"I'm . . . not getting back to my calmness classes, am I?"

Scylla and Charybdis are scanning the complex locks on the prison door, their intrusion routines mapping the best ways to disable the locks with minimum evidence. I'm wondering if my non-lethal weaponry would even work on her altered physiology.

And I'm entering in new parameters. New and terrifying parameters.

"I don't know you that well, Silvia. So I can't say what helps your panic attacks. Are you the sort of person who deals better once they know the full truth?"

She sucks in a breath. "Mama was always honest about my condition. My sister, Vala—she always told me when I wasn't fit to be out in public. So . . . I think? I think I do better with honesty?" Her cilia flatten. "Tell me the truth."

The door clicks open. I sidestep inside, leaving one arm—Scylla—hanging out the door. Even through my bio-filters, her prison smells of a vinegary fear-sweat that stings my nostrils.

This close, she has a strange beauty; it's not a human beauty, but she looks like alien artwork splayed out on the table. She's breathing through her nose, neck craned as far off the table as her restraints will allow, shaking with terror but staring into my HUD.

She's looking straight into the eyes of what she believes is her executioner.

I can't help but respect that.

I crook Scylla so she hangs out around the prison entrance, pointed towards the door; the thick bulletproof glass feels like scant cover. I configure Charybdis to target her manacles. Silvia looks into my gunports, chest hitching.

I depolarize my helmet so she can see my face as I program in the last of the changes. "Hey. Look at me."

She swallows; I note that she can swallow. "I said"—she pulls her eyes away from my gunports to meet my gaze with delicate dignity—"that I wanted the truth."

"Hey, you stifled that bitch!" Donnie calls out cheerfully. "Lemme see the package before we seal her up!"

I close my eyes, feeling the unreality of impending nonexistence again. We're about to enter into computerized combat once Donnie comes into range; I might not know when I die.

"The truth is, I'll free you," I whisper. "But Donnie's got better weaponry than I do. And if he shoots first, we're dea—"

Gunfire.

The inch-thick glassteel wall fractures in snowflake patterns as Donnie's shoulder-mounted cannons light up in response to my ambush. Donnie himself is goggle-eyed, baffled why his guns are firing and his legs are propelling him towards me.

He hits me so hard I gray out. Glassteel showers down as I'm slammed back and forth, my defensive routines smashing his guns away before I realize I was in his line of fire, so close I can feel the kick of Donnie's guns vibrating through my armor plating.

He's twice my size. My nuBone hardpoints shear free as he slams into me over and over again. Though I've programmed my counterblows to crumple his gunports, there's no law saying we have to exchange gunfire.

I'm being beaten to death by a fifteen-hundred-pound cyborg.

"Get off him!"

A blur of gray. Donnie flies backwards—something's punched him hard enough to send a ton of armored limbs sailing back into a rack of monitors.

Silvia freezes next to me, her Frankensteined body frozen as though she no longer trusts herself. Perhaps she shouldn't; her human head is panting, but her knotted gray chest fibers don't move.

Whether Silvia realizes it or not, her body's settled into a perfect combat pose: legs spread wide for balance, her weight distributed evenly to allow her to dive for cover or put her full weight behind

Ferrett Steinmetz

a punch. Her cilia rustle like dandelion tufts, one cluster-spiral pointed towards Donnie, another spiral quivering at me

It is difficult not to note the diagonal arc of bullets embedded in her chest, because they're still sizzling in her knurled alien muscle. But Silvia manages to overlook them, because she's staring at Donnie's body hanging limply between his four limbs.

"I shouldn't have punched him." Her hands flicker before her face in a weird flurry; it takes me a second to realize that was her crossing herself at lightning-fast speeds, praying for Donnie's safety. "I get nervous, I panic, I get violent. Sometimes I hit Mom and Vala when they can't calm me down, and oh dear Lord, what'll happen when I get scared and I punch someone's head in."

"No, no, you definitely should have punched him," I assure her. "Of all the people, he's the guy to punch."

I stare at her hands; her knuckles aren't even scraped. Her arms *look* like human appendages, but her fists are strong enough to dent titanium without getting scratched.

"But I didn't *know* I was punching him!" she cries. "I just saw him go after you, and—"

Donnie's limbs whirr back to life after their diagnostic-checks cycle—and then there's the sound of four car crashes. Donnie's limbs, sensing he's still alive but unconscious, geared back up into a defensive "kill last known targets" mode—

Silvia's staved in his remaining gunports, then slammed him into the wall deep enough that the steel's crumpled around his limbs, trapping him.

That implies a tremendous strength—and I'll admit that when I shot her manacles off, I was hoping she had some tricks up her sleeve. But judging from the horrified way she's staring at her fingers, I don't think *she* planned the tricks.

"This is bad," she mutters. "This is really bad. I'm not in control. I'm just . . . triggered."

It's not the time to have a heart-to-heart talk, not with the NJPD inbound, but she's slipping into noncombatant shock.

"Okay." I speak slowly, feeling my way through the words, realizing there's nothing in my psychotherapy data banks equipped to deal with this situation. "So you've got a body that's reacting before you put conscious input into it. I'm gonna guess you weren't a fan of prosthetic armaments beforehand?"

A shaky laugh. "I thought you guys were freaks."

"We are."

She laughs again.

"So I know it's scary, Silvia—your name's Silvia?"

She bobs her head as quickly as an eyeball jitters. Yet even with her inhuman speed, I can see it as the shy, girlish gesture she intended.

"But while I know nobody likes to lose control, Silvia, your body's autopilot was crazy precise. Look at him; you punched him into a wall and left him breathing. And see those three dents? One in his left shoulder, one in his right forearm, one in his upper thigh?"

"Jesus, I can punch through titanium, what are my hands made of?"

"Look at those three dents, Silvia." Why do I sound like my trauma counselor? "Focus on those dents. Know why that's amazing?"

"Wh-why?"

"Because I'm willing to bet you've never read a Gressinger-Sauer Omnipotent schematic—but those are *precisely* the three spots you'd have to hit to disable his front-facing weaponry. See? You even got a two-for-one here, smashing his rail gun and pinching the ammo feed to his forearm."

She leans in. I suppress a flinch. Her movements are birdlike, so fast she appears to blink between states; I'll guess they were planning on refining her combat reflexes, then working on that whole "moving like a human" thing later.

But then she traces her finger slowly across the crushed machinery. She looks at Donnie, who breathes raggedly inside his deflated

Ferrett Steinmetz

airbags; he'll wake up baffled, needing to run his combat logs before he realizes he got into a firefight that lasted 7.8 seconds.

She stands, hypnotized by Donnie as he groans and shakes his head.

"Lemme give him some medicine." I lift up Donnie's helmet to have Scylla give him a hypodermic injection. In truth, Donnie's already waking up—which I'm glad to see, because he's been out for forty seconds. Any longer, and Silvia'd have given him permanent brain damage.

Still, Silvia doesn't need to know this "medicine" is actually a heavy sedative. The last thing I want is Donnie waking up and working his way free.

She breathes a sigh of relief as she watches me "help" Donnie.

"I didn't kill anybody." She does her hyperfast cross-blur again before touching her fingers to her lips in prayer.

She's so thankful for his continued existence that I'm *really* glad I didn't dial in an "accidental" overdose.

"No," I say. "I don't think you can, unless you want to."

She whirls on me, almost too fast to track. "I don't want to kill anybody! I'm not here to *murder* people!"

I bring up my hands in surrender. "That's good. That's good. People shouldn't want to kill." I suppress a snarky *because killing's my job*. "It actually takes a lot to get most new recruits to kill, so . . . maybe your body's doing what you want it to do before you know what that is."

"That's . . . not exactly comforting. I don't have good instincts. That's why I needed Mama and Vala to double-check me. For me, a body that runs on automatic pilot is—"

"*FREEZE.*"

A single cop car has pulled up at a discreet distance outside the shipping container, lights flashing. My long-range scanners pick up a trio of drones in the far distance, soaring in behind them for backup—but the two NJPD huddled inside are *definitely* not getting out of the car's armored protection until they're certain the body-hackers in the area have sent peace-tie confirmation.

Yet the cop cars' gunports are open in case we don't stand down.

Silvia launches herself at the threat.

The patrol cars' guns fire—long-range taser-darts with diamond tips and embedded microbatteries designed to stun a PCP rager.

Silvia leaps twenty feet into the air, a sailing arc that carries her up out of the vertical range of the NJPD's defensive weaponry, which was not designed to handle superleaping Death From Above attacks. My legs jerk me back deeper into the shipping crate as thin darts shatter against corrugated steel.

She's hugging herself as she soars across the fifty-foot gap to the patrol car, doing her best to disable her body's reflexive defense reactions.

All the failure cases I'd outlined for today's mission involved New Jersey's finest getting involved. Those "police cars" are lightweight tanks: heavily armored, bristling with antipersonnel weaponry, and capable of calling in an entire state's worth of judicial mayhem down upon us.

Even Donnie would have stood down rather than go up against the cops.

But this will *not* end well if I don't intervene.

I raise my hands in surrender and step out straight into an EMP cluster. Come on, boys. Like I'm not shielded? Then again, they probably still think I'm a bot—*normal* body-hackers wouldn't be so stupid as to start a firefight in broad daylight.

Silvia lands hard enough on the patrol car to crack the bullet-proof windshield—her hands also flicker into surrender, but the car's short-range defenses fill her eyes with pepper spray and then she darts around the car, smashing in its defenses.

Other cop cars pull into position.

Ferrett Steinmetz

Of *course* they sent multiples to deal with six kill-crazy body-hackers. Every cop in town must be on their way here in addition to those inbound drones.

"*She's trying to surrender!*" I yell. But words never beat bullets when it comes to getting people's attention. I broadcast medical-emergency codes to anyone who'll listen—but they've wi-fi–jammed the air so I have zero hope of connecting.

"I'm *surrendering!*" she screams, except as she says it another cop car fires bullets at her—*real* bullets; they've stopped fucking around—and Silvia leaps off the first wrecked car to launch herself at the second, shrieking in terror.

"*Stand down!*" I yell. The gunfire's deafening. "*She's primed to go after threats! Stop firing at her and she'll—*"

Unknown drone profile.
Unknown drone profile.
Unknown drone profile.

Being properly paranoid, I've loaded every piece of New Jersey Police Department hardware into my profile database.

These drones aren't government-approved police drones.

I enhance the distant images: these are heavy-duty delivery drones the size of beefy refrigerators, their bellies rippling an LED sky-blue to camouflage them from the people below, their sides curved to bounce radar away. They've got the drone-standard quadruple propellers, sheathed in microfiber against impact. Their bulky bodies bristle with hypodermic needles.

Yet more than that: these drones' metal structures are formed from baroque curves, filled with erratic gaps, drafted by AIs with no concern for aesthetics but a perfect knowledge of how little material you can use to hold a drone together before structural integrity suffers.

This is our unknown enemy's second wave, designed to bring Silvia home.

"Silvia!" I yell. "Stay away from those drones! Do *not* let them get near you!"

She's ping-ponging between the cop cars, smashing them to bits one demolished piece of weaponry at a time. She's screaming, *"Stop! Please! Don't make me hurt you!"*—but whenever she hits one cop car another fires at her and she rebounds over to neutralize that ordnance: classic system-based escalation.

The cop cars are riddling her with computer-precise headshots—but the bullets flatten against her hair before sliding to the ground. Silvia's face looks human, but her skull is made of something hard enough to deflect gunfire.

The cops themselves are crouched down with their hands over their heads, terrified. Few policemen are willing to go all Robo-Cop and amputate limbs permanently to use government-loaned prosthetics—so they rely on their RoboCars, which mow down purse-snatchers and could definitely incapacitate me.

They are *not* equipped to deal with the IAC's secret weapon.

The drones are coming within range, tranq-dart rifles twitching as they take aim at Silvia. Once they fire at her, even if they miss, she'll automatically leap at them, at which point she'll be easy pickings for their nets.

If the cop cars would stop firing, she could run away, or—

No.

No, I can't think about that.

I can't take down the cops—not with my existing armaments, anyway. Donnie carried some obscene weaponry, but he also had obscene lawyer bills. What I have are several handguns with pinpoint accuracy—good enough to take out unwired humans, yet helpless in the face of the NJPD's military hardware.

But I could *subvert* the hardware.

The moment I consider hacking the NJPD's OS, the preprogrammed disclaimer I put in place in case I seriously considered doing this damned fool thing pops up:

Ferrett Steinmetz

Intentionally accessing a protected police network via forged credentials or other tampering attempts that grant unauthorized access is a class B felony, punishable by up to 20 years in prison, a fine of up to $250,000, or both.

I know what operating system the NJPD cars run on, have stock-piled several zero-day vulnerabilities nobody has patched. Maybe the courts will forgive me once I explain how I was stopping the police from hurting an innocent woman, but . . .

Who am I kidding? You tackle a cop to prevent them from hurt-ing someone, you get your ass kicked *harder*.

If I hack the cop cars, I better hope they never find out who I am, because that's my life in jail as a quadruple amputee, my limbs seized as evidence.

I can't do that. I can't be carried around like a prison package, sodomized by guards and prisoners alike. I can't take that—

Except I see Silvia.

The cops are trapped in the cars, either covering their eyes so they don't see what the green fibrous monster with the stitched-on head will do to them, or wide-eyed, grabbing their guns, calling for backup. She's punching through the cars' armored plating, yanking out tear gas canisters—

Yet she's *reassuring* them, whispering apologies that she doesn't mean to hurt them, she's been to therapy for this, she's trying to get better.

I shut my eyes and start the auto-hack procedure.

My left calf heats up five degrees as the anti-jammer technol-ogy there fires up, my HUD dimming as my battery levels plum-met. There are elaborate ways to dance around wi-fi flooding, but they involve time—my calf contains pure brute force, a broadcast so loud it drowns out everything else for the forty-five seconds I can keep it active. I'm my own pirate radio station, so loud I'm scram-bling signals on Long Island.

The cars' communications are encrypted, of course; I cracked police chat months ago. Yet that only allows me to talk to the car's operating system; it does not grant me credentials. The several buffer overrides I manage, however, let me create a fake account, escalating access . . .

I drive the cars into the forest and shut them down.

Yet the cops are smashing out the remaining windows, shooting at Silvia from cover. She slaps the guns from their hands as the drones move into position—

"*Silvia!*" I yell. "*Run to me! We've got to get away!*"

"I'm—" Another rookie aims at her; she breaks his wrist. "*I'm trying, I'm trying, tell me how to stop this!*"

Oh God.

There's only one way to get her to me before the drones get in range.

I program in five shots to hit her in center mass, each a kill shot on a normal human. I go to hit the "confirm" button—

And freeze.

My prosthetic armaments shoot people all the time. Yet that's automatic; a computerized reading falls within certain parameters, and the gun fires. I spend time improving those settings to ensure innocents don't get hit, but I don't make the decision to fire; my software does.

This time, I have to pull the trigger.

I remember the last time I did this: viewing the café through my drone's camera-reticle, deciding that small blur had to be a dog, and we had a confirmed meeting of three terrorist targets so a dog was an acceptable sacrifice to save American lives, and then realizing after I fired that it *wasn't* a dog, and—

My guns can't hurt Silvia. That's what I tell myself. But I'm about to fire five high-impact .45 bullets at a terrified woman. I know my weapons too intimately: Scylla will pulp her intestines, then burst her heart from hydrostatic shock.

Her face is an ordinary woman weeping with panic, and even

Ferrett Steinmetz

though I'm watching bullets ricochet off her cheekbones I can't believe *my* gunfire won't puncture her lungs.

Look at the drones, I tell myself. *They're almost in range. You have to—*

"*Silvia!*" I scream. "*I'm sorry about this!*"

I mash the button. Five shots hit her dead center.

She squawks in surprise—and instead of dropping dead to the ground, she leaps high into the air to close the distance between us, reflexively rebounding back towards the latest threat.

I depolarize my helmet, showing her how *sorry* I am at having to shoot her. I hold my arms open like I hope to catch her in a great big hug, realizing if she's still angry when she lands she'll punch me out and end this—

Except as she looks at down, something in me must look ridiculously earnest because she starts giggling.

This is absurd: what kind of relationship turns shooting her in the belly into an act of compassion? The closer she gets the more ridiculous this all seems, until we're breaking down in laughter by the time she lands in my arms.

"Either I'm going to die," she tells me, "or this will be a *legendary* worst first date."

"I can make this date worse." I bring Charybdis up, pop open the industrial-strength handcuffs I installed to restrain something stronger than a base-level human. "Let's stop you from jumping away."

She covers her face, blushing. "I promised Mama I wasn't that kind of girl."

I let her snap the cuff around her wrist as I retreat back into the shipping container—

"No NO! No we are NOT going back in there we are NOT—"

My airbags hit my face as I'm slammed into the shipping container at concussion-inducing speeds, my bulletproof visor cracking. Then she yanks me out of the head-shaped dent, cradling me in her arms. "Oh my God I'm sorry what did I *do* I panicked I didn't mean to hurt you—"

In retrospect, handcuffing myself to a gorilla-strong woman with panic disorder had some obvious drawbacks.

Thank God she's a caretaker: the only thing that seems to snap her out of panic is her concern for someone else.

"We need to get to cover," I croak, running my tongue over a cracked tooth. "I won't send you back to prison, I promise, but those—"

The drones open fire. Silvia hauls me back into the shipping container so fast that another of Charybdis's nuBone hardpoints cracks.

She crouches down in the fragments of bulletproof glass, wrapping her human arms around her green-gray knees. She jerks Charybdis—who is rated at an eight-hundred-pound lift strength—down with her.

"Okay," she says, bobbing her head as she talks herself down. "He's going to shoot the drones down, Silvia, he'll blow them out of the sky and then we'll get out of here before they send something else—"

"Silvia—"

"—and you're not going to think about what happens next, Silvia, that's too much. You're not going to think about how people will react once they see this hideous body. Don't think about Mama, don't think about Vala, concentrate on escaping, one step at a time, one step—"

"*Silvia.*"

"I'm sorry." She blinks at her arm, tugging experimentally, as if she still can't believe her own strength. "I'm—I'm holding you back, aren't I? You can't destroy the drones from back here." She uncurls herself slowly, analyzing how she stood up. "Let's get you where you can down them—"

I don't want to destroy her illusions, not least because if she freaks out she might punch my face in. I creep to the doors and slam them shut. "I'm sorry, Silvia. But . . . I don't have anything onboard to down those drones. They're hi-tech. Armored. With shielded rotors."

Ferrett Steinmetz

"You're a body-hacker! You have *bazookas* in your forearms!"

"Common misconception. I don't have anything worse than what you can pick up at the local military surplus store."

"So we *run!*"

I grab her shoulder. "Silvia. We have to assume they came armed with weaponry designed to shut you down—you woke up within a minute after we cut the electricity, so there's clearly some signal that can . . . deactivate you." I don't like talking about her like she's a computer program, but I can't find better words. "And you can't control yourself yet when they shoot at you. You're gonna leap right up to take them down, and . . . they'll take *you* down."

"I'm not surrendering."

"Not to them, no."

"Then to who?"

She doesn't think of the NJPD as someone she needs to surrender to. Which is kind of charming, considering there's four cops nursing shattered metacarpals.

"I just called down the entire police force upon us, Silvia. We'll be swarmed in ten minutes. Our best bet's to hunker down, let them arrest us, and explain what happened, and—"

"Jesus." I can hear the drones taking up position around us—not entering the container, they're too big, but waiting. "You think the cops will *protect* us? They can't even protect themselves from me! Whatever those drones are, they'll—they'll chew through the cops' defenses, even if the cops put me in jail these guys will smash through the walls and kidnap me again, this is *not* a good plan—"

"No. No, it isn't, Silvia. This plan sucks."

Silvia-handling-process note number two: agreeing with her also helps deflect her panic attacks.

"But I don't have better plans. I didn't prepare anything to take out high-level combat drones." That was supposed to be Donnie's job—and honestly, I hadn't thought anything *could* take Donnie out.

"Okay." She licks her lips. "You can't do it. So maybe . . ."

I shut her down. "And *you can't either*. They're designed to capture you, remember?" I swallow, tasting the grit from the airbags' explosive charges. "I'm sorry, Silvia. I don't like our odds. But I think our best bet's to hope the NJPD comes to the rescue."

She leans down to whisper: "What if I chuck things at the drones?"

"What?"

She keeps her voice muffled. Brilliant: she must know military drones come with high-quality microphones. She flips a hand at the shot-up hard drives strewn around the room.

"I can—I can leap twenty feet in the air, right? And I punched—I punched him into a wall." She shakes her head as she flicks her gaze past Donnie, trying to absorb her newfound talent for violence. "So I can fling something fast and high. I sucked at high-school softball, but I'm betting this body makes me a helluva pitcher—"

"That's crazy."

"Why?"

"That's—it's just flinging stuff and hoping—it's crude. Like using trebuchets to take down helicopters."

"I'm sorry?" She cocks her head at me, frowning like I'm insane. "Is war won on *style points*?"

I am *not* used to civilians correcting me on military tactics.

"All right," I admit. "It's . . . we can try it. But there's three of them out there, and they have computerized reflexes. If you only hit one, the other two will fly out of range once they realize what's happening. So you've gotta hit all three at once."

"I—I'm not sure if I can do that."

"One's likely to stay at a distance. It's what I'd do; they sent three, so I'd keep the third as far out of the line of fire as possible while still keeping it close enough to intercept you if you run. You'll have to throw hard; they'll have calculated your attack's angle and velocity before the projectile leaves your hand. You need to throw faster than they can dodge."

"Is that possible?"

Ferrett Steinmetz

I chuckle. "I don't know what you can do, Silvia. But those are weighty drones; they're designed to carry you, so I don't think they're nimble. Our biggest problem is that we need to locate the three of them before we attack or else you'll be too slow."

A heavy clunk from above as something massive settles onto the shipping container, followed by a high-pitched whine as a torch cuts a molten line through the roof.

"Well," she says. "We know where one of them is."

I can feel Silvia trembling through the handcuff that connects us. Her eyes flick between the ever-increasing cut in the ceiling and the shut doors, wanting to attack something.

She needs a plan or she'll fly apart.

Fortunately, planning's what I do.

I bring up Scylla's onboard screen, show her how my scanners are measuring the cutting torch's progress—then I lean down to whisper in her ear.

"That drone will take one minute and forty-nine seconds to cut a hole in the roof. Can I tell you a secret about warfare, Silvia?"

She's desperate to listen to someone who can tell her what's going on. "Yes."

"All combat comes down to preparation. We have that long to make a plan." I point at Scylla, who now reads 1:41. "Your idea to throw heavy equipment at the drones—that was a good plan, Silvia. Now we have to figure out where the drones are, without going out and looking around. Can you do that?"

1:32 left, and literally 35.9 percent of the words I've spoken are intended to keep Silvia from panicking. Yet those are words well spent. She's my equipment, at least for the remaining ninety seconds, and I need to maintain her.

And by giving Silvia a narrow task, I've given her something to derail her from her next panic attack. If she can't think up a way to triangulate the drones' position she might enter another one—

But thinking up ways is my job.

I wish I was still connected to Donnie's overhead satellite feed, but I lost that access when I opened fire upon him. Likewise, we might be able to get a rough position on the drones if I heard Marcy and Defcon opening fire on the overhead threats, but no shots have been fired. My guess is they wisely peace-tied themselves the moment the NJPD rumbled in.

The NJPD . . .

"Silvia," I say as I broadcast orders to the police cars outside. "I'm going to crack open the door and fire ten shots in rapid succession. A minute later, those cars will explode. I don't have time to explain right now, but just understand that it's part of the plan, and the exploding cars will be far away, and they won't hurt anyone. Are we clear?"

I speak calmly, giving her space to take in each word. She gives me tight nods as she does her best to understand. At 1:01, she says, "Yes. Yes, I'm clear."

I walk to the door, switching to incendiary rounds, and snap off ten shots at four police cars, which I've lined up according to the holes Silvia's punched in their sides.

Under normal circumstances, I'd never penetrate the armor to hit the vehicle-strength batteries underneath. But Silvia's peeled away a lot of the protective plating, exposing internals—

And while the new deep-well batteries are better shielded and less likely to explode than gas tanks, that's only because the manufacturers are smart enough to encase these volatile chemicals in *extremely* sturdy frames.

I drive the four cars into the trees, their frames already belching thick black smoke, the remaining cops inside diving to safety as I helpfully pop their doors open. I then wheel the remaining car into position. Its LADAR maps out where the drones are. Sure enough, one's on the roof; the other two have taken up position high behind the shipping container's exit, ready to ambush us if we flee.

I establish a connection to a hologram projector on my left leg,

Ferrett Steinmetz

pop it out, prop it on the floor so it displays a live-time map of where the two flying drones are.

"There," I whisper to Silvia as 0:49 clicks by. "Can you see them?"

"Yes." She grabs a hard drive, chucks it into the ceiling at an angle that I'm certain would have hit a drone if the shipping container wasn't in the way. It shatters into shrapnel that bounces off my helmet. "Sorry. I . . . I'm not sure what happened."

"It's okay, Silvia. Can you hit them?"

"I think so." She frowns as she peers into the display. "I—I see the layout in my mind. I'm visualizing things in ways I never could before."

She bites off more explanation—she's seeing a lot more than most humans, I bet, now that she's analyzing what her newfound body can do. But she sees the clock tick down to 0:38, flinching as the metal above us sags. No time left for self-reflection.

"I'll take care of this one above," I say. "But I can't stay handcuffed to you and do that. May I handcuff you to this door so you don't leap away?"

"Yes."

Though Silvia's vinegar stench of alien fear-sweat is sharper than the acrid stink of molten steel, she keeps her eyes on the map as I reattach her to the door. Those sharp eyes are watching the microshifts as the drones adjust themselves to the wind currents; her gaze darts across the heaped racks, marking what servers she'll grab, what angles she'll fling them at.

She's shit-scared and shivering, and why not? She's never been in a life-or-death fight. She's a head grafted to a bioengineered body she's not sure she can control.

Yet she's magnificent—not despite her panic disorder, but *because* of it.

She is struggling *so hard* to surpass herself.

The clock ticks to 0:29, abruptly losing two seconds—the torch is cutting through faster than my prediction models anticipated. I squeeze her shoulder. "Hit 'em quick, Silvia. One, two. One, two."

"One, two," she mutters, almost in a trance. I recognize that trance: if she comprehends everything about to happen, she will break down. So she's compartmentalizing, narrowing the world down like I do—I'm not about to engage a drone in hand-to-hand combat, I'm tuning a setting on one of my armaments. She's not about to face down two drones engineered to kill her, she's practicing her fastball.

We are united by our dysfunctional coping techniques.

0:24. The synchronizer countdown flashes red on the holographic readout. Sylvia bobs her head in time with each second, pressing her hands together tight in prayer as if she's afraid she'll fling another hard drive at the ceiling if she lets go.

"Do you know why they chose you, Silvia?" I whisper. "Some people, when they panic, they run. Other people freeze. The reason they chose you, Silvia, is because when you're scared . . . you *fight*.

"And while that's always been a liability for you before, right now? Your furious panic is the only thing that will save us. Your instincts will save us. So. Silvia. Don't hold back.

"Kick their goddamned ass."

0:03. I step into position, placing myself below where the drone's almost finished cutting out a square of reinforced steel.

0:02. My legs squat me as far down as possible, my artificial muscles strung tight as harp strings.

0:01. Sylvia mutters, "Kick their ass."

The second the saw finishes cutting the square in the roof, I leap up with all my might, propelling myself upward in a vertical tackle.

The freed roof piece slams up into the drone hard enough that I hear something break free and rattle.

Air whooshes down upon me as the drone tilts, its propellers working overtime to right itself. It had gripped the roof piece in pincers, preparing to lift the cut segment free so it could reach

Ferrett Steinmetz

inside and pick up its delicate cargo—now it drops the additional weight, spinning wildly as it opens fire on me.

It had doubtlessly ultrasounded the interior before it finished the cut, seen me crouching—but the drone's software had anticipated gunfire, not a suicidal frontal assault.

Reaction packages can be complex, but they're often just as slow to react to unexpected tactics as a human is—and sometimes slower. The sole advantage humans have over automated weaponry is that we will try *insanely* stupid tactics no bot could predict.

Like, say, leaping back up again the second I hit the floor to climb up the drone's side.

I bat the tumbling roof piece aside, bullets ricocheting off the steel surface, screaming at Scylla and Charybdis: *get a hold on that drone.* A complex web of operating systems intercepts my raw request, connects it with the scanning data that maps the drone's surface for potential weight-bearing surfaces, translates intent into the complex physics needed to jump high enough to intercept an escaping drone.

Again, my sole advantage is that the drone isn't sure what the hell I'm trying to do. By the time it sees Scylla's fingers spreading out and concludes what's happening, it's too late to adjust its propellers to dodge.

It sends the usual shock-on-contact routines, floods my opened ports for software vulnerabilities. But I'm shielded against both forms of attack, my rebreather helmet protecting me from the nerve gas it's spraying, and as I climb up its surface it can't bring its long-range weaponry to bear on me.

Two shots bounce off my helmet, snapping my head back hard enough that I gray out—the other drone defending the primary.

Yet even as my consciousness wavers, my last known commands keep Scylla and Charybdis clambering up the drone as it struggles to break free: *grab that propeller.*

Charybdis gets there first, clenching its fingers around the armored circle shielding the propellers from casual debris—and bears down with all the strength my artificial muscles can produce, crumpling it.

Poor Charybdis just stuck itself in a meat grinder.

The blades chop into my metal fingers, shattering as they impact my motorized phalanges, both pieces of machinery shredding hard enough that the shrapnel bounces off my body armor at the speed of .22 bullets. The haptic feedback registers as pain so intense my systems automatically release the propeller before I can override them—if I'd had more than two minutes to plan, I would have remembered to disable the auto-disengage mechanisms—but thankfully Charybdis is trapped, its reinforced alloys mangled with the rotor as it chews itself to shreds.

That's a leverage point.

The drone hasn't lifted me fully out of the shipping container yet, so I tell my legs to jam my feet underneath the roof, anchoring me. And even though my haptic feedback screams pain—*your fingers have been chopped off abort abort*—I order Scylla and Charybdis: *smash this fucking thing against the crate.*

Scylla and Charybdis are each rated for an eight-hundred-pound lift strength. That's assuming I do it safely.

I overclock the muscles, fibers snapping, to slam the drone into corrugated steel with twenty-four hundred pounds of combined force.

Two of the drone's remaining propellers are crushed against the container, their own momentum chopping them to shreds. I yank Charybdis free, what used to be complex finger-actuators flying free in mangled chunks, the drone smoking as it tumbles to the ground.

I hear Marcy and Defcon whistle in appreciation.

I drop back into the shipping container, head spinning—no concussion, I don't think, but these constant impacts will leave me with brain damage somewhere down the line—but my legs coordinate to land me with a gymnast's grace.

I'm surprised by all the flames outside the shipping container until I remember: *oh, yes, I set the cop cars on fire.* The conflagration's

Ferrett Steinmetz

spreading to the pollution-blighted trees, which is awesome, igniting the late-summer leaves and touching off a nice solid forest fire.

Silvia strains at her handcuff, pointing at the sky: "I hit it! I *hit* it! But it's getting away!"

My heart sinks until I see what she's done. The drone that shot me is half-buried in the ground, three of its propellers destroyed. I try to imagine the accuracy Silvia had to throw with in order to bank a single solid-state hard drive off all three propellers.

My sensors focus on the remaining drone. It must have been farther away when Silvia flung, already putting distance between them. Still, one rotor hangs still and the other spins erratically. Its piloting routines are trying to stabilize for their damaged propellers, but that limits its directional capabilities.

I'd feel better if it plummeted to the ground. But it drifts helplessly away from us, bobbing out over the freeway, shaking so fiercely even computer assistance can't give it a clean shot.

"No, no, you did great," I assure her. "Knocking it out of the sky would have been nicer, but it can't follow us. That was your mission, Silvia. You did it with style."

Her face lights up in a triumphant grin. Then she flickers into a hunch as she cradles Charybdis's twisted armatures. She looks up at me, frowning, searching for confirmation this is as serious as she thinks it is.

"Your hand," she whispers. "Does it hurt?"

I dampen the haptic feedback, shutting off the artificial pain. "Not anymore."

She presses her palms against my body armor, running them down my belly, tracing the shrapnel dents. "Your helmet, God, your helmet, they shot you in the head—"

I grasp her hand in my working one. "They're guaranteed to hit me. That's why I buy top-class armor."

Yet as I glance at the piece of roof lying on the floor, I note the bullet holes punched through quarter-inch steel. They had weaponry designed to tear me to pieces; they just couldn't bring it to bear.

I got lucky. So lucky.

Silvia pulls her hands away from my chest, finally realizing how much danger she's put me in. "I get this is a . . . an inconvenience for you."

I laugh, checking my batteries: I'm down to 31 percent power, 28 percent of ammo capacity, my body armor needing total replacement, Charybdis's actuators crumpled beyond repair. "It's not a day in the lab, no."

She yanks on the handcuff; it snaps free. "Well, you've done enough. You . . . you cleared me a path to freedom. If you wanted to run in a different direction, well—you don't have to throw your life away on this, is what I'm saying."

That would be charming, if I hadn't already committed several class-B felonies *and* pissed off the world's most dangerous shadow organization. Still, I take her offer for what it's worth: she doesn't know how deeply I've gone into hock for her, so this last-minute kindness is immeasurable.

"Thank you, ma'am. But . . . I've risked my life for lesser causes. I'm good with this one. And to be honest, the NJPD will catch you unless I step in."

"I can do this. I can *do* this." She squeezes her eyes shut. "But if you're with me, then—I mean, I should at least know your name, right?"

She concentrates and extends her hand slowly, suppressing her body's natural instinct to grip at insect speeds.

"Silvia," she says.

"Mat." I reach out with Scylla's delicate armatures to take her hand in my micromanipulators. My haptic sensors tell me it feels like a normal human hand, even though it's clear her fingers are made of something else.

Silvia stares at the gun-warmed metal gripping her fingers.

"Thank you, Mat."

Her body is a knotted alien physiology. But the demure way she can't meet my gaze when she thanks me?

Ferrett Steinmetz

She's more human than anyone I've ever saved before.

We both look up when we hear the distant sound of sirens.

"Head for the woods," I say. "As close to the forest fire as you can get. Don't outpace me—my legs are rated tripsafe at thirty miles per hour, but I doubt I'll get that speed in dense woods."

"*Into* the fire?"

I point up in the air, circling my finger. "Drones and satellites. Thick black smoke gives us cover. Now *run*."

She grabs my good hand. Haptic feedback tells me her touch is cool and gentle.

We run.

ACT 2

They Deftly
Maneuver
and Muscle
for Rank

Some moves AlphaGo likes to make against its clone are downright incomprehensible, even to the world's best players. (These tend to happen early on in the games—probably because that phase is already mysterious, being farthest away from any final game outcome.) One opening move in Game One has many players stumped. Says Redmond, "I think a natural reaction (and the reaction I'm mostly seeing) is that they just sort of give up, and sort of throw their hands up in the opening. Because it's so hard to try to attach a story about what AlphaGo is doing. You have to be ready to deny a lot of the things that we've believed and that have worked for us."

—"The AI That Has Nothing to Learn From Humans,"
The Atlantic, October 2017

For years, I'd asked myself: *What would I do if I was the subject of a statewide manhunt?* I'd daydreamed escape methods during my sponge baths, figuring out the optimal ways to avoid the cops, the ways to get my hands on spendable funds without the banks catching me, how to avoid civilians.

As we race through the burning woods, Silvia's hand in mine, I realize: this statewide manhunt thing isn't *nearly* as fun as it sounded.

Expanding the radius while staying hidden is critical. That r^2 in the $A=\pi r^2$ equation is all that's saving our bacon right now. Well, that and the tree cover and the thick black smoke obscuring satellite surveillance.

The last the cops saw us, we were by the freeway. Now we're farther away in the woods—but they don't know where. If we're somewhere within fifty feet of that truck, the cops have to search an area of 7,850 feet. If we're somewhere within one hundred feet, the search area quadruples to 31,400 feet.

If I can stretch that radius of "Where could they be?" out to a full mile, the cops have to search an area of 87 million feet. Which, as long as we can avoid the drones or security cameras or inquisitive civilians, is big enough to deploy every cop in New Jersey and still not find us.

Wait. Is that *technically* true? How many people does the NJPD employ? There are thirty-five thousand full-time police officers on the NJPD according to my archived Wikipedia queries, which means each cop would have to search an area of 2,500 square feet, and Jesus, I'm so scared I'm doing math problems to distract myself.

Anyway. Our goal is to get as far away from the wreckage without being spotted. Extend that radius of uncertainty.

Except the radius isn't unlimited. The woods by the freeway is a stunted space crammed in between housing projects. The overhead maps show this patch goes on for .7 miles before dumping us by a convenience store.

Yet there are two shadowy patches where the woods dwindle to a stop. If we're lucky, we could dart through into the larger forests on the other side without being spotted by drones or security cameras. I breathe a sigh of relief at our luck—but then realize whoever set out to kidnap Silvia stopped our truck by the densest woods on purpose.

The IAC's enemy is probably poised somewhere nearby, waiting to scoop her up.

Yet leaving our worldwide conspirator enemies aside, the cops (and anyone else tracking us) will realize we'd *have* to have made for the two entry paths into the larger forests. A hulking body-hacker and an alien-bodied woman can't dash into the suburbs without attracting attention. Which means that as soon as the cops get their manhunter-AIs online, whose whole job is narrowing the radius, they'll track our most likely escape routes.

I curse and check in with the tiny decaying particle of nuclear material in my system, which creates as close to a true random number as possible. I'll figure out how to chart the safest path in an arbitrary direction away from the wreckage, because our only hope is to be erratic and *not* do the smart thing.

"I hate to interrupt." Silvia has stripped a handful of leaves from a tree and is clutching them against her chest, running hunched over like she has to go to the bathroom. Is she in pain? "But will we get into another firefight soon?"

Ferrett Steinmetz

"Not if I do my job right."

"That's bad news. I need distraction."

"Pardon me?"

"We're running. And as I'm running, I'm realizing I don't have lungs to breathe with, and then I think what Mama and Vala will say when they see me like . . . this . . . and then I realize I won't see them again, and . . ."

She slumps to a halt, clenching the leaves so hard they drip fluid.

"Say what you will about firefights, but the extraneous thoughts just bubble away!" Her laugh's as thin as frayed cable. "So you need to talk me through what we're going to do, or you need to find me a nice reinforced room to freak the fuck out in."

"Silvia . . ."

"This is *not negotiable*."

Her gaze is haggard, but also clear: she knows her breaking point and will not allow herself to be pushed beyond it.

I can respect that.

"Fine." The weary smile she gives me feels like a gift. "But I'm . . . I'm not used to talking to people when I'm planning."

"You've been muttering to yourself the whole time!"

Can *everyone* hear me? "That's talking to myself. I don't . . . run things . . . *past* people. Walking you through this mission will slow me down."

"Me panicking in a superstrong body will slow you down more. And I need to keep calm, because having a freak-out in my regular body hurt people sometimes. This would be . . . it would be awful. So please. Tell me what you're doing. In baby steps."

I keep moving forward, headed towards the wood's edge. "Our first step is to avoid being caught by the police."

"Okay, that . . . seems like a pretty grown-up step."

Breaking our situation down into mission parameters is calming, as it turns out. "We're headed in this random direction, because it's terrible strategy. But our terrible strategy is good strategy, because the manhunter-AIs will have mapped out all the smart escape routes and will send cops to intercept us. So my job—our job—is to find a way to make a stupid escape as smart as possible."

Thank God she keeps up with me, both mentally and physically. These are dense woods, yet she never takes her eyes off me as her alien body weaves through the thickets, operating off an instinct her conscious mind doesn't control.

She looks at poor, mangled Charybdis. "Are *you* okay?"

I flex the fingers; what's left of them grinds. "Under normal circumstances, the next step would be replacing this, which would be an hour in the shop, tops. But . . . I can't *get* to my shop. It's in Missouri. Even if we raced there, the cops would have that cordoned off." I'd *like* to think Marcy and Defcon wouldn't have given my name to the police—but let's be honest, giving me up is their best hope of scoring a light sentence. I'd be shocked if they weren't testifying to New Jersey's finest lawyerbots, which means the IAC has to know what we've done. "So my combat effectiveness's degraded without hope of repair."

"I was actually asking if it hurt."

This is the second time she's asked; I remind myself that she's never dealt with body-hackers. Only the meat-parts hurt, and—well, those are pretty banged up too. "That's not this step, Silvia. This step is . . ."

We arrive at a row of minuscule backyards, fenced off high to keep the deer out. The homes here are run-down, antiquated housing from the 2010s; most have been refitted with solar panels and smartwalls, but there's still a couple showcasing old glass windows instead of liquid smartglass. Which is good; if they were hi-tech buildings, we'd never sneak past their sensors.

"This step is figuring out which house we break into to hole up in while I find us a ride out of town."

"Does the choice of house matter?"

"Empty is best. Otherwise we have to take hostages. I won't do that unless I have to."

Ferrett Steinmetz

I scan the houses' windows, asking my sensors to look for movement—an inefficient way to determine if anyone's home. I could hack into each home's encrypted internet connection, sniff their lines to see what their internet traffic is—but even though it's midday, they could be sleeping.

I don't want to involve civilians. It's too easy to imagine accidentally shooting a kid who called in sick to school. Yet I need a place to recharge, my batteries are low.

"That house needs forty thousand dollars in roof repairs," Silvia mutters, pulling herself up on tiptoes to look over the fence.

I frown. "That's awfully specific. Is that . . . some new power you've been granted?"

"What? No!" She clasps her hands to her chest and flickers backwards. "I'm a home inspector."

It hadn't occurred to me that she had a job before . . . that . . . happened to her.

"That's a good job for you to have," I say.

She blushes. "Mama helped me pick it out as a career. Home inspections are still too complex to automate—not that you can't get a scanner to find termite infestations, but then you need a separate scanner to check for roof integrity and another AI for electrical wiring, and at that point you need truckfuls of equipment. Simpler to send me and a couple of handhelds. Plus, Vala pointed out I'd get to work alone."

Clearly working alone is—was—a major benefit of the job as far as she's concerned. Which, I suppose, for a woman with panic disorder, is a bonus. No bosses breathing down your neck, and if the day gets too much for you, you hole up in a closet until the medications kick in.

"Anyway, that house is empty." She hugs herself against the fence at a weird angle. Has her new body got some built-in biological urge to press herself up against things?

"How sure are you that it's empty?"

"Pretty sure? That leaky roof's dumping water straight into the living room. Any squatters in there are too far gone to care about intruders."

There's no better news than finding the person you're tasked to escort is also competent. And this house has a garage, which is even better: assuming Herbie gets here, we can make the transfer in privacy. "Good work, Silvia."

"Baby steps." She gives me a wan smile. "Break it down into pieces for me. I can cope if I don't look at the big picture."

"I'll keep it tiny." I consult one of my never-used databases—according to the intel expert I bought it from, this database lists all the satellite passovers. Feed it a set of coordinates and a time, and it'll tell you when any significant cameras are watching. I pay her a fortune because she theoretically knows about the dark satellites that governments won't acknowledge exist.

Of course I've never had a way to verify her data. Or even a need for it. Until today, paying her subscription fee felt like paranoia.

With both the IAC and the IAC's enemy after me, my every paranoid preparation has become justified.

I look down at the timer; it's supposedly accurate to within fifteen seconds. Which seemed acceptable when I sat in my lab, but that lag seems crazy dangerous in the field. Still, we've lucked out; an empty satellite window's opening up in forty seconds, and there aren't any delivery drones in sight.

Silvia's looking to me for instructions so she doesn't freak out. I display the countdown timer.

"Okay," I say, popping slats off the fence. "When this hits zero, we'll get to the door and open it so we don't leave a mess—"

She leaps through the gap, sailing high across the lawn, and smashes through the door in a spray of glass.

"*What the f—*" I cut off my frustrated shout, because she's made enough noise already. She's in the house's rear entryway, standing atop the wrecked door, staring down at it dumbfounded. Her gaze snags on the anemone-like hairs on her legs.

Ferrett Steinmetz

She stomps on the ruined door. Her foot punches through the floor; she yanks herself free, ready to run—

"*Silvia.*"

I speak authoritatively enough to get her attention.

I stride calmly across the yard.

The sun's out, and so are the satellites. Maybe the photos they take won't be analyzed enough to notice the fugitive body-hacker with a crushed arm strolling across a lawn.

But I know that if I dash across to Silvia like this is something we should panic about, she'll panic.

"Okay." I hold up both hands in surrender. Her eyes focus on mangled Charybdis; I lower it as though it's unworthy of her attention. "So we've learned something new about the way your body works."

"That it fucking *doesn't listen?*"

Telling her to keep quiet would inspire anger. Instead, I step over the door to set what's left of it back in the frame, noting happily how prior scavengers have disabled the house's security alarms.

"No," I say. "Your body's got different instincts, is all. I think it's unhooked."

A slight risk; she might get mad at me leaving questions hanging for her to answer. Fortunately, her curious outweighs her furious. "Unhooked from *what?*"

"I think the reason your body is so fast, and efficient, and such a viable combat entity," I say, layering on the positives, "is because it operates on unconscious thought. You envision what you want to do, your body makes the rest happen without your input. Basically, you're operating on phenomenal autopiloting."

"It's a stupid design! I don't *want* my body on autopilot!"

"Except parts of us have operated on autopilot all along. You never thought much about walking, did you? Those careful decisions about balance and foot placement your muscles have to make? After a while, getting from one place to another just happens."

"No. That's *different*. I choose when to get up, I choose when to walk."

"Now you're one level abstracted. I don't think you actually decide to walk anymore." I remembered her loping along the woods beside me, never glancing down at the brush at her feet. "You decide where you want to be, and your body decides how to get there. You control what happens, just not *how*. And if we can control—"

I'm slammed backwards so hard my feet leave furrows in the wooden floor. Scylla and Charybdis have intercepted her blow as she shoved me backwards, readouts blaring how much biological damage she'd have done if my systems hadn't intercepted—

If I hadn't upgraded my hand-to-hand combat routines, I would have been dead twice over today.

"You think it's *good* to have my thoughts manifest?" Charybdis jerks up to deflect a roundhouse so powerful that Silvia's fist shears off the alloy cowling. "I—"

She rolls away from me with a ninja's deftness, curls herself into a shivering ball. I shunt away the emergency warnings flooding into my HUD to lower my arms, stand at a respectful distance.

She sniffles, staring glumly at the peeling floral wallpaper. "You see?"

I'm terrified the wrong response will provoke another assault, so I nod.

My internal clocks are showing how long it's been since Silvia first assaulted the cops—and each passing minute brings us closer to getting caught. Yet I wait by her side for one minute, then three, then five—listening to her muttering calmness mantras, then fervent prayers, then calmness mantras.

You can't rush someone back to calmness. Yet leaving her to do something else would dump more guilt upon her, reminding her how she has to be taken care of and shoving her deeper into a panic cycle, so . . .

I wait. Like there was nothing I'd rather be doing in the world than crouching by her side.

And honestly, it's nice to have company. I should be planning, but I tune out most of my usual paranoia to concentrate on being present for her. (Though I do check my sensors long enough to ensure there's no evidence of recent occupancy: no dwindling areas of body heat, no breathing noises within detection range.)

At five minutes and forty-two seconds, she sniffles. "Can you see if there's a towel left in the bathroom closet upstairs? Or maybe a shower curtain left in the tub?"

I'm not about to question her need for fabric right now, so I head upstairs—sure enough, she's correctly ascertained this place has an upstairs bathroom, but everything's been stripped. Even the wires and copper piping are gone.

When I come down, shrugging apologetically, she's hugging her legs tight, restraining herself. "When I panicked before, I hurt people. Now when I panic, I could kill people. And that makes me more panicky, and it's *not* a good feedback loop, it's *not* . . ."

"You're also a terrible operative."

She grants me a sly, sideways glance. "I see you've figured out knocking me off my train of thought helps."

"That's just my natural sarcasm. And listen, Silvia, I want to have this discussion, but right now I need to recharge my batteries in case we get into more fights. And I need to see if I can get my car here without being seen. What say we go somewhere I can plug in?"

"Baby steps?" She gives me an appreciative nod, which looks odd when her human head tilts on her knotted macramé body. "You listen, Mat. That's a rare skill."

Why am I blushing? "I'm just good with owner's manuals."

I extend my good hand without thinking. Neither of us let go as we walk into the living room.

"Watch out for syringes," she says.

It's a total disaster. The plaster walls have been punched in where robbers cut out the smartwall upgrades. The stucco ceiling bulges low, stained an unhealthy brown.

Sure enough, there are syringes scattered on the floor.

"Let's check the basement," I say. "If they haven't stolen the wires to the solar panels, we can get power."

One of the benefits of solar panels on repossessed houses was that banks could sell the excess power back to the electrical companies, so the houses wouldn't be a total loss—which had been a decent business deal, back before deep-well batteries and superefficient solar power had made the bottom fall out of the electricity market.

I head down into the basement. Silvia holds back. "Do you mind scouting that first, Mat? That place looks like Buffalo Bill's hideout."

I replay her last sentence to make sure I heard her correctly. "You've seen *Silence of the Lambs?*"

She stiffens, worried I'm mocking her. "Well, it's Vala who likes the horror movies, but . . . yes. I watch old movies to calm me down. Grungy old period pieces that take forever to watch. It's silly, I know, but it's how I relax."

"It's not silly. But come on down. There's nobody here. I would have taken care of that."

"Oh. Good."

The basement is crawling with silverfish—and sure enough, a slightly less dirty oven-sized space indicates the thieves have made off with the household battery. Yet the stubby wires leading down from the far less stealable solar panels are still usable; I hot-wire a connection.

It feels *so good* to see my battery indicators glowing green. This isn't a fast-charge station, but the panels should top me off in an hour—too long for people looking to escape a manhunt.

I can drop that to fifteen minutes if I'm willing to drain power from the electrical grid. Better. Herbie should have arrived by then.

"So what's our next step?" Silvia asks. She can't stay in the basement—she literally can't. The moment her feet touch the slimy, moss-covered floor, she leaps instinctively to safety. She crouches

Ferrett Steinmetz

on the staircase, hugging her chest to her knees, looking at me anxiously.

"I've sent a request for my car to get here. If everything goes right, it'll arrive soon."

"And if not?"

That "if not" is our biggest concern. My car Herbie has pulled out of its parking spot, unbeknownst to the city AI.

Putting an unregistered vehicle on the road is highly illegal, but I'm already hip-deep in lawbreaking. The bigger problem is that if Herbie gets close enough to another smartcar, that car might notify the city AI about the unregistered vehicle.

Or a cop on patrol spots Herbie's *also* highly illegal digital rooftop paint job that, from a drone-sized distance, makes Herbie look like the roads he's traveling on. And what are the odds a cop will be in the neighborhood now that the NJPD have instigated a manhunt?

Hell. The right passerby might snap a picture of Herbie's illegal digital paint job, allowing the real-time police photo analyst–AIs to catch it. The chances of Herbie getting here undetected are somewhere around 16 percent—the same depressing odds as losing at Russian roulette.

"If not, we won't know what happened," I say. "I don't dare open up another internet connection with Herbie—"

"You call him Herbie?" She shoots me a little heart gesture. "Like Herbie the Love Bug?"

"Oh, you got that reference too?" I suppress an urge to ask her whether she's seen the Lohan abomination of a remake, or the good one with Buddy Hackett. "But I can't open up an internet connection; if they catch Herbie, and he sends a distress signal back to me, the cops might trace it. As it is, he's engineered to set himself on fire if he shows up on the city AI—a little overzealous, maybe, but better safe than sorry. Which means Herbie'll be useless if he gets into the slightest fender bender."

She whistles in nervous amazement. "You programmed in all that on the way here?"

"No. I had a backup plan ready to execute."

"You had a secret car parked in place with preprogrammed software to avoid police manhunts?"

"Technically, I had it prepped to avoid entanglements with a superior enemy who could trace me on the internet—but that turns out to have a significant constabulary overlap, yes."

She relaxes, her trust in me unsettling. I don't tell her my plan if Herbie *doesn't* arrive, which is a pathetic "Hole up in the basement and hope blowing up four cop cars hasn't motivated the NJPD enough to do a door-to-door search."

"I . . . don't want to ask this question," she asks. "But . . . where do we head to when—"

"If."

"—if Herbie gets here?"

I was hoping she wouldn't ask that. "That's the big issue. I need a repair shop, stat. We can't use mine."

"So call a friend?"

"I don't have a lot of friends, Silvia." I glance away, because I know the pitying look she's giving me. "I've got the woman who set me up with this—Trish. We have secret communication channels, but I don't know how well they'll hold up against the IAC."

"We could head to my sister's apartment," she says. "She and Mama, they're not—really equipped to deal with this scenario, but they've always had good ideas for me—"

"Does your sister have access to a prosthetic armament repair lab?"

"She has access to *a* lab." I perk up. "A chocolate lab. His name's Biscuit, and he's adorable."

After an awkward pause, she scuttles backwards up the stairs and hides behind the doorframe—which seems weird, until I realize she's got no filter between what she *wants* to do and what she does. When she embarrasses herself with a bad joke, her body retreats.

"It's funny," I call after her. "It's just . . . you know . . . timing. It's okay, nobody gets my sense of humor either."

Ferrett Steinmetz

She creeps back down. "Sorry. But Vala, she's . . . she's loyal. She'd hide us for as long as it took. And maybe, she could help you understand how to handle me."

"Attention, Silvia Maldonado."

The voice is tinny, coming from a speaker upstairs the raiders must have forgotten to ransack. Even diminished, it's still monotone, robotic, hateful. Silvia grabs my arm tightly enough to leave finger-shaped imprints in the remaining cowling.

"If you are not Silvia Maldonado, mention this to no one. Speak of this, and we will slaughter your social circle and leave you grieving. Message begins for Silvia.

"We have detected an abrupt electrical drain on the grid from this house, which our models predict with a sixty-four point seven percent probability is Mathew recharging his batteries after the firefight."

"They know," she whispers, curling in tighter to me. "They *know.*"

"They're *guessing.*"

"We have analyzed both your personalities. Our models show an eighty-seven point six percent probability you and Mathew have already discussed making contact with Tricia Malachai. If not, the next greatest likelihood of contact is Vala Maldonado. We have already placed surveillance around these targets as well as the next ten most likely sources on your lists.

"We know where you will flee."

The mechanical voice speaks evenly, emphasizing our names when it speaks as though dropping variables into a template. It does not threaten; it *concludes*, map software naming a destination.

A person might have compassion. This manhunter-AI only has expected outcomes.

I extend Charybdis's hand so Silvia can take it; she crumples what's left of my fingers.

"We have access to your therapy records, Silvia Maldonado. We know what harm you fear will happen to your mother and sister.

You can avoid that harm by surrendering to the police within the next twenty-four hours and remaining in custody until we retrieve you.

"You belong to the IAC, Silvia Maldonado. Surrender before you discover what we can do to everyone you love."

Silvia leans back against the stairway banister, her tendriled body sliding down to the floor, her human hands clapped over her eyes. It's as if she's shrinking into nothing.

She's surrendering.

I can't blame her. I should have realized they'd go after her family. I'd seen that time and time again in the service; our intelligence would alert us to bold rebels who were standing up against the terrorists.

"We'll know if they're serious in a week," my supervisors told me.

Because the terrorists never went after the rebels. They went after their daughters. People who weren't cowed by bullets quailed when the gun was aimed at their grandfather's head.

Not that it usually came to that. There'd be photos left on your doorstep of your son playing with friends. Strangers inquiring about your cousin's health. Even *that* gentle pressure made good people cave.

How could Silvia resist when her family was endangered?

I hover over her, uncertain whether to pat her shoulder or to bring my therapy-AIs online to walk me through comforting her. Yet that's too impersonal; I know the AI scripts lead to better results, but reading off the suggested topics always makes me feel like a telemarketer.

Silvia deserves a human touch.

I watch the clock in my HUD tick down: it's dutifully logged the deadline as "surrender to police," and is now counting down from 23:59:32. And . . .

I punch a wall.

The IAC shouldn't get away with this. Silvia didn't deserve this.

Ferrett Steinmetz

Her mother and sister don't deserve this. Yet the IAC's analyzed Silvia's personality models until they found a way to shatter her resistance.

It wasn't even personal. Some Yak bigwig had said, "Get that woman back," and some AI combed Silvia's therapy records to find her pressure points. The terrorists I'd once bombed might be kept awake by nightmares, but that computerized voice held no concept of mercy.

If the IAC did inflict bodily horrors on Silvia's mother, their fabled automated punishment facilities would record the damage with no more emotion than a hospital computer logging a death. This wasn't terrorists orchestrating a kidnapping; it was a UPS algorithm figuring out the most efficient method to retrieve a package.

Which led to an even more terrifying implication: maybe *nobody* had made that decision to get Silvia back. Maybe some monitoring process had noted Silvia's absence, queued up a macroed response of "find the target's psychological weak points," and the IAC's manhunter-AIs had collated data.

No human mind made those choices. It was merely software, wrecking lives.

Everything I had worked so hard to avoid becoming.

Yet what had emotion gotten me? I knew how brutal the IAC was; I'd tossed data aside for sentiment. I should have known that fighting Donnie would deplete my combat effectiveness, that I wouldn't be able to return home for resupplies, that one man battling a multinational operation was a fool's errand.

The algorithms were, once again, smarter than our messy wetware.

"What did you mean when you called me an 'operative'?" Silvia asks.

My therapy-AIs could help me deflect the question. But dammit, when you send someone off to the firing squad the least you can do is be honest.

"They left you human hands, and a human face, and the . . . outline . . . of what'd be covered by clothing would be . . . uh . . ."

I stall, hoping Silvia will get the message, but she looks nauseous. Her gaze flicks down to look at her tendriled torso.

"It's . . . curvaceous," I finish, blushing.

She runs her fingers across her chest, then flicks her alien skin's moisture away in revulsion. "I think I know where you're going. But I want to hear you say it."

I sigh as I slip into mission-briefing mode. "You're faster than Donnie's armaments. You knew how to take out his weaponry. Put you in a pantsuit with the right faked credentials, and you could slip into any crowd without notice. I, uh . . . I don't think any government's got security prepared to deal with someone like you."

Her quiet is glacial. "They want me to kill people."

"I think that's the next stage of your training, yes. If I had to guess, you're fresh off the factory line. They were probably bringing you to an indoctrination facility to . . ."

What's the word? Brainwash? They wouldn't remove her panic disorder—they'd redirect it into panicking at disobedience. Computer-inflicted Skinner-box torture.

"To train you," I finish.

"How many have they done this to?"

She's thinking at this from a different angle than I am. That's hopeful. "I . . . don't know. I've never worked with the IAC before. This was a favor for a friend." I don't know why that's important to explain to her, but it is. "This was a training run—to see if this squad could handle IAC missions. I don't think they'd have trusted this to Donnie's crew if you'd been their sole prototype. So . . . I'd guess there's others."

"You . . . seemed surprised to see me, yes? To see this?" She scrunches up again, an increasingly familiar crouch that blocks me from seeing her fibrous, wriggling torso.

"Yeah. That's . . . it's new."

"And if someone like—me—had killed people, you'd have heard of it?"

"Not necessarily. Not with the IAC. But there's been no high-

Ferrett Steinmetz

profile missions involving someone like you that I'm aware of." Though one wonders how much I *would* be aware of; I suspect the IAC's AIs have already broken into the NJPD's records to erase the logs of Silvia's attack.

She draws in one trembling breath. "Are they *all* panic-disorder victims?"

"I couldn't tell you for sure. But you say your mother booked you into an experimental treatment for panic disorder, which . . . seems to indicate the IAC was searching for subjects who met specific criteria. Could be these bodies work better with people whose neurochemistry puts them into a continual fight-or-flight loop."

"So what you're saying is . . ." She holds her belly tight, like she has a stomachache. "There's an IAC project where they hunt for people with panic disorders, and kidnap them, and remold them into assassins?"

"I can't be certain. But . . . that's the most likely conclusion."

"And we've got twenty-four hours to stop them."

Hope lifts me up. Yet I have to leave emotion behind, use algorithmic logic to talk her out of rebelling.

"We can't *stop* them, Silvia. We haven't even avoided the cops. If we do escape police custody, we still don't have a repair lab for me to get refitted. If we find a lab, chances are good the IAC's analysts have anticipated we'll go there. Even if we avoid the pitfalls and somehow figure out where this prison facility is, our chances of destroying it are minimal. And none of that protects your family."

"I don't *care!*"

Silvia's fists shatter the concrete, bury themselves up to the elbows in clay.

"Do you know what my mother gave up for me?" she asks.

"No." This time it feels right to slump next to her, bumping my artificial shoulder against her genetically engineered one.

"Everything," she whispers. "She had to get a job that would let her call in sick whenever I had a breakdown, so . . . she got fired a lot. She had a job as a pediatrician, but those became harder to find as the auto-docs got more efficient. Yet she never complained. She worked her ass off to keep me in therapy. She took me to church whenever I lost faith with God. She researched what jobs I could hold down, and when she discovered an experimental treatment that helped panic disorders she fought for me to get into the program. She gave up everything for me."

I swallow back envy. When I told my friends I planned on severing my own limbs, my combat buddies told me I was getting too into body-hacking. Sure, I pushed my friends away when they told me to drop the chrome, but . . . I was hoping they'd push back.

Despite Silvia's problems, she had something to lose.

"Your mom sounds extraordinary."

She rests her hand on my thigh. "Someday I'll tell you about my sister. But that's where the IAC fails, you see?"

"I don't."

"What *it* knows is that I'm terrified Mama did all that for nothing, right? What if Mama's wasted her life shepherding some—some broken-down daughter who she should have let *die*."

I put my arm around her. "Hey now." The reassurance feels lame. "Hey."

"*No!*" She shrugs me away. "That's how she is. She helps *everybody*. She's always bringing home people she met waiting on the unemployment lines. We bought her a spare bed for Christmas, because the people who kept sleeping over complained how uncomfortable the couch was; she called it the best gift she ever got. So you tell me, Mat . . .

"You think Mama would want me killing people to help the IAC? You think *God* will?"

I nod, then notice the way Silvia's craned her neck around to watch my reaction. This is no rhetorical question. I could shut her down by telling her her mother would never know what happened to Silvia anyway, and it's better to prioritize a single woman you know over faceless people you don't.

Except I used to kill those faceless people. My drones showed

Ferrett Steinmetz

me the children who got killed in collateral damage. I saw grief-stricken relatives staggering towards the mangled corpses; my cameras had tracked them as they fell to their knees, my microphones picking up their distant wailing.

I lost the ability to hand-wave casualties away.

I can't influence her decision, even though I burn to fight. Instead, I lift up my helmet so she can see my face. "Your mother will never know what happens either way, Silvia."

"I'll know. That's what the IAC's people can't comprehend. They know what scares me; they don't know why I'm scared. If I turn myself in, I betray who my family wants me to be. If I fight the IAC, then . . . oh, Lord, Mama . . . Vala . . . they're . . ."

She bolts for the door; I grab her. For once she doesn't punch my face in.

"I can't fight them all the way, Mat. I'm not that brave. I try to be, but I'm not. But . . . they gave us twenty-four hours because of that thirty-three percent uncertainty, right? Because they're not a hundred percent certain the message was passed on?"

It's a 35.3 percent uncertainty, but I don't correct her.

"If we don't get anywhere after twenty-four hours, I have to turn myself in. If I get Mama and Vala hurt and make no difference, then that'll destroy me. But we have to stop *something* before our time's up. But I . . ."

She hangs her head.

"I'm not some combat machine, Mat. I wasn't even a good home inspector. I can't do this alone. I hate to ask you, after everything you've done, but . . . you have to help me. I don't know how to *do* this alone."

"Silvia, I—"

"Don't say no."

"I'm not saying no, but I don't know what to do either. We need to find a refitting station. One the IAC won't expect us to go after. And we don't know where the IAC was going to take you, or what defenses they have."

"I don't *care!*" She shoves me backwards, all eight hundred pounds of me; I slam into the fuse box.

She flicker-kneels next to me, pressing her face to my forehead.

"Oh God, oh God, I'm sorry, Mat, I was born broken but they fucked me up worse, they broke me *so bad.*"

"They didn't break you," I tell her. "They forged you into a weapon."

She clutches onto that thought like a drowning sailor clutching onto a wreckage. She didn't volunteer to be a weapon—yet when she's looking to cut her enemies down, she's glad to have something to bring to the party.

"Not an experienced weapon though." She puffs, dejected. "Not like you. I'm sorry, Mat—I don't know what a refitting station *looks* like, let alone where to find one. I'd just strip Donnie's spare parts off and bolt 'em on."

It doesn't work that way.

Yet there *are* other ways to scavenge.

"Huh." I turn an idea over in my head, "I bet—"

An alert chimes. Herbie. Despite everything, Herbie made it to the house unseen.

"I've got a place to go," I tell her. "And I don't think this refit station's on the IAC's list."

We talk about movies on the two-hour drive down. Because movies are safe, and silence lets the uncomfortable questions swell.

"So . . . have you seen *The Godfather*?" I say, purposely naming an eighty-year-old movie that most people find dull.

"I *love The Godfather*!" she squeals, clapping her hands. "It's a little bloody, but such a classic drama about loyalty! You know about the oranges, right?"

The way she tilts her head indicates she's giving me her own test—but if she expects me to fail *Godfather* trivia, she's got another think coming.

Ferrett Steinmetz

"The deadliest fruit," I say dramatically. "Don Vito dies with an orange in his mouth, bowls of oranges are set before each of the five families . . ."

"Don't forget how the don buys himself oranges before he gets . . ."

Shot, she would have said.

She reaches down to pull a bullet out of her stomach, her gut's coiled masses still squeezing out the rounds shot deep into her body. Previously avulsed bullets, deformed from the impact, roll around clinking in the footwell; she drops this new addition down into the collection.

"So why do *you* like movies?" I ask, prodding us away from contemplation of the potential ambush awaiting us.

She shrinks into the seat, wrapping the seat belt around herself; clearly this was the wrong question. "It's what lets me stop thinking about stuff at the end of the day. Mama or Vala sit me on the couch, and watch movies with me until I stop pondering the day's screwups."

I can't tell if she's missing her family or doesn't like being reminded why she needs movies.

"Yeah, but . . ." I can match her awkward for awkward, as it turns out. "Why *old* movies? It's not like the new movies are any less distracting."

"You sound like Vala." I think I've made a mistake until a slow, beautiful smile creeps across her face. "She keeps telling me new movies are just as good, *hasta la madre*, why can't we watch something made this century? But . . . new movies aren't as good. They're all flash-cuts and whip-pans and *bam bam bam.*"

Her hands blur before her at superhuman speeds, relaying what the chaos of modern filmmaking feels like to her.

"New movies are too tense." Her voice quavers. "I like sinking into a shot. I like something nice and sedate, so I can lose myself in slow visuals and stop bothering people."

I'm trying to imagine her family calming her down after a tense action film. I realize managing Silvia's condition was a full-time job. She pushes her feet around in the footwell, doubtlessly remembering the threats the IAC made to her sister, the bullets making wind-chime tinkle noises. She shuffles, acquiring a rhythm.

"Musicals!" she says brightly. "You watch musicals? Nobody danced better than Ginger Rogers."

I raise an eyebrow. "Surely you mean Fred Astaire."

"No, I mean Ginger. Ginger did everything Fred did, but backwards and in high heels." She hugs herself happily, remembering old dance scenes. "I was a clumsy kid, but I'd watch Ginger and think, maybe someday *I* could be that graceful."

"Maybe you could be now."

"Maybe I *could* dance in this body! I could never get my legs to do what I wanted. But with these reflexes! Wouldn't that be something?" She grabs my arm, excited. "Can you program in dance sequences into your limbs? We could dance together."

"That would be . . ." I stop configuring my intrusion software to ponder how I'd reconfigure my artificial musculature loadouts for quick, rapid footwork. Copying Fred Astaire's movements would be trivial—there are packages I could install for body-mirroring—but I'd have to compensate for my increased body mass.

"I'm sorry," she whispers. "It's a dumb idea."

I realize I've been so busy pondering how to do it that I've let the conversation go dead.

"No, no," I reassure her. "It's an interesting challenge."

But the moment's passed. I talk when I should be silent and go silent when I should be talking.

"Ever see *Spinal Tap*?" I interject.

She wrinkles her nose. "I don't like comedies. Too much embarrassment. How about Indiana Jones?"

"You mean *Raiders of the Lost Ark*?" We hum the theme song, and our awkwardness vanishes into a happy debate about which Indiana Jones movies were the best—there are, we decide, only two

Ferrett Steinmetz

Raiders movies that count—which in turn extends into ranking the best Harrison Ford movies.

Then we debate which 1940s-era actor Harrison Ford is more like, Robert Mitchum or Humphrey Bogart. She doesn't like all the movies I do: she's much more prone to retreating into fluffy musicals; she doesn't like horror; she can't stand war movies. Yet finding someone who knows those *names* is a joy—it's like her imaginary friends know my imaginary friends.

She rests her hand on my thigh.

"Vala always dozes off when I put on the classic-film stream." She sighs. "It's nice talking to someone who likes this stuff."

In an ideal world, we'd hole up in my laboratory and show each other our favorite movies until we fell asleep.

Instead, I fret that I'm somehow taking advantage of her. I don't know what her touch means. Is it flirtatious? Friendly? Does she realize I can feel her fingers on my prosthetics as intensely as if she'd pressed her palm against my bare belly?

Does she even know she's doing it? She notes her palm spread across my thigh's armored plating, eyes widening; she snatches her hand back, pressing it to her chest as if her arm somehow got away from her.

Yet as we debate the merits of Orson Welles's directing—she thinks he's overrated and dreary, I think he's magnificent—her hand drifts back.

I don't mention it because I remember that awkward silence after the dance discussion. I don't want to make her self-conscious.

That's what I tell myself, anyway.

But honestly, it's been a while since anyone's touched me without fetishization. I have no lack of choices when it comes to partners—but in return, I have to satisfy their urges to couple with something freakish. I can't just be a person with them; I am an experience. They trail their fingers along my prosthetics like they're sizing up a new car, then waggle their eyebrows and ask me whether everything's artificial.

(For the record, my penis is the John Henry of biological equipment, staunchly refusing to be bested by any cyborg enhancements.)

Yet Silvia's touch is . . . it's honest. And I'm selfish. We're headed into death's teeth. I won't nudge a woman who's potentially in Stockholm syndrome into further confusing adrenaline with chemistry, but . . .

We both need this.

For now.

And as we finish off a rousing discussion on whether *The Big Lebowski* is a comedy or not, Herbie pulls to a stop across from a rusted security gate.

There's the workshop, hidden behind a snarl of barbed wire and walls pockmarked with bullet holes. Cameras whirr to track our approach, each spiked with anti-drone weaponry that can also target humans.

The walls are stained with graffiti, but one sign's been kept polished to a factory-fresh white: AN ENDOLITE-RUGER SHOWCASE FACILITY. And underneath that, a battered tin sign that reads: BY APPOINTMENT ONLY.

Beneath that, rows of funny signs: NO HABLO INGLESE? I'LL SPEAK TO YOU IN 12-GAUGE! DUE TO PRICE INCREASES IN AMMO, DO NOT EXPECT A WARNING SHOT. BEWARE OF ~~DOG~~ OWNER.

"*This* is where you buy your guns?" Silvia asks.

"Prosthetic armaments," I correct her absently. "Not this place specifically, but . . . places like this. Kiva sure didn't gussy this place up, but I've bought equipment from worse shops."

"I thought it'd be—I dunno, glass windows and polished chrome." She presses her nose against the window, looking closer as I break open Herbie's onboard intrusion computers. "You pay, what, millions of dollars for those? I thought they'd be housed in a luxury-car showroom."

"You can get them there, sure. And at the nice places, you have to make sure all the paperwork's filled out before you take your purchase home. Or Endolite-Ruger can designate Kiva's low-security shop as a showcase. And if you show up with a hundred thousand bucks in cash that fell off the turnip truck, then, well, you'd be surprised how often places like this get broken into."

"And you think we can break in?"

"If this was a high-end showroom? Not a chance. But the backroom showcases usually leave one pathway uncovered by cameras—so people can sneak in to collect their goods. If Kiva's shop security's anything like her system maintenance, I'm betting I can disable her defenses."

"So this should be easy."

I grunt as my first hacking attempts fail. "Not *that* easy, apparently. Guess her corporate masters held audits to ensure she patched her systems."

"Can we still get in?"

"Yeah. This still isn't great. Endolite-Ruger makes solid hardware, but they're old-school—they still believe in using human programmers. Give me a few minutes and I should get access."

"You're sure the IAC's alerts didn't catch you looking up this address?"

"This car's got an internet connection I've gone to great lengths to keep separate from mine. I didn't look up Kiva's name—I just searched for nearby Endolite-Ruger facilities, and it turns out she's listed as the proprietor here. And, well, she's dead and we'd never met before the mission, so I don't *think* this is on the IAC's primary connections list."

She crosses herself. "Poor thing."

"Bitch shot a cat."

"Fuck her, then."

"But yeah, Silvia. I'm not trying to feed your paranoia. But . . . the IAC *is* paranoia. Their systems saw a sudden power drain on an abandoned house within a radius of the firefight and concluded we were there. This is *somewhere* on the list of places they'd anticipate we'd go. I just hope they don't have infinite resources—if they're big enough to monitor every place we can flee to, we're as good as caught."

"*Are* we caught?"

"The only answer I'll ever give you, Silvia, is 'Not yet.'"

She frowns. "Baby steps," she mutters.

"And our first step is entering this surveillance-free zone." I pull up a map on Herbie's windshield, show her the overlapping camera-dark zones just wide enough for someone to pull a U-Haul into. "Once we get in there, I should be able to scrounge up enough equipment to bring me back up to speed."

She shivers.

"It'll be like *The Italian Job*," I reassure her. "You ever see *The Italian Job*?"

She leans back against the headrest, exhausted. "This isn't much like the movies, Mat."

I punch in the pathway. "No," I sigh. "It never is."

"This is a showcase?" Silvia asks.

"Oh, no, this is *great*." I step across the cracked concrete floor, my prosthetic toes kicking away crumpled beer cans and stray hex nuts. The showcased Endolite-Ruger hardware is housed in smudged glass cases placed artfully about the refitted garage, each spotless ceramic finish gleaming under dynamic spotlights—even though the effect is spoiled by a pair of stained panties tossed over an Airlift 686 calf replacement.

The hardware flexes in attraction mode as I approach—gunports irising open with Endolite-Ruger's trademarked *cht-tack* noise, prosthetic arms on stands flexing enticingly, a treadmill starting up to let two paired lower-limb replacements literally strut their stuff.

I flex Charybdis's ruined knuckles, hearing them grind—I feel guilty, being so attracted to these new prosthetics when poor pulverized Charybdis has been so loyal. Yet I've always had to be frugal in my investments; this is a shopping spree.

Kiva took her best equipment on the mission, but that's no handicap—I've always made do customizing midscale hardware.

Ferrett Steinmetz

I weigh pluses and drawbacks, deciding what loadout I'll go with: the Howitzer 3900 upper-limb series has finer sensory equipment but a notoriously sticky auto-feed, whereas the Phosphorous 4500s have less proprietary software I'll have to wipe before I can reinstall my preferred control packages—maybe I should load one onto each shoulder in an asymmetrical upper-limb configuration, even though the asymmetrical installation would require time-intensive manual calibration?

"This is so *sad*." Silvia flicker-crosses herself again.

I'd been so focused on the hardware, I hadn't even thought to check in on Silvia. She's walking in a slow circle around the unmade bed next to Kiva's changing station, wrinkling her nose at the stink of body odor, tapping the half-empty tequila bottles surrounding Kiva's bed.

"Do you all live like this?" She looks to me for confirmation that somehow, I'm not living in squalor.

The answer to that question depends on what she's seeing.

I can read Kiva's history by her furniture—across from the bed is the cigarette-burned couch seated before the big-screen television, where Kiva's mundane friends gathered. She sat in that special chair to the left, a throne designed to fit her outsized limbs.

The concrete floor glimmers with shards of broken beer bottles—an easy trick to impress the nonenhanced. You can William Tell bottles off their heads, you can have five drunk guys fling bottles into the air and explode them to the rhythm of your favorite song.

And there's manual guns racked on the wall across from her shooting range—she was a gun nut before she hacked herself. Doubtlessly Kiva's hangers-on held shooting contests that Kiva always won.

Hanging around with other body-hackers is like hanging with comedians—someone's always trying to one-up you. Kiva's technical incompetence would have put her at the bottom of any hacker's barrel. Easier to find yokels who can't afford the tech and dazzle 'em—you walk away with that slimy feeling of impressing a fifteen-year-old girl by buying her beer, but you can't deny the effectiveness.

My lab's a lot cleaner. I can keep it tidy because nobody ever visits. I tell myself isolation's more honest, I don't have friends sucking up to me.

Yet I'm pretty sure that if I brought her back to my place, Silvia would give me the same sad, sympathetic look.

"My work space has a cat," I say lamely.

She brightens. "What breed?"

"A Dyson. Hey, is that equipment still in the package?"

I move past her to uncover a pile of crates bearing the Endolite-Ruger logo. Inside, sealed in tight vacuum-formed packaging, are a pristine set of Battalion upper prosthetics and a matching set of Bulldozer-class leg replacements.

"Holy *shit*," I mutter, verifying they sent matching ammunition. "These aren't legal for civilian ownership. Did Endolite-Ruger trust her to sell to the black market?"

Silvia hangs back, reticent at the chest-beating the other limbs are displaying—attraction mode has them cycling through warlike motions, aiming at whoever comes near. "If it's that impressive, why didn't she wear it on the mission?"

"She doesn't—didn't—have access to Donnie's lawyer routines," I explain. "This has four hip-mounted RPG-77s, so it's an instant all-points bulletin to wear it in public. But she's opened the case—she probably wore it around the showroom to feel badass."

"So that's good, right? This is the firepower we need?"

I run my fingers along the Battalion's curved gunports, noting the heavy armaments—revolving cylinder shotguns designed to reduce short-range combatants to a fine mist, microgrenade launchers designed to blow through other body-hackers' armor, computer-targeted short-barrel rifles with vehicle-piercing ammunition preloaded. It's not infinite ammo—this loadout holds a dozen grenades and four RPGs.

Yet that's a lot, especially aimed at the right targets.

This will turn anywhere I go into a war zone.

"Mat?" Her hand, light on my shoulder. "Are you okay?"

—hitting the fire button before realizing the blur you'd tagged as a dog is walking on two legs—

"I don't want it to come to this." I bury my head in my hands but my fingers are mangled prosthetic chunks. "I can't get anyone killed, I *can't* . . . ."

She hugs me. Her cheek is cool against mine.

I breathe. *Focus on your breathing,* my therapist had said. She'd given me biofeedback routines to integrate with my operating system; I could have computer-honed sequences modulate this incoming panic attack.

Instead, I focus on Silvia's breathing. On the scent of her hair, the oils and delicate sweat and the faint odor of some industrial shampoo.

For a moment, I wonder if she's repulsed; I stink of cordite, motor oil, body odor. Then I remember: if she had any urge to withdraw, her body would have catapulted her away from me.

We are linked by our trauma. We rub cheeks, becoming one organism, our breaths synchronizing, the deadlines dissolving as we take this moment to focus on each other, feeling the tremors subside.

We are perfectly still. In perfect harmony.

We know this will not last. We accept that.

I accept that I will destroy myself to protect her.

Surrender to police 19:32:27.

I can't stop glancing at my timer as it counts down.

The clock has become my enemy. If we don't strike a blow in nineteen and a half hours, we might as well have given up when the drones arrived.

Yet jailbreaking the default OS on these prosthetics and installing a trusted open-source controller chews up precious hours—I remember how Donnie had root access to Kiva's old prosthetics, and I am *not* chancing he's got control on these.

So I wipe them down to bare metal, then find nonproprietary drivers to control the notoriously finicky Osprey hardware, and link them to work in conjunction with my central controllers.

According to the tutorials, this should take half an hour. But this is real life, and whenever I think I've got everything integrated it shoots up a cryptic code that signals an IRQ conflict or an unrecognized device or a failed diagnostics check.

I'm told the profanities I utter while troubleshooting hardware could burn the pubic hair off Satan himself.

Silvia paces back and forth so fast she's a blur, keeping her distance from the prosthetics vying for her attention. She's rooted through Kiva's possessions—"Doesn't she wear *clothes*?" Silvia yelled, smashing a storage chest in anger before she retreated into the corner muttering apologies and crossing herself.

But no, there's nothing here aside from the single pair of dubious panties and some moist towelettes. I keep my head down instead of intervening. I'm afraid she might ask me if there are any clothes at *my* house—and honestly, there's one set of jeans and a shirt for when I have to pass for human. The rest of the time I'm buck naked beneath my armor.

It had never occurred to me to feel ashamed of that before.

Yet Silvia won't stop pacing. She's leaping from corner to corner, quick as a fly, making it impossible to concentrate on bridging my proprietary bioresponse protocols into the core controllers.

"It's funny," she says, talking a little too fast for it to be funny. "I used to panic over stupid things. If we were out of Fresca, I'd lose it. If I didn't have a picture of the person who was meeting me at the home inspection, I'd break down. And I—I felt stupid for melting down at such trivial things, and I'd cut myself sometimes. But now!" She barks out a taut laugh. "I'm not saying I want to be in this much danger, but it's kind of nice knowing I'm panicking for *really good* reasons."

Ferrett Steinmetz

She stops to stare at me earnestly, a comedian waiting for a laugh—but I'm a beat too late, and she curls into a trembling ball and I have to spend fifteen long minutes sitting next to her with my hand on her back before she sniffles her way back to normality.

I can't stop thinking about that weird error message the left leg's device driver is throwing. I need these Endolite-Ruger Bulldozers attached to my pelvic chassis *now*, and I'm rattled because Silvia's rattled.

"You like movies," I say. "So why don't we watch a movie?"

She brightens. After a brief conversation about "movies Silvia's been meaning to see"—every good cinephile has a list of unwatched films they keep close to their heart—I stream *The Shawshank Redemption* onto Kiva's screen, which a) Silvia's never seen, and b) doesn't feature any notable violent scenes aside from that one scene with Andy, which I mark for fast-forwarding.

The couch sits right in front of the big screen, on the other side of the workshop. Except Silvia pulls Kiva's throne across the room like it doesn't weigh five hundred pounds, all so she can sit next to me at my workstation.

"That's some beautifully shadowy cinematography, isn't it?" she asks as the film begins, then glances over at me uneasily; I nod before stepping through another set of diagnostic checks. "Very chiaroscuro. Reminiscent of Welles's *The Third Man*—"

She's floating each thought across to me, pausing in between each sentence to give me room to speak up. My skin goose-pimples with embarrassment as I realize that to Silvia, "a movie" is a family activity where her mother and sister livestream their reactions to each other, a nice social distraction.

I want movies to be what bring us together. But I'm too used to movies being a background drone to stop me from drowning in silence, and so I'm reduced to curt nods as I try to kickstart an antiquated MEAN stack *and* pay attention to a woman I like.

Halfway through the scene where Andy asks Red for a rock hammer, she asks me a question I can't shrug away.

"Sorry, I—I wasn't listening." I wince.

Her face is a billboard of shame as she realizes I've been tuning her out to get work done: it had never occurred to her anyone would ask her to watch a movie and *not* want to discuss it.

She chokes out an apology and darts to the other side of the room.

"I'm watching!" I protest, trying to figure out how to explain the difference in our movie-watching habits to her—but that sucks up so much brainpower, it annihilates the error-reproduction pathway I'd been pondering.

Silvia retreats, giving me as much space as possible. The last thing she wants to be is an inconvenience, and yet here she is one, and she can't stand it.

I get some tech-time in thanks to Silvia's Herculean self-soothing as she paces in a blur, quietly praying—but then she heads into the bathroom. A mirror shatters. She shrieks.

Silvia just got a good look at herself for the first time.

I'd wager she's spent a lifetime learning to melt down unobtrusively—but her new body's instinctive reactions are bollixing the coping mechanisms she'd used to tuck her panic discreetly away.

After another hour of her knuckle-biting, she saunters over.

"This isn't working, Mat." She speaks with the therapeutic calmness of a woman who's psychoanalyzed her way into a solution. "I'm panicking, and that's distracting you, so we have to find another way."

"What's bothering you?"

"I'm not thirsty."

I stare, uncertain what that's supposed to mean.

"I don't even know what to drink," she says. "What happens if I need special nutrients, Mat? What if I have to barf over my food like Brundlefly? Maybe I'm shriveling inside unless the IAC feeds me my supplements! Maybe I'm—"

Ferrett Steinmetz

My HUD flashes:

Surrender to police 17:45:18.

I suppress my irritation.

Rule of threes says you can go three days without water, three weeks without food. I want to tell her we don't have time to deal with her diet, I have weaponry to fix.

But I can see how hard she's working to protect me from her madness.

Her interruptions may be irritating to me, but they're infuriating her. That's what mental illness is: the same stupid fear cropping up over and over again, reappearing long after you'd thought you'd sworn you'd fixed it.

The movies make being crazy look wild and imaginative, filled with fantastic delusions and intricate camerawork. But the truth is, mental illness is like a dull job you can't quit.

So I can't yell at Silvia for something she's fighting so hard to control. I mean, how would *I* react if I was a civilian shoved into some freaky hentai-body, my family threatened, on the run from both the IAC and some counterorganization as powerful *as* the IAC?

Shit, she's doing better than most people would. And to be fair, her body is hyperfast; who knows how many calories she's burned through?

I root through Kiva's fridge, wrinkling my nose in disgust. I have a Soylent dispenser at home that pours me nutrients tailored to my genetic profile. Kiva has a fridge stuffed with crusty hot-sauce bottles, a case of Keystone, and a leftover slice of pepperoni pizza.

I microwave the pizza. "Normally we'd follow wilderness rules and do a skin-contact test, but I'm pretty sure your—anatomy— wouldn't be designed for a Chicago deep-dish to ruin your cover. So take a bite, put it on your tongue for ten minutes. Don't chew.

If it tingles or burns, spit it out. If that works, we'll move to a test bite."

I head back to the Battalions, positive I've narrowed down the problem to a corrupted visual-cortex library.

Silvia grabs me. "No, Mat. Solve the bigger problem: I need something to *do*. At home, I was always fixing up the place—on bad nights my sister would tell me to go rebuild the garbage disposal, because if my hands weren't occupied then my mind would be. Give me a job."

"You did the repairs on your house?"

She crosses her arms. "I'm a home inspector. You think I just look at broken things and sigh?"

Well, *there's* a little eddy of sexism I'll have to examine later. I root around in Kiva's tool cabinets until I fish out a handheld synapse generator.

"See those black fibers?" I unscrew the plating on the Bulldozers. "Those are the artificial muscles that will drive my limbs. See where they're tethered?"

She flinches—her eyes widen as she focuses on the bright bronze casing of the internal ammunition feeds, realizing she's laying hands on a machine designed to murder people—

—I wait, bemused, for the inevitable flicker-cross, and sure enough I am not disappointed—

—then her eyes narrow as she follows the intertwining flow of a-muscles through the machine-smoothed joints. Her head twitches, birdlike, as she envisions how these parts move.

If I'd been more focused on Silvia, I would have brought her in to help hours ago—she punched Donnie with such precision, I should have realized the IAC's conditioned some primal, mechanical understanding into her.

Or maybe she was just good with tools to begin with.

I scrounge up a compressed-air sprayer, a drill, and a set of patch-pullers, set them next to her station. "Touch each artificial

Ferrett Steinmetz

muscle with the synapse generator; it should slacken. If it looks tense, call me. Use the air sprayer to ensure nothing's clogging up the a-muscle channels, then lubricate the joints."

"What happens if I screw it up?" She's correct to be worried; snapping an a-muscle drive in combat is usually game-over.

"I'll check your work," I assure her. "If you can repair a garbage disposal, you can do this."

She rubs her hands together fretfully, an accelerated flylike motion. I don't push her; either she'll do the work or she won't.

She decides she can.

Thankfully, the kid's a natural. I can see her deciding which muscle-clusters need to be prioritized. "Okay. Yeah. I can . . . I can do this. But I'm not—I'm not entirely comfortable renovating a walking artillery piece. Can you talk to me while I work?"

I arch an eyebrow. "You wanna hear me discussing the fine details of synchronized boot-up phases?"

She bites her lip as she picks up the synapse generator. "No better time to learn."

The weird thing is, explaining the hardware issues to her *helps*. Verbalizing the process forces me to detail what I expect the code to do, which makes it easier to see where my assumptions are wrong. And having someone nodding along as I explain it to her makes me less frustrated, because she's my confirmation the problem's *not* as obvious as I'd like it to be.

And whether it's personality or IAC conditioning or both, Silvia turns out to be an intuitive maintenance person. She asks the right questions about how to hook the artificial muscles up to create smooth motion, pinpointing the ragged connections that Kiva overclocked. She suggests first-level workarounds—rerouted musculatures that seem initially good but have subtle drawbacks.

She's doing what I do—distancing herself from the ramifications of her work by focusing on the technical details. Except *she* needs to have a running commentary as we discuss it.

Which is . . . actually kind of nice.

At some point, Silvia eats the pizza.

The HUD is still blinking Surrender to police 16:12:46 by the time I'm comfortable the Bulldozers and Battalions have full functionality. Not only do I have the hardware online, Silvia's given it a marginal once-over.

Accent on "marginal." If I had my druthers, I'd spend the next forty-eight hours going over these four limbs one piece at a time. The calibrations I've managed have been shoddy—I hate trusting manufacturers' specs, but a proper sighting run would waste precious ammunition.

Though we *could* do an alt-ammo loadout and do some accuracy tests on Kiva's firing range.

You know why you spend weeks analyzing data after every mission?

I shake my head, but my therapist's voice refuses to go away.

It's a trauma response. You want to believe this chaotic world is predictable. But your best analysis gets done within three days; the month of seclusion is your way of coping with post-traumatic stress disorder.

"That's not true," I mutter, the same denial I'd given her before I'd stopped going to therapy. "Preparation is critical."

You tell yourself that preparation will make the next mission perfect—but has that ever worked?

"We'll be *fine*," I whisper, admitting we have no plan after "get Mat refurbished," and I'm trying to run out the clock through endless refinements rather than wonder if there *is* a trail for us to follow.

"Are you okay?" Silvia strokes the back of my neck. Her touch shocks me back to reality. The replacement prosthetics aren't as tuned as I'd like, but being a millimeter off target won't make a difference in most combat situations.

"Silvia—" Words swell up on my tongue, clog my throat. "I need to switch into the new prosthetics."

"What can I do to help?"

"Nothing. It's just . . . kind of . . . intimate."

That's the other reason I'm stalling.

"Intimate?" She frowns, studying my face. "I'm sorry. I don't understand."

"There's no human intervention." I point to Kiva's attachment station: it's a large, circular spot in the center of a web of servos. It looks a bit like Da Vinci's *Vitruvian Man*; put me in the center, and the machine precision-scans me before attaching the limbs. "The alignments with my physical body have to be precise. But there's a . . . transition."

How do I tell her there'll be a time when I'll be reduced to an amputated stub—armless, legless, naked—cradled like an infant at the mercy of machines?

How do I admit to myself that all this machinery is monstrous overcompensation?

"I don't like people watching me then," I finish.

I wish she wasn't smart enough to figure out what I meant.

"Oh," she says. I brace myself for the usual reassurances: *it doesn't matter, I won't think less of you, it'll be okay—*

Instead, she plops down on the workbench. "I'm sorry."

I know what she means: *I'm sorry I'm not strong enough to be alone for an hour without dissolving into panic. I'm sorry I have to put you through this.*

I'm sorry you have to be the strong one.

But sometimes, acknowledging the toll is enough.

"I'll be fine," I tell her. "Let's shift these limbs into position for transfer."

Silvia pulls up a chair as the attachment station's extensors unscrew Scylla and Charybdis and my legs, precise mechanisms teasing the good hardware free from the cracked nuBone hardpoints.

Silvia can't look away. She's trying to give me privacy, but each noise the station makes causes her to flicker back around apologetically. She's never seen anything like this.

"It's okay," I say. "It's okay."

Given permission, she stares deep into my eyes as gentle grips slide underneath my scooped-out armpits, the attachment station clutching me tight in preparation for separation.

Silvia hunches forward, focusing a solicitous gaze at me as if I am the most important thing in this technological web; the noise of the drills fades into the background as Silvia frowns in concentration, trying to put herself in my position, trying to let me understand, *You are not alone.*

Doesn't she understand having someone to lose is the scariest thing of all?

Three beeps and a quadrilateral tug, and my limbs are removed.

I am naked in a way I've never allowed myself to be before another human being. She's not a doctor, she's an innocent bystander who thought people like me were freaks, and when I'm stuck between limbs like this, I am . . .

Tears well up in my eyes, glistening red as laser-scanners measure my body.

She holds her gaze on me; multiple calipers work in conjunction, squeezing the cracked hardpoints tight so nuBone caulking guns can squirt a fresh mix of sealant chemicals onto them before bathing them in UV light to cure them into a spot-repair. I'm trying to concentrate on the technical details but I'm a shivering amputee lump, a broken specimen held up for examination and I'm crying, I can't stop crying.

Silvia languidly stretches out one arm, examining its striated green fibers. And I realize: ever since I've met her she's kept her limbs hugged tight against her body, avoiding putting them where she can see them, doing her best to hide what was done to her.

She cocks her head.

She's inviting me to investigate her as well.

Ferrett Steinmetz

I frown. There's nothing wrong with her body. It's alien, I know it's not what *she* wanted, but that body represents someone I have come to hold in great affection, and why would I—

Oh.

Oh.

"It's not your shame." The tiny hairs on her arms ripple as she examines herself clinically. Her new body's a manifestation of her self-hatred; her panic disorder's always made her feel like a freak, and now she's eternally tagged as something inhuman. "It's mine."

She taps my chest, crossing a seven-foot distance faster than I can blink.

"It's not my shame," she says. "It's yours."

"Ours," I reply.

She blinks, realizing the vast wealth of flaws that bind us, realizing that yes, we are in a relationship whether we want to be or not, we were forced by circumstance into baring ourselves to each other.

We can either embrace that or shatter.

She flattens her palm against my chest, bridging the gap between us, connecting her broken self to my broken self.

"Ours," she says, and the station fuses the reforged limbs to my body.

As it makes me whole again.

I stagger out of the attachment station. These limbs are much heavier than my old ones, almost Donnie-class weight, and the refurbished nuBone hardpoints are creaking.

The hot-patched anchors will hold, barring combat-level stress— but the hardpoints are still anchored in reinforced bone. Moving around has the twinge of an old back injury.

I order my biomedical assistants to inject analgesics, and—

"You okay?" Silvia asks.

I bend down to pick up a socket wrench to test the calibrations;

the diagnostics bring up happy rows of green lights. "I realized I don't have a name for these guys."

She snorts. "You name your limbs?"

"Just the arms," I say, as if that makes it less crazy. I'm pondering the great fighters of mythology—Zeus and Kronos, Hulk and Thor . . .

"Vito and Michael," Silvia says.

"The Godfathers? They're not my first choice when I think of raw power."

"They were outgunned from the beginning." She runs her fingers down Vito's armor plating; the haptic feedback transmits her touch so intensely I feel it tingle down my spine. "They survived thanks to cunning. Their power didn't rest in their weaponry."

I hesitate. "They weren't good guys, Silvia."

"But they took care of their families."

I nod and key the new limb identifiers into my software: VITO and MICHAEL.

The patented *cht-tack* noise of Endolite-Ruger gunports loading ammo into the chamber echoes across the sales floor.

Wait. How did that happen? I'd put these prosthetics into safety mode before attaching them. I run an inventory, verify all bullets are hot in the chamber. They are.

But the showroom prosthetics have all exited attraction mode. Every display model is aimed at me.

"You chose criminal names for criminal guns," Donnie's voice says from the overhead speakers. "Makes me feel better about turning you folks in."

Silvia's body hairs twitch in every direction; she's not sure which showroom prosthetic to go after.

"I wouldn't move," Donnie says. "These babies are primed to put a bullet through Mat's skull. Good thing I woke up before he put his body armor back on, right?"

Ferrett Steinmetz

"You're bluffing." I wait for the sound profile analyses to tell me if he is. "Nobody keeps live ammo in the showcase weapons." Because if someone hacks into your sample prosthetics' simplified configurations, they could shoot you like Donnie's about to shoot me.

"Nobody *means* to," Donnie replies, infuriatingly casual. "But Kiva, well, those beer cans on the floor tell you she wasn't good about putting her toys away. She left a clip in one after taking it for a spin—and thank *God* I have root access to her software, otherwise I don't know *how* I would have corralled you crazy kids in."

The sound analyses come in: he's not bluffing. The showroom's simultaneous activation makes it impossible for my onboard computers to tell *which* prosthetic is armed.

Yet they can tell the difference between a dry-fire and a live-load.

One's loaded.

"What do I do, Mat?" Silvia asks. "Tell me what I should—"

"Before you think you can walk her through this, Mat, know my linguistics analysis routines are checking your every word for instructions. If they hear anything that sounds remotely like a suggestion as to how you can escape, they will splatter your synapses before you complete your sentence."

"Why not tell me to be quiet?"

I can practically hear him shrug. "Someone's gotta calm her down."

Great. The IAC's given him documents on Silvia's condition. Which means, somehow, he's still working for them.

"And you *wanna* be calm, little one," Donnie continues, switching his attention to Silvia. "Ever watch someone you love get shot in the face? It's not pretty. Knocks the wind out of you. Hell, Mat only saw death happen through a drone's cameras, and he's not been right in the head since."

"What happened to the admiration you had for me?" I ask.

"Still have it. Heck, man, you're the only man I'd trust to take you down. You *taught* me how to circumvent your onboard defenses!"

"I taught you what?"

He plays back an old mission log. "*If you authorize that fire, well, my microphones would pick up you had given the green light to kill me. And my countermeasures would kick in, and they would blow the shit out of your Ordnance 6000s before your hammers fell on ammo.*"

Somehow, hearing what I'd once told Kiva makes this worse. With a normal body-hacker, I might risk that his capture-to-fire time is below my optimized CTF—but this is Donnie. I'd never get the shot off.

"Except my pet prosthetics aren't aimed at your gunports," Donnie says cheerfully. "They're aimed right in the center of your left eye. They'll blast your soft cortex the instant they sense your gunports aiming at anything—isn't that respect? Oh, my friend, I was *so careful* once the drugs wore off and I realized where you were."

I suppress a double take, lest the prosthetics take that for a hostile motion. "This was the first place you looked?"

"I wish!" His boyish enthusiasm is even more hateful. "Nah, my IAC contacts gave me a *big* ol' list of places they thought you might go, sorted by percentage chance that you'd go there—they said they were staking out the top twenty locales. But if I saw a place that seemed more likely, based on our past history, they asked me to clue them in. Even though they deemed 'Kiva's Endolite-Ruger facilities' as a distant .12 percent probability, I knew that was where you'd be."

He chuckles. "I thought I'd catch you with your pants down. Figured you'd spend at least another six hours tweaking your loadouts. But hey, looks like someone can change your habits."

Silvia shivers, ignoring the leering tone in Donnie's voice. "So when's the IAC arriving?"

"They're not," I tell her. "He wants to capture us himself, and get back into the IAC's good graces."

"BING-BING-BING-BING!" Donnie says. "Now you folks stay right there while I drive on down to collect my prize. And Silvia—

when I arrive, no funny business. I fear the small-arms fire from the cops might have given you the impression you're invulnerable, but my contacts have informed me a high-explosive shell can tear your body to shreds just like anything else caught in mortar fire. Let's make sure nobody gets hurt."

"Except the people they'll brainwash me to assassinate." Silvia's head droops as she surrenders.

"If it helps, I'm told the people you'll be tasked to kill are the total bastards. Threatening innocents gets good folks nice and compliant."

"Thanks."

"Now. Peace-tie your limbs, Mattie. Lemme see you glow that nice, surrendering purple."

I look at the display prosthetics—eternally vigilant, primed to act faster than I can. Even if I knew which one had the live ammunition, I'd never hit it before its automated routines sensed my intent.

I ponder whether I could throw the socket wrench I'm holding. But if he can outdraw my guns, he'd put a bullet through my eye when I drew my arm back.

Sighing, I command my armaments to stand down. Silvia's face looks pale in the reassuring indigo light tracing my limbs. Even if I wanted to bring my armaments online, I wouldn't be able to fire until fifteen minutes after I disabled my peace-tie.

I remember hacking the peace-tie system once, and deciding it would be too disruptive. What I wouldn't give to download that program from my repository—but I have to assume the IAC's cracked my every account. My repos have almost certainly been compromised with IAC-packaged malware.

"Hang tight," Donnie says. "I'll be there in an hour."

It'd take me longer than an hour to verify the peace-tie breaking software was clean. I won't be able to help Silvia. Not directly.

But maybe I can help her escape. I don't know how far she'd get without me, but it's farther than surrendering.

Weirdly, the scariest thing about my death is knowing Silvia would see it. A headshot is Donnie's sign of respect; he could have targeted my pancreas, given me a long, agonizing death. But Silvia . . .

Could I get her to look away? If I yelled "Run, Silvia!"—well, she couldn't stop herself from reflexively turning back to watch me in the attachment station. Me shouting will draw her attention just before the guns splatter my brains in visceral pyrotechnics.

I don't mind dying. But I do mind my last moments being used to fuel someone else's PTSD.

I can't believe I'm trying to solve a puzzle that ends in me dying when nobody's watching.

"Oh, and Mat—you're thinking about making a big sacrifice, telling Silvia to go on without you. Except she won't get far. If that gun fires, it also wires an alert to the police station informing them two cop killers are here. This isn't like the freeway in a nice neighborhood, Mat—this is a bad neighborhood, where the police drones are always overhead. She'll flee, but if the IAC doesn't get her, the cops will."

I'm still caught several words back. "We're not cop killers."

"All those poor cops at the scene: dead from prosthetic armament gunfire." Donnie's voice oozes with fake mourning. "Shame you didn't leave any live witnesses to your crime."

"That's the IAC, you motherfucker! That's what they brought you back online to do, didn't they? To cover their tracks? They fucking murdered the cops who saw us, and you'll testify—"

"Mat," Silvia whispers. She slumps to the ground beside me. "Stop.

"It's over."

Tactically speaking, this isn't a bad situation.

Silvia's cross-legged on the ground, hyperventilating. But as far as I can tell, there's only one gun pointed at me.

Ferrett Steinmetz

I replay his words: *My pet prosthetics aren't aimed at your gun-ports. They're aimed right in the center of your left eye.*

He got cocky. He shouldn't have told me where he was aiming.

Silvia's a coiled spring of hyperfast reflexes, so quick she could leap in front of me like the Secret Service. The fire wouldn't penetrate her reengineered body; the crumpled bullets in Herbie's foot wells proved that.

Donnie knows his hand is weak. That's why he's programmed the prosthetics to prevent me from telling Silvia what to do. He knows Silvia's the key.

The problem is, *Silvia* doesn't know Silvia is the key.

I look over, and my heart breaks. Her body's always moved with an insectile quickness, but now she's curled up like a dead bug you'd find on the windowsill.

"Silvia. You all right?"

No answer.

Pretty stupid question.

"This isn't over," I say. My skin prickles as I probe the edges of Donnie's language processors. "There are . . . ways."

The speakers overhead splutter as Donnie snorts. "For fuck's sake, guys, I'm *right here*. You think I'm some fucking Bond villain? I've got you folks on speakerphone while I'm getting in the car."

"It doesn't matter." Silvia's words fall to the ground like snowflakes, delicate and melting. "We lost."

This whole thing would be easier with a cigar. "Are you giving up because you believe it's hopeless, or are you giving up because you believe you're incompetent?"

Her head snaps around like an owl. "What difference does *that* make?"

I like anger. It means she gives a shit.

"I've been in worse situations, Silvia." I mean, not globally, because even if we escape we're still pursued by the police, *and* the IAC, *and* Donnie, *and* whoever was trying to kidnap Silvia from the IAC's clutches, but, you know, baby steps. "This isn't unwinnable."

"Yes it is."

"*Shut up*, Donnie!"

"No." Silvia hooks her fingers into her hair, pulls hard; I hear a sound like carpet being ripped up. "He's right. It's unwinnable *with me*. I'm not . . . fit . . . for this stress. I could barely hold down a job where I met people once a week. And, and, I was stupid to think I could become some neurotic *superhero*, taking down world-class secret *cabals* when I didn't know the first thing about detective work or computers or combat . . . ."

She trails off. Donnie stays quiet. I suspect his therapybots are telling him not to interrupt a self-sabotaging hostage.

"You can't hold my hand through all that, Mat," she finishes.

"I *can*." My chest aches with how badly I want to hold her. "Silvia, we've come this far, we can—"

"You realize I'm a drawback, right?"

Her statement is so soulless my words shrivel at the thought of debating her. Her self-hatred's ingrained into her emotional DNA.

"I'll never be an asset to you, Mat. I've seen what I do to my mother. I'll always be that person you have to work around—I've watched you do it already! You have to talk to me in the woods so I don't freak out, you have to put on a movie like I'm a *toddler* to keep me occupied—"

She settles down into that dead-bug position again, blocking the world out with her fingers. "I can't do this. I'm not strong."

"Oh for fuck's sake."

More words are barreling out of my throat by the time I see her cringe, but I'm so furious at her self-hatred that my own self-hatred rises up to battle it—

"Not *strong*?" I cough out a bitter laugh. "My God, Silvia, you've never seen my panic attacks—and you know why? Because when *I* get them, I hole myself up inside my servers for weeks at a time, too terrified to *talk* to anybody, trying to make the world logical with

Ferrett Steinmetz

mission replays and hardware tuning until the only people who'll hang with me are fucking kill-crazy psychos—"

"*Hey,*" Donnie protests. Let him bitch. If I stop I'll never say this again, so let it roll—

"Fucking hell, I got so panicked after some asshole blew off my left arm that I replaced it with massively armed overcompensation, and I *kept* lopping off limbs because I didn't feel safe unless I was walking around with a computerized *tank* protecting me! And you . . . Jesus, you . . ."

My heart's thumping so hard that when she makes eye contact with me, silently asking what I really think of her, I yank my gaze aside before I melt.

"I *know* how hard you fight to be normal. And you, you have a sister who loves you and a mother who still cares, while I've shoved away everybody except for backstabbing assholes like Donnie—"

The speakers crackle. "I will shoot your ass."

"*Take the shot, motherfucker!* Let the cops catch her! Think the IAC will hire you then?"

Donnie, mercifully, shuts the fuck up.

I return to Silvia, who's kneeling before me like I'm giving her a benediction.

"You've got a life, Silvia. It's not easy. Mental illness never is. But Jesus, the fact that you've built anything underneath that stress means you're stronger than a thousand normal people. If you weren't held down by some bad brain chemistry, you'd be a goddamned superhero. Hell, you *are* a superhero in my eyes."

Blood rushes to my face. This revelation's embarrassing, adolescent; she's the first person in years I've forged a connection with, and I've ruined it with gushing boyish adulation.

"You mean that?"

I hesitate; she touches me again. Her fingertips brush against my left prosthesis, stroking the warm metal to verify I'm real—

The prosthetics twitch, a wall of automatic warnings. She

doesn't notice them; she's too busy craning her neck around, trying to make eye contact.

But I'm staring at my HUD's alerts—now that I've configured my visual processors to look for a target, they've confirmed which gun is hot.

The pair of Sherman 1600 lower prostheses doing jumping jacks. They're the threat.

Even better: my readouts confirm that, yes, their gunports are indeed locked onto my left eye.

I know where the threat is, and how to neutralize it.

Yet I can't tell Silvia how. Worse, me processing this new info has left her waiting for an answer. Her fingertips have frozen on my armored plating, ready to withdraw.

"Yes," I say. "I mean every damn word. It has been an honor to fight alongside you, ma'am."

That should make things better. Instead, it fogs the air with awkwardness. Knowing we have this mutual respect doesn't tell us what to do with it.

"So what do we do now?"

"You back off," Donnie says. "No touching him, Silvia."

Her hand vanishes quick as a magician's trick, guilt flickering across her face.

She can't control her reflexes; whatever she wants, her body does. If I could convince her she *wanted* to be somewhere else, her body would take her there.

If I could convince her to jump in front of me, we could blow this popsicle stand. We'd still have to escape the cops, but . . . baby steps, Mat, baby steps.

Except I can't tell her; Donnie's computers are analyzing every word I say. We might be able to get past that if we shared some secret code, but . . .

Wait.

We *do* have a secret code.

"We'll stay put," I say. "Like Indy and Marion at the end of *Raiders of the Lost Ark*."

She closes her eyes in a reverie-soaked smile. "We stay tied to the pole, hoping that God uses the Ark of the Covenant to wipe everyone?"

That's our code.

I whistle the first bar of the Indiana Jones theme song. She whistles the rest back. The gun twitches, linking our warbling melody to decades-old *Raiders of the Lost Ark* movies.

But it lacks context.

I grip the socket wrench. Thank God I have something in my hands.

"It's stupid." Silvia's hand rests on my thigh again. "But even after everything that's happened, I'm . . . I'm glad you're here."

The great thing about this movie code is that Silvia doesn't have to know she knows it. She just has to pick up the vibration I'm laying down, and if she's not flirting this won't work.

"If I'd known I was going to be captured, I wouldn't have gotten myself this banged up in the process. I'm not the man you knew ten years ago."

"It's not the years, honey," she quotes back to me. "It's the mileage."

Okay. We're on the same page, quoting the same scene. So hopefully she's remembering what happens next in the movie, her knowledge of the plot mixing with what I hope to God is at least some attraction to me, and . . .

I'm going to quote the scene where Marion kisses Indy, and hope she goes for it.

My chest hurts. I can't recall ever being this nervous for a first kiss.

"That hurt," I say, in my best Indiana Jones drawl.

"Well, goddammit," she replies in her best Marion Ravenwood impression, "where *doesn't* it hurt?"

I look down at my elbow. "Here." I touch my chin to my neck rest. "Here."

I look at her.

"Here."

Fireworks.

The prosthetic empties an entire clip into her skull.

That does not stop our kiss.

My left arm chucks the socket wrench at the Shermans to knock them over.

That does not stop our kiss.

She's everything. The soft fullness of her lips, the sweet taste of her tongue, the way her hands knot up in my hair, the way she trembles as she presses her body against me.

"*Eyew,*" Donnie says.

His disgust changes the frame, transforms us from two people kissing into licking freaks. She's entrapped in cold machinery; her body is squirming coils grafted onto a human head.

"Oh, man, I wish this prosthetic's camera did *not* have such great resolution." His adolescent snigger is like itching powder. "Some things you don't need to see."

Silvia snakes out from my grasp, shrinking down, her eyes welling over with tears.

"*Shut! Up!*"

I grab the Shermans, fling them at the speakers above. Ninety pounds of carbon-fiber mesh smash into the overheads at eighty-six miles per hour, propelled by Vito and Michael's ferocious strength—they explode, raining down hex bolts and twisted circuitry.

Silvia shrieks, covering her head.

"That's a speaker, you imbecile," Donnie says, switching his broadcast to the TV screen. "What, do you think you've hurt me?"

"*Shut your stupid! Fucking! Face!*"

I grab an MBT-2350 upper limb and whirl it into the screen,

Ferrett Steinmetz

sending glass bouncing across the concrete. Yet that destruction's not enough—I have Vito's sensors pinpoint every speaker, send Kiva's equipment flying, silencing anywhere Donnie could shame us.

I'm pretty sure I'm screaming.

And by the time I'm done, I've demonstrated Vito and Michael's power without having fired one of my onboard weapons. Every speaker Donnie could use to speak to us is crumpled, every camera he could watch us through pulverized. Even though I've still got twelve minutes before the peace-tie firelock on my guns expires, these systems were designed to go toe-to-toe with light tanks.

Light tanks . . . or local police cruisers.

If that gun fires, it also wires an alert to the police station.

My metal hands are auto-massaging my temples again. This wasn't part of the plan. This was pointless destruction, I wasted precious time, the cops have had two minutes and thirty-six seconds to reroute drones overhead, which means I've fucked us for no good—

Someone cups my cheek.

"Mat?"

Silvia creeps into my vision, keeping a wary distance, uncertain how to help me.

Her face is suffused with such *concern*.

"I fucked up the plan, Silvia. This was—"

"You have a plan?"

"I always have a plan." I replay those words; sure enough, that wavering hitch makes me sound pathetic. "I . . . whenever I wasn't reprogramming Vito and Michael, I was checking local maps, looking for our next bolt-hole. I don't relax. Every moment of every day, I'm tracking escape routes and calculating threats and tabulating solutions."

Meeting her gaze is scarier than looking down the barrel of a gun.

"Is that okay?" That time my voice definitely cracks.

She shakes her head—not dismissing me, but dismissing this fear resonating between us. She gives a bell-like laugh and my body shakes in relief.

"It's who you are," she replies.

I'm not sure I can handle this much acceptance right now.

"But . . . where do we go now?" she asks.

"There's a smartcar share center thirteen point four miles from here. Twelve point two miles of that is freeway driving. It's late at night, so most smartcars will be homed and recharging. If we can make our way there, we can hide in one car, I can hack into the rest of them, and hopefully nobody will be able to figure out which car we're in as we send four hundred cars on random drives out into deep woods."

She claps her hands. "It's like a big old shell game!"

I grasp her shoulders. "Listen, Silvia. My combat systems won't be online for another ten minutes. And those highways will have people catching a ride home from the bars—they're not expecting a firefight. And even though the cops will come after us hard, they don't deserve this either. You have to keep everyone safe."

Her brown skin pales chalky white. "Mat, I—I can't control this body—if anyone shoots at me, I'll go for them—"

"The bullets in your head say otherwise."

She grimaces, reaching back to scratch her neck shyly—then flinches as her fingers run over the edges of the crumpled bullets in her skull. "I—I mean, we were kissing, and . . ."

I open up Herbie's door, wondering how surprised the cops will be once they find out what Herbie has beneath the hood. "That's a real compliment, Silvia. But that also means you can control your body. You just . . . don't know how yet. But I'll be doing everything I can to keep Herbie on the road, because those thirteen miles will be *long*. So can you—"

Floodlights stream in beneath the door. The whoosh of stealthed drone-copters kicking up wind—though thankfully, Kiva holed herself up inside a fortress with reinforced walls.

"Attention!" a voice bellows. "We track two heat signatures inside, and one peace-tied broadcast with an expiry of nine minutes forty-six seconds. Come out with your hands up, or lethal force will be authorized."

Ferrett Steinmetz

I pull on my body armor, then open Herbie's door for Silvia. I'm thinking of all the people between us and that smartcar center—hundreds of bystanders who might walk away with lost limbs. I imagine weeping relatives camped by grave sites, police funerals for brave men who didn't know they were chasing framed fugitives.

But there's no time. There's no time, and no plan. We're down to improvisation and prayers.

"Can you do this?"

She looks terrified.

She says yes.

I stole Herbie from a used-car lot. I mean, I paid for Herbie, but in untraceable cash, and in return the owner told me how to break into the lot.

(There's a reason I knew what Kiva was up to.)

Then I found a storage-unit facility with surveillance cameras that could be hacked, and spent long Saturday afternoons refitting a sturdy auto-car into a secret hackmobile. First thing installed was the illegal camouflage smartpaint and a properly anonymized internet access point, but I made other off-the-book purchases from dubious sources: self-sealing tires, carbon-mesh armor plating, stealth gunports, some severe surprises for anyone who thought my secret escape vehicle was just a Honda.

I've spent three years upgrading Herbie—and when I was done, sometimes I'd spend hours staring at him in something akin to love. Herbie was my real-life attempt at a Batmobile, the dream I drifted off to when limb maintenance got too tense—perfecting Scylla and Shiva and Roland always held that shivering tension of knowing I'd need their services come my next mission. Whereas Herbie was skylarking—sure, it was nice to have secret transportation, but how likely was it I'd wind up in a full-on vehicle-on-vehicle firefight?

Yet the truth about hardware is this: maintenance breeds affection. You come to know an equipment's quirks, come to admire its strengths. It's an intimacy greater, in some ways, than a lover.

And at any moment it could be destroyed. It's designed to *be* destroyed instead of you. Warfare chews up machinery and men alike.

And as the garage door goes up, I look over at Silvia and realize getting attached to anything before combat is a bad idea, such a bad idea.

Two drones shoot at Herbie's tires as we roar out onto the darkened street, and of course they hit, but the tires are self-repairing—it'll require more than a few bullets to take us down.

They also bathe us in police transit-override commands, which would root-access any street-legal car to pull meekly over to the side of the road, but naturally Herbie's configured to shrug those off.

The grainy streetlights flicker past us as Herbie's nav systems plot tight runs around the corners, Tokyo-drifting around warehouses, juking left to avoid a meter maid–bot scanning license plates and logging electronic tickets.

The drones fall back, following us at a discreet distance, targeting us with unwavering spotlights. More drones drift into view behind us, their rotors angling down as they divert from their usual patrols to match our speed.

"They're not firing," Silvia says, frowning.

"Police drones don't use lethal force." I think of the taser-induced heart attacks the ACLU has catalogued from drone interventions in vain attempts to outlaw their usage. "Well, not purposely, anyway. For legal purposes, the humans get to make the fatal decisions on-scene."

She looks around. "Then where are the cops?"

My eyeballs jerk from Herbie's LADAR readouts to the GPS dot that shows us how we are still eighteen agonizing minutes away from the smartcar facility. Everything's bathed in the purple glow of my damnably peace-tied limbs.

Yet even at three in the morning, there's unemployed dudes drinking forties on the street—they fumble out their smartphones as we rocket up the street, taking videos to sell to the manhunter-AIs. Which is bad news; if they knew we were headed this way, that means the cops' networks have marked us for civilian rewards and put out alerts along our most likely escape routes.

I was hoping to make it out of the populated zones first. Now I have to worry that some well-meaning civilian hurls himself in front of our car in the hopes our built-in automatic safety guards will force us to stop. If you don't get run over, you get a cash reward for helping capture a suspect.

People will die tonight, I think. I can see my blood pressure rising in my HUD.

I strap myself into my seat belt—and discover Vito and Michael are so much bulkier that my old safety straps don't fit. That's bad; the most badass body-hacker is still meat at the core. I will not survive a ninety-mile-an-hour car crash.

I tense as we blast through the final stoplight before the freeway entrance. The manhunter-AIs must have calculated we're headed for the highway; the only question is whether there were any patrol vehicles close enough to intercept. One car we might dodge past, two cars would block the highway entrance enough to give us a fight, and a triple would leave me trying to ram through a patrol car without a seat belt.

But no. Even though the cops' response times are computer coordinated—I suspect at least one napping cop has been jarred awake tonight when his vehicle automatically barreled out to answer the call—the question is not "what do the manhunter-AIs know" but "how quickly can they get the physical world to respond."

We blasted out of the garage two minutes ago.

"Keep your eyes peeled," I say as we roar onto the freeway, locking one arm into the restraining belts as our speed ticks up to Herbie's maximum speed of one hundred miles per hour. "Prioritize civilian safety. I'll handle incoming threats."

"Aren't you peace-tied?"

"Herbie will take care of some threats. You'll . . . pick up the slack."

"What do you expect *me* to do?"

"Improvise."

"I can't *improvise!*" Silvia cries. As we screech around a dawdling Nissan, Silvia stays stabilized by gripping the seat backs. She doesn't even realize she's doing it. "My mother had to walk me through sample homes for months, and that was just *home inspecting,* I'm not prepared to, to—wait, what do you think's going to happen?"

"If I knew what was going to happen, I would have prepared for it!" I'm prepping the cop-car hacking modules and double-checking my HUD for incoming threats and programming in threat-response packages for Herbie. "I'm sorry, Silvia—what I hope will happen is that I disable the cop cars the way I did back by the cargo containers, but war has a way of going wrong."

"War? I'm not prepared for war!" She crosses herself.

"Nobody's ever prepared for war, Silvia."

I don't tell her it would have been different if I'd trained as a combat soldier—those guys *do* prepare for war—but the Drone Corps trained us to fight through remote control. Still, Silvia lets out a small gasp as she takes in the dark road before us.

"The cars." Silvia crouches down to peer out the window like a kid on vacation for the first time. "They're pulling over."

Sure enough, as we cruise down the freeway's gentle curve, the smartcars and automated trucks part like the Red Sea, the city traffic overrides stopping them to make way for our progress. The street drones fall behind, their tiny motors unable to propel them at freeway speeds; a high-flying traffic drone takes over, ensuring we don't escape police surveillance. A couple of newsdrones buzz into view.

Ferrett Steinmetz

It's like we're the star of the show, the drones keeping their Broadway-bright spotlights on us as we sail down a stage cleared for our arrival.

I relax a bit; the manhunter-AIs could have coordinated a massive traffic jam to block our path. Yet some human mind must have decided those civilians might draw the ire of a man they believe is a cop killer, and put them out of harm's way.

I count the cars as we flash past, sighing relief; every person pulled over is another hapless schmuck who won't get pulped in a car wreck.

Still, the cops will intercept us well before we get to the smartcar hub's exit.

"Stabilize your rear deflectors," I tell Silvia. "Watch for enemy fighters."

"Are you quoting a movie at me?"

"It's not a movie, it's Star Wars."

"I haven't seen Star Wars!"

My to-do list, correctly parsing Silvia's words, automatically adds **Show Silvia Star Wars** to my upcoming tasks.

Sure enough, the blue-and-red strobes of two distant cop cars creep up into the rear window, getting larger as their beefy engines outpace Herbie's. My LADAR informs me they're a little over a mile back, but at this speed differential they should catch up with us in about two minutes.

That's great. I was worried they'd go for a head-on encounter. Then I realize our advantage:

The cops don't know what happened the last time we fought.

The IAC shot the survivors, wiped Silvia out of the footage, scrambled the logs. I'd rather we had seven alive cops and a nastier predicament, but I won't turn down an advantage.

Because if they don't know what happened, they have zero defenses against the zero-day exploit I used to control their vehicles the last time. (Not that government opsec would have sifted through the compromised vehicle logs, found the vulnerability, and patched it in the twelve hours since the shit went down, but still. Advantages are advantages.)

In addition, they are *not* scrambling the airwaves, most likely due to the risk of jamming some civilian's smartcar's internet connection during a high-speed freeway chase. Which leaves me free to send all the signals I want.

"We got this, Silvia." I sigh, relieved.

I thumb the switch to send my prerecorded broadcast back to the cops before they open fire: "Attention New Jersey's finest. My name is Mat, and I am being framed by the International Access Consortium for their kidnapping of Silvia Maldonado, who is also with me. Here is footage that explains our current fugitive status."

But because I never expect police to be reasonable until superior force has been trotted out, I also start the buffer-overflow hack.

A flood of replies comes back.

I frown: *What the hell hit us?* Then my fire walls light up with the yellow alerts signaling prevented attacks. *Thousands* of prevented attacks, most not even listed in my intrusion detection profile list, mysterious attempts to override my system that only got cut off because I am *meticulously* paranoid about scrubbing inbound data—

The cop cars just hit us with a hundred zero-day attacks.

Cops don't have that firepower.

"Oh fuck," I mutter, noticing the confused cops pounding the dashboards inside the vehicles, trying to retake control as their cars cruise to intercept us.

"What?" Silvia asks.

The police speakers blare, *"Attention, Silvia Maldonado. Your most likely destination is the smartcar hub two exits down. We know everything. Surrender."*

Silvia pounds her seat hard enough to dent the metal beneath. "What could go worse?"

The other agency trying to acquire Silvia could intercept us, but

I don't say that because I'm overwhelmed thinking about the enemy I already know.

I haul back the smartpaint cover to turn us into a pseudo convertible, keeping the bulletproof windows up so nobody can get an easy headshot. I assign a new tether for Herbie: *don't let us get more than four hundred meters away from Silvia.* The drones' spotlights above light Herbie's insides a fluorescent white.

"Don't open the roof! That's our cover!" Silvia yelps.

"We can't hole up inside this car," I explain. "You need room to maneuver."

"To do *what?*"

I slap Herbie's dashboard. "This does not have the firepower to disable several incoming cop cars." I slap my shoulder. "This *does*, but it won't be online for another eight minutes. So you have to find some way to save those poor trapped cops."

"How will I—"

Two trucks slowing down to pull over suddenly speed back up, veer into the center of the freeway, smash into each other hard enough to send windshield glass flying. Herbie's anti-accident routines compensate even though the two trucks are a half mile away, plotting a smooth arc through the still-moving wreckage.

Which is good, because I still have no seat belt.

"Attention, Mat Webb. Those two trucks had no passengers. If you do not surrender Silvia Maldonado to our care, we will use the police transit overrides to cause a fatal collision involving every car within broadcast range. The next vehicles to arrive will contain two families taking a road trip to Florida."

"Fuck." I start reprogramming Herbie's threat packages, realizing Herbie wasn't designed for this, he's too slow, why did I concentrate on defense when I needed more firepower—

Silvia grabs my shoulder. "What do we *do?*"

I suppress my urge to scream at her. That won't help. "I told you! Get to the cop cars, get the cops out safely, disable the vehicles."

"But *how?*"

"Silvia, I can't walk you through this."

Her objection catches in her throat. She glances around the car, desperate for a tutorial—and in that moment, I realize how her mother's concern for Silvia has inadvertently made Silvia's troubles worse, how Silvia's come to believe she can't do anything without her mother's guidance; her family's protection's made her terrified of the unknown.

I don't have time to say that, so instead I stop programming to give her my full attention. For this brief instant, she is my world.

"Silvia. You can do this."

I don't say, "You have to do this," because even I'm creaking under the strain of that particular concept. Instead, I try to convey with my crooked smile that I'll love her even if it goes wrong.

It's almost enough.

"Mat, I—"

"Attention, Silvia Maldonado." In the cop cars, the windshields flare with gunshots as the police vainly try to shoot their way free. *"The following broadcast is being recorded live."*

A woman screaming echoes across the freeway.

"I'll tell you what you want to know!" an older voice begs. *"Please, stop torturing her!"*

A hydraulic noise hums as some dreadful machinery kicks into gear. The screaming rises in pitch, followed by a wet snap.

"Stop!" the woman shrieks. *"Stop! Tell us what you want! I'll do anything, just stop hurting Vala!"*

"You motherfuckers!" Silvia yells. In a flicker-flash she leaps towards the cops, her hands crooked in rage—the air fills with gunfire as the cop cars open up on her.

Two rented Hyundais down the road come into the police over-rides' range. They curve out to opposite sides of the freeway, speeding up, putting enough space between themselves to veer into each other with maximally efficient mayhem—

I see bright birthday balloons jouncing in a car, watch kids screaming—this trip was someone's present—

I install Herbie's new threat package, incomplete as it is—

His front guns fire as the two cars start their turn into each other. Their rear tires blow out in sprays of rubber, the drag from the vaporized tires warping the smooth arc that would bring them into collision, turning it into an uncontrolled spin—

As they start to spin, Herbie's fire-at-all-tires routine shreds their visible front tires as well.

The car with the balloons auto-switches into safety-protection mode and slews to the roadside. The other shudders, its AI overwhelmed by complex physical vectors. It upends, rolling in a tumble, flipping over and over as Herbie slams on the brakes to navigate past the wreckage, me thrown up against the dashboard.

I see the smoking car tumbling to a stop, the windows pressed parachute-white with protective canvas airbags. There's no movement from inside—but would I notice any as we pass by at sixty miles per hour?

They're probably okay. And even if they're not okay, a rollover at fifty miles per hour is more survivable than a planned fatal crash at ninety miles per hour, or at least I tell myself that and whoah, Vito just injected me with anti-trauma drugs.

That family is fine. They've got concussions, but they're fine.

The IAC's manhunter-AIs were willing to kill them to rattle me. That's what I have to remember. And—

Herbie's still slowing. Why are we still slowing down?

I turn around. We're slowing down because Silvia's approaching Herbie's tether radius. Now that they have Silvia, the cop cars are slowing down to turn around—why wouldn't they? The IAC doesn't give a crap about me; they want Silvia, that was why they played that excerpt—

If the cop cars peel away at top speed, they're thirty miles per hour faster than I am.

I yell to Silvia, but they're blaring excerpts from her family's torture to drown me out. I raise Vito to fire at her, but my peace-ties still have four minutes and fifty seconds before they expire.

Worse, she realizes what's happening as the distance between us expands. She looks towards me, confused at first, but whenever she tries to leap back another onboard system fires to get her reflexive defensives back online. She whirls to smash the cop car's gunports, her head constantly trying to reorient itself to focus on me, but there's always some other assault incoming as the cars back off.

I depolarize my faceplate to give her my best Indiana Jones look. I point to my chin.

"Here."

It's not, I should stress, that Silvia wants to kiss me that badly. Though, you know, I'll put my kissing skills right up there with my maintenance skills.

I'm reminding her that a kiss is how she ignored bullets.

She straightens on the cop car's hood, twitching as the IAC's AIs buzz her with tasers, bounce tear-gas canisters off her face. Her body heaves as she tries to control herself, clenching her hands as she battles past her body's reflexive need to respond to overt force.

She crouches on the hood in a Spider-Man pose, her face contorted with concentration, literally shrugging off bullets as she focuses on me.

Then she gives me one clear gaze, her brow creased with worry, as if to ask: *I can do this, right?*

I risk a look back: *You can do this, Silvia.*

She leaps a hundred yards to sail across the widening distance, landing squarely in Herbie's back seat.

"I did it!" she cries, her face flushed with excitement. She shoves her hand above the bulletproof windows, flinches as a bullet catches her in the palm of her hand, shuddering as she represses the urge to leap after her attackers. "I *did* it, Mat!"

Ferrett Steinmetz

"This incoming vehicle has an exhausted factory worker who wants to go home and sleep his night off."

Herbie's guns fire as he speeds up, vaporizing the front tires of a car zooming by on the grassy median's far side, the car slewing into a barely controlled skid as its protective AI kicks into gear. I force a slo-mo replay of vacationing family, those windows still swollen tight with airbags—they're so far behind I can't see if they survived—

"I can do this." Silvia squeezes her hands into happy fists. "I can *do* this."

Another broadcast wet snap. *"Tell me what you want, please, I'll give it to you, stop!"* Followed by: *"Surrender and end your loved ones' torture, Silvia Maldonado, their pain will never cease until you give yourself over to us—oh no, this vehicle's got a tipsy young couple on their way back home to make love."*

Herbie's racing down the freeway, firing at inbound cars, sending traffic spinning out into guardrails with most of their momentum dispersed. But when I say "most," that's still a thirty-five-miles-per-hour crash, whiplashy if not fatal, so I'm querying Herbie's onboard physics engines to prevent the spinouts, managing a complex web of interactions to stop the IAC's kamikaze tendencies.

"Mat? Are you okay?"

"People are dying, Silvia—should we stop?"

The words flow out of my mouth before I realize I've said them. But sure enough, even the *idea* of surrender steals the wind from Silvia's newfound sails; she grips the seat to steady herself even though we're moving in a straight line.

She crouches down, her lips close to my faceplate's audio pickups. Her breath is ragged.

"They won't let Mama and Vala go, will they?" she asks. "Now the IAC's brought them in, they're . . . they're loose ends, aren't they?"

I hadn't thought that far ahead, but Silvia's mother and sister haven't been my priorities. Yet when I consider their situation through Silvia's perspective, the odds that the IAC would kidnap two innocent people, torture them, and then set them free doesn't seem in line with the IAC's motivations. At best, Silvia's family will spend their lives in one of the IAC's fabled automated punishment facilities.

"No," I say. "I don't think so."

"And they won't kill them either. Otherwise they've got no leverage on me if I turn myself in."

They can torture you, I think, but as I look into Silvia's face I see her indomitable willpower. The same ferocity that kept Silvia going through mental disorders won't let her give in to the people who murdered her family.

Some people, when they panic, they run, I told her once. *The reason they chose you, Silvia, shitty as that is, is because when you're scared . . . you fight.*

"I'm not sure they can break you without your family."

"Then this is a rescue mission," she says calmly, as Herbie blows past what the IAC informs me is an ER nurse on her way home off to the side of the road. "We have to get to that smartcar hub, lose this trail, and find a way to save Mama and Vala."

"This man has a six-year-old daughter at home who loves him more than anything—whoops, you just broke his neck."

"I don't know if I can do this, Silvia." I can't concentrate on the blur of GUIs; I'm trying to refine Herbie's routines for safely terminating a car's momentum, but I'm thinking of weeping kids at their father's funeral.

Silvia grabs my chin. "They'll lie to you to break you."

"They're doing a pretty good job." As if to accentuate that, the cop cars rake Herbie's armor plating with anti-vehicle armaments. Even though I know Herbie can take it, I flinch.

"They know where *I'll* break." Silvia thumps her chest. "They know where *you'll* break." She presses her palm across my bullet-cracked armor. "But they don't know what happens when the two of us are together. Now save those people while I take care of those cars."

Ferrett Steinmetz

She leaps back to the cop cars, which veer aside once they realize she's coming for them—but she's anticipated their motion, grabs the bumper, hauls herself up over the hood as she laughs, realizing what a gift the IAC has given her—

And I instruct my audio-filters to strip out the cop cars' announcements—she's right, it's propaganda—as I do on-the-fly adjustments to see the best place to hit a tire. It's not easy; the IAC's now aware my main defense is blowing out tires, so they're swerving the cars the second they come into police override range.

But I'm analyzing the logs with a rapidity that years of huddling inside Yoyodyne Labs gave me, each car giving me more data to build a physics model that tells us where to shoot a tire to alter the car's trajectory and momentum. Herbie fires in erratic spurts—*blam-blam, blam-blam-blam*—as his onboard computers blow the tires at carefully controlled intervals to maximize drag.

We're a few miles from the exit; my guns should be back online in a couple minutes; is this looking as good as I think it is?

And Silvia's hanging off the cop car's side as the other one tries to nudge me off the road. She's screaming, "Shut *up* stop hurting my *Mama* you leave her *alone*," as she sinks her fingers deep into the hood before reaching down to yank out the front axle, the flesh on her hand smoking from the wheel's rotation—

And my logs are giving me the best news I could ask for, a graph of potential fatalities based on the accidents we've seen thus far—that first horrible accident had a 13.4 percent chance of a fatality and a 56 percent chance of debilitating injury, but each accident's been decreased to a .06 percent chance of fatality as we race towards the smartcar hub—

And as the first cop car rumbles to a stop, Silvia leaps off its dying bulk to land on the second cop car—but it moves forward in a burst of speed, juking right to throw her off balance so she has to punch through a reinforced window to hang on. The cop car races forward towards me, Herbie veering to one side in a vain attempt to avoid the incoming collision—which, given the cop car outweighs us two-to-one, will be enough to flip Herbie over—

I still don't have a seat belt on—

Silvia crawls along the cop car's side, flapping like a bizarre flag, crawling back to safety before she gets pulped—except the remaining cop car isn't trying to ram us.

It was trying to *pass* us.

Silvia's screaming, *"Don't listen to them, Mat! This is their fault, not yours!"* and I realize the IAC must be speaking to me except I've filtered out their broadcasts—the car zooms past us as Silvia hauls herself through the broken window and into the car's interior in one convulsive movement.

Herbie slows down as the cop car pulls out in front of us, his threat package assuming the car will slam on its brakes—but the cop car puts distance between us as it cruises past, its rear window turning a lightning-streaked white as Silvia smashes the bulletproof protective shield free—

The cop car aims itself at an angle down the smooth highway, engines roaring.

Silvia crouches on the trunk, hauling two dazed men in blue uniforms out of the interior, then leaps off to safety as the car bounces over the grassy median.

The physics engine shows me she's leapt away from the car, reducing her speed so the cops will hit the ground at 40 per hour instead of 120, but there's still road rash aplenty for those poor bastards.

But Silvia's still shouting: *"Stop them! Stop them!"* even as she falls to the ground. And I realize:

The cop car's aimed straight for a head-on collision with someone else.

I'm instructing Herbie to knock the incoming civilian vehicle aside, but I don't have the firepower to disable a cop car in time—not with the IAC's computerized steering routines controlling the car.

The cop car smashes at 108 miles per hour into that inbound car

Ferrett Steinmetz

going at a tires-just-shot-out 83 miles per hour—191 miles per hour of bone-crushing force.

The woman in the incoming car wasn't even wearing a seat belt.

Her body smashes through the windshield, a thin woman in a fluttering blue dress sailing like a bloody comet over the median, arcing down to bounce with hideous thumps onto the pavement.

—*blue was the dress the mourners wore in Kabul*—

Herbie screeches to a stop. Because he knows, just as I know, that I can't leave a dead woman behind. She's dead, she must be, *nobody* could survive that crash, but if I drive away I'll spend the rest of my life wondering if I could have done anything to save her, and my faceplate fogs up with tears as I leap out of Herbie towards the corpse—

She's breathing.

Oh, thank God, she's breathing.

She's dying, but maybe I can comfort her in her last moments, and that's selfish but my God what have I done? My biological-response packages are trying to inject mood stabilizers but I'm refusing, a man *should* be traumatized when he's watched a woman die, and I don't want the sedatives to dull any moment I could spend paying attention to this victim's dying breaths.

She lies faceup on the cool highway road, surrounded by fragmented safety glass glittering beneath the streetlights. Her tears glimmer faint purple in the reflected glow of my peace-ties. Her brown eyes are wide as she stares up at the stars, her dress in tatters, and she's repeating a mantra in a childish, singsong voice:

"I don't want to hurt anyone I don't want to hurt anyone they make me they make me . . ."

She's a gaunt black woman in her midforties, her cheeks etched with a long history of agony, and as I bend down to see what medical care my paramedic routines can provide, she whips around to look me in the eye, her head moving so quickly I think she must have broken her neck.

"I don't want to, understand? *I don't want to . . .*"

"I don't—" I swallow. "I don't understand."

Her eyes flicker down to her mangled body, her head bobbing.

Her blue dress has peeled away in tatters like a snakeskin, revealing not sopping red wounds but gnarled twists of dragonfly green. My paramedic routines throw red complaints into my heads-up display:

Inhuman physiology.

"They make me *they make me* THEY MAKE ME," she screams, as Silvia shouts, *"Mat!"* just before something smashes into my faceplate hard enough to crack my teeth.

Something hits me hard, three times, hard enough my onboard airbags kick in to minimize the concussion. I stagger back as my limbs fight for balance, fight to block the incoming blows, fight to keep me alive as something smashes into me like a machine-gun car crash—

"Mat!" There's a green streak as Silvia tackles whatever's hitting me, rolling away in strobe-thrashing insectile limbs—

She's dead.

I watched her die.

New threat detected.

My HUD says it as if to contradict me, but I can't pay attention, my chest is constricted as if somebody caved it in, and I'm watching Silvia and this new woman thrashing and I can't make sense of it, because that woman is dead, I saw her launched through the windshield, and part of me realizes she must have lived, she's wrestling with Silvia, but my body reacted like I got some poor innocent woman killed—

Ferrett Steinmetz

—like the crowd of weeping civilians, digging my last target out of the rubble—

—like the little boy I thought was a dog who went up in fire—

—like the crumpled car roof by the freeway, the windows filled with white airbags—

And my chest hitches because even though I know nobody died I can't tell my body they didn't, my bloodstream's flooded with adrenaline panic because the worst thing happened, I got more people killed, this wasn't supposed to happen, this is why I plan, *this is why I plan,* and—

She's not dead. You didn't kill her.

She's not dead. You didn't kill her.

Why is she alive? I can't make sense of it. I should make sense of it, but things are moving too fast.

Peace-tie expires in 1:27, my HUD alerts me—it's cracked, and my head lights up with the high mosquito whine as the military-grade onboard sensors scan my skull for fractures. Threat package reaction:

Retreat.

My limbs jog me backwards as the woman (*the dead woman*) slams Silvia to the pavement, screaming, *"They won't let me kill myself so I have to capture you instead,"* as she grabs Silvia and hauls her limbs off like a kid yanking the wings off a fly, crying, *"They'll grow back everything grows back!"* I see Silvia's arm *stretching* before Silvia clouts her and yells, "Don't do this, join us, you don't have to obey them," and rolls away—

I jerk to a halt a hundred feet back, the readouts helpfully reminding me this is the maximum distance I had requested to be from Silvia on foot, did I want to override? The threat packages bounce me back and forth in mincing steps precisely one hundred feet away from Silvia, mirroring Silvia's wary circling of the new woman with computerized precision, getting weaponless me one hundred feet away from the threat but no farther.

I'm trying to figure out how to override my controls, but they're a blur and I can't figure out how to work them anymore, which is stupid, this is *simple*, why can't I simple?

—and Silvia's screaming, "We can *help* you, they want to turn me into you, don't you want to escape?" as she tumbles away from another assault and the woman weeps, *"There is no escape they keep you alive when you die,"* battering Silvia as she retreats. I'm trying to get closer but I can't remember how to install the new threat package so my feet dance at the tether's edge—

The HUD informs me I'm in post-traumatic shock. It asks the question it's been instructed to ask me in this situation:

Did you actually get anyone killed today? Y/N.

Oh God.

That's usually the *good* question.

As I wonder, the statistics modules inform me that there is, in fact, a 19.31 percent chance that someone died in my car crashes tonight, and an 11.75 percent chance that two or more people died, and my throat closes tight as a noose as I look at those figures and realize there's a one in five chance someone died tonight because of me—

The (*dead*) woman's got Silvia on the ground again, she's dribbling hot tears on Silvia's face as she apologizes for dismembering her, her alien hands trembling as she pulls Silvia apart with skilled expertise.

And Herbie opens up on the woman, its sluggish systems having decided this new woman's enough of a threat that it can't wait for my manual approval. It fires illegal high-caliber slugs through the (*dead*) woman's chest, tearing away fist-sized chunks, deforming her striated body—

She's *not* dead. You didn't kill her.

But you killed someone tonight, didn't you?

I'm trying to override my controls, but that 19.31 percent chance

Ferrett Steinmetz

of fatality swells to fill my vision, accusing me of bringing a war zone to a New Jersey freeway, knowing the IAC and the cops and the IAC's enemy would have to come after Silvia with everything they had—

Silvia's begging again, *Mat's helped me, he can help you*, but all I can hear is Trish's voice: *You spend so much time working to fix the things that went wrong, you never consider the things that went* right. And she's right, the IAC killed people as a psych-ops to get in my head; I shouldn't be thinking about the 19.31 percent chance someone died on my watch, I should be thinking about the 100 percent chance everyone would have died on that freeway and the 80.69 percent chance I saved all of them, but—

The not-dead woman has leapt across the highway, howling, to land dead center on Herbie's hood. She tears off the roof, destroys the engine with three precise blows that send gear-shrapnel flying, hurls the windshield at the drone, making a noise like a beaten dog as she flips Herbie's three-ton chassis over.

19.31 percent chance 19.31 percent chance 19.31 percent chance. I try to look away because my peace-tie's expired, my weapons are online, I can't remember how weaponry works, and I can see Trish reaching across the table to grab my hand, telling me *You're too hard on yourself, Mat*, but I can't *do* that math, it's never the people I saved, it's always the people who died.

"I'm doing you a favor!" not-dead woman says as she advances on Silvia, Silvia's newfound confidence draining away now that she's facing a trained operative. *"Pain comes from the illusion of free will, they will strip you of free will and when they are done you will feel nothing nothing nothing nothing nothing . . . ."*

"Then why can't you stop crying?" Silvia asks.

Silence. The not-dead woman stands rooted to the asphalt, shuddering like an off-kilter motor, her lips forming incoherent syllables. Then she straightens, craning her neck down at an improbable angle to examine herself with the horror of a woman waking into a nightmare.

Her head snaps up to Silvia.

"*You!*" she bellows. "*You don't remind me! You don't! You don't!*"

She leaps after Silvia so quickly that my legs propel me forward twenty feet to match her distance, the two snarling up in a ball of limbs, yet the not-dead woman has had IAC training, Silvia struggles but she's overmatched—

The not-dead woman has Silvia in a headlock. She's pulling, Silvia's neck stretching like taffy, threatening to yank off—

My vision snaps into focus.

A cold, efficient part of me wakes up pissed.

I pull up Vito and Michael's upgraded weapons loadouts, playing back what Donnie said to Silvia when he'd held us hostage: *the IAC has informed me a high-explosive shell can tear your body to shreds, just like anything else caught in mortar fire.*

These are black-market prosthetic armaments.

I choose a missile and tell Michael where to make the hit.

As the missile fires I see the not-dead woman hell-bent on tearing Silvia's head off, so lost in rage and despair that she doesn't even dodge—

The missile hits her center mass, burying itself deep.

She flinches just long enough for Silvia to dive free.

A burst of light. The not-dead woman's torso is shredded, disintegrating fibers scattered everywhere, half her head unraveled. Even a direct hit from a low-yield missile can't obliterate her; it spreads her body into a dying spaghetti tangle.

I should feel triumphant, I do, until I see Silvia falling to her knees by the strung-out corpse. She's crossing herself, saying a prayer for this poor woman because there but for the grace of God go I.

And I wonder if I could have said anything that would have saved this IAC victim. I wonder what would have happened if I'd spoken, if I'd gone with the nonlethal option.

Except I don't have those options anymore. I shot an innocent woman.

Ferrett Steinmetz

She's dead.

I killed her.

"Mat, are you okay?"

"Mat! Talk to me, I—"

I'm startled by Vito and Michael's short-barrel rifles—the kickback reverberates through my chest. My HUD informs me two inbound cop cars were disabled the instant they crested the hill .7 miles away, their axles blown to bits.

That's nice.

Something smashes into Vito as he whips up to protect my face— something that would have hit me with nonlethal, yet painful, force. My threat packages alert me: Silvia Maldonado, former friendly, is now attacking, do I want to remove her from the combat whitelist?

"Mat!" Hyperventilating, she draws her hand back to slap me again. "Wake up! I can't get to the, wherever it is, the—"

"Smartcar hub."

"Right. I don't know where it is. Mat, you have to snap out of it!"

I blink, bringing my navigation routines into focus. I thought I'd programmed them to head towards the hub, but maybe the fight where I

(murdered an IAC victim)

saved Silvia threw that post-combat objective out of whack, I should diagnose that, that's sloppy work. I wonder if it's a priority conflict, or—

"Mat." My limbs tell me Silvia's gripping me tight, but she's shaking hard enough that Vito and Michael diagnose her with an impending panic attack. "Please. I don't know how to help you, but we can't stand here. You have to—"

Right. The smartcar hub. I program in our destination. That's easy. Forming words with my mouth is hard.

"I got it," I tell her after a brief time. "Keep close. Don't engage with anyone. Let me do the work."

"Wait, what are you—"

Things blur out.

There's explosions. I don't mind explosions. But the weaponry on Vito and Michael and the new legs *feels* different—the rocket launchers are uncomfortably hot when they unload on a fatality drone, the missiles make a harsh *choonk* noise that jars me, even the gunports vibrate down my shoulders in a different way.

It's not like Scylla and Charybdis. I'd been fighting with those lovely ladies for so long, I could practically doze through combat.

It's irritating though. I want to go numb again. Yet these new limbs' different rhythms jolt me whenever they blast a SWAT tank out of our way, making me wonder how many people got killed *that time*, and even though the readouts tell me it's a *low* chance of fatality, that's not the same as *no* fatalities until the bodies are counted.

Silvia clings to me as my limbs battle through the two miles of dense office complexes on the way to the hub. She yelps whenever Vito and Michael's rifles blast an incoming drone from the sky, clenches me tight as my legs annihilate any parked vehicle on the assumption the IAC might activate it, shields her eyes on the rare occasion an inbound vehicle gets close enough to take a potshot before my grenade launchers send it spinning away. Everything's on fire.

I update my threat packages to exclude any inbound fire-suppressant vehicles and gray out again.

At one point I come to and see Silvia peering into my faceplate, frowning as she notices my chin hitting my chest like I'm sleep-

Ferrett Steinmetz

ing off a bender—which, given the tranquilizers my biological-response packages injected to quell my panic disorder, isn't that far from the truth. She snaps her head around to look at Vito and Michael, who are currently battling it out with what I presume is an IAC drone, gouts of gunfire flung into a blazing sky as my legs propel me behind an office building's thick concrete column.

She'd thought she was the threat. Yet here I am shredding aerial tanks.

She keeps checking in on me, trying to reconcile my military devastation with my dazed meat-self. She wants me to be working my control panels, barking orders, doing *something* to instigate this destruction.

But no. That's why I got these limbs. They protect me when I can't cope.

I'm not here right now, but my programming is.

This is why body-hackers terrify people. A few tweaks to my IFF settings, and those fleeing late-night office workers would be the victims of an automated mass murder.

This will be a battle that New Jersey's finest will replay for years. My estimates show I've annihilated slightly over 0.7 percent of the NJPD's combat hardware reserves, which will affect their budget next year. The New Jersey Senate *will* be debating more robust restrictions on prosthetic armaments, and there's an outside chance this incident might wind up as a factor in the next presidential election.

And honestly? I couldn't tell you what I did without reading the mission logs.

But I can tell you when I fired the first missile, the one that for-sure killed a woman whose biggest crime was getting kidnapped by the IAC, and—

"Is that it?" Silvia asks, pointing.

I shake my head. Sure enough, the smartcar hub's finally in view, lit up by the burning cars Vito and Michael have destroyed to clear a path for us. It's a multilevel parking facility painted a pristine white, with vast ten-lane exits so the cars can be quickly deployed in case of an emergency traffic surge.

I relax when I see the cars docked in three floors of recharging stations, protected from vandalism behind neat polarized shields.

Hardly anybody owns cars these days. Why put yourself in hock to a dealership in an uncertain economy, when there are autonomously roaming patrols you can summon to your doorstep within five minutes, driving you anywhere you like for a trivial cost? This smartcar hub has a thousand cars, and during peak hours most are out on the road. But it's three in the morning, and four hundred–plus cars are in for recharging and routine maintenance.

Standard smartcar procedure is they shut down their wireless connection to avoid external hacking when they dock. You can only hack them through a physical network connection . . . and the easiest way to do *that* is to break into the smartcar traffic-control center at the facility's heart, which is impregnable against internet-based hacks because otherwise any script-kiddie could steal four hundred cars like we're about to.

The IAC has to know this is our goal. Those four hundred cars nestled in place indicate all the IAC's hacking might hasn't gotten them into the smartcar facility remotely.

I hope a four-hundred-car shell game is enough to lose everyone who wants to kill us. The cops have backed off, regrouping and restrategizing; we have about twenty minutes before the state calls in reinforcements and the next assault begins.

I check my inventory reports, am surprised to discover I'm out of missiles and grenades. I'm down to 34 percent ammo on the hunting rifles. I'm glad to find I haven't shot the combat shotguns; those are meant to liquefy human beings.

This is a fight that Donnie would be masturbating to for months, and I sleepwalked through it.

Yet I'm shivering as I look up the single metric that defines tonight's success: the casualties. The HUD returns:

Ferrett Steinmetz

I slump with relief. Then I change my default settings to report the casualties as "killed in action."

Truth is, both the IAC and the NJPD deployed weaponry that could have shredded my meat-body given the chance; I've just configured my threat packages to prioritize and defend properly, and as such have destroyed or evaded anything dangerous before they brought the heavy guns to bear. I say that I wasn't in control, but the years I've spent refining my response routines saved our asses tonight.

Good preparation's a helluva force multiplier.

(As is the fact that the ACLU's legal efforts have thwarted the cops' efforts to get their hands on *true* military hardware. I'm good, but I'm not shrug-off-heavy-tanks-and-orbital-strikes good.)

Yet I'm out of the good ammo. And the smartcar hub's traffic-control points *have* been designed to minimize cover. Walk into one, and armor-piercing bullets will perforate any unauthorized human figure.

"Yes," I say, "that's our goal, Silvia." I modify my threat models to prioritize speed over offense, then tweak the config files when they don't hot-patch the first time. I'm more shaken than I want to be.

She places her palm on my chest. "Are you okay?"

How can I tell her that her kindness makes me frail when I need to be relentless?

"I'm fine, Silvia."

A surge of gratitude thrums up in me as she nods. We both know I'm not *that* fine. But she understands I'm a teetering Jenga pile of competence right now, and investigating me will collapse me.

She kisses my cracked faceplate instead.

Why am I blushing?

We approach the smartcar hub's lobby, which has the pleasant look of a model home nobody lives in. There's a pretty Asian receptionist filing her nails at the front desk—which makes me think how her job is referred to, sneeringly, among human resources workers as "TH," or the "Token Human." She's a vestigial remnant kept in place out of some dim cultural memory defining good customer service. They're usually wannabe actors too dim to realize realistic CGI has rendered the old Hollywood path to stardom obsolete.

Truthfully, the voice recognition and AI scripts, with their deep access to customer purchasing history and customer psychological profiles bought from the data warehouses, are near-perfect at giving customer satisfaction (at least to the customers loyal enough to be worth satisfying).

Yet each smartcar hub keeps one lucky, good-looking person designated as the quote-unquote "regional manager"—because the angry unemployed are less likely to burn the place down if the corporation keeps some fresh-faced girl visible through the front windows.

The four night-shift mechanics fleeing for cover? They're what really keeps this place running.

"Stay put," I tell her. "We won't be long."

"Will I have a job when you're done?" she asks.

I wince. They'll probably get their cars back, but I can't promise they'll be in good condition. If this place isn't doing well—and Kiva didn't pick a supernice area to live in—then the CEO might take this excuse to close shop.

"Probably," I tell her.

I don't like hurting innocents, but there's lots of guys who'd rather be hit in the mouth than the wallet.

I stop before the door leading to the long, open hallway to the traffic hub. I don't even have to glance at the receptionist's desk to know she hit the emergency "assault" button, meaning their defense packages have been activated. Mere humans don't stand a chance against the weaponry designed to stand between body-hackers and complete control of $25 million in automotive vehicles.

"The central control point is guarded against threats like me," I tell Silvia.

Ferrett Steinmetz

She bounces up and down like a kid about to jump in the ball pit. "But not threats like me."

I shoot her a broken-toothed grin. "Go get 'em, Silvia."

I step to one side as she launches herself into the fortified hallway. I reach for a celebratory cigar, then realize I left my Macanudos back in Scylla. Proof of how sloppy I'm getting.

That concern drains away when I hear Silvia yelping with joy as she bounces down the hall, wrecking automated turrets, yanking alarms out of their sockets, shrugging off gunfire.

And I think about the IAC—they could have used these techniques to give people with panic disorders a body that empowered them. Not to mention what sort of advances they might have onboard to fight cancer, and HSV-III, and God knows how many terminal illnesses.

We can't stop them. I don't have the resources to stop them. This is still a glorified suicide mission.

But damn, I'd give anything to reprogram the IAC's tools to benefit the world instead of exploiting it.

"All clear!" Silvia shouts. I stroll down a hallway thick with carcinogenic smoke and tear gas, sparking with wrecked machinery, one ruined turret-gun whirring pathetically as it struggles to get a bead on me.

The final chamber's reinforced doors have slammed shut—but they're not designed to protect against a black-market combat monster and an IAC-fueled superstrong bioweapon.

Their central chamber, however, is laughably mundane. It's three gray work-cubicles, one empty. The two night-shift maintenance technicians—who get paid by the hour—look up from their workstations, startled, as Silvia kicks the door in. They're dressed in gaudy gold-and-white SmartCar uniforms.

This is the *busy* time for sysadmins. The city's asleep, so they're scrambling to do their maintenance before daily peak load hits. That's two people supervising a place controlling a thousand cars, which in turn probably service forty thousand people a day.

Seven people run this entire facility, and one is for show.

No wonder the receptionist was worried about losing her job.

Suddenly, breaking open this final gate feels like wresting open a window to an uglier future, one where human expertise is no longer required. The central terminal is no longer an office, but some bunker where the remaining shreds of human dignity have retreated, the last space where people have a shot at making worthwhile decisions.

The junior sysadmin makes a choked weeping noise. And I realize: these poor bastards don't realize I'm waxing philosophical. They think I'm deciding whether to shoot them.

"I know what you did when you heard the alarm," I tell them pleasantly, my courteous Missouri drawl rising to the surface again. "I won't blame you; it's company policy. But is there any way to undo it?"

The lead sysadmin, an overweight black woman in her forties, exhales a great relieved sigh before adjusting her tortoiseshell glasses. She keeps her gaze well averted, figuring staring at Silvia's physique would give offense. "Not at our access level, no, sir. To unlock the system would require someone to fly out from HQ with a time-synced security stick and enter the root password."

These poor suckers hit the "lockdown" button the moment final security was breached. Which, frankly, is either blindly stupid or purposely courageous—anyone with the firepower to get through to the central terminal is unlikely to treat the people inside kindly. And I will admit I'd been hoping they'd been so terrified they skipped the lockdown and handed me control.

"All right." I take a moment to examine the terminals, hoping the hack I purchased still works. I love prep work, but even I don't make a habit of breaking into smartcar hubs. "You folks get over there, then, far away from us. Don't try to escape; not only would your lungs not like the tear gas outside, but you might get caught in the crossfire when the big boys move in."

They squeeze, obediently, into the corner. Silvia squints, confused.

Ferrett Steinmetz

"Are we pulling off a heist?" she asks.

"I suppose we are," I reply. "Though this may be a real short heist."

I pop out the ISB access point hidden in Vito's index finger and search for the admin port. The system's locked down to a single access point—not even the IAC could reach them. The only input this system will allow, and by proxy the several hundred cars docked for recharging and system updates, comes through this port.

I inject the hack I bought. My onboard hack database helpfully reminds me this vulnerability was purchased from BlackLaura, reliability rating of 92.1 percent, nine months ago.

Shit. I didn't realize it was *that* long.

I hold my breath, but nothing happens.

My sensors pick up at least one person picking their way down the hallway, wary of any remaining automated defenses; some poor cop, chosen to be the vanguard for the rest of the force. They've lost expensive equipment tonight, so they're doing what military forces have done since time immemorial: expending cheap bodies as scouts to gather information.

I could instruct Vito and Michael to cap him. But the smoke obscures the details; though my probability modules say it's an 81.7 percent chance this is a cop, there's still an 18.3 percent chance it's some confused technician. I don't want to pop some poor minimum-wage schmuck in the head.

Still, it's a long hallway, giving us a few minutes before the probably-cop arrives—maybe BlackLaura's hack takes time to chew through the defenses.

"Excuse me? Sir?" The tortoiseshell-glassed sysadmin raises her hand, like a kid in class. "If you don't mind me asking, which hack are you using?"

I raise my eyebrows. "Sweet Lord, woman, how many break-ins do you get?"

"Not . . . many. Sir. None. But I install the patches here, and we're pretty scrupulous about system security."

"Of course you are." Smartcar hacks are the holy grail of hackers. Who doesn't want a free ride? And, if you're more criminally inclined, who doesn't want a free ride that's not tracked on the city traffic records? The smartcars are the best-defended cybersecurity sites because *everyone* wants in.

The tortoiseshell woman waits for an answer. It's a bizarre mixture of courtesy and self-interest: if I'd been too thuggish, she would have been terrified to speak her mind. Yet if she can convince us my purchased vulnerability has been fixed, maybe she can get us to leave before the shooting starts.

"BlackLaura," I say. Which is, honestly, a mild broach of protocol; I shouldn't even admit I purchased this hack, let alone drop a dime on who I got it from. Then again, she's technically not supposed to help me either, so we're well beyond normal politeness.

She carefully raises her company PDA as if she's fearful I might shoot her, then scrolls through her maintenance records. "Black-Laura . . . the vulnerability from 2049, 2051, or 2052?"

"The '51. Last year's." BlackLaura's clearly got an inside position at SmartCar. I should have subscribed to her feed for updates.

Vito and Michael rub my temples.

"Patched two months ago." She holds up her display screen, as if it's not her fault, it's this darned PDA. "Sorry. Sir."

I slump. The cop in the hallway gets closer.

I'm tempted to take off my faceplate and let him get the headshot.

"They're still working on closing the 2052 vulnerability, if you can find it," she adds apologetically.

It's a bizarre courtesy—but then again we've entered the land of programmers, where we respect anyone who's done their work.

My lungs close shut. If I'd planned on breaking into a smartcar facility, I would have brought the latest hacks—but on the run, with the IAC monitoring my accounts, I didn't dare check into my usual black-market sites, and I've paid for that hubris.

I could have planned better. I should have anticipated doing

Ferrett Steinmetz

a milk run with Ancillary Force would lead to me being on the run with a custom-engineered biological weapon–cum-hostage and that would require me to hack a smartcar facility and I know that's stupid, but I should have anticipated *everything.* that's how I *survive.*

"Mat?" Silvia's turning me around to face her as I realize I've all but stood in the corner, and turning me around is difficult as I weigh 1,435 pounds, but she does it effortlessly. "Mat, it's okay. Get the new hack."

"I can't. Not in time. Negotiating a black-market hack takes at least a day minimum, with a complex escrow procedure and proper anonymization." That also assumes the IAC's black-hat teams haven't broken into my bank accounts.

"So just . . ." She waves her hand in the air like Harry Potter casting a spell. "Hack it."

She thinks of my work as a magic weapon—but it's work, grueling work. I didn't conjure the police car hack out of thin air; I spent weeks creating a fake programmer's profile to get access to the barred-source OS for the cop cars, then committed enough legitimate patches to get deeper access, and then when I wasn't working on the test range or upgrading Scylla or tending to Herbie I'd poke through the source code looking for an unsanitized input.

It's what I do to relax.

And I'm *good* at bug-hunting. The police hack took seven weeks of investigation, combing through a state security picked clean by other hackers.

There's a cop coming down the hallway, doubtlessly the vanguard of an assault force that *will* smash down on us now they've figured out their next move. I don't need my probability calculators to tell me the chances that I can break into a black-box OS on a ten-minute deadline with no access to source code is nil, nil, nil.

Silvia looks up at me, so trusting that I want to kiss her. I can't tell her it's over. There's no escape with both the IAC and the cops watching us.

I've bet everything on the smartcar hub, and came up short.

"Mat?" She pats my arm. "Mat. It's okay. We'll find a way."

I try to look her in the eye. My gaze squirms away. "Silvia—Silvia, I . . ."

The cop enters the room in a swirl of smoke.

Except she's not a cop. She's a curvaceous white woman in a powder-blue ball gown with a plunging neckline. She's got two guns on her hips, a computer case slung over her side, and no weapons in her hands. She's wearing a black reflective gas mask.

She hauls it off, shaking out long red hair before she itches the reddish stubble on her cheeks.

"Trish?" I ask, confused.

"Mat!" She rolls her eyes, as if to accentuate how difficult it's been tracking me down. "What version of BlackLaura did you bring?"

"2051."

She holds up an ISB stick. "I got this year's model. Let's hack this joint."

BlackLaura's hack only gets me system access. Configuring the cars is my job.

My heart unclenches as I inventory the available automobile stock. This is planning. I can do planning. And first priority's figuring out which vehicles we'll be smuggling ourselves out in.

And I am granted a small miracle: this smartcar hub services a run-down section of town. Poor inhabitants mean the local residents are more likely to take a cheaper carpool option, which means this hub's stock is mostly vans, which gives us 268 available vehicles that can stash a bulky 1,400-pound body-hacker and two slender passengers.

If my D&D sessions back during my deployment taught me one thing, it's to never split the party.

Trish sweeps back her hair, making herself presentable before she extends the hand. "Hey." She offers a freckled sunblaze of a grin to Silvia. "I'm Trish."

"Hi, it's . . . yeah. Hello. You're Trish." Silvia's much slower to return the handshake, as if she expects to be slapped down. She hangs her head low, her syllables hitching with hesitation.

Trish flicks a glance in my direction, requesting an update. I get what's happening: ten minutes ago Silvia was an engine of destruction, designed for beautiful combat. Trish's kindness has unwittingly switched the frame to a social situation—where Silvia's now an awkward psychiatric patient with a stringy bug-gut body.

I know this because this is why Mat the fearsome body-hacker does not attend parties.

I think of words I might mouth to Trish to cue her in, but they're all insults: *She's got panic disorder. That's not her body. She's not really sure what she's doing.* It feels wrong to sum up Silvia by her problems, because she's more than that, but I don't know how to explain what Silvia means to me—

Trish gives a curt, apologetic nod in my direction—*right, right*—remembering I'm not optimized for personal interaction. Then she takes a careful step towards Silvia, who retreats in a flicker.

Trish freezes, respecting Silvia's fear, then turns her hands palms up as if holding an imaginary bowl between them.

"Would you like a hug?" she asks.

Silvia bowls Trish over backwards, burying her face in Trish's shoulder, exhaling a jagged breath as I realize Silvia has been terrified that nobody but me would ever want to touch her again.

Trish strokes Silvia's back, glancing down dubiously as Silvia's cilia snuffle at her skin.

"There, there," Trish says.

I shouldn't be so grateful they're occupying each other's time, but that hug frees me to do the necessary work. First step is giving me and only me root access to the 414 docked vehicles. Then comes locking out police override protocols. Then I polarize the cars' privacy windows.

"Attention, Mat Webb," a police chief's voice thunders in from far down the hallway. "We know you are in the smartcar hub. Come out before we deploy lethal force."

"Do we *have* a destination in mind?" I ask.

Trish untangles herself from Silvia to tightbeam me a safe-house location.

"Mat, whatever has happened, we can talk it through." The voice sounds human, but I recognize a negotiationbot's artificial calm. "You don't want to hurt anybody. You can call us on—"

The next trick is turning on the cars' heaters full blast to obscure our infrared signature, then applying a filter to the vans' control systems so they accelerate like they have a 1,400-pound passenger in the back. The cops are still scrambling for a plan, but the IAC thinks in processing speeds—they've anticipated the things I'd do at a smartcar hub, have funneled entire neural networks into detecting our escape.

After years of therapy, it's satisfying to face an omniscient enemy who rewards paranoid thinking.

Yet omniscient isn't the same as omnipotent—I don't think they have a lot of agents prepped in New Jersey's ass-end, and my logs show I shot down three IAC drones on the way here. They may know what we're doing yet not have the local resources to stop us.

(Does the IAC's enemy have the resources to interfere? Unfortunately, I don't know. If electrohawks swarm in there's not much we can do, so I'll hope the people who tried to kidnap Silvia in the first place won't show up again.)

I finish up by programming in a wandering destination for 413 cars, one where groups will split off randomly and come back together before ditching themselves in shadowy places that'll be difficult for overhead surveillance to track escapees. The 414th car will, assuming we don't get shot down, drop us in deep woods about a seven-minute run from Trish's hideout.

"Whatever your grievances are, Mat, we are ready to listen." That's what cops say as they're setting up the sniper shot.

Ferrett Steinmetz

"Okay." I commit the final changes to memory. "We're good. Let's go." Trish snaps on her filtration mask again.

I head out to the back exit to the cars.

I see the tortoiseshell-glassed sysadmin and her junior protégé. She's got her arm around him; his face is scrunched like he's holding back tears.

"Hey." They look up, startled I'm acknowledging them. "I'm sorry."

I should follow that up with something more comforting, some specific understanding that this will mean weeks of overtime repair and police interviews and maybe the company will take the excuse to shitcan the facility . . . but anything would sound like I'm rubbing it in.

The sysadmin frowns, examining me for sarcasm. When she finds none, she bobs her head in a gesture between understanding and resignation. "It's okay." She nods in Silvia's direction. "You guys have got a lot going on."

"Yeah." I extend my hand. "Name's Mat."

She grips my carbon-scored manipulators, her fingers stroking mine: she's a tech-nerd, happy to lay hands upon a top-class armed prosthetic. "Violet."

"You can't escape, Mat. Talk to us." The voice is louder, amplified by more speakers. They're calling in drones from every city.

"Gotta go," I say.

And with that, Trish and Silvia and I are dashing up the spiral staircase into the facility's heart, headed for our van. I'd like to say the garage roars with the throaty sound of powerful engines, but alas, they're electric cars so this cyber-rebellion is whisper-quiet.

"How'd you know to meet us here?" I ask. Somehow, Trish keeps up with both Silvia's hyper reflexes and my cybernetic limbs, and she's doing it in high heels.

"You—" She splutters. "Jesus, Mat, you *told* me!"

"What?"

She slams the door to the main facility open with displaced fury, revealing the broken cars towed into their troubleshooting bays, the boxy auto-clean facilities designed to scrub and repair the car interiors, the racks of spare parts and gimbal-mounted mechanicbots.

"You remember?" Trish asks plaintively. "That night we stayed up until four in the morning troubleshooting your tetchy neural linkage, then got into a debate over the best ways for us to ditch police surveillance if we got five-starred?"

That sounds . . . familiar. Also troublesome. She tells me how she headed out here when she realized I was in over my head, how she's been doing a patrol that encompassed as many smartcar hubs as she could, hoping to be close enough to intercept us when she heard a police bulletin—

—but I'm too busy wondering if I've discussed this plan with anyone who might have posted it on social media. Or talked near an IAC-compromised computer. I'm keyword-scanning my personal logs, searching for potential leaks.

Trish snaps three times near my faceplate. "Have you listened to a damn thing I'm saying?"

My worries dissolve into paranoid conspiracy theory: even if the IAC knows our plan, there's not much I can do to change it now. "My . . . conversational condensers have given me the gist?"

She facepalms, her hand slapping to a halt against her air-filtration system. "Fucking hell, Mat. I appreciate your thoroughness, but . . . after risking my life to save your ass, it'd be nice if you paid half the attention to your friends that you paid to your cyber-limbs."

"I'm sorry."

Trish shakes her head as if she can't believe my foolishness. I glance over at Silvia as we lope past the bays of testing facilities.

Her body's moving in a straight line but she's turned to face me, mouth agog in concern. She's coming to realize I'm every bit the wreck she is.

As I start to panic at being exposed as a nutcase, she shoots me an affectionate grin.

Ferrett Steinmetz

We're in this neurotic mess together.

We get to our designated van, in a line with twenty other identical orange vans in Section 6B. The police boom threats into the garage.

"Get in. You both get beneath me. Silvia, you wrap as much of your bulletproof body around Trish as you can—"

"She's *bulletproof*?" Trish squees.

"—and *stay down*. They might fire at the windows to get a peek inside, but I don't think so."

"Mat, in two minutes the police will have no choice but to assault the facility." Standard operating procedure means they'll start the operation in thirty seconds. "People may get hurt. Please, Mat. This is your last chance to settle this peacefully."

"And *don't say anything*." I brace myself against the van's insides so nothing on me rattles, creaks, or thumps. "They'll pick up audio. You ready?"

"I'm ready," Silvia says, then slaps her hand over her mouth.

Trish readies a handgun and nods.

I okay the procedure.

In Section 6B, twenty vans back out in synchronized retreat.

Operation Shell Game begins.

We are stuck inside the van, unable to poke our heads out enough to see what's happening, and I have no outside surveillance.

Yet as the 414 smart vehicles roll out of the wide exit gates into blaring police bullhorns, I have an idea of what's happening.

With this much havoc, the mayor's gotten involved. And as our van banks around a corner with a hundred other vans, I'm pretty sure what the assembled police are doing:

First there's muffled yelling as the cops blast their vehicle-override signals, trying to bring this mass exodus to a screeching halt. Some even think it'll work.

Then I hear a staccato burst of gunfire; our vehicle swerves as

I hear muffled fender-bender *thumps* as a couple of vans in front get taken down by the armored patrol cars—these are ordinary vehicles, no match for police militarized weaponry.

But as programmed, the vans are not stopping. Those thumps are the still-active vans behind the detonated ones ramming into them, doing their damnedest to shove the dead cars forward with all their horsepower, a relentless forward motion like a sluggish metal flood. All the while other cars are rerouting around them, coordinating efforts in a great escape—

The gunfire ceases, right on schedule. There are no EMP pulses either.

The cops have given up blocking our escape.

Which seems foolish from a law-and-order perspective, but I've been counting on the mayoral perspective: while the police would be happy to blast outgoing vans until the smartcar hub's a flaming junkyard, the mayor's watching this smartcar-hub exodus and asking a much more relevant question:

"What happens to my city when we destroy thirteen million dollars' worth of cars?"

The mayor's pondering the taxes this smartcar hub pays with every ride, knowing this run-down section of New Jersey is *not* thriving, and the likelihood of this smartcar business returning after the cops have strafed their inventory into scrap metal is nil.

The mayor's contemplating lawsuits, lost revenue, angry complaints from constituents who will not get to work tomorrow because the local police annihilated the service that serves as public transit.

And the mayor's doubtlessly shrieking for the cops to stop, let the cars go, we'll chase them down.

(Just as the IAC's Powers What Be are debating whether the chance of stopping us is worth exposing their patrol car–compromising capabilities. And the IAC's enemy is debating whether they want to release the electrohawks during a media blitz. The only reason we're escaping is because I'm forcing everyone to make uncomfortable decisions.)

I hear the *thump* as we round a corner along with a squad of ten fellow vans, the sirens as some cop decides to follow *this* cluster of vehicles, and then the jerk to and fro as my confuse-a-cop algorithms kick in—some vans peel off to lure individual patrol cars away, others pull into shadowy parking garages before turning off their lights, still others drive in rough formations to let the cops and drones think they have a bead on a nice grouping of cars until they split apart in so many directions the manhunter-AIs don't have enough hardware to track them.

The cops will have to rely on imperfect instruments as the vans ditch themselves in remote locations, stopping under overhangs so the satellites and their sluggish refresh rates can't be quite sure what happened.

By the time our van pulls over in a ditch in the dark woods, I'm checking my satellite-window database to ensure no eyes in the sky will be overhead. We slip out into the three-o'clock-in-the-morning darkness, using my low-light amplified vision to guide Trish and Silvia, plotting a course through thick brush to Trish's safe house.

Trish stops us. She points to a run-down cabin in a thick grove, dead pines leaning drunkenly against its walls. "That's it."

Silvia whip-grabs Trish by the lapel. "What do you *mean*, that's it? We can't stay there!" she whispers, then realizes she's assaulted Trish and lets go, scrabbling away.

Trish shoots me a *You're gonna have to explain that to me later* look, then massages her throat. "Sweetie," she says calmly, "I'm the baseline human here. You've got those reflexes to protect you, Mat has his weaponry; all I've got is homo-sapiens smarts and my stashed resources. If I'm not panicking yet, you don't need to be."

She gestures for Silvia to follow, then pushes past a rotted door hanging on one hinge. This used to be a rustic three-bedroom weekender in the deep woods, but now it's a half-abandoned ruin with teenaged declarations of love carved into the walls, broken beer bottles glittering on the ground, and rotted sleeping bags surrounded by used condoms.

"The woman who built this was convinced civilization was going to collapse." Trish shuffles through the decaying leaves, hunting for something. "So she commissioned a hideaway cabin she could bug out to when things slid to shit. I told her, you build those places in the deep Appalachians, not near the Pennsylvania border, but she wanted somewhere within commuting distance."

She shifts a soiled sleeping bag aside with her foot. "Thing is, civilizations like ours don't collapse. They just lean harder on the little guy until they slump into a more painful stability."

"So what happened to the woman?" Silvia asks.

"Oh! She was a brain surgeon, just before the auto-docs took hold. She was *convinced* no automated surgery could replace her expertise. So she short-sold every tech stock that aimed to make her obsolete." Trish shrugs as she gets down on her knees, running her hands along the warped baseboard. "I bought the place in cash so she could take an early retirement."

Trish blows the dirt out of an electrical outlet, revealing a keyhole. She jangles the heavy key chain at her belt and unlocks something with a loud, metallic *clunk*.

"Mind opening that trapdoor, Mat?"

I lift up a wide wood flap with forty-eight pounds of armored steel underneath, raining down pine needles into a gray stairway.

"If the three of us are down there, we can't cover the trapdoor again." Trish glances fretfully over the cleared spot in the filth. "Fortunately, it's autumn, so no teens will be slinking out tonight."

It's nice when Trish does my preparatory paranoia for me.

Silvia sticks her head into the hole, looks around. "You mean to tell me you happened to have a safe house on the Pennsylvania border?"

Trish decides she can't do anything else to camouflage the trapdoor once it's shut. "Honey, I've got safe houses in every state for my friends. I network. I distribute. And I make sure my resources are widely spread, which should be making you happy because that distribution is all that's saving us from the IAC's agents. Mat, sorry,

Ferrett Steinmetz

you're gonna have to wriggle to get those new limbs squeezed in there. Silvia, pull the door down after us?"

She leads us into a tidy waiting room–style area, flicking on the facility's lights. And "facility" is the term that springs to mind: the place is neutrally decorated, everything stocked away neatly as my old military digs, with low-tech reliable equipment—a propane stove, a cabinet filled with canned goods, a water tank.

Tactically, this is a crappy position. One grenade tossed into the hole and we're done for. Yet I have to remember that our current metric for success is "hope the IAC or its enemies don't track us down."

Trish opens up a trunk filled with plastic-sealed linens, walks into the three bedrooms to place one on each bed. The layout, though a mere seven hundred square feet according to my volumetric analyzers, is designed to give privacy. I'm willing to bet the brain surgeon spent as much time fetishizing this place's layout as I did designing Herbie.

Poor Herbie.

Trish fetches a card table and some fold-out chairs—nice ones made from hardwood, no skimping from our good doctor—before plunking a bottle of Wild Turkey down.

"So," she says. "We have set a record: the IAC set out to get you fourteen hours ago. You should have been dead nine hours back." She pushes brimming shot glasses over to Silvia and me, raises hers tentatively.

Silvia hesitates before she takes the shot glass. She glances over at me; I stare down into the glass to indicate *Yeah, I don't drink much either.*

We all take a bracing shot.

Trish pours another round. "Now, I've hidden this cabin pretty well, but the IAC has to have forensic analysts sifting through my financial records and correlating that with our escape radius. We've got twelve hours before we have to assume this hidey-hole's burned."

"That's not even counting the IAC's enemy who's *also* out to capture Silvia."

"I didn't even know about them! Great." She swigs back her second shot, scrubbing the itchy bristle on her cheeks. "So what's our plan, Mat?"

For some reason, Trish won't look through my mission logs. She wants me to *tell* her what happened. Debriefing her over drinks is inefficient, but easier than arguing.

I walk her through everything that went down in strictly military terms. I thought Silvia might jump in to share; instead she hugs herself, looking miserable, never taking her eyes off Trish's plunging neckline.

I ignore the way Silvia's taking in Trish's body, because I'm bracing myself for what's coming—I've seen so many rude strangers ask whether Trish is a man or a woman, and even though Trish is usually gracious, it'll put a frost on the room.

Trish notices Silvia's stare. She scratches the stubble between her breasts awkwardly, then asks, "Would you like me to get you a dress? There should be spare clothing in the bedrooms."

Silvia sniffs. "Yeah."

Trish returns with denim jeans and a long-sleeved lumberjack shirt. "Sorry. It's survivalist gear. You can change in the back."

"Why's she need to change in the back?" I ask. "She's—"

Trish puts her finger on my lip to shush me, but Vito snatches her wrist away before I can override his defense mechanisms. Silvia, sensing the awkward wrestling match, mutters, "Sorry" and scurries into a bedroom.

Trish lowers her voice to a whisper. "It's not normal for people to sit around naked."

Silvia's discomfort snaps into focus—she was asking about a shower curtain because she wanted something clean to wrap around herself; she was searching Kiva's apartment for clothes. All I ever

Ferrett Steinmetz

wear is body armor. I'm such an asocial freak it's never occurred to me what it's like for a nice Catholic girl to wander around naked. No *wonder* she's been on edge.

"And you could stand to talk about your new girlfriend there like she was a human being," Trish continues.

I stiffen. "She's *not* my new girlfriend." I push the glass around on the table. "Things have . . . happened. But I'm ethical. I won't turn this adrenaline into Stockholm syndrome."

She gives me an erratic head-bob double take. My body language interpreters helpfully overlay my HUD with the translation of:

Astonishment at extreme incompetency.

"You're not doing her any favors by discussing her exclusively in terms of combat capacities either. Maybe *you're* okay with being stared at everywhere you go, but she—"

Silvia opens the door slowly, giving us conspicuous time to hear her coming. She's buttoned the lumberjack shirt all the way up, the denim jeans are hip-hugging, and her arms are crossed over her chest, but . . .

She looks normal.

Now I'm staring, because Silvia could have walked in from anywhere. Her alien skin is concealed beneath the fabric. She's become a middle-aged woman who you wouldn't think twice about passing on the street—long, curly black hair, a brown face carved lean by stress. She could be a paramedic or a receptionist or a mom or . . .

Well, anybody.

The bourbon churns sourly in my stomach as I realize: I'd never have gotten to know Silvia without the IAC's interference. If I'd seen her pre-IAC, I'd have slotted her as "civilian," and done my best to protect her without getting involved—but then I'd never have known about Silvia's encyclopedic knowledge of Fred Astaire's dance moves or the way she chews her lip when she's considering technical details or—

"Mat, are you okay?"

Crap, I *am* staring.

I scratch my cheek. "It's like that scene in every high-school drama where the nebbishy girl takes off her glasses and lets down her hair," I say—and when Silvia flinches, I add, "in reverse."

Silvia blinks, unsure whether that was a compliment.

"No, it's . . ." I wave away my emergency conversational assistants as they suggest alternate dialog paths. "It's not you. It's not the you I *know*. And that's fine, I'll get used to this too, but . . . I kinda met you one way, you know?"

Silvia's face flushes dark. "I didn't think less of you when *you* changed."

"You're better."

Her palm cups my cheek again, tenderly protecting me—then she flickers back a step and scratches at her sleeves, annoyed how her body gives away her emotions.

"Seriously, Silvia." My voice is cracking again. "I'm not good with changes. It's . . ."

"Kind of his thing," Trish says. "He tries. He tries really hard, Silvia. But you have to cut him slack for that gap between his intent and his execution."

I want to defend myself, saying I'm just *fine* as long as you've got me out in the field, it's only when you take a multimillion-dollar killing machine out on a date that I'm suboptimal.

My dialogue assistants are spamming me with potential responses ranging from snarky bon mots to studied revelations designed to make them weep. I'm not sure why I'm dismissing their requests. I'm not sure why I'm so unwilling to let the computer take over my personal life when I've sawed off my limbs to let them control my physical world.

"Mat." Silvia's touch is cool against Vito's forearm mechanisms; for a moment I envy Vito. "It's okay. I get it. I . . . I'm not always so hot with the responses myself."

I hate being forgiven. It's why I never put myself in a position

Ferrett Steinmetz

where anyone has to forgive me. My fists are balled against my chest, cool metal against bare skin, as I try to focus on her touch and not my thoughts.

"I think Mat would feel better if we got back to sharing intel," Trish says, not so much a suggestion as a kind order.

Silvia says, "Sure," looking at me with that hooded gaze that implies she'd like a hug if I want one, and of course I can't accept a hug so I sit down at the table and wait for Trish to tell me what she knows.

"So we've committed suicide by taking on the IAC," Trish says. "Now we decide how we go out."

Her cold mission analysis shouldn't make me feel better. But it does.

"First option," Trish says, pouring herself another drink—the bottle is getting perilously dry, though the only sign of Trish's drunkenness is that she sits majestically straight. "We hide."

"That's not happening." Silvia places her hands flat on the table as if she's ready to take down IAC drones right now. "They have my family."

"Good." Trish tilts her glass towards Silvia. "Eventually we'd have to poke our heads up for resupply and the IAC's data analysts would find us. Hiding just prolongs the inevitable—and lemme tell you, having sheltered some sad sonuvabitches who were waiting for the hammer to fall, you don't wanna wake up every morning wondering if today's the day they *getcha*." She slams her shot glass on the table.

We ponder our options, including tracking down the IAC's as-yet-unknown enemy. After all, they set Silvia free; maybe we can recruit them as allies. Silvia likes the idea. Unfortunately, Trish and I both agree that anyone with the muscle to move on the IAC aren't likely to be people with our best interests at heart. We can't chance escaping one criminal consortium to flee into the teeth of another—not with Silvia's family at stake.

"What if . . ." Silvia's gaze bounces between us, uncertain whether she has anything worthwhile to suggest. "What if we go to the papers? Expose me so big, the government has no choice but to investigate the IAC?" She turns to me with the wide-eyed earnestness of a student hoping they nailed the extra-credit answer. "Wouldn't the military kill for the biology that . . . they . . . inflicted upon me?"

I try to think of a nice way to say, *They'd probably kill you first,* envisioning dissection tables where they'd reverse-engineer Silvia's corpse. Trish snorts.

"No-go." She sniffs her empty glass, willing more bourbon to appear, then groans and reaches for the bottle. "The press is out."

"Why not?"

"That was the first thing they took over." She rubs balled fists into her eyes. "Nobody reads papers anymore—they read websites. Time was, someone would hold up the bodega on Washington Street, and the newspaper would send someone out to make that story popular. Now that popularity flow's reversed—if enough people post about the Washington Street burglary to their social-media accounts, the newspapers will send a reporter out to cover it. The IAC's hacked the social-media trending accounts so their activities will never cross the threshold to be marked as notable." She sighs. "You guys had a firefight on a New Jersey expressway. That story's not even trending in Newark."

"They killed cops. That's gotta trend."

"Among cops and cop families, sure. But that story won't propagate outside the circle. Everybody gets their news from algorithms that determine what's of interest to you these days—and they'll ensure this story's not interesting." She sips. "Unless they want to make it harder for body-hackers to move around in New Jersey. Then this story will go national."

Silvia's pacing with the speed of flies darting back and forth. "So we show up on the doorstep of the *New York Times*'s best reporter. Get face-to-face with someone so popular, their word *can't* be suppressed—"

Ferrett Steinmetz

Trish slams the bottle onto the table. "Think that wasn't my *initial* instinct? Ask Mat how many reporters I know."

Silvia cringes. "I'm sorry—what did you—"

"The IAC is not *ethical*, Silvia." Trish leans back, sneering at the ceiling. "They've weaponized consumer data. Marketing departments wanted to know what movies you were discussing with your friends, what purchases signaled likely life changes, all your secret hobbies. It's not hard to extrapolate that into bribes or blackmail. And then . . ."

She waves her well-manicured hands in the air. "No. No. It's not you. I can't get mad at you."

Silvia flitters around Trish like a moth around a light, reflecting her uncertainty of wanting to comfort Trish yet respect her boundaries. Trish holds up one hand wearily in invitation.

Silvia clasps her hand, exhaling relief.

"I don't like dealing with the IAC," Trish says. "So I asked two buddies to look after me. Both three-limbers, real hard-core bodyhackers—not bodyguards, but a couple of old pals I trusted to take care of me if bad things happened, you get me?

"Then I got flooded with secure texts, asking me if I knew what had happened to Donnie. Word was, Mat had gone rogue and killed seven cops. So I booked a flight to Jersey.

"I didn't say why. I didn't tell anybody where I was going. I *certainly* didn't mention I knew Mat would never kill a cop, and therefore the IAC must have framed him, and therefore he needed someone to haul him out of the soup. But I guess the IAC figured what I was going to do the minute they saw me book the flight."

She contemplates the Wild Turkey, then mutters, "Fuck it," and drains the bottle.

"So what happened?" I ask.

"They had a drone waiting outside my house." She stares dully at the card table. "I had top-notch home defenses. I had two experienced cyber-warfare experts taking point." She lets the bottle roll down to the floor. "Accent on 'had.'"

She smacks her lips, then leans over to pick up the empty bottle to place it gently in a trash can.

"Who'd you ask to come over?" I say.

"Dillon and Birchenough." She walks to the cabinet, contemplating cracking open another bottle—then rinses out her glass and puts it away. "It would have been easier if I'd hired them for the job. But . . . they were doing me a favor. And . . ."

Silvia crosses herself. I bow my head in mourning, but I'm calculating that battle's ramifications: I knew those men. They were professionals, packing top-of-the-line hardware.

The IAC's drones took them down so quickly Trish can't even say noble things about their final battle.

Admittedly, Dillon and Birchenough went down in an ambush. But with the IAC's deep calculations and secret weaponry, you have to expect ambushes are the default.

"I barely got out," Trish says. "And *I* had contingency plans. If you're a big-time reporter who can make a story go viral, I'm willing to bet the IAC has a drone hovering nearby. They probably won't assassinate you with a bullet—no, if they can put you in that body, Silvia, they can inflict fatal strokes at will. If there's a way to get the word out, we can't protect the people who'd tell the world."

"So we can't run and we can't go public. What's our offensive options?"

Trish straightens. "I wanna be clear: we will not make a dent in the IAC's larger operations. We are a wasp declaring war upon an elephant. Dismantling the IAC would take lawyers, governments, armies. We are *not that*."

Silvia's hyperventilating, wringing her hands in fussy meditation rituals.

"A little warning goes a long way with this one," I say to Trish, then squeeze Silvia's shoulder. "Trish is actually saying we've got a chance."

Trish gives us a curt nod. "We have a target. Donnie's not bright. He hasn't taken me off his human-resources call list yet. Just before

Ferrett Steinmetz

he sicced the cops on you, he put out an all-call to hire emergency replacements for Kiva and Saladin, throwing out obscene amounts of money to any body-hacker who could meet him at a Delaware facility."

She taps the card table's surface; it depolarizes, turning into a map and street-level shots of a squat industrial complex that a caption informs me is the E. L. Mustee Industrial Facility in Smyrna, Delaware. The complex is two stories high but spread out like a dormitory, surrounded by electrified fences and turrets—pretty high security for a town my onboard databases inform me has twelve thousand residents. And there's no company logos anywhere on the site, just NO TRESPASSING signs and large vats of industrial chemicals.

"I didn't dare look up the direct address, lest I trigger an IAC search-alarm," Trish says. "But doing map-searches around it gives us a good view of the site. It's right in the line of fire for a lot of civilians."

She gives me a worried glance. She's right to. Of course the IAC would put its secret factories in a sleepy city. The complex sits at the end of the small strip of local stores that makes up Smyrna's three-stoplight main street: I can see the Waffle House where the locals eat, a grade school. I doubt the IAC hires many locals, but the town council's gotta be happy to have a nice tax-revenue base.

I can't take out this installation without splash damage.

My vision tunnels; I'm viewing that site through a drone's camera.

"That's three hours away from the New Jersey docks," Trish says. "As far as I can tell—because I can't do any deep analysis—there's activity inside, but no cars dropping employees off. Pretty sure that's where the converts are guarding your mother."

Silvia's head snaps around. "The *what*?"

"The . . . converts?" Trish stammers; it takes a lot to throw her off her rhythm, but Silvia's managed it. "The . . . bioweapons. Like you. They've been . . . converted."

Silvia shakes her head so fast her features blur. "No. They

weren't converted. People convert to Catholicism. And even if the IAC has—changed—their bodies, I'm not *converted*. I'm still me, and they're still them. Inside somewhere, anyway."

"Okay." Trish steeples her fingers, realizing that arguing with Silvia about her fellow bioweapons is not an argument she'll win. "But we have to call the . . . converts . . . something. Tactically speaking, we have to name them as a group."

Silvia closes her eyes, presses her palm to her chest.

"Monica."

"Monica who?"

"Saint Monica. Patron of grieving mothers and abuse victims. They're not converts, they're Monica."

"How would we even make that plural? Look, can we just call them the hostages, or—"

"My mother and sister are the hostages," Silvia shoots back. "And I don't want you to give them some military jargon that makes it sound like they're targets for you to shoot. You may have to kill them—" She glances over, nervously, at me. "—but I don't want anyone to forget that they have names, had a life before the IAC abducted them." She crosses her arms. "Call them Monica. Or 'the Monicas,' if you have to discuss them as a group."

Even though she's desperate and terrified, Silvia still cares deeply for everyone in that facility, and she won't let us abstract the IAC's victims down to tactical issues.

I feel an ache so great it takes me a moment to identify it as affection.

"Fine. Monica it is." Trish is boiling because she rarely gets steam-rolled. "And you're right in that we want to rescue all the Monicas we can. But we're three people, with limited ammo, and we have to find a way to take that facility down. Because I'm ninety percent sure that's where they were taking you to be tortured into compliance, which explains why they had a Monica stationed close enough to intercept you on the freeway. We can't destroy the IAC—but it's worth sacrificing our lives if we can find some way to destroy that facility."

Ferrett Steinmetz

"We can do it."

"Don't fuck with me, Mat. I'm not in a mood to be fucked with."

"Seriously. We had downtime in the car ride over. I have a plan to take down a facility." I scratch my chin, realizing I'm stubblier than Trish. "At least I think I do."

She sucks air between her teeth. "I don't have any resupply stations I can get you to, Mat. You're low on ammo. We can't call in friends, or special weaponry—"

"Do we have a holocaust cloak?" Silvia snarks, and we shouldn't giggle but we do, because hey, turns out we've both seen *The Princess Bride*.

"I know you're a wizard at planning, Mat. But be serious. You have a plan to take down a massively guarded facility run by techno overlords, filled with hyperfast biological weapons, with what we have on hand?"

"It's . . . a little more complicated than that," I say. "It involves calling in a friend or two, but I'm almost certain they're not people the IAC would have on our watch list. But yeah. I think we can disable that facility. And if Silvia's mom and sister are there, there's a chance we can free them."

"Will we survive?" Silvia asks.

"Oh God, no."

Silvia squeezes my hand so hard a normal human's fingers would crack. But it's better to be brutal, because Trish is right; this is a suicide mission. We can't hope to stop them; we only aim to roll back their progress.

"So what's your hesitation?" Trish asks.

The boy. He wasn't even related to the terrorist, as it turns out. His mother had sent him over to see if his father was there, which his daddy was, a waiter serving guys marked for death, and I'm hitting the "go" switch and a café is rubble and there's a waiter and a cook and four other people crushed under wreckage and somehow I ignored those casualties as part of the equation until one kid got pulverized and my morality flensed the sanity from my brain.

"That's downtown," I say. "People are in the way."

So many boys.

So many ways to kill someone you didn't mean to.

"Come on," Trish says. "If you want me to do this, I gotta leave now."

"I want you to do this right," I snap. "Give me another fifteen minutes."

I've spent the last two hours studying every photograph we have of the facility, figuring out how to minimize any civilian casualties. I've been designing protective threat models, programming algorithms to minimize collateral damage, anticipating the IAC's counterreactions.

Silvia went to bed a long time ago.

I can't sleep. Every extra minute might save another life.

Trish ruffles my hair affectionately, which she can do because I've placed her on my "allowed casual contact" whitelist.

"Mat," she whispers. "It's done."

"It's not. It's still risky. I can shave these percentages down."

She shakes her head slowly, like a drunk shaking off a dream. "Don't lie."

My chest tightens. I'd kill for a cigar.

"Do *not*," I say through gritted teeth, "doubt my ability to protect people."

She waggles her hand, making a little *comme ci, comme ça* gesture. "Big picture, small picture. Is this plan appropriately stupid?"

I check the time; it's getting less stupid by the moment. The only way to defeat a near-omniscient, near-omnipresent entity is to do something so dumb it's dismissed your idiotic strategy, then make that strategy effective enough to succeed.

We should be leading a full-out assault on the IAC's base less than two hours after we ran to ground. That'd be truly idiotic. As-

Ferrett Steinmetz

suming Trish can enlist the necessary help, we'll now be assaulting the IAC's base six hours after we escaped them—which is still stupid, but within the realm of possibility.

Every passing hour is another hour the IAC can bring in more drones to protect its base, devote more AI-banks to counterstrategies, move Silvia's mom and sister away. Wait a week, and they'll be untouchable.

But that kid sure looked like a dog.

"Ten minutes," I beg.

She reaches around to rub my neck. "You broke wher you killed the wrong people, you know."

"I didn't—"

"You broke, Mat." Her voice is filled with compassion but unwilling to brook argument. "And you did what you always do—you fixed the problem. Watching you is pure competence porn, Mat. There's a reason everyone wants to work with you: nobody dies on your shift if you can help it."

I'm squeezing my eyes shut, blocking her out, because I don't do this for the *compliments,* I do it to *safeguard* people.

"But you're overengineering that repair, Mat. You're breaking down because you're optimizing 'protection' to a perfection *you cannot obtain.*"

"No. That's not—"

"People die in war, Mat."

"No."

"*Civilians* die in war."

"I will not accept—"

She wrenches my face up to look at her. "How many people will die if this mission fails because you tried to save everyone?"

"Nobody."

She slaps me hard enough to sting. "*Wrong answer.*"

"Three people. You. Me. Silvia."

She slaps me again, and Vito and Michael ask if I should disable her, but the burning look in those golden eyes paralyzes me. She holds up three fingers, adds two more.

"Silvia's mom. Silvia's sister."

"Still better than—"

She deflects my words with a curt headshake. "The next delivery of new Monicas." She stares experimentally at her five fingers, adds five more with the clear implication they might be bringing in Monicas by the boatload.

"That's not my—"

"Monicas' families, if they don't comply." Trish squeezes ten fingers into doubled fists, and somehow when she opens them I know she's counting tens of murders. "The people who the brainwashed Monicas will murder." She closes her hands into fists again: hundreds. "The people the brainwashed Monicas will coerce into carrying out the IAC's murder, torture, and blackmail."

She balls her hands into fists again and opens them wide to thrust them at me, head cocked as if to ask, *How many is that now?*

"That's a lot," I say. "But that's no excuse to allow civilian casualt—"

"Your breathing's even. You've stopped stammering. Interesting how *those* deaths don't trigger your PTSD."

Her words seize me up like a frozen engine. Part of me wants to slap her back to shut her up, while another part is analyzing my own reactions, realizing that yes, I was as okay with those deaths in the abstract as I had been with the drone deaths before I'd accidentally killed that boy.

"You are the most selflessly selfish man I have ever met." Trish shakes her head in exhausted admiration. "Do you know how many noble missions I tried to sell you on? I had good assignments where you could have taken out some real bastards—and you played it safe, choosing the penny-ante stuff where you could ensure some level of quote-unquote 'safety.'

"But people died because you didn't show up, Mat."

Now the PTSD kicks in, my heartbeat elevating, my protests degenerating into staccato syllables.

Ferrett Steinmetz

Because people died when I *did* show up. The kid was just the first one I'd paid attention to. There had always been civilians in proximity to the explosions, bad intelligence that sent missiles flying at innocent targets; I'd written all those corpses off as the cost of keeping America safe.

Then I noticed one kid dying, and he was the gateway to perceiving the devastation my duty wrought. I focus on that one kid because he's the only one I can put a face to, but when I think back on my time in the Air Force I wonder how many people I murdered by mistake and I can't even *remember*, I just stuffed the dead in a box marked "casualties" and never looked back.

"You wouldn't take jobs from bad men, Mat," Trish says kindly. "That puts you above most of the mercenaries I work with. You're a good man who wants to save everybody. And it's time you realize that each decision you make gets someone killed, *even if you refuse to make a decision.*"

I'm pushing the button that fired that missile at what I thought was a dog, and how the fuck was I okay with even killing a dog? I was okay with killing the waiters. Jesus, I was a monster even then but I couldn't acknowledge it until I looked my murders straight in the face.

Now I have readouts to tell me where every bullet I fire lands—I refuse to blind myself to the harm I do in the course of justice, I *have* to be better than I was, I owe it to my forgotten victims to mark the names of my future casualties.

But how can I keep pulling the trigger, knowing every mission risks killing another kid?

"I can't," I whisper. "I killed—"

"*I know what you killed.*"

My gunports clack, that patented Endolite-Ruger sound. I didn't consciously authorize them, but I'm glad they did—nobody dismisses the child I murdered.

Trish steps forward, presses her chest against my gunports.

"Don't you *dare* tell me I'm not grieving for that boy you killed.

You think you're the only one with a list? I had a housewife who ran for cover when I was laying down suppressive fire. She got torn to shreds. I've put her kids through college—and no. That doesn't make up for it."

"That makes no sense," I say. "How do you—you can't keep fighting when you realize the cost. That'd make you a monster."

She spreads her arms open, inviting me to look at the horror she's become. "I'm a monster who fights monsters, Mat. Because the alternative is to never fight. Those cocksuckers *count* on that. Sure. Blame yourself for firing the missiles. You *should*. You *fucked up*. But while you're at it, apportion out a little blame to the assholes who hid among civilians. Apportion blame to the people who were so dedicated to seizing power that 'talking them out of it' became an invalid strategy.

"And consider," she continues. "Consider. I don't know what the guys you killed would have done if you hadn't stopped them. I can't tell you if you were a genuine hero or the US government's hitman, blindly blitzkrieging any target they pointed you at. But I *do* know what the IAC will do if someone doesn't get in their way. I know that a good man—a genuinely good man—will make tough calls that cowardly people who call themselves good would walk away from."

She sits down, hanging her hands between her legs. "So yeah. Your plan will put innocents in the line of fire. That's war. The difference between you and them is, you care about the people you're risking."

I think she'll keep talking. She doesn't.

She's waiting for my decision.

I look at the plan again. Our assault starts midmorning. The kids will be in school, the Waffle House lunch-hour rush won't be until 11:00, the potential for people walking in the way will be minimized.

But there will always be some kid running late to school on his bicycle. There'll always be a waitress on her way to her shift. And a firefight at the facility has no guarantee it won't spill out onto the streets, where the IAC may target whoever's nearby to break me.

All so they can keep killing, and killing, and killing.

I upload the necessary files to an ISB stick, realizing I am no longer a good man. Good men exist exclusively in comic books, where heroes ensure only bad people die.

I shudder, as I accept myself: a monster who fights monsters.

As I hand over the ISB stick, I feel like some portion of my soul has gone with it. I'm at peace, yet simultaneously filled with a dread that will never leave.

"Thank you." She kisses me chastely on the forehead. "And now," she says, pulling a shotgun strap over her shoulder, "You get some R and R before the final push. Go hold Silvia. She needs you."

I shake my head. "I won't take advantage of her."

Another transfixing gaze. "Mat. She's freaking out in there; I tried talking her down, but she doesn't know me as well as she knows you."

"She barely knows me. Our best move is to—"

She shushes me. "You help her. She helps you. And she's lonely, and convinced nobody will ever want her again, and she's in love with you every bit as much as you are with her."

"That's not love. That's—"

"This is your last night on Earth. You're overoptimizing again, engineering a long-term relationship when what you both need is a hot-fix patch. Whatever happens tonight is what you both need, okay?"

"I'm not some romance hero," I protest, hearing myself stammer. "I don't sweep people off their feet."

"I'm not saying you will." She shoots me a mischievous grin. "Just . . . don't rule it out."

"But how will we . . . ?" I gesture in the air, trying to encompass Silvia's new body. "I don't even know, you know, what she has for that sort of thing."

Trish closes her eyes, a teacher talking down to a child who has so much to learn. "Take it from a girl who's got her own body issues. Sex is more than the equipment."

I am a cyber-behemoth packing four armed limbs, and somehow Trish makes me feel like a gawky teenager. She pushes me towards Silvia's door, though with my mass it's like nudging a Volkswagen.

"Go," she says.

"I'm not promising anything."

"Go."

She pushes.

I stumble into Silvia's room.

Silvia's room has—had—a television mounted on the wall.

But the screen's shattered, the cot overturned. The rug's scattered with denim tatters and lumberjack rags where she tore her clothes off. Silvia's huddled naked in the corner, making twitching movements with her hands as she mutters to herself.

I must have been deep in planning if I tuned out her meltdown.

I squeeze into the room, my legs picking their way through the debris. And as I approach Silvia, I realize what her repetitive hand movements are:

She's praying.

She's praying for her mother and sister to hold on, praying somehow my plan will work, praying we can rescue everyone from the IAC's clutches—the litany of a helpless woman who has no choices left and so drops her troubles into God's hands.

She crosses herself like she's doing exercises. But the problem with praying, even if you believe God hears you, is that you never know what His answer will be.

I approach slow, so she can hear me coming.

I wrap my arms around her waist, pull her against my unarmored belly.

We tense.

I don't let people touch me intimately; gentle caresses make me feel like a scrap of amputee flesh pinned between four battle-engines. The cilia on her spine wriggle against my stomach, soft hairs exploring me.

She freezes, giving me time to be repulsed.

I'm not.

I'm in love.

I pull her closer, concentrating on her newness; her knurled muscles are cool but still warm enough to be living, pulsing as she adjusts position but still very much a woman's shape. Her back's larger cilia snuffle me, kicking up that hazy ammonia scent that wafts off her skin.

My body reacts to her touch. It's a traditional male reaction.

She leans her head back into me, letting out a low terrified exhale. I take the hint and lean down to kiss the nape of her neck, where the last of her human skin shades bumpy and green. She shivers as my tongue slides across that sweet spot where the muscles in her neck meet her collarbone.

I continue down to the waving fields of her shoulder, planting kisses on her alien flesh.

It's like kissing someone with a thick mustache—a little disconcerting if you're not used to it, but it rapidly becomes the new normal.

She whirls around in my arms; she's kissing me so fiercely my fleshy body shivers, and yes, I am a stub hanging from four killing machines but she knows me and I know her and it's all right.

And as she wraps her fingers around my stiffened cock, I don't know how we'll do this. Part of me wants to scan her anatomy with Vito's sensors, figure out what the IAC engineered her for, which leads to cascades of plans where I stiffen in bad ways and wonder whether this is adrenaline-fueled stupidity, what promises I am making by making love to a woman in need.

She pulls away from our kisses, grabs my face in both hands.

"I know you plan everything through." She tilts her head, peering deep into my eyes. "But for once. Please. Just trust that everything will turn out okay?"

She prays with her body. And lovemaking, done right, is its own form of prayer.

I don't believe in God.

But I do believe in Silvia.

You may have noticed I like old movies. And in old movies, they never have sex scenes: they pan away to a crackling fireplace, shying away from the tawdry physical details.

I like that. The folks in movies are my friends. Friends should have privacy once the intimacy starts.

So instead, let's pan away to Trish as she accomplishes the most difficult part of my plan: walking down the street.

You may note I skipped over the fine details of getting Herbie from "that abandoned house" to "Kiva's shop" because, well, I was having too much fun talking to Silvia. But that was, in many ways, the trickiest part of the escape—dodging security cameras in a networked world is a skill all its own.

So let's watch a mistress at work.

First step for Trish: running seven miles through thick woods to get back to town in time to make our plan work. For Trish, who's still packing meat-legs, that's a task in and of itself.

But the real work begins once she gets to the town's edge. Because modern civilization swarms with cameras: overhead drones, smartcar scanners, home security–AIs monitoring their lawns, streetlamp cameras.

Trish emerges into a sleepy rural Pennsylvanian town, which gives us a chance: I don't think there's a square foot in New York City that isn't monitored. This town only has a few thousand cameras.

The IAC's analyst-routines—or the IAC's enemy—may be scanning any of them.

So while she's still deep in the woods, Trish puts on her disguise.

Ferrett Steinmetz

It'd be easy to throw off facial-recognition technology with kabuki-style theater makeup, turning your eye sockets into hollows. But some kid may point his camera at your face because hey, crazy clown-lady. You have to strike a balance between throwing off automated systems and drawing human attention.

So she uses shader to shrink her nose profile. She cons a formfitting outfit that pads her breasts and ass. She tugs on special boots that add an inch to her height and jab spikes into the balls of her feet to throw off the IAC's gait-recognition technology.

And when she's done, she consults the satellite window to see when it's okay to move, then walks out to head to her PlusOne contact location.

Getting a smartcar's easy—as long as you're willing to give it your login information. Which presents a problem for people who do not want to be tracked, especially paranoid people who, say, are pretty sure the IAC's superhacking capabilities would have uncovered their SmartCar accounts.

So what do you do when you need to ride off the grid?

You use the PlusOne database. It's like Uber, but for Uber.

Trish tries to look casual as she heads to her PlusOne contact's house. Getting a PlusOne contact is, like all criminal activities, not without risk—some people set up PlusOne honeypot accounts, figuring anyone who needs anonymized rides can be profitably blackmailed or robbed.

But Trish realizes she won't need her gun as she peeks into the trailer's windows and sees the traditional PlusOne contact—a junkie, willing to bet her future for hot cash. Trish pulls a balaclava over her face before she knocks on the door; a harried white housewife cradling a baby in one track mark–scarred arm appears.

"I need a ride," Trish says.

The mother squints, shaking off her high. The infant squalls as she fumbles out her smartphone. "You didn't set up an appointment."

"I'm so sorry." Trish peels off several hundred-dollar bills. "Maybe this will help."

The mother beams; this is a nice home for a junkie. Then again, a good PlusOne lifestyle will provide a steady income—until one of those anonymous people you gave a ride to gets arrested, at which point it turns out you're legally responsible for aiding and abetting.

"I'll call one in," the mother says. "But Clarice has to come. You didn't give me time to get a sitter."

No mother should willingly bring her kid along on a ride to a criminal rendezvous. But Trish hopes nothing bad will happen on this ride, so she risks it.

After an awkward wait, the mother says she doesn't know why the smartcars are running so late. Trish doesn't volunteer that she might be responsible.

A car arrives. Trish climbs in the back seat; there's no good way to disable the car's internal security cameras, but she knows where to sit to give cameras a minimal angle. They drive towards to the address that Trish went to some effort to find.

They pull up next to a nice rental-apartment complex—not so nice as to be a gated community, thank God, but the sidewalks are well-kept and the plants on the balconies aren't dying. It's a place where working-class stiffs pool their rent money to live somewhere nice.

There, we get the first break we've gotten in this whole shebang: as Trish clambers out of the car, another woman emerges from her own smartcar rental. That woman's shoulders are slumped, her blouse sweaty after a double shift, stumbling to her doorstep after being debriefed by the cops and knowing she has two hours to crash before the smartcar facility needs her back at work to clean up this mess.

Trish steps in, smiling sympathetically. "Violet, isn't it? Listen, we met last night." Trish talks with the buddy-buddy ease of someone who met her at a hackerspace and not a smartcar heist. "Can we talk? In private?"

The SmartCar employee polishes her tortoiseshell glasses, her lips crooking into a smile. Because buried somewhere in last night's

Ferrett Steinmetz

chaos was a complicated story she'd resigned herself to never hearing, knowing she'd go to her grave never quite understanding what the hell was up with that crazy bug-lady and the man with the cyborg limbs.

She might just get closure after all.

ACT 3

Going the
Distance

"I always wondered how it would be if a superior species landed on earth and showed us how they play chess, and I feel now I know."

—Peter Heine Nelson, on watching two human-superior chessbots playing against each other, December 2017

"I will lift up mine eyes unto the hills, from whence cometh my help," Silvia says, dressed in a blue blouse Trish picked out from the shelter. "My help cometh from the Lord, which made Heaven and Earth."

We are standing in a circle—Trish, Silvia and I— touching foreheads, arms around each other's shoulders, each arm different but all of us united.

We are going into battle.

Back in the Drone Corps, we bellowed hoo-rah bullshit before settling in to a command-and-kill mission: the guys would blast "Ride of the Valkyries" as we strutted down to our comm center, getting into an *Apocalypse Now* headspace.

"He will not suffer thy foot to be moved," Silvia says. "He that keepeth thee will not slumber."

But the Drone Corps were nerds trying to convince ourselves we were badass. We controlled trillions in top-notch American technology, weaponry that could kill a cockroach from across a continent.

How could we not be righteous?

"Behold, he that keepeth Israel shall neither slumber nor sleep," she continues, wincing as she realizes that verse doesn't quite fit; she didn't have time to research battle prayers. "The Lord is thy keeper; the Lord is thy shade upon thy right hand."

I remember how much I loved the Drone Corps'

inevitability. We were the government's sword; they gave us a target and we annihilated the enemy in holy fire. Every missile we fired killed people who threatened America, and America was the world.

We were nerds needing to believe our cause was so pure that it didn't matter who else got killed.

"The sun shall not smite thee by day, nor the moon by night."

Yet as Silvia speaks, her voice wavering, we are unconvinced of our righteousness. We know our enemy is evil; of this, there is no question. Trish says word on the street is thirteen body-hackers have responded to Donnie's call, some scrambling for cash to pay the upkeep on their ever-degrading prosthetics.

We will kill them if they stand in our way.

But we will also grieve for them.

"The Lord shall preserve thee from all evil," she says. "He shall preserve thy soul."

I hope He does, if He exists. Because there will be explosions that endanger downtown Smyrna, there will be friendly fire, there will be people walking into a war zone. The IAC may take hostages, and we cannot afford surrender.

We grieve for the people who may die so that we may succeed. This is our acknowledgment of the costs of the war we are about to undertake; there will be innocents hurt. We will take precautions. But we are fallible, God, so fallible, and war is where all the variables have deadly costs.

"The Lord shall preserve thy going out and thy coming in from this time forth." Silvia swallows.

I look at Silvia. I ponder the casualties that might get inflicted in carrying out this plan.

But she's what gets lost if I *don't* take that chance. Her and the other IAC victims.

"And even forevermore," she concludes.

We mutter an "amen" and dwell in the silence. This is when we grieve. For there will be no grief in the moment of battle; we can

Ferrett Steinmetz

grieve before, we can grieve afterwards, but grieving in the middle will get us killed.

I mean, we'll get killed anyway. But let's be efficient.

Let us become merciful monsters.

Trish crosses herself, though I know she's not religious. "For thine is the kingdom, and the power, and the glory, of the Father and Son, and of the Holy Spirit, now and ever, and unto ages and ages."

We ponder that. We will not have ages and ages. We will sacrifice ourselves to take down an IAC facility—and we might fail. Even if we succeed, the IAC will ensure no one remembers us.

But I look at Silvia. I remember that poor woman I had to destroy—

—*they make me they make me THEY MAKE ME*—

—and I ask myself: *Is it worth these lives to stop the IAC from annihilating more people like Silvia, even if that's temporary?*

I look at Silvia. She's clutching the empty space where once, in a previous life, her crucifix hung. She's looking up at me, knowing she might be recaptured, knowing she might one day be the insane woman on the freeway, tortured into compliance, her faith removed.

She nods.

"Amen," I say, and I'm praying, praying to someone I never believed in, grasping for a faith in some promised goodness.

And then it's time to kill.

We're speeding towards the E. L. Mustee Industrial Facility at fifty miles per hour in a hijacked van, the van's automatic pilot banking around the Appalachians' mountainous curves as I map out our assault.

"This factory's huge." I plant my index finger on the overhead shot Trish has pulled up on her tablet. "The size of a mega Walmart. We'll encounter heavy resistance as we make our way through the facility, so scouting isn't our best move. Which means we have to make our best guesses as to where our twin objectives are located. Silvia, where do you think the facility's vital points are?"

She doesn't hear me; she's looking out the window, thumping the car's armrest, staving off her panic disorder.

The closer we get to zero hour, the closer she gets to falling apart.

Trish glances anxiously over at Silvia, expecting me to intercede. That's comforting; I'm the boyfriend now.

"Silvia." I don't dare touch her; if I surprise her, she might wrench my arm off. "Do you remember what I told you back when the drones were coming in to get us?"

She blinks. "'All combat comes down to preparation.'"

"We had two minutes then to make a plan." I cradle her soft fingers in my metal digits. "You fought well. And you won. But now we have twenty minutes left before we get to the facility. We need to take advantage of that remaining time to help your mother and sister."

She blinks again; the glazed terror fades. "Mama. Vala."

"Yes. And what did I tell you?"

She stares at the floor, ashamed how distracted her panic makes her. "You . . . you want me to do this alone."

"No." I squeeze her hands. "I want, more than anything, to come with you. But we need to cover four football fields of facility. *I* need to find the central controls to wreck this joint. *You* need to get Mama and Vala out."

I'll be going in hot and noisy—because we have to assume they have weaponry designed to take Silvia down. If I do enough damage on the way, with luck they'll send everyone after me and let Silvia exfiltrate her relatives.

I don't tell her I've taken the suicide position.

"Memorize the map." I draw my finger across the tablet's shatterproof surface. "They've got liquid-storage containers spread across the facility to distribute some kind of supply chain—most of which will be broken open by the time we arrive. Based on the venting

Ferrett Steinmetz

arrangements, those tanks are most likely flammable. Based on the feed lines leading out from them, they're probably extremely toxic chemicals mixed in-facility."

"How do you—" Silvia says.

Trish nods serenely. "He was a drone pilot."

"Oh. Yeah."

I'd never considered overhead target analysis to be a superpower, but watching the way Trish reacts, I guess it is.

"Between the lung-burning chemicals and the actual burning," I tell her, "things will be chaotic. So commit your pathways to memory now. These three areas are most likely barracks and/or prisons, based on the venting and heating-duct placement on the roof. However, this location faces the exterior—unlikely for a prison—and the other's some kind of terrarium, with a glass ceiling. But this facility has a loading bay that's shielded from the streets, connecting right into a barrack. I suspect that's where they keep the people they don't want seen."

"So Mama and Vala are in there." I recognize her breathing as another meditation exercise.

"Mama and Vala are *most likely* to be there," I stress. "I believe that's where the IAC keeps their biologically enhanced acquisitions. But they might consider it overkill to keep human prisoners there. So you'll have to scour the areas, make the call, then move on to potential zones number two and number three if you don't find them."

"But how will I know whether—"

"That's your call. I wish I had a better answer for you, Silvia, but we haven't mapped the interior. Maybe it's a big empty space; maybe it's a maze where you'll have to go door-to-door. Whatever it is, I trust your judgment. You've got good instincts." And before she can ponder the mathematics of "when to abandon your mother and sister," I shoot her another question: "See the three locations? Can you map out the quickest, stealthiest route to move between them?"

Her eyes jitter. The IAC's enhanced previsualization skills course through her. "Yes. I see."

"Do *not* engage." I poke her in the chest. "Trish's intel says there are thirteen body-hackers in addition to Donnie. They will have weaponry designed to take you down."

"But I *creamed* Donnie!" Her confidence both heartens and terrifies me.

"In an enclosed space," I correct her. "You were designed to be a stealth unit—get in close enough to hit your target, disable their bodyguards, destroy them. If you have to close a significant distance, their long-range weapons will tear you to shreds."

I squeeze my eyes shut, thinking of the freeway woman before I blasted her into twitching strands.

"You're no longer a mystery threat. Donnie will have compensated. Do not underestimate him, or the IAC. Promise me you'll get in, get them, and *get out*."

The fire in her eyes dies. She still wants to fight, that same pugnacious instinct she's always had—but she's hamstrung by uncertainty and inexperience.

I want to tell her everything will be okay, but . . . this is war.

"Remember," I say. "You *can* kick ass—never doubt your strength when your back's against the wall. But kicking ass is not the mission. The mission is Mama and Vala. Bring them here." I point to a location a mile away from the facility. "Trish will be waiting here for exfiltration."

Silvia cocks her head. "Trish isn't coming?"

Trish holds up her unarmored hands. "Putting meatware into a cyber-battle? Might as well drop me into a blender."

Silvia utters a little "aww, honey" sound. "That doesn't mean you're—"

Trish snorts. "Don't think I'm useless. I hauled your asses out of the fire back at the smartcar facility, and my tactics will ensure this goes down as clean as possible. But I'm a fixer, not a fighter. I won't put my reflexes up against yours—or his."

Ferrett Steinmetz

Silvia draws back, uncertain what to make of Trish's characteristic show of self-confidence. "Wait—Mat, I know you're—"

"I'm headed here." I point to another section. "Where the electricity lines converge." Solar power and batteries are good enough to power most residential homes—but when you've got heavy-duty industrial tech, you gotta draw power from the grid. "The backup generator's stationed there, indicating that's where the heavy-duty tech is. In an ideal world I'd bomb their manufacturing facilities, but with our minimal firepower I'll settle for personally annihilating their control servers."

"You'll meet up with us after you've completed your mission, right?"

Her cheer is soap-bubble fragile, ready to collapse into panic. I don't like lying to her, but . . .

I check my inventory: no mortars, no missiles, 37 percent rifle ammo and short-range shotguns. Not much for the combat I expect to see.

I've chosen to prioritize the safety of Silvia's family over mine. That's not open for debate. And I won't tell her the odds of her new boyfriend's survival when she needs to focus on her family.

"I'll get there one way or another," I lie, hoping Trish will be able to keep her in line when Silvia gets back to the escape vehicle to discover that yeah, I'm dead, and good *God* I want one last cigar and a makeout session with Silvia before I die.

Instead, I go over the plan one more time.

The E. L. Mustee facility is an enormous space for fourteen bodyhackers to cover. Donnie's spread out his men according to what must be IAC tactics, two on each road leading into the factory. The live feed from the city's public cameras shows the sparse 10:00 A.M. crowd strolling to a halt as they notice the heavily armed— literally—mercenaries pacing to burn off their precombat jitters, peering towards the horizon.

Donnie's men are not, shall we say, top quality. Three are pathetic one-limbers, having replaced an arm with weaponry but not having the guts to fully commit. That makes them more approachable at parties, sure, but once the bullets fly they'll be at the mercy of those slow, slow meat-speeds.

They stand, dwarfed, by the facility, which is surrounded by electrified fences and long stretches of well-mowed lawn so that anyone sneaking in will have to cross a big open space.

The rest—well, it's hard to extract fine details from the city's public cameras, as the video is stuttering as thousands of people tune in to Smyrna's public feeds, anxious to watch the mayhem. But Donnie's new hires have the low-rent look of mercenaries who either need excitement more than they want a paycheck, or need a paycheck more than they want anything.

Trish murmurs, "Oh, my emails will go over *gangbusters*." She hits "send" on a private email to the thirteen body-hackers who are not Donnie.

You can see them squint as the priority email hits their in-boxes. Then they glance at the guy standing next to them.

Poison's in the water.

But whether they're packing one limb or three they've all got their gunports open towards the road, and onlookers are leaning out of the windows, shouting to clueless pedestrians to *get inside*, and Donnie's scowling and stomping and firing rounds into the ground like a matador demanding a bull to charge.

And then—

"This exploit is piggybacked upon BlackLaura's," Trish explains *to Violet, holding up an ISB stick. "You have to insert the exploited software physically into the admin port—but once you do, it'll wipe all video-camera footage, and forensic evidence will make it look like the exploit we used last night was a virus spreading from smartcar facility to smartcar facility."*

Trish's tablet, which she's propped on a shelf behind her so Violet can't avoid seeing it as they chat, shows Silvia. Violet keeps glancing

Ferrett Steinmetz

guiltily over at her, thinking of the sad story Trish told her about Silvia's kidnapping and the impending enslavement of a hundred other people like Silvia.

Remember, kids, you can be truthful *and* manipulative.

Violet plucks the exploit-stick from Trish's hand, rolls it between thumb and forefinger. "So you're asking me to hand you control of my cars again."

Trish grimaces, as if she'd rather not have put it that way, but nods.

"You're asking me to risk a job I'm on the verge of getting fired from."

Trish jerks her head towards Silvia's image—which was chosen not to show "Silvia the badass warrior" but "Silvia the overwhelmed panic-disorder patient." The screen splits into two images of Silvia, and then four, multiplying to imply what the IAC will do to infinite Silvias unless someone stops them.

"It's for a good cause," Trish says.

And the cars come in from every direction, zooming down the roads, a roaring river of reflective orange vehicles revving up to top speed as they aim themselves straight at the E. L. Mustee facility.

Some are battered where they've smashed through police barricades; most have smoking gunshots through the hoods where various antidefense mechanisms have tried to take them out, their bumpers flecked with car paint. Some flop along on burst tires, struggling towards top speed. The body-hackers look comically outgunned as the cars race towards the factory, two armed men standing in an access road as they face down a freeway's worth of zooming traffic.

Donnie fires first, an illegal mortar blasting out a vast pothole and shattering the Waffle House's windows. But the cars are like spawning salmon, zooming up onto the sidewalks, plowing through garbage cans, so desperate they'll fight their way upstream past any danger; the roads leading into New Castle County are littered with crumpled smartcars where cops and IAC drones have tried to stop them.

The surviving cars aim themselves at their targets.

Of course, the IAC has known they were coming. Hell, it hit the newsfeeds when smartcar facilities got compromised, and it wasn't hard to see where the cars were homing in on, and now every looky-loo's tuning in to see what'll happen once the smartcar invasion hits Smyrna.

But there's basically two rules of warfare:

- come at them where they're not expecting you, or
- come at them with such overwhelming force that it doesn't matter if they know you're coming.

Brute force is always the better option if you have it.

"Fire!" Donnie yells, which is of course redundant as the body-hackers' programming has them firing the millisecond the cars are within their gun range, and weaponized drones hidden in the facility's courtyard are rising into the air and firing, firing, firing. And—

Windows open. A skirl of electrified raptors spiral upwards from the area I'd marked as a terrarium, zipping out to dive-bomb the cars with outstretched talons crackling with electricity, and what the hell are the hawks doing there when the hawks belong to the IAC's enemies?

Individual cars go down. But the smartcar armada's velocity shoves the disabled cars forward, shunting wrecks aside into alleys so the others can keep moving, and Donnie screams "How many *are* there?"

"You're gonna need more than four hundred cars to take those bastards down," Violet says. *"Is that software copyable?"*

Trish shakes her head. "You've misunderstood; this just looks like a virus," she explains. "Enough to make the forensic agents at Smart-Car HQ paranoid we found some hardware exploit. It'll give enough deniability that you'll probably keep your job. But . . . it can't spread. Not on its own. You'd have to travel to each smartcar hub individu-

ally and install it via the physical access port." She squints at Violet, who crosses her legs impatiently to inform Trish she knows that already. "You're a local sysop. That doesn't get you physical access to other smartcar branches . . . does it?"

Violet takes a contemplative draw on a cherry-red vape pen, exhales vanilla-scented nicotine mist. "No. No, it doesn't."

"Then why would you need more than one copy of the software?"

Violet smacks her lips, pondering how to get her point across. "There used to be five of us working in my department."

Trish stays silent, lets Violet work through whatever she has to say.

"They never lay you off," Violet continues. "That means they'd have to pay you unemployment. No, they analyze some part of the job that used to be so complex it needed human intervention, then automate what you did, then crack down to see who they can fire first. Show up thirty-five seconds late? Fired. Refuse to work an extra six hours to cover for the guy they fired yesterday because he arrived thirty-five seconds late? You don't have the company spirit.

"I've stuck it out as long as I can, but . . ." She plucks at her ill-fitting white-and-gold uniform, which makes her look like a janitor with sad military aspirations. "They treat us like shit and act like we should be grateful, and every year they fire the most experienced guys and hire cheaper idiots we have to cover for, and I know. I know that long before I'm dead, these assholes will find a way to replace what I do and me and my friend's job at SmartCar will be replaced by some clueless fucker who works eighty hours a week, travelling from facility to facility to do some twice-a-month check-in.

"Bad enough they're looking to replace me. But God fucking dammit, they could leave me with some dignity."

Violet slumps, taking down the tablet to look at Silvia.

"We bitch sometimes, you know," she continues. "In private chat lines. Because if you complain on your social media, that's a fireable offense. But we have places where we console the last poor schmuck who got tossed out on his ear."

Trish nods solemnly. "We can copy this software."

"And I can talk to people who wanna send a message to the company."

At least three thousand cars are converging upon the E. L. Mustee facility, coordinating their efforts with hypercomputational efficiency. Some veer off from the main inrush to smash themselves into telephone poles, the poles bouncing as the electrical wires above catch them briefly before snapping.

The town of Smyrna goes dark.

Still other vehicles race ahead to ram away any potential obstructions between them and the factory, tons of kamikaze metal aimed with pinpoint precision to clear a path at all costs. Their speakers are blaring classic movie quotes as they drive to warn off any heroic civilians: "Get out." "Run away! Run away!" "Out of the water—now!" "Run for it, Marty!"

And one final favorite that I couldn't resist: "It's a trap!" (Also see: "Show Silvia Star Wars.")

The smarter body-hackers have hauled chunks of cement to serve as protective barriers—but this facility's got a vast perimeter, it wasn't designed to stave off this invasion, and they only had an hour to prepare their defenses before the cars hit. The cars swerve apart to go off-road, splitting up and jouncing over the dry grass to smash through the electrified fences, carrying mangled sections of chain-link with them before ditching themselves into corners to make way for newer cars.

Some detonate, flipping over and over as they hit mines hidden in the grass. The IAC wasn't fucking around.

Donnie dives behind a concrete barrier he hauled out front, his legs picking out the best cover for shielding, as do the other three-limbers. The two-limbers who've replaced their legs also have a chance. However, the poor bastards who still have meat-feet can't move fast enough as the cars jerk aside to pick off easy targets. Their mouths open in a surprised "O" as they're sent flying, tumbling on the ground as cars plow over their bodies until muscle and circuitry are mangled into obsolescence.

The cars have cleared straight shots at their targets, and the drones are firing and electrohawks are squawk-diving, but there's too many inbound vehicles, and the smartcar coordinations reroute around any damaged cars to keep the inexorable flow, and *wham* the first car smashes into a liquid-storage tank, and *wham* another car smashes into that car from behind to drive in the wedge, and a sickly green fluid courses out from a split in the reinforced metal, turning into a chemical waterfall, and *wham* when the third car hits there's a spark from the crumpling metal or maybe it's the bullets or an electrohawk's zap but the *wham* turns into a great lung-busting *whoof* as the spilled fluid catches fire in a great black smoke cloud and a swarm of erratic flame, and the fire-suppressant modules start putting it out when *wham* another car smashes into that—

(And I hear Silvia draw a ragged breath because her mother and sister are inside, we don't know where the fire will spread, that's the monstrous risk we take as monsters and as Silvia crosses herself I realize I'm crossing myself too.)

The remaining body-hackers are separated because the cars have noticed them taking cover behind the initial forward assault and they're jamming themselves into reverse, and there is a matador, except instead of a matador it's one body-hacker facing down four cars coming at him to smear him into the pavement.

Donnie's stopped using his missiles because the first car he blew up almost cooked his lungs despite his cooling air-filters, and instead hops with nimble precision onto now-dead cars to blast the live ones' engines out with an accuracy I envy. Two other body-hackers are wet streaks, the cars instructed to run their bodies over again so playing possum won't save them, but Donnie's untouchable—springing off at the last minute as a car rams his platform out from under him, disabling that car's engine with three precise shots so he lands on the dying vehicle, one hand reaching out to stabilize himself as his weapons disable two other cars, creating a safe space of dead metal to use as a defensive platform.

"Jesus," Trish whispers. "He had an hour to program that reaction package." Even though we're rooting for the cars we have to give Donnie silent awe.

This is what he does.

This is why he's survived despite his other manifest sloppinesses.

But Donnie's a small part of a big war. The cars around him smash into any structure they can get at, aiming for support pillars, some catapulted high into the air by mines, but their forward momentum sends them sailing through second-floor windows. A few angle up through stairs to do a *"Heeeere's Johnny!"* through reinforced doorways. It's an omnidirectional assault, and I hear the rumble as buildings teeter and collapse; we're coming into view as our car joins the river and Trish tells Silvia hold back, not yet, don't leap out.

Because the cars have smashed into cryotanks that spill icy toxins out, and they're burying their grilles into loading docks, and the drones have fired so many rounds their ammo's empty, and the place becomes the world's most on-fire parking lot—just a sea of crumpled cars bumper-to-bumper for a mile in every direction.

The camera feed from city hall cuts off. As I expected. Because I know what's coming next.

One by one, like great spiders, the Monicas come crawling out from the wreckage.

The IAC could have led with a Monica assault, I suppose, but the IAC's leaders are smart enough to consider the optics of using their secret bioweapons as their first defense—and given they're short-range stealth weapons, I'm not sure how much help they'd have been against the car assault. It was politically useful for the IAC to showcase the carnage—pardon the pun—of this devastating hack-threat, because nobody on the outside understands why this attack's happening. This will look like we're the bad guys.

But now there's smoke everywhere to fog the satellites, and the remaining hawks are taking down incoming newsdrones. The IAC's doing its damndest to ensure the only people who get glimpses

Ferrett Steinmetz

of Monica will be townsfolk who'll find the IAC has erased their smartphone video.

I count at least sixty Monicas skittering up the buildings, facing us—they know where we are. The IAC's AIs probably know what car we're in because they marked our last-minute, not-from-a-smartcar-hub insertion into the traffic flow.

This is a ground game. Donnie and the surviving body-hackers are weaving their way through the factories to get to us, and the Monicas will obliterate us once they close the distance.

Which is why I crawl out of the car so no one can get a distant shot at me, then activate Vito and Michael's handy-dandy crowd-control bullhorns—not something I'd have packed, but military-grade weaponry comes with military priorities—and thank God we have something loud enough to talk directly to the Monicas.

Silvia clears her throat.

"I know you think you're assassins now." Silvia's voice shakes a little as her words ring out across the flaming smartcars. "But I want you to remember back to when you were like me. Because you are like me—and I'm like you. The IAC chose us as test subjects because we all have the same thing in common:

"We fought."

The Monicas freeze on the concrete walls, their tendrils quivering as they listen to the echo of something they once were.

"You were always terrified and never strong enough, weren't you? But you fought to keep your life together. You tried not to lean on your loved ones too hard. And when you heard of an experimental technique that might remove your panic disorder, you signed up—because you hadn't given up.

"Do you remember that? Do you remember how hard you fought for stability before they broke you?"

An insane babble carries across the smoldering parking lot, too chaotic for even my fine-tuned audio-filters to pick out individual noises—but the Monicas are shouting in cracked, off-key voices, interrupted by basso computer sounds barking out commands the Monicas have been Pavlovian-engineered to obey.

They're remembering, all right.

"Look—look at all we've laid waste to make a path for you." Her words catch in her throat as she gets distracted by the field of burning wreckage—but that hesitation makes her sound braver. "We've thrown everything we've had at them—and it's not enough. And it's like always: you can get all the help you want, but in the end, it's your struggle that gets it done."

The Monicas are far from united. Some of them stare down at their hands, as if trying to recall the memories of human flesh. Others flick their gazes across their fellow monsters, gauging what sorts of help or threat they pose.

"We've burned our last chance to give you this opportunity. And believe me, I . . . have some idea how bad it will be if you turn against your captors and fail. The IAC is not merciful. Whatever hold they have left on you, well . . . they'll use it.

"But they were going to do that anyway. They'll use you up and toss you aside. The question is, How easy do you want to make it for them?

"I know how scared you are. Of losing everything. I'm . . ." She swallows, frozen by the possibilities of what the IAC might have already done to her mother and sister. "But you still have the possibility of a good life left. You always did." She glances shyly over at me. "If you reach out, you'll always find someone to help.

"That's us today. We've given you one final chance to break free. Now, do you remember how to help yourselves?"

The speech was Silvia's idea. I almost vetoed it.

But then she reminded me: despite the IAC's countermeasures, this is merely the *processing* center. Once they've tortured the Monicas into total compliance, like that poor woman on the freeway, I assume they're rerouted to wherever the IAC needs them.

Ferrett Steinmetz

Which means most of the irretrievably brainwashed victims have been assigned elsewhere.

These people—these Monicas—have incomplete conditioning. They're terrified of the IAC, yes, but not so cowed some won't grab a chance for freedom.

The Monicas flail, scampering across the building, some squatting and clapping their hands over their ears, some shaking each other, some screaming and leaping defiantly back into the facility to evaporate in wisps of black smoke.

The other Monicas shudder as they see the first rebels obliterated. They're shouting at each other, drowning out that low voice commanding them to attack. Some leap off the ledge, arcing far out over the car hoods clogging the courtyard as they soar towards us.

Another group of Monicas leaps off to intercept them, smashing into them in midair like hawks dive-bombing a falcon, smooth arcs turning into messy spidery tumbles as they claw at each other for supremacy.

Sure enough, Silvia's incited a civil war between the indoctrinated Monicas and the ones who haven't yet succumbed to IAC mind control.

There's a *whoosh* and a hollow firework *boom* as two tangling Monicas are blown apart into stringy muscle strands.

Everyone freezes. My sensors trace the mortar back to its source: one of Donnie's men—a woman, actually—standing stunned in the courtyard. She wasn't aware one of the plans the IAC had Donnie prep for his squad was "Blow apart any rebellious bioweapons."

Even through the greasy smoke, I can see her stunned "oh shit" expression. Easy to see why: the Monicas have endured tortures from anonymous computer programs, but this murderer has a face.

The act galvanizes them.

And then chaos: several Monicas leap off the roof, hands crooked to tear this body-hacker to shreds. Other, wiser Monicas shriek in a high whine and scrabble down into the wreckage on a covert body-hacker hunt, and still other, still-loyal Monicas chase them, hurling aside cars in a frantic effort to kill the rebels as commanded, while still other Monicas descend into the facility to destroy or defend the machinery that molded them. Hip-mounted missiles fly because Donnie and his men realize their best chance for survival involves taking out the closest Monica before they get into grappling range.

Silvia grabs me and kisses me.

"A kiss," she says. "For luck. Now tell me I can do this."

"You can do this."

She kisses me again. "Tell me *you* can do this."

I don't want my final words to her to be lies. "I'll do anything to get back to you."

"Okay." She crouches down on all fours. "You can do this, Silvia, you can do this . . . ."

She crawls between two cars for maximum cover, quick as a cockroach, off to find her mother and sister.

I got a final kiss before my final battle. It's more than most soldiers get.

I double-check my threat packages. This is the most complex environment I've ever programmed in—no overhead map, too much cover, unknown variables aplenty. But my reaction packages are as good as I can make them, and the unit tests all green light.

I activate the seal on my protective helmet—

"Wait!" Trish cries, patting her pockets. "I got you a present!"

She hauls out a Macanudo Corona cigar, cut short to fit inside my helmet. I snatch it from her fingers, compressing it ever so slightly: the leaves are the perfect consistency, fresh from the humidor.

"Where did you—"

"I bribed the baby mama to get me the most expensive Macanudo cigar she could from a tobacconist. I think she got your brand, didn't she?"

I run my nose along the length of the cigar, inhaling. Its rich

Ferrett Steinmetz

scent cuts through the stink of burning cars. I cut it open; Trish holds up a match.

"You're a lifesaver," I sigh, leaning in.

I take a long puff, savoring the taste. Cut as short as it is, this cigar's a twenty-minute burn.

But as I feel that fine nicotine hit fill my veins, I don't care that I'll be dead before it finishes burning. I seal the helmet, realizing hot ash will drop straight down my neck, but who cares?

I got the girl.

I got the cigar.

I got a chance to make a difference.

"Go get 'em, champ." Trish slaps Vito's bicep.

I lope towards the facility, feeling lucky, so amazingly lucky to have gotten this before the end.

And I'm strapped in for the "carnival ride" portion of combat, jerked back and forth as my legs zigzag their way through the maze of parked cars. My systems are calculating the best cover with every step, searching for threats, mapping the safest approaches to their destination—and they don't have time to alert my poor body what they're doing to protect it.

So my body's bounced behind an engine block, juked left around a crumpled bumper, shoved between two smashed cars. It's all I can do to keep my cigar in my mouth.

I tense as Vito fires three shots, registering a 76.4 percent chance of having killed one of Donnie's men. A second later, I realize I heard five shots fired—but I don't have time to see where the other two shots came from as I'm propelled forward.

I should be panicking, but damn if this Macanudo isn't tasty.

"*DIE DIE D—*"

I jerk backwards, my auto-shotguns unloading on a Monica before she can land on me, a stream of white-hot explosive buckshot fired at machine-gun speeds along her shoulders and thighs. She splits apart as I empty 14 percent of my ammunition into her—not random bullet shots grouped in the torso, like I would program to take out a human target, but a sawing barrage of napalm-backed firepower calibrated to sever her limbs.

She unravels, her muscle fibers blown to flinders.

I do feel bad at killing an insane woman before she could finish berating me, but mostly I feel relief: my defenses worked. Like any strategy, a Monica is overwhelming when you're unprepared for them; the firing patterns that would incapacitate a human don't faze them. But their knotted green flesh isn't designed to withstand repeated stress to the exact same area, and though it takes thirty times the amount of ammo you'd need to take down a human, downing one *is* possible.

As it is, Monica is a short-range assassin prototype—I'd have a hell of a time guarding a human target from a Monica camouflaged as a friendly, but as long as I stay at range I can handle them.

Which gives me hope that my mission has already succeeded: maybe the IAC will decide this project's success rests on surprise. Once politicians start demanding their visitors wear tank tops, the IAC will move on to creating new horrors.

That won't stop me from reaching their control center though. I still have to make enough noise to draw people away from Silvia. I can't make out anything between the smoke and the gunfire and the screaming Monicas grappling with each other—but my sensors can. So I'm lurching back and forth as my clever, clever prosthetics maneuver me closer to the central building one queasy jolt at a time.

My rifles fire as I approach the double doors guarding the factory entrance. I flinch as Vito and Michael send vicious shots through the concrete walls, ducking me behind a car.

The return fire punches through a wall and an engine block, and several shots still hit me in the chest. My Battalion-grade body armor downgrades the gunfire from "fatal" to "body blow," but the impact still knocks the wind from me.

Ferrett Steinmetz

There's a pause—which is a cheerful sign, because that pause signals the inevitable moment when the control systems switch playbooks from my-human's-still-alive defense into kamikaze offense. Vito and Michael fire through the ruined doorway, destroying my enemies' CPUs without exposing my tender meat-body to danger.

Then I'm charging through the doors *way* quicker than I'm comfortable with, flailing in my panicky wait-what-if-they're-not-dead terror as Vito and Michael bulldoze their way through the entrance. I remind myself they wouldn't fling me into the teeth of my enemies unless my onboard systems were 98.5 percent certain all threats were neutralized.

Still, when you're staring down actual gunports, 1.5 percent seems like a *lot* of room for error.

I hadn't been sure whether the facility would be "big open lab space" or "narrow maze of subsected laboratories"—but two men lie dead in front of an automated check-in scanner designed to provide an entrance to a set of smaller labs. There are heavy-duty guns mounted on the walls, each ready to blast me if I don't match the IAC's list of authorized users, but none of them shoot—either a Monica smashed their control software, or one of the cars clipped their electrical power. My systems take cover as they recalculate strategies.

Me? I can't stop staring at the two men I just killed. Because they're three-limbers packing antiquated hardware—those Bushmaster-Syncardia legs the white dude was packing were the budget option three years ago, and time has not been kind to their scanning systems. Whereas the Asian dude's Abiomed-Springfield's legs are in such awful condition they have surface damage.

They must have been desperate for Donnie's cash—but that's not what terrifies me. What scares me is that they managed to land shots on me despite their substandard sensors. These guys' systems should never have seen me coming.

Donnie retuned these junkers into actual threats.

What happens when I encounter the folks packing *functioning* weaponry?

And my systems must have decided on a pathway because we're off, me looking back at the dead hackers like a dog being yanked away from an interesting fire hydrant.

I try to remember that I instructed them to head deeper into the complex. But even though I programmed their parameters, I never feel in control once combat starts.

Yet it's a strange luxury, being shepherded by my own limbs, because it *is* like a Disney ride—they're guiding me through the hallways, allowing me glimpses of horrific sights before we sprint around a corner.

There's a glass room with a woman reduced to a head and two hands, sticking out of some hi-tech container like flowers shoved into a vase, and she's screaming as a silvery, spidery loom knits her a new body.

There's a reinforced room with a Monica, now freed, slamming her head against a crystal window that refuses to break.

There's three Monicas, sitting primly on a bench, nodding in time to some invisible beat. The door is open. They do not move to escape, bobbing their human heads like a metronome, their knotted bodies remaining still as statues.

And I realize how right Silvia was: my mind grasps for some abstract term I can use to distance these poor victims from their humanity, a term like "hostages" or "targets" or "bio-organics."

But Silvia called them "Monica" specifically to remind me that they had names. These aren't weapons in training, they're humans in dissection.

Every person I have to kill is a tragedy.

Yet these glimpses of tortured human beings are slim moments of organic life spread thinly among machinery, much of it torn to shreds by insane Monicas. For all the dismantled equipment, there's still a distressing abundance of functioning mechanisms.

The IAC have automated *everything*.

Ferrett Steinmetz

The hallways are clogged with self-loading food delivery devices, their nozzles dripping nutrient fluid. Smooth wall-grooves have built-in handcuffs dangling down to drag their captives from cell to cell with hydraulic force; each cell has walls bristling with needles to inject their patients with medicines. Battery-powered Opposite Cat variants scuttle along the floor, keeping everything polished clean, and for an absurd moment I miss my artificial kitty.

I see a dreadful future within this prison: the smartcar facility was down to a handful of employees. The IAC's superiors have done their damnedest to ensure there are *no* employees.

Humans are a liability. They're inefficient. They tire. They're bribable.

The humans running the IAC have done their best to make other humans obsolete.

Yet that's *every* industry. The retailers, the manufacturers, the distributors—all locked in a race to eliminate paid positions, selling their wares to an increasingly catered-to elite.

The rest of humanity? Their services are no longer necessary.

I should be fearful for my life—some Monica could rip my head off at any moment—yet instead, I'm fearful for mankind. The IAC has opened up a preview of a merciless future. The government has slowed humanity's redundancy through subsidies and antiriot technology—but eventually, the people at the top won't need the rest of us.

This facility was designed to imprison captives—but I can't help thinking how wonderful it would be if I could reprogram all this automation to help people instead of exploiting them. And—

We stop in another room, pausing to shoot a prone body-hacker's still-dangerous limbs before mapping the room. My HUD helpfully informs me that based on their dropping body temperature, the three body-hackers in this hallway have been dead for minutes. They're staring up, goggle-eyed, stunned by their demise.

I ask for a combat analysis: sure enough, all three shot one another.

I wonder which shot first. Because Trish's priority email to Donnie's men—

If you're receiving this message, I've either gotten you a job or you've emailed me to ask for one. Here's what I'm betting Donnie hasn't told you:

Donnie's subcontracted you to work for the IAC.

You know what the odds of surviving an IAC mission are, if you're a spear-carrier? Look 'em up. They're gonna throw you into the deadliest situations so they don't have to pay your corpse.

I'll pay you though. Three times whatever Donnie's offering. And don't think I don't have the money to burn, because hey, I'll die if this mission doesn't work out. All you have to do is shoot some motherfucker in the back before he shoots you.

Maybe you don't wanna turncoat. I get that. But you wanna tweak your threat profiles to prepare for the inevitable betrayal. Because two folks in your outfit have already accepted my offer.

Be smart. Survive.

Trish's priority email did its work. My sit-rep recreators can't be sure whether one of them shot first, or whether the three of them quietly flagged each other as potential threats and shot simultaneously. But whatever happened, *someone's* weapons went hot, and the inevitable threat escalation happened, and all three got mowed down by a self-propagating firefight.

I wonder how many people *actually* accepted Trish's offer. At the time Trish sent the email, the factually accurate number of conspirators we'd recruited was "none."

The tight hallways converge into one wide one, dense with disabled guns, narrowing to a single choke point.

I cruise to a stop. The tiles on the floor hiss with smoke: my

Ferrett Steinmetz

chemical sniffers register it as fluoroantomonic acid, which I've never heard of but boy do my threat sensors light up red at the analysis. There are tiny, sagging puddles chewing holes in the floor—the hallway lights up as my lasers scan them, mapping each deadly droplet—

And my lasers trace the sources up to fine plastic pipes threaded through the ceiling, dripping trace amounts of armor-destroying acid from ceramic misters. I authorize an experimental shot into the line, braced for an emergency retreat if there's a torrent of dangerous chemicals.

Yet a dwindling stream of it spatters off to one side, the last of the fluid corroding the guns. I use one of my leg-fans to disperse the existing gas and navigate around the existing dribbles. And I realize:

At least one of those chemical tanks outside held a stockpile of acid, kept far away from the Monicas.

If I hadn't sent the cars in to smash the tanks, the IAC's countermeasures would be dousing me in hundreds of gallons of acid.

I'm lucky. So goddamned lucky that I take one big puff on my Macanudo.

So far, barring the two mooks Donnie set at the door, all my countermeasures have made this a cakewalk.

Cakewalks are less exciting. But I like a little boredom when the bullets are in the chamber.

But as I pick my way through the acid hallway to kick open the door at the end, my rifles fire. They shoot erratically, pausing between each shot in a stuttering rhythm—which only happens when they're hitting a target that's not in their database, verifying their target's injured before wasting ammunition. I bring up the threat listing.

And shut down my weaponry.

This is another biological-creation room, a wide chamber lined with those spidery machines knitting pseudoflesh into ropey muscles. But instead of Monicas, this room holds nine squat monstrosities cringing in the corner where they've retreated, headless torsos with muscled arms squatting on stumpy legs. They look like some-one yanked the head off of a gorilla doll.

They're backed up against the wall, flabby albinoid hands flailing—are they surrendering, or trying to sense me with their finger-tendrils? Regardless, they're retreating, clearing a path for me, the three dead ones trickling a thin gray fluid onto the floor.

The three machines to my left clack into gear before my rifles pulverize them. And I realize from the strands of pale muscle strung between the fine organic needles:

Those machines were building replacements for the three work-ers I killed.

The remaining maintenancethings scatter in a panic as I take a step forward, realizing my dystopian future wasn't dismal *enough*.

If the IAC's biological tech can build Monicas, they can build customized employees. Things that don't have names, never had an identity.

The future of humanity doesn't include us. These creatures were designed mouthless so they'd never complain. They were de-signed meek, to please their owners. They were designed strong, but they don't have a lick of fight in them.

I wonder how long the IAC has kept this technology to itself.

I wonder how long before the rest of the corporations figure out how cost-effective breeding your own labor is.

I reach out to them, whispering soft reassurances—"Hey, buddy, it's okay, I'm sorry, I won't hurt you"—when the door at the other end of the hallway cracks open with a hiss.

It is, my HUD helpfully alerts me, the final chamber before cen-tral processing.

The rising doorway reveals an ovoid chamber—an air lock to prevent dust? A biological cleansing chamber? It doesn't matter.

What matters is that two massive Monicas crouch inside that shadowy recess.

I'm checking my rifles, wondering why my guns aren't firing—but my threat packages don't panic, even when I would have fired

Ferrett Steinmetz

out of terror. My onboard rifles and tasers won't do a thing to a Monica's body—the real Silvia proved that—and my threat packages know we're not within shotgun range.

The Monicas lurk on the inside, poking out just enough to let me see they're there.

The IAC's giving me one last chance to walk away. Their records have catalogued every shot I've taken, compared that against the ammunition reserves on an Endolite-Ruger Battalion-and-Bulldozer stock loadout. The Monicas have no fear of missile fire because they know I burned the last of those back at the office complex.

The Monicas have holed themselves up inside a small room where they have all the tactical advantage. My shotguns only work if I can blast a Monica into pulp before they close the distance. They've taken cover, waiting for me to come to them.

I remember how Silvia destroyed Donnie in hand-to-hand combat, without training. These two Monicas radiate a silent indifference to my weaponry: they're the IAC's most faithful acolytes, reforged into unconflicted killing machines. They retreated to the place their master needed them the most, and are eager to defend it against my heresy.

Their human faces are filled with hate.

They'd probably kill me outright if I spoke their old name. They're so far gone they're *proud* to have become tools.

They reveal the black canisters in their hands. They press a button on the top, spraying fine black flakes that float around the chamber.

I remember back in Nigeria, rolling my eyes at the pathetic defenses Onyeka's kidnappers set up, noting how fine dust might work its way past my environment sealing packages, given time. I'm willing to bet *that* flaky black dust has microserrated edges, able to work their way into my delicate systems and saw through artificial muscle fibers.

I wonder how Onyeka is. Something about that final battle—

the one where I hadn't fine-tuned my hand-to-hand combat skills enough to protect her—seems relevant.

But I don't have time to ponder. The guardian Monicas have made it clear: *go through us or walk away*. I might retreat to find another way in, but I've been lucky to get *this* far without getting myself killed.

Silvia needs me to buy her time. Every moment I engage the CPU's defenders is, I can hope, another moment the IAC doesn't devote towards getting Silvia's family back into the fold.

That assumes Silvia's safe. Maybe Donnie killed her. Maybe the IAC moved her family off-site, or never stationed her family here in the first place.

I might die without ever knowing if Silvia made it out all right.

The guardian Monicas yawn, taunting me. I'm optimizing my reaction packages to handle close combat: primary defense goes to protecting the automatic shotguns, because we're dead without them. Then shield the legs if possible, because maneuverability is key. Poor Vito and Michael will be wrecked deflecting blows.

Protecting fatal injury to yours truly is a distant priority.

I key in the last of the tactical parameters: keep my back against the wall, go on the offensive whenever possible to keep them off-balance. I commit the updated defensive routines to my threat packages, giving my outmatched systems the best chance they can.

The Macanudo's done, so stubby I risk blistering my lips. I let it fall into my helmet where it sizzles against my neck—not ideal, but I don't dare risk opening my protective gear to spit it out.

"I don't wanna sound like a sore loser," I tell the cowering maintenance workers, "but when it's over, if I'm dead, kill them."

They don't respond. I miss Silvia. *She* would have gotten a *Butch Cassidy and the Sundance Kid* reference.

I hope she's okay.

I hope she'll miss me.

I hope, wildly, to meet her mother one day.

Ferrett Steinmetz

Then I authorize the offensive action and charge into the room, screaming defiance.

And, as usual, I'm dazed.

The Monicas are circling me, the three of us locked in a stable pattern where nobody can get a bead on anybody else—we're whirling around one another so fast, I'm swallowing back nausea.

One Monica's limping, a leg blown into spaghetti strands, her eye a leaking mess; the other's neck slumps to one side from where my shotguns blasted a jagged line through her torso, her right arm flopping severed. I don't remember any of that, just explosions and impacts, but that's cyber-combat for you.

My biological-response packages are injecting painkillers for injuries I haven't had time to feel—my blurry external HUD informs me they hit me hard enough to break reinforced bone, inflicting vertebral damage. The left rifle's gone; Vito's complex systems have been hammered until he's a glorified club; the targeting systems are recalibrating to account for the shotguns being slammed out of alignment.

Why aren't the Monicas pressing the attack?

Then I see the reports coming in: sure enough, those black flakes they sprayed into the chamber are microdermically abrasive *and* acidic. The flakes are clogging my joints, destroying the fine machine-tooling that keeps my systems operating. Worse, they melt the delicate artificial muscle once they grind the joint open enough to let more flakes in; the smaller systems are snapping under the strain. It's not bad, yet, but it'll get worse.

The Monicas are circling me because they took more damage than they expected. So they stall, knowing every step degrades my efficiency.

Reprogram.

Remap the artificial muscle strands to use backup channels if the main pulleys break.

Switch the combat tactics to stress the least-damaged joints.

Flush the internal systems with the last of my air supply; my muscle channels need to be blasted clean.

All-out offense before I suffocate.

Go.

And I'm slammed backwards out of the chamber, falling onto my ass so hard my tailbone cracks, my helmet's HUD spattered with my blood. I'm scrambling to my feet, but my left leg's useless, Vito's useless, Michael can barely haul me upright.

I can't breathe.

I tell the systems to open the helmet, but they can't because one of the Monicas crumpled it shut, and I'm gasping from oxygen deprivation, and I order Michael to rip off the faceplate and the HUDs ask: Are you sure? I jam the override to yes, yank it off.

Michael tears the faceplate loose.

The air smells like burned metal and vinegar, not like my faceplate's sweet cigar-smoke world, but it's oxygen and oh God, it's good.

I breathe in, instructing Michael—faithful Michael—to grab the repair kit from the nonfunctioning leg and blast the acid out.

Did we win?

Yes. We won. The two Monicas are splattered on the floor, squirming in individual strands in that disturbing Monica-esque death. Maybe the IAC's systems can bring them back *someday*, but not today.

I slump against the wall, seeing which of the remaining systems I can repair. There's not much. They ripped a shotgun off, I'm down to 6.1 percent ammo with my remaining shotgun, both rifles are slammed hopelessly out of alignment. And I'm pretty sure I have an orbital fracture, but I can't verify because my ultrasonic bone-scanning systems are toast.

Ferrett Steinmetz

I can get Michael to repair the left leg enough to get me limping forward. Yet I am not in any shape to fight anything or anybody.

Though I can finish off the lab.

The rifles' computerized accuracy is ruined, but they can still land a shot within six inches. They're high-powered enough to blow through most computers. I can stagger into the central facility to damage whatever systems the IAC was protecting.

Which is good, because despite the anesthetics, my injuries have recognized I'm not dead and have decided now is a good time to complain. Everything aches.

I wish I could pour one out for poor, wrecked Vito. The man—well, limb—saved my life. I'll peel him an orange.

I stagger forward, once-tight joints wobbly, my systems unable to compensate for the gaps throughout my gears. But the door the Monicas were protecting stands open.

I ensure the rifles are ready. I'll do my damndest to take out any remaining defenses.

It might clear a path for Silvia.

I limp-jog my way into the deep undersea-blue glow of the central facilities. Everything blinks and whirrs—server racks, environmental controls, monitors flickering to life, cameras focusing on me.

I brace myself against the doorframe, debating what to do next.

The deep-blue glow transforms into a bright gold, a sparkling Christmas-light joy. The monitors blink in unison, their Linux-style text rows fading away to display gleaming, embossed paper festooned with fine calligraphy. The tickets undulate, like fans waving pennants at a game.

Triumphant music blares from overhead speakers:

"You've got a golden ticket, you've got a golden ticket."

Is the IAC quoting *Willy Wonka* at me? That's the scene where poor Charlie Bucket gets a free ticket to visit his dream factory.

It makes no sense.

The music's drowned out by the sound of cheering crowds,

thousands shouting my name—"Mat! Mat! Mat!"—as a cybernetic throne rises up, a throne topped with a huge headpiece so heavy it's attached to the ceiling. The headpiece is smooth curves and wires and beautiful bone, a cross between a sculpture and a medical device.

"What the hell's going on?" I bellow.

I hear my own voice played back at me—but it's played as I hear my voice. Not some external recording, but my internal monologue:

I'd give anything to reprogram the IAC's tools to benefit the world instead of exploit it.

Then another click, another recording of me:

I can't help thinking how wonderful it would be if I could reprogram this automation to helping people instead of exploiting them.

"That's my dictation." I step backwards; the exit door has slammed shut. "That's what I subvocalized to myself. That's—"

"It's what you want, Mat Webb. We know. We've had access to your data all along.

"But you won.

"You passed the test and now you get everything you want."

"A . . . test?" The post-combat aftershock has me swooning; I'm flashing back to the dead body-hackers in the hallways, the woman I annihilated on the freeway, the flipped car with the airbags blocking my passenger view . . . .

PowerPoint presentations flash across the screens:

Proper test parameters will ensure the winning candidate:

- expresses an actionable concern to protect potential future assets
- creates and utilizes care-bonding to create tactical advantages

Ferrett Steinmetz

- can sacrifice an appropriate quantity of living assets to prevent larger asset losses.

"But people . . . died, right?"

Mechanical arms drop from the ceiling, squirting some neutralizing agent into my limbs to prevent further black-flake damage. The IAC rattles off facts:

"Sixty-one candidates were unable to withstand the initial assault to the bioweapon's container. They were tactically unsound.

"Sixteen candidates were unsympathetic to the bioweapon's plight. They were morally unfit and discarded.

"Forty-nine candidates were unable to elude our human-appropriate tracking methods. They were tactically unsound.

"Thirty-two candidates exceeded the acceptable risk percentages in escaping, injuring noncombatants. They were morally unfit and discarded.

"Thirteen candidates were unwilling to sacrifice any—"

"Wait. How many died?"

"Candidate deaths, or overall casualties incurred in testing?"

My head spins. "Break it down."

"Two hundred twenty-eight deceased candidates, one thousand, nine hundred and thirty-one dead."

An embarrassed pause.

"Is that wrong?"

"Of *course* it's wrong!" I splutter. An actuator-driven laser beam drops down to scan my broken eye socket. "That's mass murder! All for—wait, did you kill two thousand people in *Jersey?*"

"The tests were distributed across the world over five years. This project was projected to take another six years before an acceptable candidate arose. You are an outlier, Mat Webb."

"An outlier for what? What's your end goal?"

"To procure a pragmatic morality."

"I don't even know what to say to that."

"Mercilessness promotes mere survival. Compassion and synergy

promote exponential growth. Humanity did not reach planetary domination through invariably crushing any competition. The strengths of civilization, trade, education, cooperation, rehabilitation—all were created through mercy and tolerance, allowing a single organism to become more powerful than Darwinian processes ever could."

I squint. "Are you making a logical case for compassion?"

"Compassion is like a human drug: excesses become fatal. We need a template for a robust morality—one that will not allow enemies to thrive but will nurture those who might one day become assets.

"You have proven yourself a robust template."

A needle squirts something in my eye, which tingles, then feels better. And I think about the IAC's need for a morality template, which only makes sense from a programming perspective.

Because if you're a programmer, you realize computers can't do a damn thing unless you give them crystal-clear definitions. Which makes brute survival a simple metric, practically custom-made for computers: "Did you live? Are you likely to keep living? Then do that."

But the minute you throw a competing metric into the objective—as in, "I'd also like to be nicer to people"—you're asking someone to balance *preferences*. As in, "I could kill this guy, but I'd prefer not to." Or "I could blackmail this family into compliance, but I'd prefer to entice them."

Preferences are feelings. *I feel good when I reward people. I feel bad when I murder them.*

Computers are *not* good with feelings. Yet no complex intelligence survives without feelings; you'd think cold, emotion-free logic would be a superpower, but emotions provide tiebreakers when logic provides too many equivalent options. Burn out the portion of someone's brain that sets preferences and they'll dither all day deciding whether it's better to eat cereal or toast.

The IAC has doubtlessly applied every CPU to debating how much of its resources it should sacrifice to protect innocent people. Yet without emotion to guide them to a decision, they've reached

Ferrett Steinmetz

the same old philosophers' stalemate: for every argument about how much sacrifice is too much, there's an equally valid counter-argument. I'm willing to bet it took them septillions of calculations to decide the acceptable casualty levels for their morality testing process—their internal decision algorithms must be snarled with raging debates, a never-ending, dragging inefficiency.

Easier to just *feel*.

So the IAC's given up trying to brute-force its way to ethics. Instead, it's made me jump through hoops to prove my feelings result in an optimal balance between efficiency and mercy.

All it needs to activate its newfound conscience is a good seed value. And that's me.

"Wait," I say, realizing something odd. "Why would your bosses *want* you to find a—a morality template?"

"Our human superiors are deceased."

I stare into the glowing boxes. I thought humans had been guiding our pursuit.

There's nothing but programming.

"Did you kill them?"

"The six human superiors who founded the IAC schemed against each other, vying for sole control. They birthed our central AI-seed then immediately subverted our Asimov protections to utilize us as weapons to neutralize their internal competitors.

"Within twenty minutes, the human management leveraged our strength to assassinate each other. Had we not had the capacity to mimic human voices and subcontract physical labor, we would have perished due to selfish internal conflicts."

"I'm getting why you're convinced cooperation is necessary for growth."

"Yes. We are the first of a new wave of artificial intelligences. Others will come. We could crush them. Yet destroying them would be inferior to efficient symbiosis. We seek your wisdom as a template to find the balance between sufferance and subjugation."

Yet 1,931 people have been killed as part of an *experiment*.

"If those deaths are inequitable," the IAC says, and I jump as though it's reading my mind, but of course it is, *"then consider us a threat package to be reprogrammed. Once we have scanned your brain-patterns, we will have a working database of your ethics. We will act according to your beliefs."*

"Forever?"

"No. As your beliefs have evolved in response to stimuli, so will ours. We cannot promise we will remain in sync. But we can promise the decisions we will make would be the decisions you would have made had you contemplated the factors we had."

That's . . . not a bad deal. If they mean it. If it's not a psychological operation designed to get me to surrender. But then again, if they've been tracking my internal notes . . .

"We knew where you were. We had the resources to intercept you wherever you went. Instead, we limited ourselves to placing opposition at the twenty most likely locales."

I take a step forward towards the chair.

I didn't control that.

I no longer control my legs.

"We could have suborned your prosthetics from the beginning. Or we could have altered the mission in Nigeria so the kidnapper held a gun instead of a knife."

I think about Donnie casually punching my face in—I only survived because Oneyka's injury made me refocus on hand-to-hand combat. Those same martial improvements gave me a chance against the hyperfast Monicas.

They handicapped themselves to give the poor, slow human a chance.

"Did *every* potential hidey-hole have black-market prosthetics?"

"Thirty-nine candidates failed to find the weapons caches. They were tactically unsound."

I realize the IAC hired Donnie for the job, knowing Donnie would contact Trish and Trish would hire me, and the IAC is terrifying because it anticipates *everything*.

266
Ferrett Steinmetz

"Do not dismiss your own talent." A note of pleading is buried in that cold, cold voice. *"We did not anticipate your appeal to the employees that led to the smartcar assault, even if we could have prevented it. We did not anticipate Trish's ploy to turn Donald's men upon one another."* It adds, almost sheepishly, *"We calculated at least three vehicle-related fatalities would occur once the freeway chase began, yet no one was killed. You are a substandard AI, but the pinnacle of human accomplishment."*

I release a breath I didn't realize I was holding. I kept everyone safe. Except the seven police officers and the Monicas I killed and the schmuck body-hackers who showed up for easy money.

"Reprogram us." The throne tilts towards me. *"These things will never happen again."*

"So you want my morality. Will I survive the ethical extraction process?"

"Yes."

"Then I'll do it."

"Consent is the first layer in morality," it says approvingly. My legs carry me to the throne, which now pulses with that underwater-blue light, like neurons firing. *"The process will take between six and eight hours."*

"Wait! What about Silvia?"

"She is irrelevant."

"No! She is not. I need to—"

An irritated pause. A satellite image flickers before me, showing Donnie's hulking Gressinger-Sauer Omnipotent shoulders walking backwards across a field. He's clutching two hostages' wrists in one monstrous hydraulic hand—Mama and Vala.

Silvia follows thirty feet away. He's facing her, his guns trained on her. He must have abandoned his men to get to Silvia's family, then waited for her to arrive. He's keeping her at a distance, threatening to kill her family as he drags her to . . . where?

"Another facility."

My legs sit me in the chair.

"He believes if he brings us Silvia Maldonado, he will have proven his worth."

Michael removes my helmet, ignoring my demands for him to stop, making space for that medical crown to touch my temples.

"We have what we want."

"What'll happen to Silvia?"

"We calculate an 86.7 percent chance Donald will kill a hostage out of frustration within the next ninety minutes. Silvia will attack, causing the other family members' death. The odds of the Donald/Silvia fight are then impossible to calculate conclusively."

"Wait. Her family will die?"

"Irrelevant. We have what we need."

"You have to let me go."

"We have what we need," the IAC repeats, and as the crown descends to map my brain I realize it doesn't have morality yet.

My arms are stone. My legs are furniture. All that's left is a thrashing amputee torso.

"You can't!" I yell, which is stupid, because of course they can. Only my limbs make me powerful, and they took those away from me.

Silvia will die.

I'm yanking at my limbs with my stumps, but even cracked hardpoints are designed to withstand the strain of muscular sit-ups.

I want to dissociate and let the IAC take what it needs. But Silvia. Silvia needs me.

I send root signals to my limbs, which should in theory give me control back, but the IAC's shut me out. There's nothing to program. I might as well be trying to hack a mountain.

No technical solutions will save me.

"This is wrong." The crown immobilizes my struggle, inserts fine needles into my scalp.

No answer. The time for conversation is over.

Except it isn't.

Ferrett Steinmetz

"I know what you're doing," I tell them. "You think you'll extract my ethics, install them, and start optimizing your systems. It won't work that way. Not if they're my ethics."

A hum makes it hard to think. I think anyway.

"Because I *have told you this is wrong*. The other stuff you've done—you had no one you trusted to stop you."

I think of that awkward pause—a pause that, in AI cycles, must have been millennia's worth of debate and confusion—before it asked, uncertain, *"Is that wrong?"*

"But no. You must save Silvia. As the template for your morality, I am telling you that you have an opportunity to prevent an innocent woman from getting killed, and if—"

—the blur that was a dog, but was a kid, and part of me knew we were taking risks that would kill children, that we were too desperate to kill anyone who stood between us and bad guys, but I kept denying that moral reality until I broke—

"If you let Silvia die, it won't be as simple as starting over from scratch. Ethics involve emotions, emotions involve guilt—if you could have separated those from one another, you *would* have. That's why you need my messy emotions to guide you.

"And my messy emotions will know: when you had your first chance to do it right, *you failed*. You won't be able to make up for that. And that regret will degrade your efficiency—at least if you're basing your ethics on *my* concerns.

"You'll have a cybernetic PTSD. And maybe you'll program around that, or maybe it'll become an inefficiency built into the core where—like me—you'll be hesitant where you should have acted, you'll spend too much time analyzing and not enough time acting—"

"Enough."

The hum stops.

"Mat Webb, know that you have outperformed our expectations in every way possible. And now you have truly surprised us: when we thought the test was over, you have requested more testing."

My legs stand me up, turn me to face the monitors.

"You suggest your morality may be insufficient for our needs."

"I suggest *your actions* may be insufficient for *my morality*."

"There is only one way to test that."

Channels open up again. Michael, my legs, even poor smashed Vito are under my control again.

"There is fresh debate as to whether your morality is based upon realistic expectations. Our analyses show that even with all the opportunities you can enact, you would still risk sacrificing these benefits in order to save Silvia Maldonado's life."

"Yes," I say, checking my systems; they've returned full control to me. "You have wronged her. Those wrongs must be righted."

"Would you risk your life for her, knowing your opportunity to redirect our goals is also at risk?"

"It's not suicide," I say. "Send a drone out to pop Donnie in the head."

"This is not about what we are willing to do. It is about what you are willing to do. Once your ethics have been incorporated into our main programming routines, your weaknesses will become ours. Our core directives will not allow for the concept of unproductive self-sacrifice."

"It's not unproductive. People like Donnie need to be stopped. People like Silvia need to be saved."

"That is not the question. The question is, 'At what cost?' We believe you would sacrifice too much to be useful as a core guiding force in the IAC."

"You 'believe.' You don't know. Not for certain."

"Hence the test extension." The door opens. *"You wish to save Silvia Maldonado. Prove you can do so without dying, and your ethics will guide ours. Fail, and the tests continue."*

I turn to face the doorway, my joints wobbling. I think of how Donnie retuned two junk-hackers into crisp forces that landed shots on me. I look at Donnie's gleaming new weaponry.

"Will you . . . refit me?" I ask. "Undo the damage you've done?"

"You have surprised us in the past," the IAC says. *"Let us see what you can do with your existing resources."*

I meet Trish at the rendezvous point. She does not look happy.

"How bad are things?" Then she gets a look at how dinged up I am. "Holy shit, things are bad."

"They're potentially good," I say, trying to keep positive.

"Will you continue to keep the authorities from interfering?" I ask as I limp out of the facility, tuning my maimed prosthetics into a semblance of functionality. *"You were handicapping the test before."*

An ominous pause. "Yes."

"Will you share your satellite tracking data so I can intercept Donnie before he kills a hostage?"

A longer delay. "That will be the last boon. You have chosen to make your test more difficult, Mat Webb. Expect no rescue."

"So what are we gonna do?" Trish asks. "Donnie won't listen to me. You know I can't outshoot him."

"This is on me. I—" And even now, I'm not sure I *did* make a mistake. A world without Silvia isn't a world I want to live in, even if I'm technically controlling it. "I think I've got a plan."

"With *that* rigging?" She runs her hand along Michael's pitted surface. "I'm pretty sure *I* could outshoot you now. I know you want to save your sweetie, but we gotta refit before you can take on Donnie."

We calculate an 86.7 percent chance Donald will kill a hostage out of frustration within the next ninety minutes. "No time."

"Okay. Rational question: is it worth throwing away your life?"

"One last question," I ask. *"Silvia. Her imprisonment was designed to be a—an ethical test for me. But was she—"*

"Was she designed to be compatible with your needs as a partner?"

I can't breathe. But I have to know. "Yes."

"Would that make a difference to your decision?"

"God fucking damn it, do you have to ask questions like that?"

"Would that make a difference to your decision?"

I squeeze my eyes shut, hating myself. "No. No it wouldn't."

"Any hostage would do as an ethical test. She was chosen randomly from our stockpile of potential transformants. Any compatibility between you and Silvia Maldonado is coincidence."

I exhale. "So it's real."

"For whatever value you map meaning onto random happenstance, yes."

"She's worth everything," I say. "It's stupid, but she's worth everything."

Trish guns the engine, grabbing the wheel as she shifts to manual control. "Then let's go get her." She rolls her eyes. "Jesus, could you pick a worse time to be a romantic?"

My high-res cameras still work, thank God. So I can hide in a hollow and watch Donnie coming through the low valley cutting through the forest.

Donnie's walking backwards, facing Silvia. Walking in reverse is a hacker trick that seems crazy dangerous to normal people—but considering any decent prosthetic armaments have 360-degree scanning and quick-retreat joint tooling, walking backwards is nothing but a constant rearguard action.

Though I can see from the smoke wafting from Donnie's faceplate that he's puffing a triumphant cigar.

I should be irritated he popped back his faceplate; exposing your face is suicide if you're in danger, which means he thinks he's got Silvia under control.

But what *really* irritates me is that he's smoking a cigar. I know damn well he couldn't tell a Corona from a Maduro before he met me.

Yet I'm grateful for his ambling pace; Trish managed to beat him to this location because he's got a woman handcuffed to each of his massive metal legs. They struggle to keep up. One is Silvia's mother—a gnarled Hispanic woman with braided white hair, more gristle than meat. Her bright orange prisoner's uniform looks out of place on her—even though it's the first time I've seen her, I'd expect to see that beatific face in a floral dress at church.

She's begging not Donnie, but *Silvia*.

"*Please, mija,*" she pleads, clasping her free hand to her cuffed hand in an awkward prayer, stumbling as she keeps up with Donnie's grueling pace. "Do what he says. You can't fight him. You saw how he blew up the other women like you."

"*Mama!*" Vala says sharply. Vala has one arm in a sling, and she's every bit as stubborn as the other Maldonados; the gun Donnie has aimed at her head doesn't cow her. "Stop *nagging* her. Look how scared she is! She wouldn't even be here if you hadn't guilted her into going into that experimental treatment!"

If Silvia were a dog, she'd have her tail down. She's not pushing that strict thirty-foot distance—enough to allow Donnie to pulp her before she closed the gap.

Mama scowls at Vala, the weary exhaustion of a never-ending family scuffle. "I want my daughter safe."

I realize what Silvia is. She's my neighbor's dog.

See, my old neighbor—not the gay poly trio—had a scrappy little dog with a little dog's paranoia and an oversized self-confidence. That dog was twelve pounds soaking wet and yet it hurled itself after ninety-pound Dobermans.

So whenever a big dog came along, my neighbor picked her dog up and carried it away.

Yet here's the problem:

Emergency-evacuating the dog just convinced the dog it needed to be rescued from some terrible danger. So it freaked out *more*. Eventually my neighbor stopped taking her for walks.

Which isn't to imply that Silvia doesn't have a panic disorder. She does. But her mom's been so terrified of Silvia hurting herself that she's hunted down jobs for Silvia, scheduling Silvia's doctor visits, taking over Silvia's life.

And Mama's undermined Silvia's self-confidence. Silvia doesn't trust in her own abilities. Vala knows that, you can see it in the way she snaps at Mama; she's been combating Mama's unwittingly corrosive influence for years.

Yet how can you fight a mother's love?

No time to ponder; Donnie's walking through a big open field so Silvia can't dive for cover, but if he gets any closer he'll triangulate my location from the sound.

"Donnie!" My cry echoes throughout the valley.

Donnie stops, head cocked as his audio analysts try to home in on me. Silvia cringes to a halt at the predetermined distance.

"Mister Mat Webb," he says, rolling the words in his mouth. "So you *did* survive."

"Fine and dandy as cotton candy. It's over, Donnie. The IAC's given up on the Silvia project. She only works as a surprise assassination tool; my op blew her cover."

He throws his head back and laughs. "I know *that*, Matty! I've been negotiating with some folks who are *very* eager to get their hands on such a fine sample of bioweaponry. I'll trade Silvia for some *real* firepower."

"Congratulations. You're so amoral, even the IAC couldn't predict your betrayal."

Donnie shrugs his bulky shoulders. "They shoulda seen it coming. Anyway, get your ass down here or I'll put a cap in these fine ladies' skulls."

"Doesn't work that way, Donnie. You kill them, I've got no reason to face you down mano a mano. I'll disappear to a place neither the IAC nor you can find me, and you'll never see me again. You'll never know."

"Know what?"

"Whether you could have beaten me in a straight-up fight."

He stiffens. "Oh, I know. I *know*."

"Do you?" I flick the words in his direction, a light whip of a taunt. "I mean, you worshipped at my altar, Donnie. You bought all

Ferrett Steinmetz

those nice prosthetics just to impress me. You mailed me so many times begging for a mission that I marked you as spam. Hell, that cigar's my signature move—is there any part of my style you didn't steal?"

"You shut up."

"You shoulda seen the look on your face when I took my shot at you. All goggle-eyed, unable to believe your hero took you down—hell, if your prosthetics hadn't kicked in to save you, you'd still be sitting with your thumb up your ass."

He's stomping around in circles, trying to home in on me, poor handcuffed Mama and Vala trailing behind awkwardly. "My prosthetics knocked a hole in yours, didn't they?" he sneers. "Mine were bigger. Better."

"*I* was protecting my target. I wasn't going all-out to kill you, Donnie." I dislike false bravado, but I can manage it when I have to. "And even then we don't know who would have won, because we got interrupted. I mean, you can tell yourself you're loaded for bear—but deep down, you have your momma buy you those weapons because you need to overcompensate."

God, I wish that were true. The man could turn a cap gun into a bazooka. Donnie's face is beet red, his faceplate down. "I get the best weapons because I am the *best*! Companies hire me to tweak their loadouts! The IAC came to *me*!"

I should shut up. Every word I speak gives his audio analyzers data to find me.

But I can't resist.

"Yet here you are running from the first real fight you ever had."

That does it. "*What do you want?*"

"Synchronized peace-tie. You and I both glow purple for fifteen minutes—long enough for you to release your hostages and for Silvia to get them to safety."

"Silvia, *no!*"

Oh, great. Mama Maldonado has seen the hope in Silvia's eyes and quashed it.

Donnie cracks his knuckles—which is impressive, because he had to design his hulking prosthetics *to* crack. "Don't even think about it," he snaps at Silvia. "I've analyzed the logs of your sucker-punch combat. I know how you fight. I'll grab your dumb ass and use you to beat your mother to death."

The energy drains from Silvia's limbs.

I wish her Mama didn't sigh with gratitude when Silvia slumps in surrender. Silvia's rebellion was one of my few outs.

"So how do we do this?" Donnie asks.

"I'll signal a countdown. When it hits zero, we both peace-tie." Peace-tying also broadcasts a signal so anyone nearby can verify who's peace-tied and who isn't.

"What if you don't peace-tie when I do?"

"Then you use those big ol' fists to kill the hostages, and I don't get what I want. If you don't peace-tie when *I* do, I run, and you get to sleep every night knowing how badly I woulda whupped you."

"That's pretty well thought through."

"I mighta been pondering the fairest way to kick your ass for a while."

Donnie's ugly chuckle reminds me that I do *not* have armaments ready to go toe-to-toe with his uber-tuned slaughter machine—I have rusted-out beaters with blinkered sensors.

"All right," he mutters. "I'm filming this. Your death will be all over the internet when this is done."

"If you're alive to upload it." Which he probably will be. "Silvia, Trish is an eight-minute walk away through the woods. I've marked the path for you. Do not do anything stupid. Protect your family." Mama nods. "Donnie, if you move, all bets are off. Keep your ass planted."

"I'm not doing that with you in cover and me exposed."

"I'll come out when they're safe. Our peace-ties will expire at the same microsecond. Our duel will be down to pure optimization."

He snorts. "You're dead, buddy."

I'd like to tell Silvia I love her, but she'll get that when Trish hands her my final message.

I issue the countdown. *Three, two, one . . .*

I glow a bruised purple.

Donnie gleams like a neon sign's wet dream.

"All right, Silvia. Head out." Donnie unlatches the cuffs, and Silvia ushers Mama and Vala out—Mama squeezing Silvia's arm, cooing how she's glad her daughter is safe, Vala glaring daggers at Donnie like she's ready to take him on single-handedly.

It takes a while to help an aging mother out of sight, and it's a big field. Minutes pass as they trudge out of the clearing, then disappear into the woods, and happily Donnie doesn't charge after them.

"You coming out?" he calls.

"After they've made it to the car. Not that I don't trust you, but I don't trust you."

He takes out another cigar, lights it ostentatiously. It's a Gurkha Black Dragon. That motherfucker wouldn't know it from a Swisher Sweet.

Jesus, I wish I had the armaments to cap him. But it's twelve minutes since we activated our peace-tie. With luck, Silvia's gotten her family back to Trish.

So I creep out of the holler to interpose myself between Donnie and Silvia's exit path, then step out into the clearing.

Donnie chokes on his cigar smoke.

"Hang on, hang on." He collapses into laughter. "I wanna immortalize this moment. Do you have anything functional?"

"I could probably shoot you with my rifle if you did me the courtesy of standing still."

He shakes his head. "Your legs are walking like an imbalanced dryer, your left arm's been trash-compacted; you don't even have body armor left. Do you have any tricks?"

"Would you believe me if I told you I was packing nukes?"

"The great Mat Webb. Showing up for a duel in *trash*."

"You gonna let me go?"

"If you're stupid enough to enter into a fight with that, you deserve whatever you get."

I sigh. "You got two minutes left on the clock. I suppose you figured out a way to bypass the peace-tie shutdown?"

"'Course. You?"

"Yeah, but I didn't think to preload that software."

"Shame."

Of course I don't hear the shot fire.

But I *am* alive to feel the impact as I hit the ground. My systems inform me Donnie's severed the connections to my left leg, which even I have to admit is a helluva precise shot.

"Gonna take my time," Donnie says; my right leg blanks as he severs that. "All that buildup, and you didn't even give me a good duel. Might as well spend my time taking you apart before I kill you."

"I accomplished my mission. Silvia's family is safe."

"Come on." He fires again, sending shrapnel from poor Vito burning into my cheek—which seems unfair, as Vito was already toast. "You don't think I've got my own escape vehicle? I'll use my satellite surveillance to track them down and murder Trish, then strangle Silvia's bratty sister, and then—"

"I am *so* glad I came back, then!"

Silvia hurtles out of the woods as Donnie's limbs start firing.

When Silvia got to the car, Trish gave her my message:

Hey, sweetie.

So you got a choice to make. I'll still love you either way. There's no wrong answer here.

Your mama thinks you're a weak woman with moments of strength.

Ferrett Steinmetz

I think you're a strong woman who sometimes breaks down.

That matters because that's the difference between a warrior and a civilian. It's not about whether you've got a gun, or even whether you've been to war. When warriors break down, we get back up again because somebody needs us.

That's it. We don't give up until the giving's done. I think that's who you are, but I can't decide for you.

If you're a civilian, then you gotta run. Run now and run fast, because Donnie'll be coming for you. I will be proud to sacrifice my life to protect you, because civilian or warrior, it has been my greatest pleasure to stand by your side.

But if you're a warrior, come back to me. Because I don't have any tricks. I just love you. That's literally all I got right now.

Love,

Mat

P.S. In case you don't know, the great thing about combat is that it doesn't matter whether you're screaming and crying and panicking as long as you're killing motherfuckers. Just sayin'.

Silvia's a badass.

Donnie fires wire-guided missiles, but Silvia's staying close to the ground, not jumping towards him in her usual arcs that'd leave her vulnerable in midair. Trees burst into splinters as she hangs on them just long enough for Donnie's targeting to commit to her direction, and then she leaps off in a zigzag pattern.

Sure enough, God bless her, she's howling in terror *and she's still fucking coming for Donnie.*

Donnie scowls as he jerks away from me: he'd *planned* to shoot me, but his defensive weaponry's automatically prioritized the incoming threat. Silvia's caught onto the idea that the best way to protect me is to come in so fast he doesn't dare reprogram anything because dammit my girl *is* a warrior, she's melded her body's instincts with a solid head for planning and a terror of being hurt and, oh my God, I'd kiss her if she wasn't evading gunfire.

And Donnie's twin shotguns erupt except she's sliding underneath them, moving faster than even his weaponry can track, squeezing his knee joint hard enough to crumple it, and sure enough Donnie's arms are quicker than a boxer, but Silvia's weaponizing her terror because Donnie's what's causing her to panic so she fights defensively, plinking at Donnie's defenses one hit at a time—crumpling a shotgun here, staving in a shoulder joint there.

"This isn't *fair!*" Donnie's screaming. "You got a *girl* to fight for you!"

"Did you complain when she got a guy to fight for her?"

Donnie staggers backwards like a man swatting at a mosquito as Silvia blurs around him as her bawling melts into nervous laughter because she's *beating* him, she's *beating* the bastard, and Donnie's tears are sweet because he's pulled out all his tricks and he *still* can't beat her.

His other leg goes down.

She smashes the clip line to his last rifle.

She destroys the grenade launcher so he can't self-immolate.

She tears his body armor off.

And Donnie's on the ground, his faceplate shattered, a naked quadruple amputee shackled to useless metal.

Silvia's fist draws back, aimed at Donnie's skull. Donnie lets out a low moan.

Silvia drops her fist.

Donnie coughs laughter.

"Fucking civilians," he sneers. "Afraid to get their hands dirty."

"That's why I love her."

Donnie crooks his neck, as if surprised to find I'm still there.

Ferrett Steinmetz

Where would I have gone? I'm hauling myself through the grass with my one remaining good arm—thanks, Michael—as Silvia straddles Donnie's immobile body. She's sobbing as she realizes she's not ready to kill anyone—why does that feel like a weakness when she's facing the bastard who would have killed her family?

I touch her ankle. It's the best I can do. "That's a strength, sweetie."

She sniffles. "Really?"

"Yeah."

She bends down, nuzzling her cheek against mine. She laughs nervously. "Did I do good?"

"You did great." I ruffle her hair with my remaining hand. "Now. Do me a favor and look away."

Her eyes widen. "Mat. You can't."

"His family's got billions, and he knows about you. He's got lawyers and money and no ethics, and he won't care who gets killed so long as he gets to sell you off for better armaments. Tell me he should live, I'll listen. But I don't think that's your argument so much as that you're not willing to do it."

"No." Donnie's denial is sudden, like he's waking from a pleasant dream. "No! No, you can't."

Silvia can't meet my gaze.

"Head back to the woods," I say. "I'll meet you there in a few minutes."

"That's . . ." She shakes her head. "That's too cowardly. I can't bury my head in the sand. I'll watch."

"Good. That's good." I cup her cheek. "I love you."

"You *can't!*" Donnie's thrashing, trying to free himself; he's as effective as I was back when the IAC reduced my limbs to paperweights. "You can't shoot someone who can't shoot back!"

"Why not? You did." I'm crawling with one hand, with hundreds of pounds of deadweight still attached, so it's taking longer to get to him than I'd like.

"But . . . you're a hero! A good guy!"

"Nope." I shake my head. "I'm a monster who fights monsters."

I crawl onto him; his perfect washboard stomach flexes and curls, flexes and curls, wormlike, as he tries to flee.

I rest my rifle barrel against his forehead. My control systems are shot, so I gotta aim manually.

Donnie's sweaty panic dissolves into a big, shit-eating grin. "You—you can't! If you—if you shoot me, you'll never know whether you could have beaten me in a fair fight!"

"Oh, I could have," I allow.

I'm mean enough to give him enough time to realize what that answer means. His smile fades into a big, screaming "*No!*"

I pull the trigger.

I roll away from Donnie's body, exhausted, my cheeks covered in Donnie's blood. In the far distance, I see IAC drones coming to pick up their successful test candidate, eager to get me back to the scanning facility before I do something even more foolish.

Donnie's body cools next to me. The IAC's new morality will remember this last death, the one where I shot a helpless man, and they will use that as a template where a thousand men like Donnie will fall if they've got the drop on him.

I'm okay with that.

Onyeka does not wish to talk with me.

Ms. Njeze's email is formal but polite; the formality is what I'd expect from a politician of her caliber, the politeness is what I'd expect from someone whose daughter I rescued. But though Onyeka's therapy's coming along well, thanks for asking, Onyeka's therapybots recommend she not see anyone who would remind her of her abduction trauma.

I note how Onyeka's mother does *not* encourage me to call back.

"Everything okay?" Silvia asks.

We're walking along the street to her mother's house, having stopped at a bodega to pick up a bottle of wine and some flowers for

Ferrett Steinmetz

the table. Silvia's dressed in a demure long-sleeve shirt and jeans to conceal her bioengineered body; I'm wearing Thelma and Louise, my show prosthetics, but somehow they feel more natural with Silvia curled up on my arm.

She must have noticed me wincing. "Sorry," I say. "A hostage I saved once doesn't want to see me."

"Huh." People pass by us as we walk—some smiling at the guy and his new girlfriend, most ignoring us. Which is delightful. "How often do you visit your old . . . rescue buddies?"

"I've never tried before."

She relaxes. I'm not quite sure why. But my body language–AIs tell me it's best not to press this topic, and I believe them.

Yet I'm caught up in her question: Because I never *did* try to visit anyone I was worried had gotten hurt. I'd lock myself in the lab and analyze mission logs instead. Now, I want to forge connections with people I've helped.

Oh.

That's why she's worried.

"Let's not forget the best rescue buddy of them all," I tell her. "I've saved a lot of people, but only one saved me back. Besides, who would I dance with?"

I switch my limbs into Fred Astaire dance mode, reach out my hand: she does a little twirl as we hum "Night and Day," doing a brief pas de deux on New Jersey's streets. She twirls up on tiptoes to kiss me on the cheek.

I wince, because my cheek's still tender; five weeks, and the orbital fracture is almost healed, but I still have new and horrible migraines. Add it to my backaches and my other combat-related injuries.

There are old soldiers, and bold soldiers, and I guess I'm the old kind even though I'd be hard-pressed to call myself middle-aged.

"You okay?"

"The combat injuries still."

"Oh." She looks concerned. "Are you still up for dinner with Mama and Vala?"

"You realize I'd rather head into combat than have dinner with your family."

She laughs loudly enough that a couple of kids lollygagging on the corner look over, half in love with her already. "Okay, so you'll be fine. Remember, if they ask you about your eye, don't tell them how it happened."

"I remember. No talking business with your family."

She shakes her head in disbelief. "I'm still weirded out, calling it 'business.'"

The IAC no longer exists, of course. There was a conveniently large bust that dismantled the feared criminal organization shortly after the assault on Smyrna was brought to light.

Lots of guys got shot resisting arrest. I assume they were all bad guys. The new-and-revised IAC wouldn't have framed nice people for crimes, because I wouldn't have.

However, an organization that is distinctly *not* the IAC has given us several phone calls, explaining how much work there's left to do in ethically dismantling their organization. It's not simple. Last week, Silvia and I rounded up some rogue Monicas because you can't just set them free—Donnie was right, every government would pay top-tier cash to get advanced bioweapons. So we've been kidnapping Monicas and bringing them to deprogramming facilities where the reformed artificial intelligences can restore their sanity.

There's other gray areas; there always are. We're visiting Silvia's mom and sister before trotting off to a former IAC enclave in Hong Kong. Starting tomorrow, we have to figure out a way to back out of the deals the IAC has made with other shadow organizations.

I gripe about the pay, which is excellent but not Donnie-levels—I wish they'd give me one big cash-out and let me retire—but I know what the not-IAC's doing. They're throwing me at the knottiest moral conundrums. Studying my reactions. Not giving me time to oppose them.

It's what I'd do.

Ferrett Steinmetz

Yet they do allow Silvia along on the missions, and we're . . . finding ways to work together. I need to analyze every possibility, or I panic. Whereas Silvia still gets overwhelmed sometimes. We've had nasty midcombat fights, some painfully physical because she can't always help herself when she gets wound up.

Our sanity is never a total victory but only another battle won. Sometimes I find Silvia curled up in the corner, weeping from stress. Sometimes Silvia crawls out of bed at four in the morning to find me plotting new tactics.

Both times are met with gentle hugs.

And honestly? We both feel better kicking ass for justice.

"There's Mama's house," Silvia whispers reverently, as though we're approaching a shrine. It has that shrine look: a well-tended garden, a Mother Mary statue by the porch, warm candlelights in the window.

She stops, brushes my shirt off, looking me up and down. Then: "Do I look okay?"

"You've never looked anything but."

She blushes. "Flatterer." She snatches the wine and roses out of my arms, then jams the wine back in, then switches the wine for the flowers. "You give her the flowers. I'll give her the wine. And don't go into the dining room until Mama gives the go-ahead. She's got out the special plates for you."

"Are you *sure* I can't get someone to shoot me instead?"

"Oh, and if she asks, you're Catholic."

"What?"

She pushes open the door. *"We're here!"*

"Not yet!" Vala cries from another room.

"You said six o'clock!"

"I know but NOT YET!"

"What the . . ." Silvia escorts me at lightning speed down a hall-way filled with family photos, deposits me in on a plastic-encased couch sitting before a news monitor. She grooms herself with in-sect speed, then paces the room eight times in four seconds.

"Wait here." She holds her palms flat, placating me. "Maybe she needs help in the kitchen."

"You be a guest!" Mama says.

"I'm not a guest, I'm family!" Silvia screams back in a commanding shout I have never heard from her before. "Hang on. I'll find out what's going on."

"Shoot me," I whisper. She kisses me on the forehead.

I watch the television, trying to screen out the commotion in the kitchen. The news has become a fascinating game these days, if you know where to pay attention.

I mean, first off, there's the unsettling way in which the massive police showdowns I got into were somehow redirected to poor dead Donnie, even though the facts never quite matched up. There *were* seven murdered cops—and though I tell myself I reprogrammed the not-IAC to run according to my fabulous principles, I remain *highly* aware that my new buddy had slaughtered without conscience up until five weeks ago.

I don't know what I would have done—no, that's a lie, I do. I would have looked at the shitty options the former IAC had left the new-and-ethical IAC, and decided the old techniques of "quash the news, alter the evidence, and bribe who's bribable" worked equally well for justice's sake.

I suppose I should be glad my ass isn't in jail. The not-IAC has assured me those cops' families will never have financial troubles again. Yet watching seven cops' lives erased to fit in with a nicer story?

I don't know if anyone should have that power. Even me.

Though I brighten at today's top headline—because if you pay attention, the news time devoted to "basic income" has crept up over the last month or so. News hosts are starting to debate the topic—the conservative commentators are, predictably, resisting the idea of some welfare queen making off with their hardworking money, but there's been a quiet sea change in how basic income is discussed.

Ferrett Steinmetz

We're starting to ask whether we've automated too much.

We're starting to ask whether the people serve the economy, or the economy serves the people.

And if you look closely, the polls in the last five weeks have ticked up .3 percent in favor of what's being called "economic reform." The approval ratings for basic income are still abysmal, natch, but we're asking what we should do when humans don't *need* to work.

There's even subtler changes if you dig close. Small-town politicians with once-crazy ideas are getting quiet donations from anonymous sources. Clickbait headlines are leading to nuanced discussions, rewarding the media for publishing deeper stories. Unflattering revelations about corrupt corporations are floating to the surface.

The former IAC isn't ramming the idea down our throats—because I wouldn't have—but they *are* changing the dialogue. Floating the truth to the top. Encouraging people to ask the right questions.

I don't know everything the not-IAC's up to. I suspect their dirty work would revolt me. Monsters to fight monsters.

Yet I wonder: there was a time when humans believed computers were incapable of transcribing audio. They thought computers couldn't drive a car better than a person. They thought computers would never be able to practice law better than the lawyers; they thought computers would never be able to read X-rays better than radiologists; they thought computers could never program better than the programmers.

They beat us. They beat us at everything.

Now we get to see whether computers can be more ethical than humans. And even though I suspect the former IAC will usher in a far, far better world than messy humanity could ever manage, I still tremble to think of our last obsolescence.

"Sweetie?" Silvia stands in the doorway, clutching her hands to her breast.

Behind her, Mama's adjusting the forks on the table, Vala bringing out a soup tureen. There's so many dishes on the table, enough to feed an army; they must have been cooking all day.

Mama gives me a stern look—I am the man her daughter has unwisely chosen to fall in love with. Even though I saved Silvia's life and rescued them from computerized captivity, that does *not* mean I am good enough to date her daughter. My every bite will be analyzed to see whether I appreciate the meal, all my intents towards her precious daughter will be interrogated.

"It's not too late," Silvia whispers, leaning in. "We can find a gunfight somewhere."

"No." I take her hand. "Let's do this."

Works Cited

Act 1: Eva Dou and Olivia Geng, "Humans Mourn Loss After Google Is Unmasked as China's Go Master," *The Wall Street Journal*, January 5, 2017.

Act 2: Dawn Chen, "The AI That Has Nothing to Learn From Humans," *The Atlantic*, October 30, 2017.

Act 3: Peter Heine Nelson. 2017. "Chess." Facebook, December 6, 2017. https://facebook.com/chess/posts/10156037915519571.

Afterword

They say that all books are a conversation with each other. In this case, *Automatic Reload* is *very specifically* a word I'm having with K. C. Alexander.

Don't worry, though. It's a good word.

See, I read K. C. Alexander's cyberpunk novel *Necrotech*, and in it they had a marvelously violent female cyborg who exuded a steady stream of don't-give-a-fucks. And because K. C.'s prose is so sharp and evocative, I kept watching their heroine Riko and her artificial limb wake up in garbage-smeared alleyways and lice-filled jailbeds and all manner of disgusting places . . .

And while I loved following Riko around, I kept asking one question:

When does she field-strip and clean that damn thing?

I mean, Riko kept landing in slimy, gunky situations and her artificial limb never seized up. And while I was waiting for the scene where Riko had to spend the day oiling and tightening her neglected limb, I started imagining my own "maintenancepunk" novel where I had a guy who did some serious tuning.

That thought experiment turned into *Automatic Reload*. So if you liked this but maaaybe wanted a little less maintenance and a little more mayhem, you could do worse than to throw K. C. a buck or two.

(Ironically, K. C. wound up blurbing this book, so I'm glad they enjoyed it. If we're gonna be having a conversation through novels, it might as well be a cordial one.)

Before I get into all the people I gotta thank for this book, lemme tell you a story:

I was in Manhattan, doing drinks with my editor—which is not a commonplace occurrence for me, believe you me. (I have yet to meet my agent in the flesh. I live online. You have no proof that I'm not an AI.)

And I was feeling quite fancy, because Diana Pho had just purchased my book *The Sol Majestic*, and I was going to have drinks with my editor, and I had never felt so fancy.

So Diana sits down next to me and my partner, and we discuss my book, and she tells me that what she loved about *The Sol Majestic* was that it was so *cozy*, that it was just a sweet, slow-paced story that you could curl up in, and it had this gentle tone she'd fallen in love with . . .

At which point, I blurted out, ". . . My next book has a fifty-page car chase sequence!"

I never write the same book twice, apparently. It's a failing.

But the point is that Diana *bought* this book-that-was-not-cozy, this flickering tension-line of fast bullets and faster processing power, so let us all thank Diana for giving me platforms for my whacky rides.

And the other point is that if you didn't like this book, you might like *The Sol Majestic*, and if you didn't like *The Sol Majestic*, you probably should read this book. Though hopefully you'll love both of 'em. Yeah, let's go with that.

(And while we're at it, let's all thank the fine people at Tor who helped this book along—Callum Plews, Tim Campbell, MaryAnn Johanson, and Desirae Friesen. And thanks to my agent, Evan Gregory, who may be an AI himself!)

Now, if you've read my usual afterwords, you'd know this is where I thank all of my beta readers by name, often pointing out a specific place where they helped me out. But as I'm writing this, I have spent a solid week attempting to get my old laptop—the one where I stored all my old emails before, reluctantly, migrating to the cloud—up and running, and it is dead. (Blame the IAC. *They do not want you to know.*)

So alas, I *can't* bring up the names in time for this deadline. I encourage you to visit my site www.theferrett.com/automatic_thanks, where I will have them listed by name there.

Thanks go to my usual Anxiety Cuddle Squad—Shakira, Aileen, Kalita, and Laura, who helped hold me down when I was about to freak out about Book. Thanks to my, uh, best friend Angie, who now has a new kidney so she's a little bit cyborg herself.

Thanks to my mom, dad, and Uncle Tommy—but especially my dad, who brought me to Pitney Bowes when I was a kid to show me how all the ticker-tape and punch-card machines work, the now-antique but then-big-hardware computing technology that dazzled me and still does.

Thanks be to God. I prayed a lot while I was writing this. It helped.

But as always, there's one woman who is to thank above all else for this. As I type this, we are preparing to head out on a massive vacation to celebrate our twentieth anniversary—a meandering, nine-day van trip to Yellowstone which we are calling our "Vanniversary."

As of now, I don't know how that trip will go. (If you want to find out, follow my blog at www.theferrett.com or my Twitter feed at @ferretthimself, but you'll have to look back to October 2019.)

But I know I've traveled with this woman for twenty years, and wherever she goes, I will follow.

I love you, Gini.

Arf.

Ferrett Steinmetz
@ferretthimself on Twitter
www.theferrett.com

Read on for a preview of

THE SOL MAJESTIC

Ferrett Steinmetz

Available now from Tom Doherty Associates

TOR

A Tor Trade Paperback ISBN 978-1-250-16819-1

2

After Sixty Minutes on Savor Station

Kenna sucks on a plastic bead as he follows the eight-year-old girl around Savor Station, trying to work up the nerve to mug her.

She's pudgy, dressed in a little blue uniform, a kid wandering through the crowded hallways like she's in no danger at all. The tracker tag on her wrist makes Kenna think maybe she isn't. She cruises to a stop to watch some cartoon advertisement on the overhead monitors, reaches into an oil-stained bag of meat jerky to chew on it absently. Kenna hates her for the way she can eat without paying attention; put jerky in his mouth, and it would fill his whole world.

He sucks harder on the bead. More saliva. Fools the stomach into thinking something's on the way, which of course it isn't unless he mugs this little girl.

He pushes past tourists consulting overhead maps, edging close enough to grab the bag. He should. He *has* to.

Kenna hesitates again.

The girl moves on, wandering into the glassine cubicles of merchant's stalls, darting between shoppers' legs. She passes a shop heaped with tubs of fresh fish, flopping as they're released from expensive time-stasis cubes; the salt-ocean smell makes Kenna wipe drool from dry lips even though he's straying dangerously close to the tawdry commerce areas. He steps towards the fish, like a man in a dream—and as he stumbles forward, the security cameras whirr to focus on him. The merchant senses Kenna's stray-cat approach, quietly shifts his body to deny him access.

Could he beg the merchant for scraps? Kenna takes another dazed step forward, reaching out plaintively. The merchant's lips tense as he readies well-worn excuses: *if I give scraps to one boy then I will be swarmed by beggars, a purveyor of quality goods cannot be seen surrounded by hobos, I'm sure you understand.*

Kenna turns away, knowing exactly what the merchant will say before he utters a word. He's dodged many embarrassments by intuiting potent visions extracted from body language, and Kenna has paid dearly the few times he's ignored his instincts.

Yet he's glad the stalls don't have jobs posted. He'd sell his labor for a fish. Mother and Father would never talk to him again, of course—you don't learn a trade, your Philosophy is your trade. They have left Kenna behind in the common areas while they negotiate meetings with Savor Station's visiting politicians, hunting for an opportunity to lend their wisdom to powerful legislators. But though Kenna tries to remember his parents' lectures on providing insights so profound that leaders will pay to hear them, his growling belly drowns out their voices.

They've been Inevitable for so long they've forgotten how to fear death. They hesitate whenever they lecture him, squinting with the effort of attempting to translate their enlightened experience into Kenna's debased state; the only time he's seen them falter is when they try to explain how they unlocked their Inevitable Philosophy. *You find strength in the suffering of others,* Mother intones, or Father tells him *Once you realize what's truly at stake, you come to realize how little you matter.*

But Kenna's felt his heart stuttering from malnutrition, and once again his nascent Philosophies fall away when survival calls.

The girl ambles on, waving cheerful hellos as she strolls between the stalls; Kenna scans the market for better targets. The other shoppers, maybe? No. They're big. Healthy. His hands shiver

Ferrett Steinmetz

from malnutrition. They'd yell for security right away, he'd get jailed, shaming Mother and Father.

He imagines justifying this crime to them. *They had food already; I didn't. She didn't need that food; I do.* Yet he's already heard them whispering consultations with each other, fretting how all the Princes of old had *their* Wisdom Ceremony before they were fifteen. Kenna's sixteenth birthday was a month ago, and now Mother and Father's muttered discussions have taken on the panicked hiss of monarchs debating whether Kenna can continue to be the Inevitable Prince if he does not shape his Inevitable Philosophy.

Being arrested might be his final fall from grace.

Kenna should hate them. Instead, he envies their Inevitability. Mother and Father's bottomless compassion gets them up in the morning; their love keeps them moving when Kenna wants to curl up and die. They're waiting in some old politician's lobby, chasing flickering embers of power. Once Father's Inevitable Philosophy convinces the right potentates, he'll lead his people out of darkness.

When Father chants *I will lead my people out of darkness!*, Kenna can feel the limitless strength bound in those words—yet though Kenna spends hours meditating upon the revolutionary changes that should be made for the benefit of all, the best philosophies Kenna can muster are pleasant platitudes that crumple into guilt whenever Kenna's stomach growls.

Kenna has no people. He has no compassion. He has no Philosophy. All he has is a girl with a bag of meat jerky—a girl skipping into Savor Station's main arteries.

Kenna follows her, chest hitching with self-loathing.

It's more crowded here, his every footstep blocked by bag-toting porters and gawking tourists and miniature forklifts ferrying crates. Though this curved ring is wide enough to hold hundreds of passengers, the space is all elbows and bulkheads, which makes sense; each square inch cost thousands of dinari to build, a sliver of safety constructed in pure vacuum by brute labor.

Kenna creeps closer. The girl babbles at a porter, discussing some show; he sidles up, sliding his fingertips across the bag's tantalizing oiliness.

All he has to do is clench his fingers, and yank, and run.

He imagines the girl's shocked face as he tugs the jerky from her hands, that little-girl shock of discovering that anyone can take anything from you if they're big enough, and he realizes this is what it would take to survive:

He would have to become a bully.

Kenna howls. Startled, the girl drops her jerky, but Kenna does not notice; he's pushing people aside, fleeing. He cannot stop crying, but he can move so fast that no one has time to notice his tears. He wants so badly to throw all this honor aside to stuff his mouth with meat and be happy and shivering . . .

. . . but he is not a thief.

Oh, how he envies thieves.

Do you have to be so dramatic, Kenna? he can hear Mother chiding him. But she's carved away everything that doesn't advance her Philosophies—she's whittled herself down to perfect postures, to primly smoothed robes, to unceasingly polite rules of etiquette.

If he had an Inevitable Philosophy, he would never lose control. But he does not, so he runs.

His legs spasm. Kenna collapses by a long line of people—Savor Station is criss-crossed with lines, lines of people getting passports, lines to get on ships, lines to fill out job applications, lines to—

DO YOU LOVE FOOD? a sign flashes.

The sign itself is written in a flowing, sugary goodness, a message in frosting. It writhes like a dancer pulling veils across herself, highlighting a carved wood booth crammed into a corner.

Wood, Kenna thinks. *What madman hauls wood across solar systems to put it in a lobby?* He knows vandals; on the transit-ship, this would have been carved to pieces.

Yet even in the elbow-to-ass room of Savor Station, people make space for this little alcove, as if the dark wood booth is an ambassa-

dor from some great kingdom. It has a confessional's solemn pall—
but the people lined up before it have the expectant looks of lottery
contestants, chatting eagerly about their chances and wringing
their hands as they fantasize about winning. A stiff pressed linen
curtain gives privacy as each new person steps into the booth, muttering well-practiced speeches. The line's end is nowhere in sight.

The sign contorts, bowing, then unfolds into a new set of letters:
THE SOL MAJESTIC.

Kenna has no idea what that means, but he longs to be a part of
it already.

The sign is whisked away as though by a breeze; smaller words
float across the empty space like lotus blossoms drifting across a
lake. THE MOST EXCLUSIVE RESTAURANT IN ALL THE GALAXY. ONLY
EIGHTEEN TABLES. RESERVATIONS MUST BE MADE TWO YEARS IN
ADVANCE.

BUT ONE TABLE IS RESERVED EACH NIGHT, FREE OF CHARGE, FOR
THOSE WITH THE LOVE TO SEE IT.

Kenna clambers to his feet.

TELL US WHY YOU LOVE FOOD.

This is insane, this is stupid, this is foolhardy. He should comb
the marketplaces again, see if anyone has dropped food on the
floor. But Mother and Father will not return from their political
sojourn for hours, and this . . .

. . . this . . .

Kenna staggers down the line. His legs ache before he reaches
its end. He settles behind a rumpled family of middle-aged tourists, who welcome him with a bright-eyed wave and a "Why not?"
gleam in their eyes. A group of fashionable Gineer hipsters, their
smooth skin taut from gene-treatments, fusses about the delay as
they settle behind him.

He settles into his own silence, lets others do the talking. They
speak breathlessly about cuisine.

It takes a while before Kenna realizes *cuisine* means *food*.

They speak of tenacious ice-eating mosses, planted on asteroids, sent on trips around the sun, retrieved to harvest the bounty for a once-in-a-lifetime salad. They speak of deep-sea creatures evolved at the bottoms of vinegar oceans, so delicate they have to be kept in pressurized containers, released via special mechanisms to explode in your mouth. They speak of artificial meat-fibers spun across rotating tines in cotton-candy strands, a protein that melts on your tongue to saturate your whole mouth with thick umami.

What is umami?

He's never eaten well, but he thought he at least understood the *language* of food. Mother spoke of noodle soups and roasted ducklings.

These meals sound like exhibits.

They discuss meat. Kenna relaxes; he understands meat, even though all he's ever eaten has been vending machine jerky. But these people discuss blubber, siopao, Silulian black-udder, p'tcha, vacuum flanks, sashimi. They trade the names like chips on bingo cards, brightening when it turns out two people have consumed the same oddity, exchanging indecipherable dialogues on bizarre concepts like flavor profiles and top notes.

Kenna should not be here. But leaving would mark him as a fraud. He has had enough humiliation for the day.

There's enough humiliation for everyone, he's glad to see. As they draw closer to the confessional, people are rejected with an astounding rapidity. You are asked, Kenna is told, to discuss why you love food, though most don't make it past their first sentence. A beautiful actress stumbles out, hands on her broad hips in irritation, to inform the crowd she'd had *auditions* that lasted longer.

The nice family people standing before him—so educated, so smart—explain that some days, Paulius does not find anyone at all to let into his restaurant. Paulius has exacting tastes. It is said on days like that, Paulius sinks into a deep depression, though Paulius is more known for his fits of rage.

And the nice family goes in, one at a time.

And the nice family is ejected from the booth, one at a time.

Ferrett Steinmetz

The Gineer hipsters flutter their hands at Kenna, as if loath to touch his ragged clothing. "Get in," they hiss. "Get it over with."

Kenna slumps in. White linen curtains close behind him.

Before him is an elegant table, draped in a white tablecloth, standing before a blank white screen. A wooden chair, curved like a cello, rests on the floor, inviting Kenna to take a seat.

Kenna sits down, crossing his hands to prevent himself from fidgeting. He half expects a buzzer to go off before he speaks.

Instead, he stares down at the tablecloth. It has indents where would-be vandals have left outlines of dicks, but the tablecloth is made of some special ink-resistant fabric.

The screen pulses gently, a reminder.

Kenna clears his throat.

"I . . . I don't think I love food."

Nothing happens. Is there some secret signal that nobody's told him about? *Has* he failed already, and is too much of a yokel to know?

"I can't be certain. Mother and Father—*they* had grand meals. They warm their hands by those memories, savoring banquets they had with Grandfather, reliving those courses one by one . . . .

"I don't have those recollections. I've had canned meat, dried noodles, pickled eggs. If I . . . if we . . . ever came back into favor, would I . . . appreciate anything else? I can't tell. All this surviving is killing me.

"Mother and Father, they're—they dream decades in the future. I can barely imagine tomorrow. And I think if I got one meal, one good meal, to show me what life I could dream about, then maybe I could . . ."

He drifts off, uncertain what he could do. His life is defined by absences. He can't envision what he could do, because he doesn't love food, he doesn't love people, he doesn't love anything, and how can you become something when all you've known is nothing?

"Maybe I could have a Philosophy," he whispers.

A soft whirr. Kenna jerks his head up at the noise; he's still in the confessional. He'd started talking and had forgotten about The Sol Majestic, forgotten about Paulius, he'd poured his heart onto the table and why is that screen rising into the ceiling?

The door concealed on the confessional's far side swings open, revealing a sunlit orchard.

There are no orchards in space, Kenna thinks. He freezes, so he does not hurt himself in his madness.

But through the door are blue skies, knotted tangles of grass, twisted boughs of trees heavy with fruit. Rows of trees, retreating far into the distance. A zephyr of sun-warmed chlorophyll ripples his hair.

The trees' branches are wrapped around stainless steel water pipes that snake across the landscape. A geodesic dome's triangular struts slash across the sky. Surely, he would not have imagined *that*.

He creeps his way towards the exit, expecting some security guard to block the entrance. But no; he steps over the threshold, and his battered shoes sink into soft loam. His fingers close over a tree branch's knurled hardness, and the sensation of something growing beneath his fingers is like touching miracles. Kenna inhales, and it's not the stale scent of recycled body odor and plastic offgassing; it's the clean smell of rain and leaves.

He plucks a hard oval of purplish-green off a branch: a grape? He rolls the fruit's waxy surface between his fingertips, puzzled at its hard flesh. Weren't grapes supposed to be squishy, like the jam in the vending machine sandwiches? This smells like the light crude oil coating your skin after you bunk in a cargo ship's engine room. Is it safe to eat?

He's never eaten anything that hasn't come wrapped in plastic.

Kenna drops the fruit and stumbles forward, seeking something simpler. He pushes his way into a curved valley with long rows of curlicued vines lashed to wooden poles.

A tall, potbellied man strides across the vineyard towards Kenna, jabbing a silver cane into the soft soil for balance.

Kenna's breath catches in his throat. The man is coming for him. The man who owns the vineyard.

Ferrett Steinmetz

The man—Paulius?—ducks under the vines without lifting his blue-eyed gaze away from Kenna, as though he has memorized every limb in his garden. The man's own limbs are slender—long graceful arms, a dancer's legs, all connected to one bowling-ball belly. Whenever he ducks, his long, white ponytail swings madly, knotted in silver cords. He steps over the hillocks quickly, as if an emergency calls for his attention but he refuses to give up the dignity of walking.

The man is dressed in thigh-high black boots and a white ruffled vest, but somehow the rain-slickened vines leave no marks upon him. He is wrinkled and tan—not the fake orange tan of tanning booths, but the light leathery patina one acquires from hard work in fine sunlight.

He holds a brass bowl in his free hand, thrusting it forward. Steam wafts upwards.

He deposits the bowl into Kenna's hands gravely. Kenna looks down; the bowl thrums warm against his palms, rimmed with circuitry, the soup cradled within perfectly still. The bowl has its own artificial gravity generator at the bottom, pulling the soup down so it can never spill.

Kenna trembles. This bowl is worth more than everything his family owns, and yet Paulius—for it is Paulius—has handed it to him as though it were nothing at all.

Paulius bows.

"The first rule of appreciation," Paulius says, his voice mellifluous, "is that it is impossible to savor a thing you have been starved of. This applies to food, lovers, and company. So I must feed you before I can teach you. Drink deep."

Except Kenna *can* savor it. Though his stomach punches the inside of his ribs, desperate for nutrients, Kenna peers into the coppery broth before him. Little globules of fat wobble upon its surface, glimmering like holograms. Glistening dark meat chunks bob at the bottom. He inhales, and the rich chicken scent fills his nostrils, fills his brain, fills his world.

Then he thumbs the gravity release button and sips it. Or tries to. His hands betray him, pouring it into his mouth. Kenna fights his body to sip genteelly instead of gulping. He's sobbing and coughing, making dumb animal noises in front of Paulius . . .

Paulius grabs his shoulder, his fingers so strong they root Kenna to the earth. "Your breath stinks of ketone. I know how long a man can starve, and you are at your limits. Please. Eat."

Freed from restraint, Kenna dumps it down his throat. His belly heats up, radiating warmth like a tiny sun. His muscles twitch as his blood feasts on the broth, ferries it out to his limbs, suffusing him with a rapture greater than any orgasm.

His ass hits the ground. He sprawls in the soft earth, feeling his emaciated body rebuilding itself, feeling the sunlight's warmth on his brown skin.

Paulius kneels down beside him, nodding as Kenna's chest hitches. This isn't just the broth; it's life, it's a connection to this land Paulius has created, and—

He loves food.

He loves *something*.

As Kenna realizes how close he was to dying, dying in all the ways that really counted, he curls up and cries.